Richard Wright

SIGNS OF RACE

Series Editors: Arthur L. Little, Jr. and Gary Taylor

RICHARD WRIGHT

NEW READINGS IN THE 21ST CENTURY

*Edited by Alice Mikal Craven and
William E. Dow*

palgrave
macmillan

First published in 2011 by
PALGRAVE MACMILLAN®
in the United States—a division of St. Martin's Press LLC,
175 Fifth Avenue, New York, NY 10010.

Where this book is distributed in the UK, Europe and the rest of the world,
this is by Palgrave Macmillan, a division of Macmillan Publishers Limited,
registered in England, company number 785998, of Houndmills,
Basingstoke, Hampshire RG21 6XS.

Palgrave Macmillan is the global academic imprint of the above companies
and has companies and representatives throughout the world.

Palgrave® and Macmillan® are registered trademarks in the United States,
the United Kingdom, Europe and other countries.

ISBN: 978–0–230–11281–0

Library of Congress Cataloging-in-Publication Data

Richard Wright : new readings in the 21st century / edited by Alice
Mikal Craven and William E. Dow.
    p. cm.
  ISBN 978–0–230–11281–0 (hardback)
    1. Wright, Richard, 1908–1960—Criticism and interpretation.
  2. African Americans in literature. I. Craven, Alice Mikal. II. Dow, William
(William E.)

PS3545.R815Z818 2011
813'.52—dc22   2011002903

A catalogue record of the book is available from the British Library.

Design by Newgen Imaging Systems (P) Ltd., Chennai, India.

First edition: July 2011

10 9 8 7 6 5 4 3 2 1

Printed in the United States of America.

Contents

Series Editors' Preface

The first thing you see when you enter the permanent exhibits at the Birmingham Civil Rights Institute is a pair of drinking fountains. Over one hangs a sign that says "White." Over the other hangs a sign that says "Colored."

To the extent that every social identity is to some degree local, the meanings of race in Birmingham, Alabama, necessarily differ, in some demographic and historical particulars, from the meanings of race in North Dakota and Northern Ireland, New York and New South Wales, Cape Town and Calcutta. But the same questions can be asked everywhere in the English-speaking world.

> How do people signal a racial identity?
> What does that racial identity signify?

This series examines the complex relationships between race, ethnicity, and culture in the English-speaking world from the early modern period (when the English language first began to move from its home island into the wider world) into the postcolonial present, when English has become the dominant language of an increasingly globalized culture. English is now the medium of a great variety of literatures, spoken and written by many ethnic groups. The racial and ethnic divisions between (and within) such groups are not only reflected in but also shaped by the language we share and contest.

Indeed, such conflicts in part determine what counts as "literature" or "culture."

Every volume in the series approaches race from a transracial, interdisciplinary, and intercultural perspective. Each volume focuses on one aspect of the cross-cultural performance of race, exploring the ways in which "race" remains stubbornly local, personal, and present.

We no longer hang racial signs over drinking fountains. But the fact that the signs of race have become less obvious does not mean that they have disappeared, or that we can or do ignore them. It is the purpose of this series to make us more conscious, and more critical, readers of the signs that have separated, and still separate, one group of human beings from another.

GARY TAYLOR

ACKNOWLEDGMENTS

Richard Wright: New Readings in the 21ˢᵗ Century has expanded vastly beyond its roots in a centenary conference held in June 2008. Many scholars, artists, and critics have helped us while we worked on this book and as we discovered and rediscovered the vitality of Richard Wright's work for our current century, and indeed, millennium. We would like to thank The American University of Paris for allowing us to host the Richard Wright Centennial, and to extend sincere thanks to all speakers who participated in this historic event. We are grateful for the generous assistance of Roberta Vellvé, Brenda Torney, Mark Rostollan, Olivier Serafinowicz, Ann Borel, John Gbajumo, Aline Mondavan, Deborah First-Quao, and Bernadette Ameye; the financial support of the U.S. Embassy in Paris; the support of the American Church in Paris; and the continuing encouragement and critical advice of Joyce Ann Joyce and Leonard Cassuto. Our deepest thanks go to Yoko Nakamura for her invaluable editorial work and her unwavering efficiency and patience.

An earlier version of Robert Butler's "Seeking Salvation in a Naturalistic Universe: Richard Wright's Use of His Southern Religious Background in *Black Boy* (*American Hunger*)" appeared in *Southern Quarterly* 46.2 (Winter 2009): 46–60. Parts of John Lowe's "Richard Wright and the CircumCaribbean" were first published in "Palette of Fire: The Aesthetics of Propaganda in *Black Boy* and *In the Castle of My Skin*," in *The Mississippi Quarterly* 61.4 (2008): 553–80. An earlier version of Isabel Soto's "'White People to the Other Side': *Native Son* and the Poetics of Space" was published in *The Black Scholar* 39.1–2 (Spring-Summer 2009): 23–26. A shorter version of Thadious Davis's "Becoming Richard Wright: Space and the WPA" was published in *The Black Scholar* 39.1 (Spring-Summer 2009): 11–16. An earlier version of Leonard Cassuto's essay was published in *The Chronicle of Higher Education* 54.46 (July 25, 2008): B12–13.

ALICE MIKAL CRAVEN AND WILLIAM E. DOW

INTRODUCTION

Alice Mikal Craven and William E. Dow

For years, Richard Wright has been known as the writer of *Native Son* and *Black Boy*. These powerful classics have helped shape the twentieth-century African American literary tradition, but the study of Wright's oeuvre needs to go beyond these seminal works to encompass his other writings, especially the rich and varied works of his later years. Though it does not ignore his best-known works by any means, this collection is the first to focus on this later body of works. *Richard Wright: New Readings in the 21ˢᵗ Century* offers fresh approaches to Wright's work for new times. It traces and gives far-reaching analyses of his creative direction as he reached beyond the safe boundaries and successes of the early works, which largely define his legacy today.

In postwar America, Richard Wright charted distinctive lines of black transnationalism while also writing about the struggles of blacks in the United States and about his own conflicted American identity. He wrote a first-person, subjective narrative of the people and the revolutionary movement of the Gold Coast (present-day Ghana) entitled *Black Power* (1954), while contemporaneously experimenting with African American fictional forms of melodrama and violent revolt in the *The Outsider* (1953) and *Savage Holiday* (1954), both set in the United States. He "saw Africa for the first time with frontal vision—black life was everywhere" but "[t]he soil was a rich red like that of Georgia or Mississippi—and, for brief moments, [he] could almost delude himself into thinking that [he] was back in the American South" (*Black Power* 52, 55). He was able to move himself into "the sphere of conscious history" (*Black Voices* 147), but only by positioning himself alongside the twenty-seven nations meeting together at the 1955 Bandung conference in Jakarta, Indonesia. As he explains in *The Color Curtain* (1956):

> . . . I feel that my life has given me some keys to what they would say or do. I'm an American Negro; as such, I've had the burden of race consciousness. So have these people. I worked in my youth as a common

laborer and I've a class consciousness. So have these people. I grew
up in the Methodist and Seventh Day Adventist churches and I saw
and observed religion in my childhood; and these people are religious.
(440–41)

In his fiction, nonfiction, and autobiographical writings, Wright offers
his own experiences as a template for contemporary history and his
"political and psychological rebellion" (441) as a conception of reality
that attempted to resist the chaos and repression of his American experience. He derived new readings of his Southern folk tradition by inter-
preting them through the lens of a communal, transnational heritage.
Richard Wright: New Readings in the 21st Century takes up the
visions seen through that lens and also makes a claim for Wright "as
the figurative father for the African American novel since World War
II," as so eloquently argued by R. Baxter Miller in this collection.
In Gary E. Holcomb's words, Wright can equally be seen as "a self-
exiled, prodigal, *transnative* son." The combination of these two critical currents unites the articles in this volume. By foregrounding these
two approaches, *Richard Wright: New Readings in the 21st Century*
is able to rethink Wright's contributions to American modernism,
social realism, and popular media. The collection takes Wright studies
into new directions by not only stressing his formal contributions—
his pulp modernism and extensive use of European literatures— to
American and world fiction but also providing evidence that postwar
Paris was indeed, as William J. Maxwell notes here, "an incubator of
new black selves of international importance." Paris brought Wright
back to America while at the same time making him see "both worlds
from another and third point of view" (*White Man Listen!* 706). The
perspectives offered in this collection join others such as those of
Michel Fabre, Paul Gilroy, and Jerry Ward in arguing that rather than
impoverishing Richard Wright's work, his late exile years allowed him
to write from a richer and more complete historical and psychological
perspective. Throughout his lifetime, Wright presented new aesthetic-
political challenges to his critics.

Contributed by international, European, and American voices,
the essays reexamine the complex story of Wright's Americanism and
internationalism and his constructions of more self-aware and complex
collectivities. By exploring Wright's connections to Caribbean writer
George Lamming and Jamaican writer Claude McKay, this volume
asserts that Wright's *theories* on contemporary history and literature
become indivisible from the *forms* he created in order to validate those
theories. His literary texts interface with nonliterary forms while also

inviting interdisciplinary readings that move beyond strictly defined literary genres. Contributors touch upon unexplored themes and theoretical constructs derived from the literary significance of transitional and interracial housing, Wright's role in such key historical formations as the Works Progress Administration (WPA), the cold war, and the civil rights movements as well as Wright's exile and his cold war cosmopolitanism. With their disparate approaches to his work, these essays present readers with arguments that at once analyze Wright's cultural positions and clarify the rich legacy of his writings.

Indeed, one irony has beleaguered Richard Wright's legacy: the idea that he was overrated because he was a *Negro* American writer and equally underrated because he was a Negro American *writer*. Certainly in his early career and even beyond, he was expected to represent the authentic voice of the American Negro and nothing else. Despite this constraint, he never stopped struggling to create his own authorial voice as a writer, a voice that he viewed as being shaped by many factors over and above his racial and geographic roots. As Paul Gilroy suggests in his 1996 introduction to *Eight Men*, some viewed "his immersion in Parisian intellectual and political life as regrettable because it led the world's preeminent Negro writer far away from the vital roots of his creativity in the Southern Black Belt" (xi). Gilroy sums up one of the central debates concerning Wright's ultimate value as an American writer: Wright's experience as an exile "contaminated the version of literary authenticity that he had established by articulating African-American experiences in a way that was universally resonant" (xii).

In short, Wright wove an identity with the threads of his own life experience and his talents as a writer, while still being measured by the distorting mirrors that ostensibly reflected the authentic life possibilities for an American black man of his generation. As Wright's own intellectual growth reached beyond the borders of those expectations, the critical question of how to evaluate his literary legacy became more complex. Was he more importantly a Negro able to write about the struggles of the American Negro or a writer who evolved his worldview based on his exile, his broad-based self-education, and his roots as a black man in the Southern United States? Maryemma Graham articulates the contingent debate concerning the reception of the African American novel of Wright's generation: the so-called distinction between the realism of Wright's work *versus* the "high modernism" of Ralph Ellison's work (6). In so doing, she captures ironic tensions of the Wright critical tradition even more concretely. Because Ralph Ellison's status as the high modernist black writer was so unequivocal, Wright was often consequently relegated to the role of black Social Realist writer.

As the contributions to this volume show, the conundrums presented by the constantly changing perspectives on Wright's work remind the twenty-first-century reader that his writing career traces one of the most complicated periods in American history, particularly with respect to the African American citizen's role in that history. Wright's work reflects the birth pangs of an American modernism that had to match itself up against the concept of aesthetic distance so crucial to European modernist movements of a parallel period. With his connections and continuities between America, Europe, Africa, and Asia, Wright is uniquely placed to instruct a twenty-first-century reader about the traumatic origins of the African American novel. Conversely, to understand the full trauma of those origins is to learn to appreciate Richard Wright's lifetime as a writer in strikingly new ways.

What unites the critical voices in *Richard Wright: New Readings in the 21st Century* is a willingness to think about Wright's literary continuity in addition to his ruptures and conflicts. Ranging from Wright's earliest works to his posthumously published novel *A Father's Law*, the chapters in this volume create a space for critical reflection about Wright's accomplishments and unfinished goals as a black man writing both in America and in an international setting. The essays in this volume, contributed by both well-established and emergent Wright scholars, explore the roots of *his* necessities during his intellectual and visionary growth as an artist. The editors have chosen essays that analyze primarily his fictional works because we want to stress the importance of taking these works outside the frameworks of the realist *versus* modernist debates in order to reevaluate Wright's place in the canon of American and European modernist literature. As some of our contributors assert, Wright was already paving the way to the twenty-first century with its myriad of creative forms and technologically evolved ways of communicating to a mass audience. His fiction was a fiction of a future generation.

Although *Native Son* and *Black Boy* figure prominently, the volume wishes to resist their long-standing power to encompass Wright's lifelong project as a writer. Weaving between earlier works (*Native Son*) and late ones (*Island of Hallucination*) and connecting the canonical texts with others such as *Savage Holiday*, *The Long Dream*, and the recently published *A Father's Law*, the volume affirms a longer and broader view of twentieth-century African American writing. Indeed, the prescience of Richard Wright's work lies in how he placed himself not only geographically and generically but also in terms of his own possibilities for individual expression and self-representation. These essays illuminate new angles on Wright's place in the literary tradition, stressing that the contemporary reader needs to look anew at the critical commonplaces applied to Wright and to his writerly evolution.

A fitting tribute to Wright's centenary, *Richard Wright: New Readings in the 21st Century* also reaffirms Wright's status as a major American writer. The essays go beyond the black-white binary to consider more nuanced models of comparative racialization. The national, international, and transnational spaces that Wright occupied in the twentieth century are touchstones for considering the intersection between race and place and for redefining his representations of a modernism that announces its troubling properties even as he himself sought to confront and overcome them through his writing. Collectively emphasizing post-New Deal, postwar, and extraterritorial works, the essays seek a counterpoint to the critical tradition of readings of Wright's transnationalism from within the precincts of African/diaspora studies, which tend to dismiss the importance of these works.

The volume is divided into four parts, each of which will be prefaced by a summary of their guiding arguments. Taken together, the four parts reevaluate Wright's own writerly evolution as well as his anticipation of crucial tendencies in the modernist aesthetic, and position his body of works for comparative study with other literatures of the twenty-first century. Such an agenda can only be fully realized by beginning, as this volume does, with a reassessment of what has been undervalued in earlier critical appreciations of Wright's prescient move toward modernist themes and styles.

Wright's modernism results from the radical nature of his political and social necessities, fuelled by his untiring energy for experimentation. His engagement was always and most emphatically with a modern racial world still in the making. As he himself put it in his last recorded public appearance at the American Church of Paris, before his untimely death, "I was learning to live as a Negro the hard way. It seemed impossible to me that other Negroes would not or could not react to life as I did, but I was overlooking our difference in background" (10). What Wright signaled in this and other comments throughout this presentation, "The Negro Intellectual and Artist in the United States Today," which traces his attempts to assimilate to a life of expatriation, was that even though he may have shared geographic spaces with other Negroes in the Southern United States or social and political conditions with black men and women in other parts of the world, he could only very reluctantly accept that his voice was counted as just one of many voices "among the writers of his race" (18).

To learn to live as a Negro the hard way implied needing to embrace demanding social and political necessities while simultaneously trying to transcend the importance of those necessities on his struggles to find a unique and powerful voice. To express acceptance that his voice belonged alongside others of his race *only with great reluctance* was not, as this volume insists in various ways, to relinquish the responsibilities linked to his race. Rather, it was a reluctance based on a realization that a writer's identity is determined through a myriad of conditions coupled with a series of events, some of which are fortuitous, haphazard, or damningly stereotypical. Given such uncertainties, the power of a truly original voice perpetually runs the risk of being muted.

Wright, in "The Negro Intellectual and Artist in the United States Today," claimed that he was ultimately saved by the fact that the society of his time fundamentally rejected the idea of a Negro from his background in the Southern United States as someone capable of intellectual growth. Ironically, the white Southern neglect and indifference to black education left Wright free to cultivate his own intellectual capacities in whatever soil he planted himself. He was therefore spared the indoctrinating forces imposed on many Negroes of his generation and discovered in his rootless existence and eventual exile a freedom that will, in the words of Billie Holiday, bear "strange fruit."

Some critics have viewed Wright's last space in Paris as a wayward homelessness that vitiated the authenticity of his voice as a black American writer. *Richard Wright: New Readings in the 21st Century* asserts that this last phase constituted a new kind of hemispheric existence—the ironic plight and freedom of the exile he became. As the boundaries of Richard Wright's life and works are more thoroughly examined, a stronger ground emerges for understanding how and why he must be considered as the "figurative father for the African American novel since World War II." The essays in this volume likewise suggest that Wright's construction of the American modernist aesthetics of identity may be used productively in analyzing the literary voice of oppressed populations in new ways. Acerbic though it may be, Wright's work needs to be read as part of the study of global literary movements. *Richard Wright: New Readings in the 21st Century* can help in showing the way to such new readings. We hope that this volume will allow the legacy of Richard Wright to function on new and different aesthetic and political levels.

Bibliography

Fabre, Michel. *The Unfinished Quest of Richard Wright*. Trans. Isabel Barzun. New York: Morrow, 1973.

Gilroy, Paul. Introduction. *Eight Men*. By Richard Wright. New York: Harper Perennial, 1996.

Graham, Maryemma. *The Cambridge Companion to the African American Novel*. Cambridge: Cambridge UP, 2004.

Wright, Richard. *Black Power. Three Books from Exile:* Black Power; The Color Curtain; *and* White Man Listen! New York: Harper Perennial, 2008.

———. "The Negro Intellectual and Artist in the United States Today." Typescript by Helen M. White of tape recording by Clayton Machmar. American Library of Paris Special Collection. November 1960.

———. *12 Million Black Voices*. New York: Basic Books, 2002.

Part I

(Re)Placing Richard Wright

Without attempting to be comprehensive or definitive, the essays in part 1 question certain categorizations of Richard Wright's work and reposition them by finding new continuities between his early and late writings. Interrogating the themes of Wright's modernism and postmodernism, and his "aesthetic distance," R. Baxter Miller's "Modern and Postmodern Eden: Richard Wright" considers how Wright struggles to invent a "New Chicago language encapsulating the repressed rage of disempowered peoples…of African descent, in the Americas, Europe, and Africa." Miller suggests that Wright's literary trajectory from *Native Son* (1940) to *The Outsider* (1953) reveals how high-modernist culture is dismantled by a more demotic, reader-friendly art while at the same time struggling toward a broadening of community and a search for cultural connections. Wright's "literary world became postmodern" because existing modernistic forms could not supply the formal meanings required to renovate conventional middle-class values and prejudices. Emblematizing the African American working class, Wright's "new language" blends with realism and surrealism to mark off Chicago, "the modern locus of modern memory," and New York as the vectors of modernist urban idioms. While accounting for mutated forms of city life, Wright's "aesthetic distance" at once challenges the conventions of racial categories and literary realism. Miller situates Wright's work as not only anticipating a new aesthetic space but also demanding that the works of black modernism require a new critical framework. The essay serves as a significant starting point for the volume by asserting the specter of race as an agency driving the modernist literary experiment.

William Maxwell's "Wright among the G-Men" replaces Wright from Chicago and New York to the spy-filled, state-sleuthing Paris, the "cultural capitol of the cold war." Maxwell offers an unprecedented reading of Wright's typescript novel *Island of Hallucination*, a fittingly secretive text that "unveils [Wright's] most incisive reflections on black cosmopolitanism under pressure from state espionage." Maxwell argues that Wright shows Paris less as the capital of modernity and more as a capital of the cold war, the international headquarters of intellectual struggles between U.S. capitalism, Soviet communism, and Wright's "third way," as developed, for example, in *The Color Curtain*. In so doing, he demonstrates that Wright did not simply inhabit Paris as an American expatriate but he also provided analyses of his adopted space that only someone in his position could offer. In *Island of Hallucination*, Wright's discourses on internationalism proliferate not only through public acts of cross-diasporic translation but also through the plots of literary impersonation, dreams of a postracial Paris, and diverse counterintelligence efforts. Infused with pulp and hard-boiled noir, *Island of Hallucination* equips itself in an era of cold war surveillance and political repression for an advanced experiment in Afro-modern—and modernistic—self-renovation.

Leonard Cassuto's "*A Father's Law*, 1950s Masculinity, and Richard Wright's Agony over Integration" locates Wright within the concerns of "corporate" masculinity and twentieth-century American middle-class domesticity. Extending Maxwell's cold war espionage fears to a more generalized fear of surveillance derived from the Red Scare, Cassuto traces how *A Father's Law* introduces new questions about Wright's cosmopolitan deracination and his ambivalent attitudes toward the American civil rights movement. Cassuto takes up Miller's "figurative father" claim by placing Wright's work in a literary historical tension between sentimental suffering and violent outrage. As Cassuto argues, Wright is the "figurative father of some of the most violent and disturbing stories in all of American literature." Wright's social representation within American modernism, intimating the hazards of creating a new self, combines "murderous language" with a vernacular, mass-mediated modernism in unprecedented ways.

Robert Butler's contribution here reconstitutes Wright's Southern religious background, long viewed as limiting Wright's work, as a source of strength for his evolving fiction. Butler reassesses the limitations on Wright as a result of the religious training he was subjected to in his youth, and effectively argues that Wright's religious background is no hindrance. Rather it actually enables Wright's metaphorical language. Butler asserts that the imaginative experience generated by Wright's reading of literature serves "a quasi-religious function," enabling Wright to experience "the conversion in his personal life which he was unable to achieve in an institutional church." By arguing that *Black Boy* can be seen as part of the long tradition of "Christian conversion narratives," Butler goes against the general critical consensus concerning Wright's rejection of fundamentalist religion—and contributes a new view.

1

FROM *NEW CHICAGO RENAISSANCE* FROM *WRIGHT TO FAIR* MODERN AND POSTMODERN EDEN: RICHARD WRIGHT

R. Baxter Miller

The dreary stretches of Chicago passed before his window; it was dim, dead, dumb, sleeping city wrapped in a dream, a dream born of his frozen impulses. Could he awaken this world from its sleep? He recalled that pale of steaming garbage , the refuse the world had rejected; and he had rejected himself and was bowed, like that heap of garbage, under the weight of endurance and time.

—Richard Wright, *The Outsider*

The young radical Lorraine Hansberry considered Cross Damon to be "the symbol of Wright's new philosophy—the glorification of—nothingness."

Indeed, in a moment of ideological correctness, Hansberry accused *The Outsider* of being "a propaganda piece for the enemies of the Negro people, of working people and of peace and Wright of having become a writer who negated the reality of the black struggle for freedom."

—Jerry W. Ward, Jr., "Everybody's Protest Novel:
The Era of Richard Wright," *The Cambridge Companion
to the African American Novel*

Actually, both Richard Wright and Lorraine Hansberry sought to invent a New Chicago language encapsulating the repressed rage of the African American working class and therefore the disempowered people, particularly of African descent, in the Americas, Europe, and Africa. Wright, who was born on September 4, 1908, on a plantation in Roxie, Mississippi, twenty-two miles east of Natchez, was Lorraine Hansberry's senior by twenty-two years, Ronald L. Fair's by twenty-four, and Gwendolyn Brook's by only nine. Eventually all would voice several individuated angles on the city. All would recognize the human promise that needed to awaken new dreams and resources that, once dismissed as public refuse, would need to be reclaimed. All would reach for a revolutionary language to depict a city that had either broken or tried to smash the spirits of its black citizens.

Wright's fiction is modern in the sense that it takes root historically in Chicago after the inventions of the telegraph, telephone, bicycle, and automobile. Since the late nineteenth and early twentieth century, the world's technology suddenly seemed very old. So did the evolution of the human species. Especially since *Native Son* in 1940 to *The Outsider* in 1953, Wright's literary world became postmodern by suggesting that the old order of Cook County politics—indeed, the very form of the modern novel—would have to become more meaningful than the decadent fragments salvaged from the scrap heap of modern faith. Far more than T. S. Eliot and Ezra Pound, Wright believed that the mutated forms of city life must be accounted for and redeemed. Personal horror and racial terror could not be easily dismissed as a leisurely malaise, a luxury of the privileged class. The horror within the American self confirmed the socially immediate terror beyond it. Its very existence threatened to drive African Americans insane.

Richard Wright ranks among the foremost authors of fiction in the literary history of Chicago and the modern world. He becomes one of the leading authors to make a seamless transition from modernity to postmodernity. He advances, in other words, from the literary documentation of Chicago and New York to the awareness that the cultures of world cities must be deconstructed back into the spiritual and intellectual foundations of human desire. Then cities must, in his view, be reconstructed into experimental opportunities for new life forms beyond the traditional rituals and laws. Civilization must therefore retrace its consciousness and its raison d'être. Indeed, the continuation of existential outsiders calls into question the continued viability of evolution itself.

Perhaps it would be helpful to clarify connections between a few critical concepts and interpretive strategies. In the third decade of his career, Wright had certainly become a modernist who was more than flirting with the deconstructive tendencies of postmodernism. Rather than presenting the modernist story of metropolitan worlds in which things fall apart (laws, racial structures, and criminal investigations), he wanted to retrace the postmodern reasons for a resurgent rage that apparently was so imprinted on the human DNA. In a sense he was a *progressive modernist,* a precocious postmodernist who so many others would never catch up to.

Though *Native Son* had been his most systematic inquiry into a supposed pathology (and yes the often-ignored redemption of a criminal mind), *The Outsider* becomes the intellectual center of his philosophical speculation. For it is here that Wright creates the material space of two major cities as a synecdoche, a focused sign, of alienated space. Modernity, of course, marks precisely the space, but postmodernity claims that its own existence transcends the temporal realm. Wright's fictive world, *The Outsider,* asserts that allegorical space, an imagined window beyond American and modern global limits, conflicts with the material reality of the Chicago and New York courts. There persists an ironic tension between the imagined space and the modern world.

In many ways, Wright was the first black novelist to narrate the experience of the urban masses and to write major fiction in the naturalistic tradition. The figurative father for the African American novel since World War II, he foreshadowed so many others whose anger would later resemble his during the sixties. He left his imprint on the worldview and metaphors that were eventually to emerge as rich completions in the fiction of Ralph Ellison, James Baldwin, and Toni Morrison. Wright represented African American alienation from the racial roots in the American South. In balancing stories about secular violence with an intuitive faith, he showed great epiphany. Just as he faced the social justice of the racist South and subsequently of the North, he inquired into the cosmic questions of human existence. Personally, he represented the talented individual who challenges the folk community that helped produce the creative quest. He was a communal artist who claimed to be his own man.

Perhaps it will help to remember the context of what his visionary and formal contribution is. He provides a theory for retracing African American roots. To begin, his work completes a vitally liberating process of thought. Initially, blacks define themselves as unblossomed flowers in the wasteland of the South (*Black Boy,* 1945). Then they recognize their beauty as being threatened by American violence (*Uncle Tom's Children,* 1938). Third, they seek the literary power to articulate and liberate themselves from American terror (*Native Son,* 1940). Fourth, they withstand a postmodern French seduction to write only about an existential protagonist who would transcend the trivial limits of racial memory (*The Outsider,* 1953). Fifth, they identify with the metonyms—related symbols of meaning—of the bullfighter, priest, and artist, all of whom see themselves within the expansive mirror of their larger existence (*Pagan Spain,* 1957; *Eight Men,* 1961). Sixth, though blacks reclaim a positive self-esteem in the American

South (*The Long Dream*, 1958), they finally serve as a human test of whether the public law, or the arbitrary theory of personal experimentation, is a more viable theory for political advancement (*A Father's Law*, posthumously 2008). Here I focus on Wright's typography of Chicago and his figurative testing of European existentialism against an implied backdrop of the Chicago Popular Fronts. There develops a need first to establish some working contexts of modernism and postmodernism within a historical and political context.

Often, research on Wright reflects the scholarly methods of the decades considered. From the 1970s through the 1990s, Michel Fabre, Dan McCall, Keneth Kinnamon, and Yoshinobu Hakutani emphasized historical sources. Though Fabre reported the importance of Wright in the existentialist thought of the West (529), particularly of France, New Historicists or postmodernists such as Jeffrey Atteberry (2005), Heather Andrade (2006), and Sarah Relyea (2006), advanced the implicit claims in Paul Gilroy's *The Black Atlantic: Modernity and Double Consciousness* (1993). Hence all argue that Wright belongs with the Germanic intellectual elite of Heidegger, Kierkegaard, and Nietzsche.

In addition, according to the postmodernist view, a communist would focus on the consequences of social policy for those in a low social class, but an existentialist would consider the moral burdens of individual responsibility in the society. Each position implies a binary. While the imaginary self in Wright was inspired by the proletariat of the thirties, the potential criminal in him accepted the idea of human law. Notable exceptions to the historical tendencies in research are Jerry Ward, Jr. (2004), who helped return the critical discussion to the political and social contexts of the African American novel, and Tara Green (2002), who perceived feminist theme as crucial to an understanding of Wright's fiction.

As now needs to be understood anew, Wright became a definitive voice within the American Left of Langston Hughes and the Popular Front of Jack Conroy as well as Nelson Algren. To Wright, the figure of the outsider, as a metaphor for literary deconstruction and for postmodernity (and as proposed so fashionably since 2000), may have violated his idea of causality. Presuming that political history produced a response in popular culture (the Chicago School of Sociology), Wright imagined protagonists beyond the Left Front of the thirties. Certainly he contributed to a popular literary advance from social realism through modernity to postmodernity. But, beyond the American and European intellectual contexts, however, he voiced an urban humanity of race within the modern idiom, resisting the expedient erasure of African American culture. A New Historicist in a way, he understood that fiction often became an imaginary mirror of political reality. If communism posed a bond between the individual and the masses, and if existentialism implied a connection between a hypothetical criminal and the American law, African American fiction encapsulated a response between the literary artists and the Left Front politicians (The Communist Party).

Both the modernist and postmodernist camps have reasons for disinterest in restoring the critical reputation of Richard Wright. The first would see him as telling a political and cultural story, which high modernism bans as being aesthetically intrusive; the second would perceive him as representing a racial essence and public democracy so unfashionable for a universe presumably now without a moral and civic center. In fact, the second group would not see a metaphysical universe as existent. In a sense, both of the critical camps repudiate a concept of periodicity. The modernists do so because history must be relegated to the periphery of literary form while the postmodernists do so because the idea of history has disappeared from their critical discourse altogether. According to my extrapolation of the theory by Madelyn Detloff (8), Wright narrates or predicts the *migration* of blacks from the South to the North during the first half of the twentieth century,[1] the *mutation* of the political discrimination against the urban poor and blacks of the thirties into an evolved penal system of the seventies (and indeed now), and the *translation* of the socioeconomic inequity of the thirties into a theory of job discrimination.[2]

In English, the word "modern" derives from *modernus* translated as "just now" in sixth-century Latin (Eoyang). Later, the term denoted the phrase, "now existing," which, according to the Oxford English Dictionary, is rare or obsolete (119). By the sixteenth century, the adjective implied "present time" as distinct from the remote past. According to the Germanic roots of the expression, "die moderne" could refer to both modern*ity* in the political and social sense or modern*ism* in the aesthetic and cultural one. Especially since the early nineteenth century, modernism has come to mean a radical response to a cultural crisis that was initiated by the disintegration of providential belief; the ravages of capitalist imperialism; the crumbling of traditional faith in self and character after the unsettling thought of Darwin (evolution), Freud (subconscious), and Nietzsche (dead God); and the destabilization of long-term assumptions about verbal communication and actuality (Giles 176, my extrapolation).[3]

Today, the definitions continue to be largely Eurocentric. According to Peter Nicholls in *Modernisms* (1995, 2009), the concept derived from the great French symbolists—Baudelaire, Mallarmé, Rimbaud, and Breton—who sought to establish an interior landscape to substitute for lost terrain of social representation (11). From the very beginning, therefore, European modernism was theoretically opposed to the kind of social representation that was to emerge in the New Chicago Renaissance. Though Europe had a proletarian measure as represented in France by Emile Balzac and in England by George Eliot in the late nineteenth century, the United States was far more ethnically diverse. By the time the New Chicago Renaissance of 1935–1972 developed, it represented a maturation of an urban idiom, not only of the nation's traditional naturalists and realists since 1880 (in other words, of *low* modernism) but of American democracy itself. Even prior to World War I, modernists had honed a conservative ideology to subvert the egalitarian theory of the French Revolution. Traditionalists such as T. E. Hulme, Irving Babbitt, Wyndham Lewis, and T. S. Eliot had already attacked the romantic legacy of Jean-Jacques Rousseau. By the end of World War II, modernist writers had become much more interested in the ways that vast corporations used to manipulate mass democracies (7). A defining tenet of high modernism was an erasure of public history.

Now, too, black modernism requires a new critical apparatus. Postmodernism, according to Eoyang, may well represent a recent advance in which a new thought tends to reject a previous idea only to replace it (122). Often, the four tentative tenets of postmodernism may conflict indeed: (1) the dismissal of high modernism as a claim for aesthetic populism; (2) the recognition that modernism has run its course; (3) the insistence on radicalism "different in kind from modernism"; and (4) the intensification of modernist qualities that persist and define postmodernism (Giles 179–81). In a sense, postmodernism ideologically opposes the political and historical frameworks in which it exists. Postmodernism is therefore to modernism as high culture was to the Popular Fronts. In each instance, an intellectual position denied and possibly even defied the context that actually produced it.

Postmodernist theory would discredit the reason of the Enlightenment while opening up personal and social subjectivities (x). While modernism had sought to separate the historical thirties from the real Chicago, Wright represented the city as a defining center in the public idiom. In other words, he wrote as a Chicago writer historically. He recognized a disparity between the elite depiction of urban space and the public perception of those who inhabited it. Rather profoundly he understood that those who lived in discrete spaces rarely doubted that a monolithic force shaped their destinies. Politics remained an often hidden dynamic (Brown and Irwin 21) of African American literary art.

By the time of *The Outsider* (1953), Wright expresses his symbolic recovery of a human language, of political history, as a tale of two cities—Chicago and New York. Indeed the work becomes an extremely raw, yet revealing, expression of profundity. Many of his deepest themes appear here, including the vital importance of Chicago as the Eden of modern African American consciousness, the emergence of the racial and metaphysical outsider as a consequence of modernity, the dysfunction of existentialism as a modern or postmodern philosophy for African Americans, and the failure of religion in a world in which intellectual outlaws usurp the prerogative of God. Here, the coldly windy city functions as a *locus,* a landscape of memory, for the imaginative resolution of detective intrigue. In a sense, *The Outsider* is therefore Wright's *King Lear,* his *Brothers Karamazov,* his *In the Mecca,* or his *Song of Solomon.*

On November 8, 1948, Wright had written to his editor Paul Reynolds about the desire to revise the urban novel. Recent trips to the United States and Argentina, along with increasing political concerns and existentialist reading, helped him reconsider the destiny of modern humanity. By turning his attention momentarily from Europe to the third world, he prepared himself in 1952 for a return to the art of writing. In the United Kingdom, he completed the novel three months after a delay of nearly six years (Fabre 365–66). Originally, he had opened the work on a description of Cross Damon, the protagonist, during a workday at a Chicago post office bustling with collegial conversation (Fabre 366–67). The suggestions had been that the novel would provide a pleasing presentation of African American urban life. To seven possible titles recommended by John Fischer of Harper's, on August 7, 1952, Wright added five, including one that was *The Outsider.*[4] In November 1952, a Harper's salesman decided on the final title. While Wright's significant step from the racial to metaphysical novel may seem impulsive, the tendency had appeared in "The Man Who Lived Underground." His pervasive theme of police brutality was already developing from his early fiction, *Uncle Tom's Children* (1938), to his next-to-last novel, *The Long Dream* (1958). Much of the racial discourse was excised from the original draft, which was, upon the recommendation of Fischer, reduced from approximately 220,000 words to 150,000. The typescript decreased to nearly 620 pages (Hakutani 134).

The transcendent universality tested in the literary world fails because the black criminal life derived from Chicago remains inescapably bound to it. The landscape appears as a contextual imagery of network news set against a backdrop of the train, along with the latent animalism reminiscent of the stockyards. There is the desperate place of comic relief in the cinema, yet the drugs and alcohol outside as well. It is the vestige of American Gothicism—the Gilded Age—and of the towers of modern alienation. Chicago is the figured underground through which the subway rockets as external objects seem to fly by a viewing window. Wright places the city in the context of the Americas and Europe as Lorraine Hansberry would eventually situate the metropolis within Africa and the Americas. But it is Wright (and later Gwendolyn Brooks) who emerges as a founder of a new black American literary renaissance in the city. Initially, Wright sets up the modern landscape of Chicago; then, he reconsiders the displacement of the terrain by the postmodern landscape of New York; and third, he achieves an aesthetic distance, evincing a persistence of modern form (Eva's drawings). Despite a distraction of nearly eighty-three pages of recitations (shades of *Native Son*), he achieves a unity of place and memory. He reestablishes Chicago as the ancestral locus of modern memory and the Eden of African American consciousness.

A subway accident allows for Cross (Christ) Damon (Daemon, Demon), who has impregnated the minor Dorothy Powers in Chicago, to reinvent his life (New Eden) as Lionel Lane in New York. As the intrigue unravels, the narrator voices a compelling critique of the communist party (Ward 180–81). By the time that Damon concludes his horrific rampage, various people become his murder victims for different reasons. Joe Thomas, a fellow postal clerk, becomes a cheerful john in the wrong whorehouse at the wrong time, as Damon prepares to escape the city. Two others, Gil Blount (Eva's husband) and John Hilton, incite retribution at Damon's hands for being communist leaders obsessed with their godly obedience to blind authority. (They are too much like him.) Langley Herndon, the fourth casualty, comes off as a fascist straw man who exposes the hypocrisy of the communist affection for the black masses. Hence, the twin cities become the narrative hub of so many theoretical outsiders, including Hilton, the communist deceiver; Ely Houston, the state attorney; Gilbert Blount, the manipulative husband; and, of course, Eva Blount, the abused artist. It is only the fourth (Eve) who would have any meaningful role in Damon's new heaven and new earth, which actually becomes his postmodern hell.

Several complementary structures unify the efficacy of the double Eden according to Wright's expressed intention. A five-part design underlies the sequence of (1) Dread, (2) Dream, (3) Descent, (4) Despair, and (5) Decision. But the protagonist's reascent from the figured hell remains incomplete. In Wright's world, a way out certainly becomes intuited rather than assured. Chicago becomes the urban site of a *rise in dramatic action* toward an eventual *climax* of a fictive drama played out in the New York streets. Eventually there emerges a convenient denouement in which the detective clues for three of the four murders are eventually solved. There exists the underlying structure of the author's life, leading from Chicago through Harlem to the Village (Fabre 366). Margaret Walker writes that *The Outsider* is the most autobiographical work by a self-obsessed writer telling his own story (230). For here the narrator relates an account in which the grim landscape of Chicago—one displaced only temporarily by Eva's imaginative paintings—defines the locus of African American modernity. European existentialism fails a racial test so rooted in its American redesign and consequently in historical memory. Even the popular European theory cannot account for Wright's very practical ethics of African American survival. In a sense, it is the same pattern that has appeared so in the original crime scene of *Native Son*.

After the subway accident on Saturday, the narrator describes the metropolis in *The Outsider* through the imagery of winter while implying a renunciation of Easter.[5] On Sunday morning, the landscape appears clearly cold while a sharply freezing wind blows across the city from Lake Michigan. Damon, curious as to whether his mother has badly received the news of his feigned death, hides in her neighborhood to catch a glimpse of her during her departure for the Church of the Good Shepherd. Smoking a cigarette and toying with a glass of beer, the protagonist keeps his eyes fixed on the doorway of her home. By 11:45 A. M., she exits to make gentle treks in the snow toward the church. Her face remains cloaked by a veil. He continues to worry that something may go wrong with the staged burial. Perhaps his deserted wife Gladys would challenge the authenticity of the mistaken corpse; or maybe the real wife of the unidentified dead would do so. By Monday morning, the brightly cold terrain freezes at a temperature of ten degrees below zero. With windy gusts sweeping in from the Lake Michigan, snow eddies pile up, as the *Chicago World* reports that the corpse mistaken for Damon's lies in state at the Jefferson Resting Home. Cross, now smug about his powers of deception, views the entire scene from the top floor of a rented building opposite the church.

New Chicago appears as from behind a veil, as in the parables of Plato and Du Bois. Often the image appears secondarily through the windows of modern edifices or trains. Indeed, the windows share the semitransparent glass properties of the fabricated device holding the drinking beer in Damon's hand. Chicago signifies a frozen world, the renunciation of promise more than the prophecy of hope, of Easter redemption. In the tradition of African American fiction, as old as Charles Chesnutt, the potential resurrection of the locale is doubtful.

Eva's abstract paintings represent her artistic distancing from the details of the urban site. Despite her general sympathy toward African Americans and the universally oppressed, she manages a racial slip. During a private lunch with Cross in the Blount apartment, she doubts that he might appreciate her "nonobjective" painting, since African Americans, according to her, are "so realistic and drenched in life, the world (204)...Colored people [she says to Cross] are so robustly healthy." By replying "*some* of us are," he subverts the traditional stereotype that a single rule applies to all blacks. Rather, he theorizes that some people become immersed in the urban environment while others are compelled to flee it. Once he shows himself as flexible regarding his personal aesthetics, she leads him into a jumbled, grimy room behind the kitchen. Nearly all of the dissociated forms of her painting, including meteors, cubes, squares, triangles, trapezoids, planes, crystals, and spirals, shine in achromatic tints. When Damon advances toward a canvas of her work on a huge easel, he encounters a surge of fragmented forms, moving almost lyrically in "*mysterious light stemming from an unseen source*" (204, emphasis added). Eva radiates brightness by being a locus for the emergent tones and patterns of her story.

Her positioning herself as a painter symbolizes Wright's own posture as a postmodern writer. Indeed, the two become metonyms of each other. Duped by the Party into a marriage of convenience with Gil, she has not had her own work exhibited in more than a year. Somewhat unsettled by having revealed to Cross so much of her private story, she leaves the room awkwardly in haste. For the next two hours, he examines every canvas in the room from varied angles in space and light. He fancies himself at the center of her private ego. So acquainted with the starkness of her aloneness, he recognizes the way that her haunted images are compelled to appear on the page. "At least she's lucky to be able to say her terrors and agonies in form and color," he admires enviously (205). Eva is, indeed, his figurative sister. Wright constructs a variety of literary lenses to filter out all but the precise colors of race and nation represented in his fiction. His writing becomes a localized prism that projects a distinctive vision and color of inner-city reality. He converts protocols of existentialist realism so as to reconstitute his African American voice. To him, sound and light become the complementary dimensions for expressing his unfinished quest. His narrating tone sounds almost silently within the reader's consciousness, but the light projects itself beyond the human grasp. Sound means present time, but light means future time. Light expresses the literary imagination.

Perhaps the problem is that the path to such symbolic light leads through fire—purgation through suffering. Eden must be redeemed. As the classical dramatist Aeschylus once theorized about the Greek King Agamemnon, at least wisdom emerges from the spiritual conflagration. More realistic concerns motivate Cross to track the communist leader John Hilton to the Edward Hotel in New York in order to murder him. Well, if murder is not the immediate intent, it is certainly the final result. On a fact-finding mission, Damon discovers that John Hilton has found and hidden the bloody handkerchief that Cross believes he himself had burned in a building incinerator (also shades of *Native Son*). Meanwhile, a new police search occurs after the double murder of Blount and Herndon. It seems that some literally incombustible evidence—ghosts from the city's past—nearly always resurfaces to indict Wright's murderers. Killers may end up on death row or be murdered in the streets within the gangster tradition of Al Capone, but they may never go free. As clarified by Wright in *Black Boy,* crime carries with it its own punishment. If Wright achieves, as suggested by his friend and erstwhile lover Margaret Walker, a daemonic genius, it is a brilliance checked by an honest conscience, indeed one tortured in the agony of its own fallen vision.

Cross is furious at the Party's mechanical deceit that epitomizes the downfall of the New Eden. The organization's purpose is to control him for social reasons more than have him captured as a criminal. In doing so, the Party would dominate his consciousness. Both the party and the city represent the industrialization that dehumanizes the postal worker. Both are indifferent; both silently ruthless. Each is sentimentally cold; each produces tragic torment. "Why," Cross asks Hilton, "all this meaningless suffering" (301). Cross, who is livid that Hilton has had the black communist Bob Hunter deported to Trinidad, eventually shoots Hilton in the head. A pillow placed strategically at the victim's temple helps mute the sound. "Cross's eyes were unblinking, seeing not Hilton sitting there staring at him, but Eva's diary, those pages telling of deception, of shame, of fear; and, too, he was remembering his own agonies in Chicago" (301).

In his reply to Ely Houston in the police station, (Adam) Damon discovers his own voice to be displaced. The aesthetic distance confirms Wright's structural device as the posturing of the outsider, the deconstructive voyeur. At once the voice exists within modernity while not necessarily accepting the alienation of it. Effectively, the author lays bare the soul of the urban masses of all colors and creeds. The outsider, though privy to all modern knowledge, either rejects it or escapes much of its pervasive influence. So much more than only an atheist, he is a pagan without the need to worship gods at all. Whether his proposed universe is polytheistic or monotheistic is certainly inconsequential for him. He avoids classical beliefs every bit as much as Judaic and Christian attitudes. What modern and postmodern worlds must account for is his terrible revival as the ancient man: "Nothing at all but his own desires, which would be his only values" (316). Wright tests an anarchical theory of reducing humanity to its original nakedness of the individual's desire. But he finds the individual self-imprisoned by a strange hegemony, the merciless god of the self.

Especially during the final part of *The Outsider*, the coarseness of Chicago resurfaces within the more refined culture of New York. In a sense, both cities are already lost. Everywhere, the ceremony of innocence is drowned and the human fall repeated. During the last recitation in the district attorney's office, even Damon sympathizes with the "origin of their [the fellow citizens'] power and authority and scope of their duties" (378). Though he makes the confession of his crimes in New York, the disclosure refers to Chicago. Within a more ancient context, Houston speaks to Cross about his own personal fall into postmodern awareness: "I wish to God I hadn't met you on that train, or hadn't talked to you. It would make my task easier" (378). It is the same train, of course, that symbolically reinfects humanity with the disease of itself; on every trip it is the disturbing awareness that horror remains within the evil heart of American whiteness. In postmodern fashion, Houston urges Damon to recommence the murder story from the origin. Then Houston leads off with an earlier starting date for it of a month and a half, February 8. But actually the grim tale dates back to the Fall of Man. Even the closure of the novel completes a unity of epic returns. To identify Cross, Houston brings in Finch, a worker from the Chicago Post Office, who had once offered Damon a loan to pay off the silence money to Dorothy Powers. Soon Cross learns that his mother was so astonished to hear about his survival as to die of the shock. He "remembers her as he had seen her that last time, walking with faltering steps over the snow in front of the church, going to get into the car that was to bear his supposed body to the cemetery for burial" (379). It is a masterstroke of lost, elapsed, and recovered time, a motion measured by ticks on the clock. And it is the church that seeks to redeem Eden (human meaning) from Time—a march toward demise—and the Chicago burial of the dead.

In the moment of reckoning, the ghosts of the past—indeed the species—may be hidden. But they remain as real as the horrific moments restored shockingly to memory. We find ourselves startled in the unmistakable reckoning, the forgotten complicity, in the unpardonable crime of being human. As Cross tells Houston, "A man today who believes that he cannot live by the articles of faith of his society is a criminal and you know it, even though Congress has not got around to making such into law" (387). When Cross returns to see Eva now in Sarah Hunt's apartment in Harlem, she verifies that he is indeed the fugitive who left his family behind in Chicago. What terrifies the characters about playing out their bit parts in the horror film of sorts is that devolution into anarchy has become so easy. And it is precisely the ease that makes the repression of ancestral memory and desire so vital. In the tortured relationship with Cross, Eva accepts the horror of what he has once told her about Chicago. Consequently, she plummets six flights to her suicide death in Harlem. As the toes of her shoes point skyward, her face lies buried in the snow. Someone has crushed a lock of her dirtied blonde hair into the ice.

In a moment of startled awareness, citizens come to accept their mutual accountability to each other. Chicago is the fallen garden in which the fellow postal workers witness the signs, if not the specifics, of personal crimes. As with Damon's mother, we seek to atone for the sins during a spiritual trek to the church. On the path we find ourselves marking our limited lives. We encounter the human borders imposed on us by our own mortality. This is the ultimate recognition that the narrator represents as the freezing wind.

Both the narrator and the communist propose to record an objective truth about the fallen Eden. Menti rushes to the corpse on the sidewalk to ask Damon why Eva has died. And Cross, without a sign of having heard him, only stares into his eyes. As police cars screech around the corners, the ice and snow make them skid into stops. When the blue-coated officers exit the police cars, the communist rises, detaches himself from the gathering, and advances into a candy store down the sidewalk. He calls in his report to the Party. As rarely true in Wright's fiction, someone other than the narrator achieves the aesthetic distance this time. Both the white communist and the black narrator look for an advantage in repeating the story. The socialist seeks to account for the trail of death that has followed Damon since his arrival in New York while the narrator traces the pattern of the seeker's desire.

The socialist rushes into the New York streets to maintain order as well as to engineer American history and postmodernity. The narrator, rather, observes the deathly scene in order to reveal the moral result of Damon's murders. While the socialist only records that Eva (innocence) has died, the storyteller implies that Cross has killed her as an indirect consequence of his crimes. If the socialist proposes to manipulate history, the narrator insists rather on revealing the truth of the human interior. Socialists may be limited to sniffing out the realistic trail of the murder, but artists concern themselves with the mythic patterns of human history. Both the social engineer and the didactic narrator have hidden agendas; but the storyteller commands the force of language. Only the artist inquires into the human heart.

Margaret Walker, who had known Wright in Chicago and had helped complete much of the preliminary research for *Native Son*, writes,

> Wright was an outsider all his life. As a boy growing up in Mississippi, he felt himself outside the pale of a loving, understanding, and protecting family. He felt himself outside the accepted world of privileged, the educated, the dominant white culture, the bourgeois class. He had lived in dire poverty among the bigots, fanatics, and insensitive people who believed in the primacy of skin color, in money and privilege and despised all those who were different, or who thought differently. (234)

Wright, she says, was absolutely sure about the hell of the black American experience but uncertain about the mystical promise of heaven. He considered himself a forced exile from his homeland because of racism and terror. "He believed," she says, "that he would lose his mind if he stayed, that many people in America did lose their minds because of the terrible racism that afflicted the psyche and spirit of all Americans. Either one must kill or be killed or become insane..." (234). Though she recognizes in his fiction a process of daemonic spirit, his work is really about a *redemptive genius* that civilizes ancient instinct—almost magically suspending it through his imaginative will to faith.

Wright emerged in part from the political order of the Popular Fronts, yet created imaginary constructions in literary form. Even more than the experimental traditionalists Carl Sandburg, Frank Norris, and Theodore Dreiser, he transformed social realism through symbolic infusions of a deeper meaning. Beneath the factual account of Robert Nixon, a political source for Bigger Thomas in *Native Son*, there remained the fatal (and perhaps redemptive) story of Adam. And it set into relief the postmodern speculation of whether a recurring pattern in Wright's fiction—the artistic redemption of the political life—would ever be vindicated in God's Law. Wright's explosive originality derives from a narrative blend of urban realism with surrealistic nightmare. Ultimately, he tests the literary devices of existential terror (*The Outsider*) only to find them untenable for African American survival. Beyond an inquiry into the mental health of the black masses, he achieves a detached posture of the bemused interloper. His surprising craftsmanship belies his reputation when he refines his fictive shapes well within and beyond the sociological theory of Chicago (socioeconomics produce a response in formal culture); his technical limitations are by choice more than by failure. Hence, he often repeats the very errors critics blame him for. Despite the tendency in the closures of his stories to lecture rather than chisel a fiction of revelation, he carves out verbal figures of unexpected beauty. He emerges as the cornerstone of a New Chicago Renaissance.

NOTES

1. See Baker.
2. As apparent below, the categories are Detloff's, but in this instance the application is entirely mine.
3. The implications regarding the thinkers are mine.
4. Other possibilities were "Between Dreams," "Out of This World," "Man Upside Down," "Last Man," and "Colored Man"; later "The Outsider," "God's Slave," "Two Thousand Years," "The Crime of Cross," "Beyond Freedom," and "Innocence at Home."
5. In a sense, it is the same pattern that appeared so well in the original crime scene of *Native Son*. Says Hilton to Cross, "Was he your brother or something?" (298).

BIBLIOGRAPHY

Andrade, Heather Russell. "Poetry, Prose, and Politics." *American Literature* 78.1 (2006): 168–78. Print.

Atteberry, Jeffrey. "Entering the Politics of the Outside: Richard Wright's Critique of Marxism and Existentialism." *Modern Fiction Studies* 51.4 (2005): 873–95. Print.

Baker, Houston A., Jr. *Turning South Again*. Durham, NC: Duke UP, 2001. Print.

Brooks, Gwendolyn. *In the Mecca*. New York: Harper, 1968. Print.

Brown, Peter, and Michael Irwin, eds. *Littérature et Place: 1800–2000*. Bern: Lang, 2006. Print.

Detloff, Madelyn. *The Persistence of Modernism*. Cambridge: Cambridge UP, 2009. Print.

Djelal, Kadir, and Dorothea Löbberman. *Other Modernisms in an Age of Globalization*. Heidelberg: Universitätsverlag, 2002. Print.

Dostoyevsky, Fyodor. *The Brothers Karamazov*. Trans. Constance Garnett. 1880. New York: New American Library, 1957. Print.

Eoyang, Eugene Chen. "A Crosscultural Perspective on the Modern and the Postmodern." *Other Modernisms in an Age of Globalization*. Eds. Kadir Djelal and Dorothea Löbberman. Heidelberg: Universitätsverlag, 2002. Print.

Fabre, Michel. *The Unfinished Quest of Richard Wright*. 1973. Urbana: U of Illinois P, 1993. Print.

Giles, Steve. *Theorizing Modernism: Essays in Critical Theory*. New York: Routledge, 1993. Print.

Hakutani, Yoshinobu. *Richard Wright and Racial Discourse*. Columbia: U of Missouri P, 1996. Print.

Kinnamon, Keneth. *The Emergence of Richard Wright: A Study in Literature and Society*. 1973. Urbana: U of Illinois P, 1993. Print.

McCall, Dan. *The Example of Richard Wright*. New York: Harcourt, 1969. Print.

Miller, R. Baxter. "A Revised Southern Memory for Blyden." *The Artistry of Memory*. Ed. R. Baxter Miller. Lewiston: Mellen, 2008. 241–52. Print.

Mullen, Bill V. *Popular Fronts: Chicago and African American Cultural Politics, 1935–1946*. Urbana: U of Illinois P, 1999. Print.

Nicholls, Peter. *Modernism: A Literary Guide*. New York: Palgrave Macmillan, 1993. Print.

Potter, Rachel. *Modernism and Democracy: Literary Culture 1900–1930*. New York: Oxford UP, 2006. Print.

Relyea, Sarah. *Outsider Citizens: The Remaking of Postwar Identity in Wright, Beauvoir, and Baldwin*. New York: Routledge, 2006. Print.

———. "The Vanguard of Modernity: Richard Wright's The Outsider." *Texas Literature and Language* 48.3 (2006): 187–219. Print.

Shakespeare, William. *King Lear. The Complete Works*. Ed. G. B. Harrison. New York: Harcourt, 1968. Print.

Walker, Margaret. *Richard Wright: Daemonic Genius*. New York: Warner, 1988. Print.

Ward, Jerry W., Jr. "Everybody's Protest Novel: The Era of Richard Wright." *The Cambridge Companion to the African American Novel*. Ed. Maryemma Graham. Cambridge: Cambridge UP, 2004. Print.

Wright, Richard. *Black Boy*. 1945. New York: Harper, 1991. Print.

———. *Eight Men*. 1961. New York: Thunder's Mouth, 1987. Print.

———. *A Father's Law*. New York: Harper's, 2008. Print.

———. *The Long Dream*. 1958. New York: Harper, 1987. Print.

———. *The Outsider*. New York: Harper, 1953. Print.

———. *Uncle Tom's Children*. 1938. New York: Harper's, 1991. Print.

2

WRIGHT AMONG THE "G-MEN": HOW THE FBI FRAMED *PARIS NOIR*

William J. Maxwell

If histories of African Americans in Paris cohere into a full-blown literary genre, that genre is a modernist arraignment of racial antiquity, a movable feast exposing the past-frozen provincialism of American apartheid. And if that genre mandates a mise-en-scène, it is the Parisian café-turned-ecumenical black church, the quarter refuge crossed with the diasporan contact zone. In Tyler Stovall's exemplary book *Paris Noir: African Americans in the City of Light* (1996), the affective architecture of the café locates and symbolizes the freedom enjoyed by the colony of black Americans who settled the Left Bank after World War II. Assimilating the everyday life of their French hosts more gamely than the earlier postwar generation of Gertrude Stein and her Imagist pupils, these second-wave expatriates went native to choose carefully among terraces and proprietors, settling on the Tournon outside the Luxembourg Gardens and the Monaco on the rue Monsieur-le-Prince, not coincidentally the same street on which pioneer émigré Richard Wright discovered his most comfortable Paris apartment. Once dug in, the literary wing of black Paris employed its favored cafés as both workplaces and social clubs, tending sequentially to coffee, page counts, alcohol, serious conversation, and sexual pursuit. In this double occupation of café space, African American writers proved their receptiveness to several strains and moments of Parisian café culture: they paid their respects to the proletarian "people's parliaments" of the nineteenth century, busy intersections of "the worlds of work and leisure" (Haine 3), even as they cemented their ties to the postoccupation existentialist network of Simone de Beauvoir and Jean Paul Sartre, so identified with punctual writing hours and

romantic assignations at the Café de Flore and the Deux Magots that
the latter advertised itself in Parisian papers as the "[r]endez-vous de
l'élite intellectuelle" (qtd. in Campbell, *Exiled* 85). No less vital for
Stovall than his subjects' Francophilic adoption of full-spectrum café
sociability, however, is their distinctive use of café space to nurture the
confident openness of their desegregated urbanity. "Black Americans
of all descriptions, from tourists to GIs on weekend passes to students,
soon learned that one could go to certain cafes" in the Latin Quarter
and Saint-Germain-des-Prés to watch "and meet well known figures"
of intellectual distinction, he reports (189). Greeting Wright at work
on a manuscript or on the Tournon's sticky pinball machine, black
newcomers to the City of Light were invited to enter what Stovall
labels "a new type of black community, one based on positive affinities
and experiences rather than the negative limitations of segregation,
one that included a wide variety of individuals yet at the same time
celebrated black culture" (xv).

So rests Stovall's self-declared "tale of romance and freedom," a
candid articulation of the penchant to volunteer black Paris as a lesson to a primitive U.S. home front, a "vision of complete human liberation," as Stovall has it, "bequeathed...across the sea" (xvi). Yet it
remains the case that the very openness of Stovall's novel community,
founded on the accessible pluralism of the Tournon and the Monaco,
exposed it to a specter that arrived along with the modern Parisian
café in the revolutionary upheaval of 1789—namely, the political spy.
As I've suggested elsewhere, with the speedup of cold war winds in
the late 1950s, the *Rive noire* of the city Brent Edwards influentially
honored as the emblem of "black transnational interaction, exchange,
and dialogue" was jeopardized by partition, information hoarding,
and raw denunciation (5). "Everybody thought everybody else was
informing on someone or other for somebody," confessed an eyewit-
ness of the Tournon scene, once a spot where post-nationals drank
off American racial masks, now a magnet for anxiety over American
state sleuthing (qtd. in Campbell, *Exiled* 91). Spy stories ricocheted
around the walls and stained everyone inside. Regulars disagreed on
who betrayed whom for which intelligence agency, but jointly worried that black café intellectuals took cues from Sartre's generic café
waiter in *Being and Nothingness* (1943), guilty of bad faith's self-
slaving impostures.

Chester Himes, lured to Paris by Wright in 1953, rehearsed his
Harlem detective fiction by investigating if William Gardner Smith,
novelist and journalist at Agence France-Press, received payments
from the CIA. Both charged essayist and cartoonist Ollie Harrington,

Wright favorite and easygoing hardcore leftist, with undercover work. Wright expressed grave doubts about the loyalties of Smith ally Richard Gibson, and only slightly less concern about everyone else with whom he spoke or slept. For his trouble, Wright was suspected of being either a G-Man or a diplomatic mole. "There is a story, a rumor about you that is going about," Kay Boyle warned in a letter all the way from Connecticut, "you are known to be working with the State Department, or the FBI" (qtd. in Campbell, *Exiled* 197). The rumor was half-true where State was concerned: troubled by Soviet leverage in Ghana, Wright had submitted a confidential four-page analysis to the department in 1953, confiding that Kwame Nkrumah slept beneath a portrait of Lenin (Rowley 437). When it came to J. Edgar Hoover's anticommunist bureaucracy, by contrast, Wright in fact offered nothing resembling collaboration. Along with the declassified FBI files I've collected for most of the Tournon group— Himes, Smith, Harrington, James Baldwin—Wright's dossier exhibits his place on the Bureau's Custodial Detention index, an ideological rogues' gallery exposing him to summary arrest, surrender of habeas corpus, and indefinite confinement in a U.S. concentration camp, should Hoover's will align with international calamity and presidential consent (Richard Wright file). Tournon habitués were thus not hysterical in fearing that if American federal intelligence divided and conquered, black writing in every genre might become a type of prison literature.

The tangle of surveillance and suspicion at the Tournon became the centerpiece of black Paris with the so-called Gibson Affair of 1957, a mysterious case of ghostwriting under Harrington's signature calculated to heighten the guilty contradiction between black expatriate sympathy for Algerian independence and black expatriate reluctance to risk expulsion from thin-skinned metropolitan France. The tangle exploded after Wright's sudden death in 1960, a tragedy that Harrington was only the first to credit, probably too creatively, to Hoover's henchmen. In even the most skeptical assessment of its French connections, however, American intelligence must be credited with persuading the residents of *Paris noir* that their harbor was navigable by repressive powers of their abandoned country. Imported late-McCarthyite "[r]acism and cloak-and-dagger terrorism," Wright lamented, "was poisoning the climate around the expatriate . . . community" (qtd. in Campbell, *Exiled* 196). The Paris lover who once discovered more freedom in one square block of the city than in the whole of the United States lived his final Left Bank years demanding the seemingly inalienable right to "refus[e] to 'inform' and 'spy' on my neighbor…" (qtd. in Campbell, *Exiled* 97). American politics had arrived to make African American literary history even when that history slipped the nation's bonds.

The still-emerging details of the Gibson Affair and of Wright's ordeal at the hands of the national security state are discussed in a number of life studies—by Addison Gayle, Jr., James Campbell, and Hazel Rowley—researched since the archival liberation of the U.S. Freedom of Information Act. Yet these details have yet to renovate the premises of the blacks-in-Paris genre, not excluding recent French-speaking variants by Edwards, Bennetta Jules-Rosette, and T. Denean Sharpley-Whiting inclined to target the fantasy of a color-blind, benevolently imperial Hexagon. Where to begin, in this case, opening the blacks-in-Paris genre to the full openness of *Paris noir*, a district whose radical welcome invited a small army of informers as well as a beloved community of difference to occupy an axis of the Black Atlantic? Fortunately, Richard Wright, this community's foremost icon and talent agent, offers provocative clues in the form of his typescript novel *Island of Hallucination*, a fittingly secretive text unlocked at Yale University's Beinecke Library only in 1996. Completed in 1959, *Island of Hallucination* qualifies as Wright's sole fiction of Paris and, after the 2008 appearance of *A Father's Law*, his last major book to remain unpublished. Instructively, it retools literary-critical satire, the score-settling novel with a key, and the pulp modernism of the hard-boiled detective narrative to imagine the black city within a city as a den of worldly spies. The Paris known by the latest lost generation, the novel submits, is no longer so much the capital of modernity as the culture capital of the cold war, ground zero for intellectual jousting among U.S. capitalism, Soviet communism, and many of the cells and forces probing for a third way. Black exiles enter this struggle as prey and agents of one side or several, retraining homegrown double vision on world-historical counterintelligence. Their discourses of internationalism proliferate not only through public acts of cross-diasporic translation but also through shadowy plots of literary impersonation.

In the process, Wright's novel suggests that black Paris must be mapped beyond bright lines of transatlantic comparison, beyond service as an edifying annulment of racism American style. On Wright's island in the Seine, black cosmopolitans lose the U.S.-minded bargaining chip of the French idyll but gain a place in the cockpit of cold war history. What Jonathan Eburne and Jeremy Braddock might call Wright's "wish image" of *Paris noir* complements a crowded field of representations employing the French *métropole* as a token of separation from all deemed archaic in black life (733). Yet lush dreams of universalist Paris are themselves wished into the past in Wright's dream work, couched as late-model detritus to be escaped in the city's accelerating contemporaneity. The coded advice to black transnational theory contained within Wright's closeted text—this essay's ultimate concern—thus entails both parodic negation and imaginative optimism. *Island of Hallucination* offers a corrective guidebook to a black Atlantic nerve center infiltrated by state-of-the-art surveillance yet thereby equipped for advancements in Afro-modern self-renovation.

For all its distinctiveness as a wish image of black expatriation, *Island of Hallucination* was not the first Wright text to explore the buried links between black transnationalism and state intelligence. Aboard the SS *Uruguay* in 1949, sailing to Argentina for the filming of *Native Son*, Wright interrupted his rejuvenation in international waters long enough to compose a lyric tribute to the FBI, his intimate enemy since the early 1940s. In the poem "The FB Eye Blues," Wright turned the tables on Bureau note-taking, filling classic blues stanzas with wry digs at the intimacy of spy-sight. Living under Bureau inspection, the poem joked, was uncomfortably close to sleeping—and cowriting—with the enemy:

> Woke up this morning
> FB eye under my bed
> Said I woke up this morning
> FB eye under my bed
> Told me all I dreamed last night, every word I said. (ll. 6–10)

Wright's compulsion to box with Hoover's shadow even while steaming toward foreign film stardom reveals his suspicion that American intelligence was just as able as he to board a chronotope of black Atlantic mobility and sail beyond the limits of the nation-state. The opening chapters of *Island of Hallucination*, conceived nearly a decade later, testify that this suspicion burgeoned into a primary narrative matrix when exposed to Paris in the age of the Gibson Affair. The novel's recycled protagonist, Mississippi-born teenager Rex "Fishbelly" Tucker, enters *Island*'s French circle in flight from his father's American text—Wright's 1958 novel *The Long Dream*—and from his father's too-American fate, murder at the hands of a cracker police chief. He carries the baggage of a resumé borrowed from Chester Himes—black bourgeois upbringing, incisive intelligence deflected into hustling and prison time—and arrives on a plane packed with unburied national terrors. Fishbelly's American seatmates comprise a gallery of lynchers in button-downs. "That nigger's being spoilt as sure as God made green apples and when he gets back home he'll be fit for only tar and feathers," hisses one typical passenger (Wright, *Island* 2). Fishbelly's first French acquaintances, meanwhile, also encountered on Wright's klannish airliner, reveal themselves as classic American confidence men who happen to have been born under the Eiffel Tower. Preying on Fishbelly's desire for cheap housing and instant repatriation, the husband-and-wife grifters Jacques and Nicole relieve him of two thousand dollars, their weapons cognac, juke-box jazz, and Nicole's seductive grasp of segregation's sexual politics. "He had, of course, heard of the confidence game," reflects Fishbelly in the aftermath, "but he had never heard of its being used against black men with sex as the bait, with racial balm as the lure, and sympathy as the come-on" (46).

Warped and interested sympathy is likewise the weapon of Fishbelly's first African American chaperone in Paris, a night-crawling café intellectual nicknamed Mechanical. With "[m]echanized laughter and windshield wiper hand" (*Island* 53), Mechanical steers the new arrival to a Pigalle prostitute with paraffin breasts and a missing navel, a fellow automaton too deadened to have been born to Baudelaire's diseased sources of "light and life" (Baudelaire l. 15). The sexual transaction is brutally consummated beneath "a faded painting of a French soldier," the traffic between decaying French erotic and imperial authorities staring Wright's hero—and Wright's reader—in the face (*Island* 56). For its part, the political initiation of Wright's protagonist is completed with an episode Ellen Wright liked enough to release for the posthumous anthology *Soon, One Morning*. Zooted to the nines for a Sunday promenade in a "dark gray felt hat" with a "speckled orange and black band" (76), Fishbelly strolls into a mob of Sorbonne radicals picketing the Paris visit of U.S. General Matthew Ridgeway, a historical figure linked to germ warfare in North Korea and violently protested by the actual French Left in May 1951. The distinctions between Fishbelly's and Ridgeway's ornamented Yankee caps are easily overlooked; dreamlike, without hesitation, the demonstrators turn their derision on the black flaneur and revise their chant from "RIDGEWAY, GO HOME!" to "QUEL CHAPEAU AMERICAIN!" (77–78). Reframing the polemical tableau of the French soldier and Pigalle prostitute, Wright ironically dramatizes the equation of U.S. military and cultural imperialisms through a Franco-modernist intertext. Fishbelly learns that imported African American style is associated with U.S. hyperpower by reprising the role of Flaubert's Charles Bovary, similarly schooled by mocking French students in charivari, or ritualized anarchy, for the sin of "[c]omposite" headgear divided by a gaudy "red band" (Flaubert 4). The bitter-comic program behind all of these early incidents is to undermine the blacks-in-Paris romance, as ripely familiar a modern classic, Wright implies, as Flaubert's novel of Paris-revering adultery. Every set piece of this romance is shaken, from the progressive de-Americanization of the journey to the frank sympathy of the Parisian public, from the emotional rescue of flesh-first interracialism to the fail-safe embrace of black Americans by the anticolonial left. The reigning mode of the novel's first and early second books, named "Ghosts" and "False Faces," respectively, is thus satirical. And the primary hallucination these books puncture is that of Paris the dream city, a paradise island isolated from American phantoms and their dodgy French relatives.

The pleasures of Paris that survive Wright's ungainly omniscient narrator gradually surface as book two flows into book three, titled "Time Bombs." The city hints at its sophisticated earthiness; its lifting of the social death sentence, if not all racist supervision, from the backs of transplanted black southerners; its promise as a daily Bandung of mingled "Africans, Chinese, Indonesians" (Wright, *Island* 75). With this improvement in urban lenses, the reigning mode shifts from literary-critical satire to roman à clef, a development that partly explains the Wright estate's reluctance to oversee *Island*'s full publication. The few prior readings of the novel—the best by James Campbell ("The Island"), Rebecca Ruquist, and a suspiciously sensible Richard Gibson, aging VIP of the Gibson Affair—note Wright's finally misleading claim that "the book is true" (qtd. in Campbell, "The Island"). The cast of characters, they stipulate, could be lifted from a Tournon seating chart. *Island*'s Bill Hart, an experienced agent provocateur taking cover as a fascist, is modeled on possible intelligence agent Richard Gibson, or so says Gibson himself (Gibson 906). The character Cato, an imposing, idiosyncratic Trotskyist theorist "smooth black of skin, graying at the temples, big boned, stooped of shoulders" (Wright, *Island* 359), is C. L. R. James, called Nello by close comrades. Nell*ie*, Cato's disciplined lieutenant and the only female character in the novel to escape the part of pneumatic national icon, is derived from Pamela Oline, a white expatriate red-baited while a diplomat in Mexico (Gibson 910). The Café de Tournon itself, meanwhile, makes several poorly disguised appearances, its "yellow awning" sheltering what Mechanical describes as the "headquarters where we talk politics. Man, everything happens here between men and women except marriage, but even that has been known to take place" (*Island* 100).

In truth, the most significant couplings under the café's sway involve male characters, and scramble the novel's otherwise efficient one-to-one key matching literary and historical types. Ned Harrison, Fishbelly's impossibly wise tutor, conflates features of Ollie Harrington with those of the mature Richard Wright, thus allowing *Island*'s author function to offer its less experienced protagonist tips on surviving a black Paris bildungsroman. Mechanical, formerly known as Charles Oxford Brown, blends the imagined worst of Richard Gibson and William Gardner Smith with that of Wright's rebel mentee James Baldwin. Ransacking Baldwin's essay "Equal in Paris," Mechanical treats a purloined bedsheet as the madeleine of his French education. If any veteran of *Paris noir* deserved to charge *Island of Hallucination* with libel, it is thus Baldwin, not Gibson, as usually supposed. Baldwin's edgy caricature, addicted to an Aunt Jemima-style pancake mix, can only satisfy his shamefaced queerness through opportunistic masochism. "[T]his bastard loved to be punished," discovers Fishbelly, sensing "that it was impossible to deal with such a man" (*Island* 182). Wright does not shy from charging his abject Baldwin with authorship of the Gibson Affair: Mechanical is the Tournon spy who ghostwrites a revolutionary letter to the editor of *Life* magazine, menacing the Wright-like character Ned Harrison with deportation for a false revelation of true convictions. "Ned's *cooked*," enthuses Mechanical over his typewriter, his "robot's straggling eyes glow[ing] with ecstasy" (386). Wright's revenge on Baldwin is just as crudely ecstatic, an overdetermined cocktail of pre-*Soul on Ice* homophobia and long-delayed intertextual reckoning with the oedipal brilliance of "Everybody's Protest Novel" (1949) and "Many Thousands Gone" (1951). Considered purely as a mechanism of *Island*'s revisionist history, however, this revenge is complexly ingenious. At one malicious swoop, Wright's entanglement of Baldwin in the Gibson Affair analogizes literary infidelity with political treason, likening clandestine dependence on a rejected style with cloak-and-dagger double agency. More overtly, this entanglement follows the Ridgeway riot in tracing the spy plot of black Paris to the immediate postwar era, the factual setting of Baldwin's break with Wright's protestant naturalism. In the heart of *Island*'s books two and three, faith in a golden age of postoccupation *Paris noir*, banked away for service in some future round of metro-racial renaissancism, thus numbers among the hallucinations under fire.

The sensational interest of the novel's final movement, spread between book three and the concluding book, titled "Kinship," stems from another of Wright's changes to the historical record. The subject of Mechanical's forgery is not the Algerian War, as in the original Gibson Affair, but the cold war that distorts its stakes. For the secretly Trotskyist Mechanical, the grinding battle between the first and second worlds is a mere rehearsal for a hot war between two evils: Russian communism as "shamed and perverted" by Stalin, and "the formless, predatory, naive American capitalist system…" (Wright, *Island* 391). All the same, Mechanical joins the rest of Wright's Tournon crew in theorizing that the cold war makes their adopted city a junction point of global history. "Paris is the center of the Cold War," recites Ned Harrison, Wright's idealized double, "UNESCO's here.…NATO's here. Paris is a crossroad of the world in thought, art, politics, pleasure" (*Island* 209). In this transposition of municipal and global maps, *Island* anticipates later analyses of the specifically cultural cold war, an unlikely struggle for world artistic supremacy whose European theater centered on the French capital. Alongside the American Embassy and the FBI's Paris legation, the Congress for Cultural Freedom, the CIA's subtlest front group, in fact rented space in the city, the better to seed influential abstract expressions of anticommunism (Saunders). Distinguishing Wright's early telling of the historical tale, however, *Island's* self-expatriated black intelligentsia ranks as a key prize and threat to the Eurocentric war of words, notes, and brushstrokes. The Cold War State Department might strategically export Satchmo, Dizzy, and other musical "jambassadors" to the continent's Sovietized hotspots (Von Eschen). Wright's diplomats without portfolio, self-importing African American letters to Paris, would in turn reopen the East-West dialectic of cold war recruitment of black culture, honing abroad a U.S.-born cosmopolitanism better poised to test the fault lines between rising American and falling European empires.

Seen from the perspective of the novel's Left Bank, the cultural cold war intensifies the modern commodification of intelligence and creates a local seller's market, lucrative and uncannily literary, for its black procurers. "Information is needed about everything, everybody, everywhere," counsels Mechanical, "You can get fifty dollars just for going into any of the little offices scattered all over Paris and writing all you know on a given subject" (Wright, *Island* 157). African American writer-expatriates, Wright's logic continues, are exceptional producers of such wordy espionage. "[R]oughly prepared" in double vision by "bitter race wars" at home (214), they are expected overseas to hang "around a café all day and night," an occupation ideal for exploiting the institution's publicly accessible privacy (210). Hired not only by the CIA and FBI but also by their rough French equivalent, the Sûreté Nationale, black operatives polish their skills against the Parisian perfecters of the trade, and threaten to outdo their instructors. "You're prejudiced in favor of American Negroes," observes Fishbelly to one slippery French radical, "That being the case, wouldn't we make the best spies?" (295).

The answer to Fishbelly's rhetorical question is plain by the novel's close, infused in its last book and a half with a melodramatic mode of hard-boiled noir. Mechanical, running scared from his cell of black Trotskyists pretending to be interracial Stalinists pretending to work for American capitalists, hangs himself from a gargoyle on the Notre Dame cathedral, a pale crowd howling as his corpse tumbles to the paving stones. His self-lynching caps a series of reflections on the moral hazards of black undercover work, and rivals the "QUEL CHAPEAU" incident in its intertextual transparency. Bookending the novel with a second deep bow to the French canon, Mechanical's suicide mimics the gothic crash landing of *Notre-Dame de Paris* (1831), in which Victor Hugo launches Quasimodo's tormentor Frollo from cathedral to pavement. Yet the secondhand spectacle of Mechanical's death retains the power to shock Fishbelly into self-authorship, jolting him from small-time pimping to textbook existential accountability. "When you can accept responsibility for what you do," Harrison praises Wright's young protagonist, "then you are starting to grow up, to be free" (514). The social extension of Fishbelly's subjective freedom, Wright proposes, will negate and reinvent Mechanical's dizzying taste for spying on spies. The future of liberated Paris will belong to "bebop sleuths with a Louis Armstrong cover!" (241), surveyors of less-taken boulevards beyond two clumsy "historical giants, America and Russia..." (392). The spies sharpened in struggle with these giants and with the lesser evil of discriminating French Negrophilia will become spies-for-themselves, architects of a counterculture of the cold war built over a black Atlantic counterculture of modernity.

Despite the fearful landscape of Wright's last years, the deciding thrust of his Paris novel is therefore antiparanoid. According to Dorothy Padmore, Wright met his death convinced he was "the victim of a plot, evidence of which he had gathered, and which implicated the French security, the American FBI (and perhaps CIA) and ex-Trotskists" (qtd. in Campbell, *Exiled* 243). *Island of Hallucination* enmeshes all these pursuers within a counterplot under Wright's control, a three-dimensional investigation of the scene of the Gibson Affair, its café, city, and world. By the resolution of Inspector Wright's novelized counterfile, both of his incarnations—Fishbelly and Harrison—go free, as does greater black Paris, vividly purged, with Mechanical's self-destruction, of the crime of spying-for-others.

Island of Hallucination, more than a vengeance-seeking roman à clef, accordingly deserves publication as a willful redrafting of *Paris noir* in the transformative grip of the cold war. Wright's final spy fiction sketches his favored alternative to the premature death he may have seen coming. It answers the once-common claim that expatriation severed his connection to timely racial subject matter with a case for cold war Paris as an incubator of new black selves of international consequence. And it gives evidence, more abstractly, of the value of integrating the vector of state surveillance into prevailing models of black transnationalism. Among other things, such integration would entail enhanced attention to the uneven development of the black Atlantic. The remaking of *Paris noir* by cold war espionage underscores the need to rethink transtemporal models of transnational black spaces. Richard Wright, for one, recognized that oceanic spheres and their metonymic ports indeed possess a variable, sometimes unredemptive history as well as a sweeping affiliative territory summoning the consolations of deep time (Warren 118–19). Such integration would also disallow easy distinctions between "horizontal," time-zone spanning black memory and "vertical," *volkish*, stay-at-home national-state memory (Hanchard 46). The better alternative to these distinctions is not merely to attend to residual and recombinant nationalisms in the self-definition of blackness. It is also to acknowledge the state's historically contingent ability to access horizontal fields of belonging, to interrupt and energize their discourses of adversarial globalism. As *Island of Hallucination* does its best to reveal, the cold war national security state itself reserved the right to think and feel beyond the nation.

BIBLIOGRAPHY

Baudelaire, Charles. "Le Crépuscule du Soir." 1857. Trans. David Paul. *Flowers of Evil: A Selection*. Eds. Marthiel Mathews and Jackson Mathews. New York: New Directions, 1958. 97–99. Print.

Campbell, James. *Exiled in Paris: Richard Wright, James Baldwin, Samuel Beckett, and Others on the Left Bank*. 1995. Berkeley: U of California P, 2003. Print.

———. "The Island Affair: Richard Wright's Unpublished Last Novel." *Syncopations: Beats, New Yorkers, and Writers in the Dark*. Berkeley: U of California P, 2008. 103–11. Print.

Eburne, Jonathan B., and Jeremy Braddock. "Introduction: Paris, Capital of the Black Atlantic." *Modern Fiction Studies* 51.4 (2005): 731–40. Print.

Edwards, Brent Hayes. *The Practice of Diaspora: Literature, Translation, and the Rise of Black Internationalism*. Cambridge, MA: Harvard UP, 2003. Print.

Flaubert, Gustave. *Madame Bovary*. 1857. Trans. Geoffrey Wall. New York: Penguin, 2003. Print.

Gayle, Addison, Jr. *Richard Wright: Ordeal of a Native Son*. New York: Doubleday, 1980. Print.

Gibson, Richard. "Richard Wright's 'Island of Hallucination' and the 'Gibson Affair.'" *Modern Fiction Studies* 51.4 (2005): 896–920. Print.

Haine, W. Scott. *The World of the Paris Café: Sociability among the French Working Class, 1789–1914*. Baltimore: Johns Hopkins UP, 1996. Print.

Hanchard, Michael. "Black Memory versus State Memory: Notes toward a Method." *Small Axe* 26 (2008): 45–62. Print.

Jules-Rosette, Bennetta. *Black Paris: The African Writers' Landscape*. Urbana: U of Illinois P, 1998. Print.

Rowley, Hazel. *Richard Wright: The Life and Times*. New York: Holt, 2001. Print.

Ruquist, Rebecca. "*Non, Nous ne Jouons pas la Trompette*: Richard Wright in Paris." *Contemporary French and Francophone Studies* 8.3 (2004): 285–303. Print.

Saunders, Frances Stonor. *The Cultural Cold War: The CIA and the World of Arts and Letters*. 1999. New York: New Press, 2000. Print.

Sharpley-Whiting, T. Denean. *Negritude Women*. Minneapolis: U of Minnesota P, 2002. Print.

Stovall, Tyler. *Paris Noir: African Americans in the City of Light*. Boston: Houghton, 1996. Print.

Von Eschen, Penny M. *Satchmo Blows Up the World: Jazz Ambassadors Play the Cold War*. Cambridge, MA: Harvard UP, 2004. Print.

Warren, Kenneth W. "Taking the Measure of the Black Atlantic." *States of Emergency: The Object of American Studies*. Eds. Russ Castronovo and Susan Gilman. Chapel Hill: U of North Carolina P, 2009. 116–23. Print.

Wright, Richard. "The FB Eye Blues." 1949. *Richard Wright Reader*. Eds. Ellen Wright and Michel Fabre. New York: Harper & Row, 1978. 249–50. Print.

——. *Island of Hallucination*. Ts. Box 34, Folder 472. James Weldon Johnson Collection. Beinecke Rare Book and Manuscript Library, Yale University. Print.

——. Richard Wright file obtained under provisions of the Freedom of Information Act, Federal Bureau of Investigation, United States. Assorted documents dated 9 Dec. 1942 to 9 May 1963. Internal case file no. 100-157464. Print.

3

A Father's Law, 1950s Masculinity, and Richard Wright's Agony over Integration

Leonard Cassuto

Richard Wright's literary career begins with a lynching and ends with a serial murderer. "Big Boy Leaves Home," the 1936 story that leads off Wright's first book, *Uncle Tom's Children* (1938), renders the vicious mob execution of a young black man falsely accused of rape. *A Father's Law*, Wright's last novel, left unfinished at his unexpected death in 1960 and published in 2008 on the centennial of his birth, centers on a murderer terrorizing the Chicago suburb of Brentwood Park.

In between those bookends lie some of the most violent and disturbing stories in all of American literature—and also the postwar suburbanization of the United States, a new model of corporate masculinity that went with it, and the flowering of the American civil rights movement. *A Father's Law* introduces a black organization man, a policeman, to Wright's canon, and examines his particular discontents. At the same time, the novel raises new questions, along with familiar old ones, about Wright's ambivalent global revolutionary politics and his uncomfortable relationship with the American civil rights movement. I'll be threading these apparently disparate lines of thought together in the following pages, using *A Father's Law* as a loom upon which to weave together some of Wright's main concerns during his last decade. Wright's curious relation to the civil rights movement can finally help us to understand not only his problematic 1950s writings but also the rage-filled stories he wrote before World War II.

I

I will start with the historical and critical commonplace that Wright's work helped to enable the civil rights movement. *Native Son* not only made Wright immediately famous but also took the debate over race relations in the United States into new (and often uncomfortable) territory. *Black Boy*, Wright's terrifying 1945 memoir of growing up in the segregated South, became a literary landmark of the U.S. color line despite his publisher's amputation of part of the manuscript to eliminate the account of Wright's flirtation with the Communist Party. Wright also wrote essays, poetry, drama, and travel narratives, but it was by wedding the undecorous realism of naturalist fiction to the experience of a subjugated race that he redirected the course of African American storytelling. After *Native Son* appeared in 1940, African American literature embraced not just lonely rural but also urban experience. It also abandoned a longtime reliance on Christian forbearance, meeting fear with anger and resistance.

That forbearance has its own history in African American fiction, and it's worth pausing for a brief moment to limn that history. The opposition between sentimentalism and violent revolt quickly crystallized in the American fiction about race and slavery during the 1850s, when the first African American novelists began publishing. Roughly speaking, the debate was between the appeal to conscience represented by Harriet Beecher Stowe's *Uncle Tom's Cabin* (1852) and the defiant rebellion of Frederick Douglass's *The Heroic Slave* (1854) or Martin Delany's *Blake* (1859), to name two of Uncle Tom's most visible antagonists. (A novel like William Wells Brown's *Clotel* (1853), which has many characters and represents multiple points of view without overtly reconciling them, may be located somewhere in the middle.) Early African American fiction borrows heavily from the sentimental forms that were popular at the time, but always does so in a way that pointedly (and often aggressively) questions the efficacy of the "win by losing" logic of sentimentalism that is originally embodied in Uncle Tom's stoic resistance to slavery and final spiritual transcendence of it. The question of whether sentimental sympathy could effect social change more readily than active, militant resistance animates African American fiction well beyond the Civil War as well, with the novels and stories of the postbellum era (by the likes of Pauline Hopkins, Charles W. Chesnutt, and others) depicting this central conflict after Reconstruction. Black writers have understandably suspected the strategic abjection—centered in the seeking of white sympathy and approval—that the sentimental pose can involve.

Nevertheless, African American fiction has always taken sentimentality seriously.

The opposition between sentimental stoicism and violent resistance receives particularly rigorous and thoughtful attention in the early work of Richard Wright. Wright's first short stories, published in the late 1930s and collected in *Uncle Tom's Children*, show by the collection's title alone the continuing vitality of the opposition between sympathy and rebellion, and its roots in the conflicted reception of Stowe's novel. Exploring different strategies of secular sentimentalism in response to white oppression in his cycle of stories, Wright first arranged them in a sequence leading from fearful pathos to mounting political violence. In the first edition of *Uncle Tom's Children*, the concluding "Fire and Cloud" balances political protest and Uncle Tom-like sentimental suffering (the physical beating of a Christian preacher), ending with a call for physical resistance. The last line of the story is the declaration *"freedom belongst the strong!"* (180) But Wright went on to augment *Uncle Tom's Children* after its initial publication, adding the story "Bright and Morning Star" (which celebrates women who choose martyrdom) to the end of the volume. In shifting the conclusion back to symbolic suffering in this way, Wright shows how he oscillated between sentimental and violent responses to racial injustice at this point in his career. Wright thus came to prominence as a writer whose work exemplifies the central debate in African American fiction between sentimental suffering and violent revolt.[1]

By calling attention to the frightening conditions facing black people on both sides of the Mason-Dixon line and the ideological oppositions within the collective fight to oppose those conditions, Wright's books surely helped clear the way for the emergence of Martin Luther King Jr., the Southern Christian Leadership Conference, and the myriad others who fought segregation in the United States in the 1950s and 1960s.

But Wright could never join their chorus for integration. He yearned for integration in his writing, certainly. In *Black Boy,* young Richard looks up hopefully to kind white characters. Some of them help him, like the optician Mr. Crane, who hires Richard and tries unsuccessfully to defend him against the white shop employees who terrorize him and eventually drive him from the job. Others shy away, fearful of the violent reprisals that awaited white people who helped black people in the segregated South.

Bigger Thomas, the young murderer in *Native Son,* is assigned an idealistic white lawyer, Boris Max, whose emotional connection with his client provides perhaps the only hopeful moment in a bleak book.

Only to Max does Bigger make an effort to explain how committing murder made him feel human, and although Max is revulsed by Bigger's confession, he reaches out to Bigger anyway and completes an emotional circuit that constitutes Bigger's only personal legacy.

Unlike Martin Luther King and his fellow crusaders, Wright never acquired the language to imagine what integration might look like.[2] His radicalism during the 1930s and 1940s centered on the struggle for racial equality, but for Wright, that struggle was complexly intertwined with his Communist Party membership (which he held until 1942) as well as the more moderate Popular Front, among other forces. In other words, Wright created Bigger Thomas before the modern civil rights movement coalesced—and the rage that animates Bigger, along with so many of Wright's other characters, represents a nightmarish alternative to the reconciliation that civil rights workers later demanded. (Malcolm X would later occupy a similar position in King's own time, standing as the radical, violent alternative to the mainstream discourse of civil rights.) Wright's Bigger is a memorably inarticulate creature of the segregated Chicago ghetto, boiling with unchanneled resentment of the white people who restrict his movements, and with extravagant and hopeless ambition to fly airplanes he can't even approach, let alone enter. Lacking the ability to articulate what he really wants, Bigger typifies Wright's characters in that he can only speak—and act—the language of frustration, anger, and violence. Bigger thus fulfills white society's greatest fear of him, by killing the white woman he works for.

King, on the other hand, used the language of sentiment to express the goal of human connection as the emotional basis for integration. In some of the century's most memorable rhetoric, he drew repeatedly on family imagery, and his strategy of nonviolent engagement—combining peaceful confrontation with an open appeal to sympathy—reflects that choice. King used family metaphors as a way of underscoring the solidarity among black people in the face of white prejudice, but he also used the family to convey his goal of interracial harmony. Desegregate, he said in his 1963 "Letter from Birmingham Jail," not because it's the law but "because integration is morally right and because the Negro is your brother" (789).

King works with the family as a force of unity in the sentimental tradition. His integrationist argument draws force from the same kind of faith-based sentimental dynamic that fueled so much American fiction about race from the previous century. Explicitly rejecting individual self-interest, King insists that "other-preservation"—not self-preservation— "is the first law of life" (*Chaos or Community* 625).

In a 1963 speech, King declared that "everyone in the movement must lead a sacrificial life" (qtd. in *Parting the Waters* 727). Such linkage of community building to Christian sacrifice gives King's civil rights writing, which was obviously formative of the movement in general, a powerful sentimental, family-building force.

Wright—who met King and spent a day with him in Paris in 1959—spoke in a harsher tone.[3] In *Black Boy*, Richard scorns the "goddamn philosophy of meekness" (225). Or consider the title of Wright's 1957 collection of essays (focused on postcolonial Asia and Africa but steeped in Wright's experience in the American South), published two years after King's successful Montgomery, Alabama bus boycott. Wright named the book *White Man, Listen!*

Such asperity precluded the sentimental. In "How Bigger Was Born," given as a speech in 1940 and later published with editions of *Native Son*, Wright lamented that the sentimentalism he had employed in *Uncle Tom's Children* allowed "even bankers' daughters" to sympathize with the beset characters in the stories and cry over them. His readers, he complained, would read his book and "feel good about it," instead of feeling a spur to action. *Native Son,* he vowed, would avoid "the consolation of tears" (531). So it does, and the result is a gruesome crime story that Alfred Kazin described as belonging to a "cult of violence" (371).

Murderous violence, not family harmony, remained at the root of Wright's emotional lexicon for his entire career. Granted freedom from an oppressive identity by a train accident in which he is presumed killed, Cross Damon, the main character of *The Outsider* (1953), gravitates toward murder. An unemployed executive in *Savage Holiday* (1954) accidentally locks himself out of his apartment—and events cascade until he, too, becomes a murderer.

II

Living in self-imposed exile in France, Wright worked feverishly on *A Father's Law* through the last summer of his life. He put the novel aside in the fall of 1960 to work on revisions to his final collection of short stories, *Eight Men* (1961), and then died unexpectedly of a heart attack at the end of the year. Julia Wright, her father's literary executor, arranged for the publication of the incomplete draft of *A Father's Law* this year because, she explains in the preface, it may be "faulty, sketchy," and "sometimes repetitive," but it's also "fascinating" (viii, vii). (The book received mixed reviews upon publication.)

On February 1, 1960, a few months before Wright began *A Father's Law*, black students in North Carolina began a series of sit-ins at lunch counters that refused to serve them. The protesters endured beatings, arrests, and even dousings with ammonia to carry out one of the civil rights movement's iconic acts of civil disobedience. The sit-ins lasted months, spread to other Southern states, and dominated the news.[4] After making a speech in early support of the sit-in protesters, King was arrested in Alabama for tax evasion; he was acquitted at the end of May. Wright, a regular reader of the *International Herald Tribune*, would presumably have known of these events, but he never wrote a public word about them. As I will suggest, *A Father's Law* amounts to Wright's ambivalent commentary—filtered through his position as an African American man living abroad under surveillance—on the events that were transforming race relations in the United States.

A Father's Law follows a black police chief, Ruddy Turner, who stands as an apparent success story of integration. Ruddy has advanced through the police force as "a credit to his race" (32), and has taken on the conventional middle-class values of the white neighborhood where he now lives. Ruddy identifies with where he is, putting out of mind the rural South where he came from (and where "he had left a girl with a baby" [34]). Though he had once run with "gangs of boys," he now "loved being with the majority" and "loved the rules of the community with an intense and abiding passion" (34, 26).

But beneath his conformity, Ruddy nurses violent fantasies that express long-held desires to "collar the smooth, smug, clean-shaven white men who passed him with their well-fed bodies" (34). He dreams of leading a black conquering army that would impose racial equality by martial force, of becoming a merciful despot who nevertheless would not hesitate to have his opponents executed. Ruddy is a joiner, then, but he can imagine joining only in terms that also involve destruction.

Although Ruddy is glad that he need not fear "hoodlums loitering about his premises" in his otherwise white neighborhood, his security comes at a price. Plagued by nightmares of black "roustabouts" trying to cut his throat with razors, he feels a "guilty poison" coursing through him that "shimmer[s] in his nerves" and leaves him continually tense, caught between the "yearning to take a smashing potshot at society," coupled with an urgent desire "to be part of that society" (33, 35, 36). "The containment of that tension," Ruddy believes, "had been his greatest achievement" (35).

One might imagine such twinned guilt and longing as accumulating through Wright's career of enraged alienation and then searching for an outlet. "How did one talk of a guilt that came from not doing the things that one wanted so much to do?" Ruddy asks himself (35). The question sums up Ruddy very well, but it also may be viewed as Wright's retrospective on the totality of his own work.

Ruddy is the rare Wright character that fends off the temptation to commit the violent acts he dreams of. In *The Outsider*, Wright's long-awaited follow-up novel to *Native Son*, for example, Cross Damon gets to live out a fantasy of sorts when he is able to walk away from his desultory existence and disintegrating marriage with a large amount of cash. Apparently freed from social obligation, he begins killing people almost immediately. Ruddy Turner doesn't give in to such urges in *A Father's Law*. Instead, his job uncovering the guilt of others serves to quell the "silent raging" inside of him (36).

However, Ruddy's own son may be performing violent acts in his stead. Assigned to investigate a wave of killings in the suburb of Brentwood Park, Ruddy slowly comes to suspect that his son is behind them. These murders occur at random, according to no pattern that the police can discern.

Wright links these serial murders in *A Father's Law* to a generalized sense of guilt. Crucially, Wright has one of the police investigators describe the murders as "a kind of language" (141), a language that expresses a free-floating angst that moves—as Ruddy's son, Tommy, a sociology student at the University of Chicago, explains—from individual to society and back again. Ruddy and his police colleagues conclude that the murderer is "a man against the law...in the deepest sense" (144). In that respect, the murderer resembles his creator, for Wright spent his life raging against the unjust laws that held blacks down.

Earlier African American writers have shown understandable anger in their work, but few have ever approached Wright's explosive rage. One has to go back to David Walker's 1829 *Appeal* for the kind of carefully crafted yet seething anger that's present on virtually every page of Wright's work, whether on display (as in *Native Son*) or barely hidden (as in *A Father's Law*).

Indeed, Wright's fiction consistently spotlights people who explode. Crime stories are the natural place for such characters, but *A Father's Law* is the only Wright plot that takes the point of view of the police. Wright's last novel shows that the cops, too, are in constant danger of detonating. Ruddy articulates what amounts to Wright's worldview: wanting to "hit out at everybody," yet needing also to "learn to trust life again" (123). One can read Wright's oeuvre as a series of statements of that suggestion, with each book offering it from a different angle.

III

One such angle is provided by 1950s American manhood. Richard Wright has rarely been approached through the concerns of twentieth-century American middle-class domesticity for at least two reasons. First, he wrote mainly about African Americans living outside the middle class. (His last novels, *The Long Dream* [1958] and *A Father's Law*, are notable exceptions, and suggest a possible direction that Wright's writing might have taken if he had lived longer.) Second, Wright was a famous exile during the fifties, a writer who drew attention to his country's cold war politics rather than its domestic angst. Moreover, the feelings of the postwar U.S. middle class were emotions that Wright could know about only secondhand. But Wright thought more deeply than has hitherto been observed about being not just a black man, but also an American man, period—and it turns out that cold war paranoia shares an emotional lexicon with suburban ennui. Wright's generally under-noticed fifties fiction, especially *Savage Holiday,* his one novel with a white main character, offers the possibility of bringing them together.

Savage Holiday captures the widespread fear of professional and social conformity in the United States. This fear, characterized by the creation of the stereotypical homogenous suburb and the sterile corporate workplace, responded to social changes in the postwar United States. The impetus for change lay in the hundreds of thousands of servicemen returning after the war. They displaced an entire generation of women from the jobs they occupied during the Depression and the war, relegating the majority to housewifery. The U.S. economy quickly expanded during the years after World War II (aided by the destruction of European industry during the war), and American prosperity resulted in a social reorganization along the lines of the separate spheres of the previous century, in which men dominated the professional world while women managed the household sphere.

Betty Freidan famously drew attention to the plight of women trapped under this new regime in *The Feminine Mystique* (1963), but men's anxieties received attention a few years sooner, in a series of 1950s sociological studies of bureaucracy and suburbanization. These books became bestsellers and social lightning rods for discussion and debate, their popularity fueled by the interest of those who were being described (and often criticized) in their pages. A myriad of intellectuals argued collectively for the loss of American male individuality and initiative, each one entering the question through a different portal. In *The Lonely Crowd* (1950), David Riesman and Nathan Glazer documented the rise of a class of "outer-directed" Americans who had, in effect, lost the ability to think for themselves, taking their cues for living from the institutional groupthink surrounding them. In *The Affluent Society* (1958), John Kenneth Galbraith argued that people could no longer figure out what they wanted without the help of "an adman" (2). In academic crossover successes such as *White Collar* (1951) and *The Power Elite* (1956), C. Wright Mills argued that Americans had become alienated from their work by an increasingly deterministic class system that imprisoned workers in sterile professional bureaucracies, encouraged by an ambitious and overbearing government. The journalist-turned-sociologist William C. Whyte became a surprising bestseller with his analysis of those professional bureaucracies in *The Organization Man* (1956). Whyte argued that corporate life eroded the entrepreneurial individualism once been thought essential to the American spirit.

Chief among the anxieties for middle-class men was the fear of professional and social conformity and the consequent loss of individuality. The fear of conformity that prevailed during the fifties linked the Red Scare to the suburbanization and corporatization of the U.S. middle class. (This connection was forged in part by an urgent heteronormativity, with homosexuality linked to communism as a security risk.[5]) Anticommunists brandished the prospect of communist cultural indoctrination as a fearful threat to American individuality. For instance, J. Edgar Hoover described communist "culture" as "an indoctrinal spray seeking to control every part of a member's heart, mind, and soul." Hoover warned that "every facet of the member's life, even when he plays the piano, sings, goes to a movie, sees a painting, or reads a book, must be saturated with communism" (168). Minus the Gothic flourishes, though, Hoover's rendering of the communist threat is not very different from Whyte's description of the conformist culture of the corporation and the suburbs in *The Organization Man*. If anticommunists described a world in which the Party would know everyone's private business, Whyte described a suburban existence in which the same thing has already happened, where "privacy has become clandestine" (353), and people seem not to mind.

These new concerns attracted the attention of both novelists as well as social theorists. Novels set in the suburbs, such as Richard Yates's *Revolutionary Road* (1952), John Updike's *Rabbit Run* (1960), and

Sloan Wilson's *The Man in the Grey Flannel Suit* (1955), proliferated in the postwar era. These books rendered the situation of the postwar American man as a mixture of anxiety and frustration over being caught in a stifling domestic and professional existence that one leading critic has compared to a state of emotional homelessness.[6]

Richard Wright didn't know the suburbs firsthand, and he didn't write about them before *A Father's Law*. But he did know a few things about the politics of conformity from his days in the Communist Party and the backlash that it created in his life. Wright found communist discipline oppressive, but the feeling did not ease after he left the party, as the U.S. government continued to track his movements. Not surprisingly then, Wright's fiction rotates consistently about fear, guilt, and desire, with the gravitational pull of now one and now another tugging the characters to and fro in Wright's post-Freudian version of naturalistic determinism. Those themes take on distinctive and anxiety-fraught forms in the United States during the fifties, and Wright taps directly into the male concerns of the fearful fifties in *Savage Holiday*. The novel is Wright's expression of the social ennui that was being dissected in his time, expressed in his characteristic language of violence.

If *The Outsider* captures the danger of creating a new self, in *Savage Holiday* Wright explores the reverse: the desperate fear of losing one's place. The tragic movement in the novel, involving (like *Native Son*) an accidental killing and then a murder, is triggered when Erskine Fowler accidentally locks himself out of his apartment while stark naked. He tries furtive tactics to escape embarrassment, and the situation escalates, playing out within the space of forty-eight hours. But rather than focus on these events (as most critics of the novel have done), I'd like to emphasize the role of the events that precede them—that is, the importance of the professional setup.

Erskine's careening descent to murder begins with his forced "retirement" from his job as a bureaucrat at the Longevity Life Insurance Company. (Though rewarded with a generous severance, he's actually being pushed out to make room for the boss's son.) Part One of *Savage Holiday* begins with a biblical epigraph about labor that suggests not only Erskine's religious piety but also his pious devotion to his job. Unmarried and with no living relatives, Erskine Fowler is introduced as someone who "looked upon Longevity Life as his family" (14). Ashamed of the past that he had risen from—his mother was a prostitute—Erskine replaces the parent who disappointed him with an insurance company. Unlike Whyte's vaguely disillusioned organization man or Sloan Wilson's Tom Rath of *The*

Man in the Grey Flannel Suit, whose very name points to his anger, Wright's Erskine Fowler feels perfectly at home in the corporation until he loses his place in it. Erskine's affectionate ties to his corporate existence amount to a virtual parody of the fears of corporate conformity that were rife during the fifties: instead of chafing within the bureaucracy, he embraces it. He's the deliberate opposite of the discontented bureaucrat, a character of deliberate extremes.

The loss of the company to which he has devoted his entire adult life unmoors Erskine. Wright, in a 1956 interview, said, "The very fact that he feels he is free, free from any compelling obligation, is for him the most terrifying thing that ever befell him" ("Interview" 167). But if Erskine is free, he's also cut off from a business that he considers "life itself" (26). It's of more than passing significance that during moments of stress throughout the novel, Erskine's hand moves reflexively to touch the tips of the pencils—the symbol of his lost professional identity—that he still keeps in his coat pocket. "Those pencils somehow reassured him" (19), and they do so even later in the novel, when he fleetingly contemplates murdering his neighbor. Frightened by his violent thought, he touches the pencils and "his fear and moral condemnation of her fled" (though only temporarily, it turns out) (112–13).

Erskine's farewell ceremony cuts him off from his employee "brothers and sisters" (14). The locked door that thrusts him naked into the world separates him from everything else. "Frightfully nude" (41), he's literally barred from his comforting and respectable domestic interior and symbolically cut off from the Sunday School volunteer duties that anchor him. Less than a day after losing his job then, Erskine loses the rest of his meager links to what is familylike and homelike in his life. Without these supports, he's overwhelmed by fear, guilt, and rage.

Patricia Highsmith, a quintessential writer of the darker side of the American fifties, expresses the spirit of the age in numerous stories in which the guilt creates the crime rather than the other way around. In *The Blunderer* (1954), for example, the plot unfolds in reverse: a lawyer feels guilty about his dark desires even though he never acts on them. His guilty behavior leads him to be falsely accused, and then, finally, for him to commit the deeds that he's accused of. Wright uses the same device in *Savage Holiday*: before being retired, Erskine would announce to his insurance colleagues that "man was a guilty creature" (27), and it is Erskine's own sense of guilt that long ago "made him a stranger to a part of himself that he feared" (30). Freed from the "prison-cage of toil" (30), that suppressed part wells up within him.

Like Highsmith (who dealt almost exclusively in male protagonists), Wright expresses not only male anxiety but also the fear of surveillance that accompanied the Red Scare. For Wright, as for Highsmith, the fear of being exposed as an inadequate man stands for the fear of being exposed as un-American. This link of anticommunist hysteria to fifties masculinity takes explicit form in *The Outsider* when Cross's search for a comfortable identity leads him to the company of communists; in *Savage Holiday*, Erskine's inner conflict between his sense of religious duty and his fear of the exposure of his mother's prostitution represents a similar opposition.

Savage Holiday is about being a man, a worker (also a bureaucrat), and an American, all at a time when conflict simmered beneath the surface of the postwar economic boom. Whyte, Riesman, Mills and other cultural commentators were able to sell their treatises to a large readership because of a widespread perception that the postwar changes taking place in people's lives were important. Their books probably didn't much change the way people lived in the United States, but they did give form and voice to the anxieties they shared. The same may be said of *Savage Holiday*, written by an expatriate who demonstrates that he's still thinking about a range of tensions in the country that he left. Race relations will properly remain the most important point of entry into Wright's work, but *Savage Holiday* suggests that we may also read his work productively through other aspects of his times.

Savage Holiday also provides a lens through which to view Ruddy Turner in *A Father's Law*. The very emotions that Ruddy Turner succeeds in forcing down inside of himself in *A Father's Law*—fear, anger, and especially guilt—are the same ones that escape from Erskine Fowler in *Savage Holiday* and doom him. Unlike Erskine, Ruddy has a job; he feels "undressed" without his uniform (9). (His preparations for retirement are interrupted, in fact, by the opportunity to become police chief of Brentwood Park.) Ruddy works for the police because unlike Erskine, he can hold his destructive feelings in check—but like Erskine, Ruddy's son Tommy suggests what can result when that restraint is absent.

Ruddy combines the domesticity of the black sentimental tradition (which Wright directly engages at the beginning of his career) with the angst of 1950s American manhood (which he clearly considers in his later novels). Ruddy sees himself as "captain of police, colored, Catholic," in that order (15). This fusion embodies the conflict within Ruddy and, together with his contented existence in a white neighborhood where residents are "damned particular" about who lives there (15), captures Wright's ambivalence about the mid-century rhetoric of integration and the civil rights movement that generated it.

IV

Wright was a restless thinker, not a movement politician. An admirer of "those who can stand alone" (qtd. in Rowley, "Exile"), he declared himself to be "a rootless man" (*White Man* 647). Given these assertions, it's perhaps not surprising that Wright largely ignored the American civil rights movement even as it gained visibility during the fifties.

"It is only now," James Baldwin wrote in 1961, that the long "anguish, to say nothing of the rage" of American blacks, "begins, dimly, to trouble the public mind" (174–75). In a wistful combination of memoir, book review, and personal expiation, Baldwin attacked Wright a few months after the latter's death for a willful ignorance of the American "Negro problem." Wright "did not know much" about what American blacks were going through, said Baldwin, and more important, he "did not want to know" (173). Of course Wright's elemental depictions of the pain, fear, anger, and violence—both physical and emotional—of blacks helped make Baldwin's more reflective probing possible, and Baldwin acknowledges that he had used Wright's writing "as a kind of springboard into my own" (161). Beginning with its title, Baldwin's *Notes of a Native Son* (1955) pays homage to his predecessor even as it maps new paths through the broken black city. But Wright's own eye was somewhere else during that time.

Wright dwelled instead, during the fifties, on postcolonial conditions in Africa and elsewhere, but he kept a notably ambivalent distance from what he saw and wrote about. Gazing upon "the kaleidoscope of sea, jungle, nudity, mud huts, and crowded market places" in what is now Ghana, for example, Wright experiences "the strangeness of a completely different order of life" (*Black Power* 56). Elsewhere, though, he adopts a different perspective and lauds Kwame Nkrumah and other authors of the Ghanaian overthrow of British rule for leading the "spiritually homeless" who are "hungering" for "THE HOME OF THEIR HEARTS" and guiding them to "socialist thought" (*White Man* 786, 794, 795). He calls their movement a "Miracle of Nationalism."[7]

Wright's diagnosis of African culture as requiring military discipline to "sweep out the tribal cobwebs" (*Black Power* 415) and march into the twentieth century has attracted much critical disapprobation—for example, Cornel West suggests that Wright's "condescension and revulsion blind him to the rich complexity" of Ghana (x). For the present purpose, I want to note how Wright's rhetoric finally underscores his self-created distance from a revolutionary movement that he nevertheless admires a great deal. That distance mixed with admiration, I want to suggest, extends to Wright's feelings about the civil rights movement, and it is on display in *A Father's Law*.

Ruddy's son Tommy insists in *A Father's Law* that "there's in us something more powerful than love" (176). Wright put those words in Tommy's mouth at the same time that King was eloquently insisting that love had the power to reform American society and rescue it from the evil of segregation. Tommy is speaking of an individual betrayal, but he speaks of "school and church" as the places where he was taught that "love was the greatest thing on earth, that it could conquer all" (176). It's hard to believe that Wright didn't have Martin Luther King in mind when he wrote those words, but Wright's sensibilities were quite different from King's. From his earliest writings through to this last unfinished novel, he speaks from the anger felt by so many blacks of his time, an anger that lurked offstage from the main events of the civil rights movement.

Both Wright and King were spied on. (Wright's expatriate community was, says his biographer Hazel Rowley, "sprinkled with spies" ["Exile"]; William Maxwell provides details of this surveillance culture and its reflection in Wright's later writing in his essay in this volume. J. Edgar Hoover's interest in King's activities is of course well-known.) Both Wright and King fought efforts to silence and control them. But Wright, struggling to remain financially afloat in a foreign country, was manipulated to such an extent that the trip to Indonesia that resulted in his book *The Color Curtain* (1956) was actually paid for by the organization that fronted for the CIA.[8] Perhaps it is no wonder that Wright developed what Kwame Anthony Appiah calls a "paranoid hermeneutic" (181).

"I'm for black people," Wright wrote in 1954 (*Black Power* 85), but his advocacy was a lonely one staged by a writer who welcomes even a "state of abandonment" (*White Man* 647). Wright longed, in effect, for the civil rights crusaders to be right, but his writing expressed his continuing skepticism about the movement that was taking place an ocean away in what Ruddy describes as a "goddamn rotten world" that would "make you kill, for sure" (124). "What can and will conquer," says Tommy, "are fear and hate" (176). Such words amount to as close to a direct commentary on the American civil rights movement as Wright ever gives us. They unveil Wright in this final novel as an angry and anguished integrationist whose main character at the end of the novel, "can't figure things out anymore in my house, my own house" (261).

Murder thus frames Wright's fictional oeuvre and occupies everything in between. Wright's last work opposes the inclusiveness of the civil rights movement to the murders of a serial killer. Although *A Father's Law* was composed near the height of civil rights activism, it lies outside of the movement's main currents, with Wright sharing its goals but unable to fully embrace its nonviolent mission.

Notes

1. The preceding two paragraphs draw on an argument I presented in my *Hard-Boiled Sentimentality: The Secret History of American Crime Stories*, chapter 8.
2. As James Baldwin put it in 1961, "Today's racial manifestoes were being written very differently [from *Native Son*], and in many different languages" (150).
3. For a brief account of Wright's day with King, see Rowley, *Richard Wright*, 496–97.
4. For an account of the sit-in movement, see Branch, 272–97.
5. For a full elaboration, see Robert Corber's *In the Name of National Security* and *Homosexuality in Cold War America*.
6. See Jurca, *White Diaspora*.
7. The full title of the final essay in *White Man, Listen!* is "The Miracle of Nationalism in the African Gold Coast."
8. See Rowley, "Exile." This amazing paradox results, says Rowley, from Wright's anticommunism, which balanced his officially undesirable racial militancy and made him useful in what amounted to a large-scale chess game in which intellectuals were unwitting pawns. Wright never found out that the CIA bankrolled the Congress for Cultural Freedom, which funded him, but he nourished a healthy suspicion of his surroundings. In the last speech he ever gave, a month before his death, Wright described his world as a "nightmarish jungle" (Rowley, *Richard Wright* 521).

Bibliography

Appiah, Kwame Anthony. "A Long Way from Home: Richard Wright in the Gold Coast." *Richard Wright*. Ed. Harold Bloom. New York: Chelsea, 1987. 173–90. Print.

Baldwin, James. "Alas, Poor Richard." *Nobody Knows My Name: More Notes of a Native Son*. London: Michael Joseph, 1961. 149–76. Print.

Barthes, Raymond. Interview with Richard Wright (1956). Trans. Michel Fabre. *Conversations with Richard Wright*. Eds. Keneth Kinnamon and Michel Fabre. Jackson: UP of Mississippi, 1993. 166–68. Print.

Branch, Taylor. *Parting the Waters: America in the King Years 1954–63*. New York: Simon, 1988. Print.

Cassuto, Leonard. *Hard-Boiled Sentimentality: The Secret History of American Crime Stories*. New York: Columbia UP, 2009. Print.

Corber, Robert J. *Homosexuality in Cold War America: Resistance and the Crisis of Masculinity*. Durham, NC: Duke UP, 1997. Print.

———. *In the Name of National Security: Hitchcock, Homophobia, and the Political Construction of Gender*. Durham, NC: Duke UP, 1993. Print.

Galbraith, John Kenneth. *The Affluent Society*. Boston: Houghton Mifflin, 1958. Print.

Hoover, J. Edgar. *Masters of Deceit: The Story of Communism in America and How to Fight It*. New York: Holt, 1958. Print.

Jurca, Catherine. *White Diaspora: The Suburb and the Twentieth-Century American Novel*. Princeton, NJ: Princeton UP, 2001. Print.

Kazin, Alfred. *On Native Grounds: An Interpretation of Modern American Prose Literature*. New York: Harcourt, 1942. Print.

King, Martin Luther, Jr. "Letter from Birmingham Jail." 1963. *Reporting Civil Rights, Part One*. New York: Library of America, 2003. 777–94. Print.

———. "Where Do We Go from Here: Chaos Or Community?" 1967. *A Testament of Hope: The Essential Writings of Martin Luther King, Jr.* Ed. James Melvin Washington. San Francisco: Harper & Row, 1986. Print.

Rowley, Hazel. "The 'Exile' Years? How the '50s Culture Wars Destroyed Richard Wright." *Bookforum*. Dec/Jan. 2006. Web. Jan. 2009.

———. *Richard Wright: The Life and Times*. New York: Holt, 2001. Print.

West, Cornel. "Introduction." *Black Power*. By Richard Wright. New York: Harper Perennial, 2008. vii–xiii. Print.

Whyte, William H., Jr. *The Organization Man*. New York: Simon, 1956. Print.

Wright, Richard. *A Father's Law*. New York: Harper Perennial, 2008. Print.

———. *Black Boy (American Hunger)*. Restored Ed. New York: Harper Perennial, 1993. Print.

———. "How Bigger Was Born." 1940. *Native Son*. New York: Harper Perennial, 1993. 505–40. Print.

———. *Savage Holiday*. New York: Avon, 1954. Print.

———. *Uncle Tom's Children*. 1938. New York: Harper & Row, 1965. Print.

———. *White Man, Listen!* 1957. *Black Power*. New York: Harper Perennial, 2008. 631–812. Print.

4

SEEKING SALVATION IN A NATURALISTIC UNIVERSE: RICHARD WRIGHT'S USE OF HIS SOUTHERN RELIGIOUS BACKGROUND IN *BLACK BOY (AMERICAN HUNGER)*

Robert J. Butler

> The religious spirit always endures. Up to now man has always been a religious animal and secular art is a sublimation of the religious feeling.
>
> —Richard Wright (qtd. in Kinnamon and Fabre 210)

James Coleman's recent study of African American fiction, *Faithful Vision,* laments the fact that even though "religious and biblical traditions that engender faith are arguably the most important cultural feature to African Americans," the critical response to black literature, ironically, reflects very little of this because "the critics who write about black novels seldom deal with religious and biblical traditions in fiction" (1). This is particularly true of the way Richard Wright's work has been studied over the years. Surprisingly little has been written about his religious background because most scholars have assumed that his childhood exposure to fundamentalist Protestantism was so painful and extreme that he simply recoiled from religion of any kind and developed a vision of life that was essentially secular. Even Coleman argues that Wright categorically rejected black religion, forcing him to envision "a hollow, hopeless and desolate universe" (203).[1]

However, a careful examination of Wright's actual writings indicates that he, like James Joyce, Ignazio Silone, and James T. Farrell, was deeply influenced by the religious values and practices of his early childhood and made artful use of them in his major work to make important affirmations, thus avoiding the "void" (207), which Coleman sees at the center of his work. This is especially true of *Black Boy (American Hunger)*, a book that crystallizes a problem that goes to the core of Wright's vision—how to achieve a human self while inhabiting a deterministic environment that systematically denies your status as a human being? Growing up in a wide variety of locations in the Deep South and the urban North, Wright envisioned both worlds as prisons, which blocked his attempts to develop himself as a person, and hells, which attacked his soul by condemning him to "meaningless pain and endless suffering" (117). The task he set for himself in his autobiography was to "wring a meaning" (118) out of such an empty, sterile world and achieve a "new life" (296) as a morally liberated and spiritually empowered person. *Black Boy (American Hunger)* thus becomes a conversion narrative that transcends the bleak nihilism of much naturalistic literature. Wright's religious background, which he consciously rejected as a young man but made skillful literary use of as a mature writer, played a crucial role in his artistic and personal development. It was an invaluable resource providing him not only with a rich store of dramatic imagery and symbolism but also the spiritual and moral values he needed to fruitfully engage a world that he described in "How 'Bigger' Was Born" where "God no longer existed" and where "metaphysical meanings had vanished" (446). Facing the void created by a world wracked by racial terror, global depression, and oncoming world war, Wright was able to construct a durable humanistic vision of life, grounded in part in the fundamentalist religion he experienced while growing up in the Deep South.

*   *   *

Black Boy (American Hunger) employs two integrally related stories: (1) an outward narrative documenting the injustices and brutalities of the deterministic social environment that trapped him in both the South and the North and (2) an inward narrative that dramatizes his transcending that environment with his own spiritual energy and free will. Externally, the segregated South is presented as a Dantean hell in which he feels "forever condemned, ringed by walls" (296). Memphis, like Dante's Dis, is a "dead city" (11) where his family falls apart and he is threatened with starvation and condemned to emotional abandonment in an orphanage where he feels "suspended

over a void" (35) and "lost" (37). His subsequent life in a bewildering
series of locations such as West Helena, Arkansas, where his uncle is
murdered by racist whites, and Jackson, Mississippi, where he considers himself a stranger in his grandmother's stern household, serve to
reinforce his terror and isolation. As a teenager, he is acutely aware
of the racial violence and injustices of southern life, becoming deeply
alienated from a society that "casts him in the role of a non-man"
(288).

When he heads North in search of a better life, he finds different
forms of the hell he experienced in the South. Arriving in Chicago,
his "fantasies" of finding a promised land are "mocked" when he is
confronted by a city that evokes both T. S. Eliot's *The Waste Land* and
Dante's *Inferno*, "an unreal city" covered with "palls of grey smoke"
and "flashes of steam" while assaulting his senses with a constant "din"
(307). The harsh environment of this "machine city" (308) is made
even worse two years later by the onset of the Great Depression, which
condemns Wright to even more degrading forms of poverty and human
insignificance, while threatening the civilized world with chaos.

This hellish and massively deterministic outward narrative, however, is balanced by an extremely affirmative inward story, which
becomes more prominent as the autobiography develops. While Wright
was physically starved by the naturalistic environment he endured in
both the South and the North, he was nourished by tapping into a
number of resources, which helped to satisfy his psychological, moral,
and spiritual needs. As a child in Memphis, he was able to ameliorate
the terror of his external life by recoiling into himself: "I began to be
aware of myself as a distinct personality striving against others. I held
myself in…My imagination soared; I dreamed of running away"
(35). As his outward circumstances became even more intimidating,
with his mother developing a serious illness that plunged his family
into extreme poverty, and the white world became more violent and
repressive, confronting him with its "white-hot face of terror" (64),
Wright was able to secure a measure of moral balance by cultivating
an inward self nourished by his active imagination. While his outward
self remained frozen in terror, his secret life "soared" and he begins to
develop the notion that he can "run away" to a better world.

This doubleness that Wright cultivates at an early age is the key to
understanding his complexly divided reaction to the severely fundamentalist religion he experienced as a member of his grandmother
Wilson's household in Jackson from 1920 to 1925. In these extremely
formative years, he outwardly rejected the Seventh-Day Adventist religion, which she imposed upon the family, rebelling strongly against

its puritanical restrictions, rigid dogma, and authoritarian rule. But he was inwardly attracted to its highly dramatic vision of the world, seeing it as an imaginatively compelling alternative to his mother's religious stance, which was a static and passive acceptance of suffering grounded in the image of "Christ upon the Cross" (376).

He deeply resented his grandmother's reducing his reading and writing to "devil's work" (41) and her forbidding him to listen to music, dance, and play sports with his friends. He also strongly resisted her forcing him to attend the Seventh-Day Adventist School taught by his Aunt Addie and regarded as useless the "all-night ritualistic prayer meetings" (138), which his grandmother made the family attend. Moreover, he bridled at her forbidding him to work on Saturdays, the day on which Adventist services were held, because it denied him an opportunity to make the money he needed to buy decent clothes and supplement the meager diet that the Wilsons offered. Most of all, however, he was repelled by his grandmother's conception of an Old Testament God who ruled by fear and violence, since such a deity resembled too closely the white authority figures who ruled the segregated South. While in the early years of his stay in his grandmother's house on 1107 Lynch Street he made a pretense of worshipping such a God and accommodating himself to a strict religious regimen, he later explicitly spurned her religious beliefs, refusing to testify to his grandmother's faith and also rejecting her orders to attend church school and services. He physically threatened his Uncle Tom and Aunt Addie when they attempted to coerce him into obeying the severe religious demands that his grandmother made on the family. In the final year of his stay on Lynch Street, he was not on speaking terms with any family member, except his mother, and was regarded by his grandmother as a lost soul headed for eternal damnation. When he left Mississippi for Memphis in November 1925, he was motivated by a desire not only to free himself of the Deep South's harshest forms of racial discrimination and violence but also to liberate himself from his grandmother and her religion.

But another part of Wright was fascinated by the stern but imaginatively evocative vision of life embraced by Seventh-Day Adventism, and this had an enduring effect on his personal development and writing. At the beginning of chapter 4 of *Black Boy (American Hunger)*, he stresses how he was "pulled toward emotional belief" (119) by the powerful sermons he heard in church:

> The elders of her church expounded a gospel clogged with images of vast lakes of eternal fires, of seas vanishing, of valleys of dry bones, of

the sun turning to ashes, of the moon turning to blood, of stars falling to earth, of a wooden staff being transformed into a serpent, of
voices speaking out of clouds, of men walking on water, of God riding
whirlwinds, of water changing into wine, of the dead rising and living,
of the blind seeing, of the lame walking, a salvation that teemed with
fantastic beasts having multiple heads and horns and eyes and feet;
sermons of statues possessing heads of gold, shoulders of silver, legs of
brass, and feet of clay; a cosmic tale that began before time and ended
with clouds of the sky rolling away at the Second Coming of Christ;
chronicles that concluded with Armageddon; dramas thronged with
all the billions of human beings who had ever lived or died as God
judged the quick and the dead... (119)

Such dramatic images fired the young Wright's lively imagination,
fascinated him throughout his life, and played a prominent role in his
personal and artistic development. As Constance Webb has pointed
out, "Richard never tired of talking about the peculiarities of that
religion" (397) and enjoyed discussing Seventh-Day Adventism with
his friend Arna Bontemps who was also raised in that religion and
taught for a brief period in an Adventist school. Although Wright's
rational nature rejected religion as a dangerous anodyne for black
people because it provided them with fantasies that distracted them
from addressing political and social problems in the real world, the
imaginative and emotional sides of his personality were strongly
attracted to Seventh-Day Adventists for a number of reasons. On the
most literal level, its belief in "the lame walking" would provide him
with the hope that his mother could recover from the paralysis, which
had become a "symbol" in his "mind" of "meaningless pain and endless suffering" (117), a vision of life that could bring him to personal
despair. On a purely aesthetic level, the colorful images provided by
these sermons would catalyze Wright's fertile imagination, combining with the murder mysteries, gothic tales, and western stories he
had read in pulp magazines to move him to write crude horror stories
such as "The Voodoo of Hell's Half Acre." More broadly, the prospect of sinners being burned in "vast lakes of eternal fire" while the
just would rise to heaven in the Second Coming of Christ provided
Wright with an apocalyptic narrative, which would be an imaginative
foundation for his later political beliefs and literary strategies. The
fire and brimstone sermons that fascinated Wright as a boy would
become the equally fiery Jeremiads found in his early Marxist poetry
as well as Max's courtroom speeches in *Native Son*. And although
Wright stubbornly resisted the pressures of his mother and grandmother to testify to his spiritual conversion, all of his writing may

be seen as his own testifying to the racial, political, and economic injustices inflicted on people by inhumane social systems. Wright's work thus can be regarded as his attempt to make "the blind" truly "see" such a corrupt world and then reform it. From his early political poems published in radically leftist journals in the 1930s to the many haiku poems composed shortly before his death in 1960, Wright's entire oeuvre can be seen as an extended quest for "salvation" in a naturalistic universe designed to condemn people to the prison of social injustice and the hell of spiritual emptiness.

*   *   *

Fire, which Keneth Kinnamon has described in *New Essays on Wright's Native Son* as "a central metaphor of [Wright's] creative imagination" (10), plays a particularly strong role in *Black Boy (American Hunger)*. Initially it is linked with Wright's fears that he lives in a hellish world that can suddenly destroy him. The opening scene portrays Wright as a small child fascinated with the "quivering coals" in the fireplace of his grandmother's house as he attempts to relieve the boredom of remaining silent while she is recuperating from an illness. He lights a straw and touches the curtains, which then erupt in "red circles" (4) of flame that threaten to burn down the house. The scene ends with his mother punishing him with a severe beating that first reduces him to unconsciousness and then makes him "lost in a fog of fear" (7). At age four, Wright wonders which is more destructive—the physical fire that nearly destroys him and his family or the hot emotions of his mother who has "come close to killing" (8) him? As a child, therefore, Wright is already strongly imbued with a sense of the world that matches the Seventh-Day Adventist vision of the radical instability of earthly life and the ever-present danger of death and damnation by fire.

Fire is also employed in a later scene when Wright and his mother visit his father who has left the family to take up with a lover in a Memphis apartment. His father refuses to provide any support for his wife and two sons and indeed laughs at their pleas for help. This traumatic episode reduces Wright to fears of abandonment and starvation, and he is haunted for many years afterward by the hellish image of "my father and the strange woman, their faces lit by the dancing flames" (140). Here again, fire is used to suggest a world where a relatively secure existence can be suddenly destroyed by forces that the young Wright can neither understand nor control. So when his grandmother later calls him "a black little devil" (48) and strikes him when he disobeys her, he feels "an aching streak of fire burning and quavering on my skin" (48). Her later admonition that he will "burn forever in a lake of fire" (135) if he fails to accept her moral codes and religious practices reinforces strongly in his young mind that he lives in a terrifying world that can suddenly erupt with fiery violence and destroy him. (His grandmother's frighteningly severe view of the world is later ominously paralleled when Wright as a teenager hears about a black man being lynched, ritualistically hung, and burned when he is alleged to have violated the South's racial codes.)

As a young boy, Wright's only resource for psychologically coping with such a terrifying world is to protect himself by withdrawing into a compensatory inward life. He does this in his early childhood in Natchez by experiencing the simple beauties of the natural world as he responds to its "coded meanings" in "wonder" and "delight," enjoying the sights of "the dreaming waters of the Mississippi" and "the wet green garden paths in the early morning" (8). A few years later, he experienced similar pleasures vicariously when Ella, a boarder in his grandmother's house, reads him a story about Bluebeard and he becomes "enchanted and enthralled" as the story, like the fiery sermons, transforms external reality with "magical presences" (45). Here, fire becomes a purifying agent instead of a destructive force as his "imagination blazed" creating "a sense of life" which is "deepened" (45), transfigured.

Throughout the remainder of *Black Boy (American Hunger)*, the imaginative experience generated by literature serves a quasi-religious function of transforming Wright's inner self, enabling him to experience the conversion in his personal life, which he was unable to achieve in an institutional church. After dropping out of the religious school presided over by his religiously zealous Aunt Addie and enrolling in public schools, Wright experienced for the first time of his life a four-year period of unbroken formal education in which he begins to cultivate a strong habit of reading and also begins to write fiction. This proved to be a pivotal experience, which "revitalized [his] being" and opened up a productive "future" (147). He thus was able to overcome several of the traps set by his environment, which kept him in his "place" and helped him to begin a meaningful journey on his own "strange and separate road" (148).

Here again, a paradoxical linkage is established between his painful experiences as a member of the Seventh-Day Adventist Church and his liberating life as a reader and a writer. His grandmother's church requires the literacy that his father lacked because it is centered on the reading of the Bible, a book that transfigures the reader's soul and leads to a "salvation" not possible in the segregated South. In the same way, Wright's reading and writing deepens his inward life, broadens his vision, and empowers him to see his own life in salvific terms. It is no accident that some of his most meaningful, early reading experiences consist of reading the Bible in Sunday School when he lived in West Helena, and later in Jackson when he and his family read from Scripture before every meal. Achieving literacy in early-twentieth-century Mississippi, therefore, acquires some of the same meaning as it had in the slave South, becoming a kind of subversive activity, which develops important human qualities that the social system is designed to destroy. As Wright notes when he is taken aback by a white woman's negative response to his writing a story, "My environment contained nothing more alien than writing or the desire to express oneself in writing" (142). Even reading the cheap pulp fiction, which he finds in popular magazines such as *Flynn's Detective Weekly,* proves liberating since it provides a "gateway to the world" (151), which was closed to him by his social environment.

These early experiences of literacy in Mississippi prepare him for the more serious engagements with reading and writing, which he undergoes in Memphis and Chicago. Such experiences are endowed by Wright with quasi-religious significance and are explicitly linked with what he had learned as a member of the Seventh-Day Adventist Church. Just as the sermons that fascinated him tell of "the blind seeing," Wright's impassioned reading of modern fiction in Memphis "opened up new avenues of seeing and feeling" leading to a radically "new life" (296). In the same way, his literary involvements in Chicago help him to construct a transformed self, which is capable of not only clearly diagnosing the social problems that had beset him in the South but also providing him with a coherent strategy to deal productively with these problems. Here too, he lives a radically divided life, outwardly working a number of menial jobs so that he can support himself and his family and inwardly developing the enriched consciousness he needs as a writer and activist. Working a mechanical job in the Chicago Post Office by day, he reads and writes at night, as his "true feelings raced along, underground, hidden" (328). Significantly, he titles the second part of his autobiography "The Horror and The Glory," suggesting not only the split between the pain of his outward life and the rich satisfactions of his inward being, but also the Seventh-Day Adventist belief that the agonies of earthly existence will one day be redeemed by the "glory" of a conversion made possible by the Second Coming.

But whereas Wright's development of a significant inward life in the South was a largely personal affair, which he was unable to share with anyone, he was able in Chicago to make connections with like-minded people and groups that helped him to broaden his vision and give it social and political relevance. He became a member of the South Side Writers Group in 1936, a collection of young black writers and intellectuals, which included Margaret Walker, Frank Marshall Davis, Horace Cayton, and Arna Bontemps, people with whom he would establish strong friendships and would exert positive influences over his writing. As Walker stressed in her biography of Wright, he had "a great need for such associations because they ameliorated the deep alienation" (286), dating back to traumatic experiences that he had endured in the South, experiences that threatened to blight his spirit and thus cripple his imagination.

He also became a member of Chicago's John Reed Club, which Hazel Rowley has described as "Wright's University" (78), because it put him in contact with young leftists such as Herbert Gold, Jack Conroy, and Nelson Algren who saw their radical politics as a kind of "new faith" (354), which could renew the American society that the Great Depression brought to the brink of collapse. Here again, Wright used in his autobiography strongly religious terminology to express his artistic beliefs. He envisioned himself as a "witness" (398) for oppressed people, a "voice" (398) for the inarticulate and silenced masses. In Chicago, Wright took on the role of a writer who would do much more than articulate a personal vision and began to see his writing as his grandmother had envisioned her religion and church—as a powerful means of transforming the world.

* * *

Although Wright was initially skeptical of the communist speakers he heard in Washington Park in his early years in Chicago, regarding their ideas as "too simple" and "frozen" in "ignorance" (319), he gradually became strongly attracted to communist ideology because it had some of the same imaginative and emotional appeal that drew him to the sermons he heard in his grandmother's church. Marxist thought provided him with "a new faith" (355) embedded in an apocalyptic vision of history, in which capitalist "sinners" would be punished and the "righteous" proletariat would experience a kind of heaven, a classless society. A fiery revolution would bring this about, annihilating a corrupt capitalistic system, just as the lake of fire of his grandmother's religion would put an end to the old order of things and make possible the Second Coming of Christ. While Wright as a child gave his "emotional belief" to sermons, which proclaimed "the dead rising and living" (119), as a young radical he was equally drawn to communist ideology, which, in the words of the *International,* urged the dispossessed masses: "Arise, you pris'ners of starvation" (450) and "Arise, you wretched of the earth" (451).

Communism, therefore, became for Wright what it was for writers such as Ignazio Silone and Arthur Koestler, a potently attractive secular equivalent to the religion he knew as a child, a mode of personal redemption and cultural salvation. His involvements in the John Reed Club and Communist Party not only ended his isolation as a person by providing him with "the first sustained relationships in [his] life" (373) but it also made available to him a colossal vision of human solidarity by "uniting scattered but kindred people into a whole," supplying a "common bond" (374), which brought the world's people together with a transcendent ideal. For this reason, Wright compared the Communist Party to a "church" whose "myths and legends" can reveal "man's destiny on earth" (441).

Wright would eventually leave the party for some of the same reasons that he had rejected his grandmother's religion, regarding both as unacceptable encroachments on his personal life and a threat to his developing the kind of consciousness he needed in order to become a writer and a fully developed human being. Party officials, like his grandmother, had taken a dim view of his intellectual life and artistic aspirations, seeing them as encouraging heretical beliefs and an unhealthy individualism. He came to view party ideology as similar to Seventh-Day Adventist dogma, as static systems that locked its members in "militant ignorance" (390).

But Wright never became like Ross, a person who could accept his personality being "obliterated" (140) as a way of maintaining his membership in the party, which he identified as his only means of salvation. Nor did he become like Todd Clifton of Ralph Ellison's *Invisible Man,* a man who chose to commit suicide rather than live outside the party's systems of belief. For, unlike Ross and Clifton, Wright possessed important psychological and moral resources, which predated his party membership and could therefore survive his rejection of communism. Unlike Ross whose only belief system was communism, Wright can fall back upon what he terms "the spirit of the Protestant ethic," a "heritage of free thought" that calls upon man "to work and redeem himself through his own acts" (436). This spirit of independence and free inquiry, which one "suckled, figuratively, with one's mother's milk" (436), sustained Wright throughout his life, enabling him to develop new forms of spiritual and moral beliefs long after he had separated himself from institutions such as communism, which falsely claimed to support these beliefs and translate them into reality. He could thus commit himself to existentialist philosophy after rejecting Marxist ideology because it nourished the self that the Communist Party tried to eradicate. He could also commit himself to Pan-African politics after becoming disillusioned with communist politics because it could keep alive his faith in freeing oppressed people, uniting them in a third world utopia, which bears some similarity to the Seventh-Day Adventist vision of an apocalyptic second coming that will bring justice to oppressed people. And at the end of his life, when he lost most of his faith in organized systems of belief, he was able to keep his soul alive by writing over 2,000 haiku poems, as Fabre observes, "like a monk in a cell" (512) at his retreat at Moulin d'Ande. These tiny poems, which employed ordinary images from the natural world to distill spiritual essences, brought Wright's religious life full circle. They greatly resemble the prose poems in *Black Boy (American Hunger),* which he used to capture the "vague sense of the infinite" as he gazed in wonder at "the yellow dreaming waters of the Mississippi River" (8).

* * *

Late in his life, Wright wrote a long essay, "Memories of My Grandmother," which was never published and remains in the Wright Collection at the Beinecke Library at Yale University. In it, he professes a strong admiration for the woman he depicted in such negative terms in *Black Boy (American Hunger),* and he also reveals her enduring influence on his life. He stressed that the habits of mind and vision of life that he received from his grandmother's religion strongly influenced his development as a man and a writer:

> Their teachings and their religion, by encouraging me to live beyond the world, to have nothing to do with the world, to be *in* the world but not *of* the world...implanted germs of such notions in me...These events which create fear and enchantment in a young mind are the ones whose impressions last the longest; perhaps the neural paths of response made in the young form the streets, tracks, and roadways over which the vehicles of later experience run...(qtd. in Fabre 36)

Wright makes very explicit here what is implicit in *Black Boy (American Hunger):* that the seeds of his adult vision of life were planted in his childhood when Seventh-Day Adventism both fascinated and repelled him, creating in his young mind "fear and enchantment" or, what he would later call in the second part of his autobiography, "The Horror and the Glory." The "neural paths" created in his early years by his religious training did indeed provide "streets, tracks, and roadways" over which the "vehicles of later experience" did "run." Wright's religious background ultimately deepened and broadened his mature work, enabling him to transcend the shallow determinism and facile pessimism of works such as Upton Sinclair's *The Jungle* and Jack London's *The Sea Wolf,* which express naturalistic theory in a simplistic, doctrinaire manner. The spiritual and moral depth of Wright's best works such as *Uncle Tom's Children*, *Native Son*, and *Black Boy (American Hunger)* also endow these books with a thematic richness, complexity, and resonance missing in typical protest literature of 1930s, such as Clifford Odets's *Waiting for Lefty*, Jack Conroy's *The Disinherited* , and Edward Dahlberg's *Bottom Dogs.* While such dated works have become footnotes to literary history, Wright's masterworks continue to disturb and inspire modern readers.

Wright, who in "Memories of My Grandmother" also expressed a desire to explore "the living springs of religious emotion" (qtd. in Rowley 85), energized and deepened the meaning of his major work by drinking deeply from these springs. *Black Boy (American Hunger)* illustrates this vividly by describing in a powerful way Wright's emergence from the hell of American racism to experience a kind of "salvation" through the exercise of will and spirit. He transcended the world that "imprisoned" the "soul" (40) of his father and "crushed" the "spirit" (168) of his grandfather, achieving a liberating "new life" (296) as a major American writer.

NOTE

1. Surprisingly little has been written about Wright's response to his religious background and even less has been said about the literary uses he made of this background. Most of the critics and scholars who have commented on these important matters have concluded that he was so repelled by the fundamentalist religion he experienced growing up in his grandmother's Seventh-Day Adventist household that he became an atheist who categorically rejected all religious institutions and values. Constance Webb, for example, regarded the severe religious training as a

boy as damaging to his character because it resulted in his feeling "menaced by a mysterious God who seemed somewhat like hate" (183). Webb regarded this religion of fear and guilt as psychological baggage, which Wright needed to reject wholesale in order to develop as a man and an artist. Margaret Walker, likewise, argued that Wright was so repelled by his grandmother's harsh religion that it led him to reject religion in any form. She regarded Wright's grandmother Wilson and Aunt Addie, both fervent Seventh-Day Adventists, as "religious fanatics" (33) from whom Wright needed to free himself. Robert Douglas's article "Religious Skepticism and Orthodoxy in Richard Wright's *Uncle Tom's Children* and *Native Son*" argues that Wright was unable to portray religious experience coherently in these two works because he was "perplexed about the value of Christianity as a means of black salvation and liberation" (80). Douglas concludes that Wright reacted mainly to religion with "skepticism and cynicism" (84).

I wish to argue, however, that Wright's response to his religious background was powerfully and fruitfully split. At times, he consciously adopted the standard Marxist view that religion was essentially a dangerous fantasy for oppressed people, the opiate of the masses, because it dissipated their energies and distracted them from understanding and reforming the real world. However, at other times, he regarded the fundamentalist Christianity he was exposed to in his childhood as an important literary resource and repository of the spiritual values he needed to overcome the crippling effects of environment, which was designed to reduce him to the status of a "non-man" (288). Christian notions of redemptive suffering, conversion, and salvation of the individual go to the heart of Wright's vision and receive especially vivid treatment in *Black Boy (American Hunger)*.

BIBLIOGRAPHY

Coleman, James. *Faithful Vision: Treatments of the Sacred, Spiritual, and Supernatural in Twentieth-Century African American Fiction.* Baton Rouge: Louisiana State UP, 2006. Print.

Douglas, Robert. "Religious Orthodoxy and Skepticism in Richard Wright's *Uncle Tom's Children* and *Native Son.*" *Richard Wright: Myths and Realities.* Ed. C. James Trotman. New York: Garland, 1988. Print.

Fabre, Michel. *The Unfinished Quest of Richard Wright.* New York: Morrow, 1973. Print.

Kinnamon, Keneth. *New Essays on Native Son.* New York: Cambridge UP, 1990. Print.

Kinnamon, Keneth, and Michel Fabre, eds. *Conversations with Richard Wright.* Jackson: UP of Mississippi, 1993. Print.

Rowley, Hazel. *Richard Wright: The Life and Times.* New York: Holt, 2001. Print.

Walker, Margaret. *Richard Wright: Daemonic Genius.* New York: Amistad, 1988. Print.

Webb, Constance. *Richard Wright: A Biography.* New York: Putnam, 1968. Print.

Wright, Richard. *Black Boy (American Hunger).* New York: Harper Perennial, 1993. Print.

PART II

TAKING SIDES: RACISM
AND SPATIAL DIMENSIONS

In this part of the volume, Isabel Soto takes up the claim that Wright's works, once recontextualized within the modernist *versus* realist debate, call for a new emphasis on space, not time, as speaking "on behalf of a racially determined organization of the world." Her essay, along with Thadious M. Davis's "Richard Wright: Space and the WPA," reconsiders Wright's spatial anatomy of the modern as an entry into the power, social entrapment, and historical (mis-) understandings of race during the 1930s and 1940s. Isabel Soto's "'White People to Either Side': *Native Son* and the Poetics of Space" analyzes the representation and negotiation of space in *Native Son*. Soto proposes that space functions as a major structural and organizing principle of the novel, with spatializing power in the novel being determined by racial agency: "Who or what defines and controls space?" Soto shows how race and space *are* inevitably contained by socialized material boundaries—for which there *are* penalties for interracial crossings—in a repressively capitalistic America.

Thadious M. Davis argues that without the "space" provided to Wright through the existence of the Works Progress Administration (WPA), his ability to become a professional writer would not have existed. Davis further contends that The Writers Project became a way for Wright to imagine his life as a professional writer despite his "dislocation from the South and his concomitant dispersal throughout America and foreign places more hospitable to racialized subjects." Davis calls for a comparative study of racializations of space in which the intersections of race and place in *Black Boy* and *American Hunger* may be read as Wright's search to realize "a mature, masculine subjectivity" as well as to fulfill his writerly ambitions. Wright's literary portrayals of embattled masculinity and the economics of racialized patriarchy followed him to Paris as well, as revealed in *The Outsider* and *The Long Dream*.

Wright made his spaces purposeful and equated them with an aggressive writerly freedom. Beginning with the opportunity offered by the Federal Writers Project, Wright ultimately pursued transnational spaces that allowed him to reconfigure narrative as unbound to national literary forms and social relations. His own writings, especially in the 1950s, increasingly concerned themselves with diasporic and global revolutionary movements. While Davis illustrates Wright's ability to test his creative limits, the troubling interpretive limitations of American readers who were exposed to Wright's works are examined primarily through Soto's close reading of spatial metaphors in *Native Son*, where Wright uses spatial dimensions in that novel to pronounce upon American *pudeur* in relation to race and on the complex place of violence and sexual desire on the American landscape of the 1950s.

5

"White People to Either Side": *Native Son* and the Poetics of Space

Isabel Soto

The quote "white people to either side" (507), which inspires the title to this essay, is both descriptive and prophetic, anchored in the narrative's present as well as in the narrative's future. It is an accurate verbal representation of Bigger Thomas's physical situation at that moment (he is sitting in the front seat of a car flanked by two white people); the words reappear virtually unaltered in the third and final section, appropriately entitled "Fate," of Richard Wright's *Native Son* (1940), in reference to the "white […] policemen sitting to either side of him" (703). If the initial appearance of the phrase "white people to either side" is echoed in the novel's closing stages, then the narrative follows the same strategy. In full, the first sequence reveals an interracial dynamic mediated through a vocabulary of physical constraint, expressive of Bigger's sense of bodily entrapment, if not actual (desire for) obliteration:

> [Bigger] felt foolish sitting behind the steering wheel […], letting a white man hold his hand […]. He felt he had no physical existence at all […].There were white people to either side of him; he was sitting between two vast white looming walls […]. His arms and legs were aching from being cramped into so small a space, but he dared not move […] his moving would have called attention to himself and his black body. (507–09)

In the latter sequence, soon after Bigger's arrest, the complete quote reads, "He tried to move his hands and found that they were shackled by strong bands of cold steel to white wrists of policemen sitting to either side of him" (703). The realization of the former sequence in the latter—in contrast to the frustrated interracial homoeroticism—speaks to the novel's naturalist aesthetics and what Valerie Smith calls its "relentless plottedness"[1] in the first place and, second, to its engaging of space and spatial categories in order to underwrite that social determinism. Indeed, space defines Bigger's existence from the start: the famously harsh alarm clock "clang" with which the novel opens—"BRRRRRRRIIIIIIIIIIIIIIIIIIIINNG!" (447)—is transformed nine lines on into a spotlight, freezing the protagonist in a confined place: "Light flooded the room and revealed a black boy standing in a narrow space between two iron beds" (447). The premonitory imprisonment of Bigger, trapped between iron in a cramped kitchenette, imagistically survives to reappear at the very end, with Bigger now facing death and literally contained by iron bars in a prison cell. Abdul JanMohamed notes the fateful circularity that links the opening and closing scenes in *Native Son*: "If the novel opens with Bigger in a death-cell [i.e. the kitchenette] and ends with him in a different kind of death-cell, then the entire novel can be said to map the movement from one form of death to another" (84). More on the kitchenette/death-cell analogy below.

Several studies of *Native Son* have taken note of the novel's reliance on the spatial as a means to frame the narrative of Bigger Thomas's radical exclusion and isolation—Catherine Jurca's *White Diaspora: The Suburb and the Twentieth-Century American Novel* (2001) and Houston A. Baker, Jr.'s essay, "Richard Wright and the Dynamics of Place in Afro-American Literature" (1990), are but two of the most insightful. While tacitly acknowledging this previous body of work, not to mention groundbreaking sociological studies such as St. Clair Drake and Horace R. Cayton's *Black Metropolis: A Study of Negro Life in a Northern City* (1945) and for which Wright wrote the Introduction, the present essay draws more substantially on, first, liminal analysis and, second, Lacanian theory. In both, what lies *between* spaces, that is, the concept of "the threshold or border," whether material, symbolic, or perceptual, plays a central role. The first part of my discussion proposes that space, understood broadly and not explicitly distinguished from place,[2] functions as a major structural and organizing principle in Richard Wright's *Native Son*, driving the novel at the levels of plot (Bigger's movement from space to space is one of the ways in which the story gets told), theme, and rhetoric. The second part of my analysis shifts the emphasis from space as such to the negotiation *between* spaces, foregrounding the perceptual threshold that underpins self-perception or the perception of another. It is here where I find Lacan's formulation of the (self-) identificatory process involved in the move from the mirror to symbolic stage so germane to understanding Bigger Thomas's subject formation. That Bigger is assisted (as I argue) in that process through the enabling black gaze of Bessie also prompts an alternative reading of her role in the novel to that to which she has been traditionally assigned: passive, helpless, victim.

The novel provides an exploration of space as a shape-shifting category (tenement apartment, cinema, Doc's, Mary Dalton's Buick, furnace, jail, etc.), which maps, directs, and mediates events, exemplifying Michel Foucault's proposition in "Of Other Spaces" (1967) that "the present epoch will perhaps be above all the epoch of space […]. We are at a moment […] when our experience of the world is less that of a long life developing through time than that of a network that connects points and intersects with its own skein" (par. 1). It is space, then, rather than time, which organizes and gives meaning to experience. In African American experience, space is further and crucially linked to race; in African American writing, space is likewise strategically implicated in race and vice versa. Samira Kawash's insightful *Dislocating the Color Line: Identity, Hybridity, and Singularity in African American Letters* (1997) notes that in the contemporary United States, "racial politics are spatial politics; race is a fundamental element of social space" (12). The positioning of race within space is to a very large extent reflective of black-white relations in the United States, haunted as they are by a racially determined system of slavery. The slave narrators in particular take note of the spatialization of existence since, as Katherine Clay Bassard argues, slavery "order[ed] experience according to free space and captive space" (116).

Historically, then, the spatialization of power is strategically placed in African American writing and Wright's novel is no exception, providing also the occasion to explore agency and raise questions over who defines and ultimately manages space. In the passages quoted thus far, spatial entrapment is expressive of the absence of material agency: Bigger endures, even as he fails to control, bodily location and emplacement. Whereas, say, Frederick Douglass's liberatory "spaces left" (87) in the primary copybook where he learns to write, and Baby Suggs's appropriation of the Clearing in Toni Morrison's *Beloved* in order to reclaim the black body are expressive of individual and collective empowerment, in *Native Son,* space is somewhat less enabling. Space can be (at best) ambivalent or hybrid; it can also be conflicted—all of which plausibly describes Bigger. His relation to the society in which he lives is to a large measure revealed through passages such as the above, where his passive rather than active relation to space derives from a racial(ized) in-betweenness ("white people to either side"). This liminal location intensifies Bigger's passivity/powerlessness and produces a weakened sense of embodied self: "He felt he had no physical existence at all right then; [...]. It was a shadowy region, a No Man's Land, the ground that separated the white world from the black that he stood upon" (508). Valerie Smith speaks of this "gray area" as being "a realm of terror, an [...] unexplored danger zone" (78). This spatial arrangement, with Bigger occupying a "gray" place that lies between—while emphatically not connecting—white space and black space, is repeated with variations throughout *Native Son*. We might suggest that this "No Man's Land" is in (ironic) anticipation of the contact zone as formulated by Mary Louise Pratt, a space where colonizers and the colonized coexist in "radically asymmetrical relations of power" (7). For Bigger, however, the interracial "No Man's Land" aligns itself more closely to Smith's realm of terror and danger, an area fraught with potential catastrophe, than it does with any meaningful (if "asymmetrical") power dynamic.[3] Thus, space is also closely associated with death and violence, inevitably partaking also of the racial politics to which Bigger falls victim: there is white space, there is black space, and there is the shadowy and dangerous No Man's Land. JanMohamed has further noted the physical degeneration associated with (black) space in Wright, in particular, the kitchenette, which both signals Bigger's fate and is equated with the "death-cell" in later writings:

> The kitchenette, with its filth and foul air, with its one toilet for thirty or more tenants, kills our babies so fast that in many cities twice as many of them die as white babies. The kitchenette is our seed bed for scarlet fever, dysentery, typhoid, tuberculosis, gonorrhoea, syphilis, and malnutrition. The kitchenette scatters death so widely among us that our death rate exceeds our birth rate. (qtd. in JanMohamed 306n4)

The sequence of lethal events that emplots the novel—the murders of Mary and Bessie, Bigger's death sentence—is the actualization of the potential violence inherent to space as represented in *Native Son*. In particular, interracial space is flagged at various points prior to Mary's murder, and always within a context of violence, anger, or dread, or all three. Firmly and uncomfortably wedged between Mary and Jan with the latter driving through Chicago's black district, "Bigger [w]anted to seize some heavy object in his hand and grip it with all the strength in his body and in some strange way rise up and stand in naked space above the speeding car and with one final blow blot it out—with himself and [Mary and Jan] in it" (510). As soon becomes clear, it is no accident that the novel's recurring image of a spatial vacuum is frequently allied to a projected desire for self-obliteration or (violent) obliteration of others.

Later that same day, Bigger goes to the Dalton residence to take up the position of family chauffeur. He pauses to survey the house before entering: "He stopped and stood before a high, black, iron picket fence, feeling constricted inside [...]; only fear and emptiness filled him now" (486). On the one hand, there is the unstoppable thrust of the narrative, anticipating and echoing images, situations, and phrases as well as the leitmotif of an image of entrapment combined with an image of spatial nothingness; on the other, Bigger, poised at the entrance to white space, is about to insert his black body into it, effecting a measure of interracial interdependence or, at the very least, interaction. Note that the feelings of "constriction" and "emptiness" are accompanied by fear (the title of this first section) in anticipation of the violent events that follow. Black space and white space in *Native Son* "are not yet smoothly commensurable,"[4] it would seem. This lack of commensurability (reflective of a "realm of terror," as Smith puts it) tragically leads, for example, to the shattering of Mary's communist boyfriend Jan's dream of an "interracial imaginary" (Maxwell 182) as well as that of Max, Bigger's communist defense lawyer. By contrast and for good reason, Bigger is all too cognizant of the penalties exacted from those who blur racial boundaries and attempt to realize a measure of interraciality. For Bigger there is no viable "interracial imaginary," only a fraught No Man's Land.

The potentially catastrophic consequences of breaching or blurring the racial code by occupying the shadowy and liminal No Man's Land that lies between white space and black space reflect the fact that space itself signifies in relation to the racial dynamics of Bigger's world. It goes without saying, moreover, that race/space is not infinite but bounded, marked off from other races/spaces both by material boundaries (as in free/slave states, north/south, Jim Crow racial/spatial arrangements, and so on) and symbolic ones, or rather, a single symbolic boundary: the color line. Kawash notes, "The color line persists as the organizing principle of racial space, that is, the maintenance of an absolute boundary between black and white and, more especially, the exclusionary line demarcating and bounding whiteness" (12–13). The economy that inheres to this racial/spatial configuration is not lost on Bigger, as is evidenced in the early street scene where he acknowledges the racial politics of space, declaring his own enraged sense of entrapment and exclusion, and inadvertently pointing to his own end:

> Every time I think about it [white power] I feel like somebody's poking a red-hot iron down my throat [...]. We live here and they live there. We black and they white. They got things and we ain't. They do things and we can't. It's just like living in jail. Half the time I feel like

I'm on the outside of the world peeping in through a knot-hole in the fence [...]. Why they make us live in one corner of the city? (463)[5]

The "two vast white looming walls," which flank him in Mary's car and threaten his sense of self, become two pages later "the tall, dark apartment buildings looming to either side of [Bigger, Mary, and Jan]" (109), in reference to the tenement buildings occupied by black tenants (and owned, it transpires, by Mary's father, both slumlord and patronizing philanthropist). As already declared, there is white space and there is black space; both "loom"—the identical verb underscoring Bigger's powerlessness in one space and the other. The metaphor of the looming buildings, an ever-present urban dystopia, is rewritten in the novel's closing scene in a gesture of irreversible self-cancellation: "As the white mountain had once loomed over [Bigger], so now the black wall of death loomed closer with each fleeting hour" (451). The terms of the metaphor—white mountain, black wall—finally merge, connoting not resolution (or a DuBoisian tertium quid), but the preclusion of further potentiality, of life itself.

The bleakness of the story, and Bigger's strategically unsympathetic characterization,[6] is not at odds on the other hand with Bigger's small measure of personal growth and identity formation, monstrously enabled through the murders he commits: " 'But what I killed for, I *am*' " (849). The tragic paradox of self-knowledge at the expense of life itself is both the measure of Bigger's fate and, simultaneously, his challenge to it. It is also the novel's maximum expression of aporia. The existential impasse is reflected in the novel's spatial poetics, which determine Bigger's existence and define even his final moments; the novel closes, inevitably, with a spatial image of Max on the outside and Bigger on the inside of the prison cell (850–51), fulfilling Bigger's earlier insight of "feel[ing] like I'm on the outside of the world peeping in through a knot-hole in the fence." The knothole in the fence has become at the novel's end the steel bars of a prison.

Space, then, determines the aesthetic structure of *Native Son*, even as it maps Bigger's existence. Bigger can no more escape the spatial, than he can the larger structure and dynamic of power relations within which space is inscribed. While no longer subjected to plantation slavery, Bigger instinctually grasps the privileged role of the (white) controlling gaze inherent to the racialized space(s) he successively occupies. Early on in the novel, shortly after leaving the kitchenette to meet with his neighborhood friends, Bigger contemplates the putting up of a "huge [...] poster" (456) of incumbent state attorney general, Buckley. This prefigurative encounter—Buckley will represent the prosecution at the murder trial—leads Bigger to note that "the poster showed one of those faces that looked straight at you when you looked at it and all the while you were walking and turning your head to look at it it kept looking unblinkingly back at you" (456). What this scene highlights is Bigger's sense of ubiquitous surveillance. Even if (or precisely because) Bigger is in an open space, his feeling of being visually controlled "all the while" coheres with his experience of being trapped by "white people to either side." In terms of the novel's seamless determinism, the power dynamic encoded in these spatial arrangements points to a tautology: Bigger is doomed no matter what space he occupies, because it is space itself that shapes and limits his agency.

Negotiating space requires negotiating the boundaries or thresholds that determine the exit and entry points of spaces as well as their difference. The line of demarcation may work as a boundary (exerting a prohibiting function) or a threshold (exerting an enabling function), the latter almost always accompanied by potentially destructive or lethal consequences; the racialized subject who breaches the color line does so at considerable peril. Similar penalties arise from the amalgamation of black space with white space in what the narrator terms a "No Man's Land." The threshold/boundary principle further works closely with spatiality in *Native Son* to determine and underpin the novel's aesthetic organization; the story advances, as Bigger does, by crossing thresholds and traversing spaces. Thresholds or boundaries figure at the literal level, setting off one space from another, but also, and sometimes simultaneously, at the metaphorical level. Witness Bigger's crossing over into white space upon entering the Dalton residence for the first time. He is separated by a literal boundary—the "high, black, iron picket fence" (486)—which he is obliged to breach into order to take up his new job. He is, however, not merely entering an unfamiliar house; in terms of the narrative, that is, his own fate, his entering white space prompts the ensuing catastrophe. Bigger's journey to that catastrophe follows sequentially and logically from a single narrative and visual threshold. At the same time, this narrative break or caesura (JanMohamed 94) problematizes the racial border, the all-pervasive nature of which aligns it closely to the panoptical power of the racialized arrangement of space that programs the novel's unfolding.

Borders and thresholds not only determine spatial limits and points of entry or access; they can also lie between one space and another, possessing a paradoxical ability to face two directions at once. In the remainder of this essay, I will briefly analyze the dynamics of (self-) recognition inherent to Bigger's evolving subject formation. As I noted at the outset, insofar as they operate across a perceptual divide or threshold, they are reflective of the poetics of space in *Native Son* I have been exploring, and exemplify Jurca's reminder that "the psychological and the spatial are indissolubly bound" (102). The ability of the limen to engage or straddle two systems is richly exemplified throughout the novel, especially at the affective level. Witness Bigger's specular identification with Mrs. Dalton's blind yet controlling (white) gaze: on hearing himself discussed by her to Mr. Dalton, he felt "as though there were influences and presences about him which he could feel but not see. He felt strangely blind" (928). Her impeded vision is internalized by Bigger to produce a sort of truncated self-vision. Writing a generation before Wright, Du Bois set out in compelling fashion the experience of observing oneself being observed, of occupying both sides of the perceptual divide. There are similar instances in which Bigger's (self-) identification with and through the gaze of another is congruent not only with DuBoisian double-consciousness but also a post-Freudian, Lacanian framework of subject formation and expressive of the doubling strategies and (internal) spatial dynamics at play in *Native Son*. Shortly after the alarm is raised over Mary's whereabouts, Bigger is interrogated by the family's private investigator, Britten.[7] Britten peers at Bigger and "in the very look of the man's eyes Bigger saw his own personality reflected in narrow restricted terms" (588).

The external and internal measure of the self—one reflected off a white surface, the other reflective of the subject's desires—is developed in the novel's closing stages, linking not coincidentally inner and outer spaces, both real and imaginary. Awaiting his lawyer's summation, Bigger gazes out of his cell window:

> He looked out upon the world and the people about him with a double vision: one vision pictured death, an image of him, alone, sitting strapped in the electric chair and waiting for the hot current to leap through his body; and the other vision pictured life, an image of himself standing amid throngs of men, lost in the welter of their lives with the hope of emerging again, different, unafraid. (786)

Bigger's double vision juxtaposes two forms of seeing, or rather, two visual images, with which he identifies equally. In addition, the negative (self-) identification characteristic of DuBoisian theory (Bigger, through the white gaze, internalizes an image of himself "in narrow restricted terms" and "alone, sitting strapped in the electric chair") invites comparison with the imaginary or mirror identificatory phase of Lacanian theory. Here the ego identifies with a person external to the subject, usually its image in the mirror, (mis-) taking it for itself.

Crucially, Bigger encounters also a self-image in the black gaze, that is, Bessie's, introduced only after Mary's murder. Much has been written about the refracted duplication of this first murder in the sequence that ends with Bessie's killing. The latter, so the argument partly goes, is a fully-cognizant act on Bigger's part of sexual predation and murder; these two aspects had been expressed only subliminally in the former. In other words, there is a specularity between the two murders, a specularity that is carried over into the narrative sequence that introduces Bessie. Just hours after killing Mary, Bigger seeks Bessie out; he "saw her looking at him, [. . .]. He liked that look[. . .]of complete absorption on her face. It made him feel alive and gave him a heightened sense of the value of himself" (587). Bigger's "heightened sense of the value of himself," materialized in his power over Bessie occurs (con-) sequentially after murdering Mary and is confirmed by the former's gaze. Lacanian theory would argue that Bigger needs Bessie in order to complete the passage from the imaginary to the symbolic identificatory stage, in which he identifies—through Bessie's gaze—"with the very place *from where* [he is] being observed, *from where* [he] look[s] at [him]self so that [he] appear[s][. . .]likeable, worthy of love."[8] Taking his leave of Bessie, Bigger's identificatory maturity enables him to act as the controlling agent of Bessie's gaze in order to create his desired self-image:

> He looked at her without expression . . . Her eyes were fastened fearfully and distrustfully upon his face[. . .]He started off[. . .]and she overtook him and encircled him with her arms[. . .]he was still poised, wondering if she would pull him toward her, or let him fall alone. He was enjoying her agony, *seeing and feeling the worth of himself* in her bewildered desperation. (582, emphasis added)

In terms suggestive of the symbolic stage, Bigger completes here the process "in which we identify with the *position of agency* through which we are observed and judged and through which we observe and judge ourselves" (JanMohamed 307n3, emphasis added).

What these two sequences point to is that Bigger's identificatory processes are racially determined, with Britten's white gaze producing a previous and intermediary imaginary identification, associated with feelings of alienation, and in which the self remains undifferentiated from the racializing gaze. (Bigger's inability to differentiate himself from Mrs. Dalton's blind gaze anticipates this.) By contrast, Bessie's black gaze enables Bigger's differentiation from the identificatory dependence of the mirror stage, thus completing his subject formation to enter the realm of the Symbolic. Bigger's increasingly confident use—indeed, discovery—of language is consistent with his entry into the Symbolic, which is closely associated with the cleaving of the subject by language into "I" and "you" subject positions. The discovery of the self-as-other, insofar as it involves the progression from one (subjective) space to another, coheres with the spatial poetics that dominates the rest of the novel.

The question that presents itself has to do with the narrative motivation behind Bessie's sexual, racial and, ultimately, identificatory role. On the one hand, the literalization of a rape-murder is part of the deterministic progress of the narrative: Bessie's rape would realize, on the third attempt, two prior nonliteral rapes, Gus's and Mary's, which are relegated to the subliminal by the gender, racial, and sexual (and editorial) prohibitions of the day (JanMohamed 113). In the case of Bessie, a black woman, these gender/racial/sexual boundaries are not enforced, their breaching additionally allowing Bigger to establish his masculinity (JanMohamed 114). On the other hand, what this otherwise persuasive analysis overlooks is Bessie's role in Bigger's identificatory development. In terms of the identificatory logic of *Native Son*, commentaries tend to focus on Bigger's dynamic with the white power structure and his internalization of its repressive injunctions. Hence Bigger's experience of double-consciousness in response to the white coercive gaze; it is also a response that, as I have argued, plausibly accommodates Lacanian analysis. Yet after Mary's murder, Bigger's identificatory dynamic with the white gaze only takes him so far; he cannot go beyond an imaginary (self-) identification. The white gaze casts back an image of himself that is narrow and restricted, or alone and awaiting execution. Bigger needs the *black* gaze in order to literalize not only the narrative's prior and nonliteral rape(s)-murder but also, and crucially, to enable Bigger's identificatory maturity. While not diminishing Bigger's morally unacceptable manipulation and killing of Bessie, this reading would invest her with a greater agential status in the racial economy of the novel. Thanks to her, Bigger gains a "heightened sense of the value of himself" and "[saw] and [felt] the worth of himself." Thus, in terms of *Native Son's* narrative logic, as a black *woman* Bessie provides Bigger with the occasion to make real his previous fantasies of sexual violence; in terms of the novel's racialized identificatory logic, as a *black* woman[9] she further enables Bigger to progress from the imaginary to the symbolic stage of (self-) identification.[10]

This essay has considered the use of the spatial in determining the aesthetic and philosophical concerns of *Native Son*. The novel is reflective of a peculiarly modern conception of reality that privileges the spatial over the temporal, even while Wright's work richly participates in a discursive tradition where space speaks on behalf of a racially determined organization of the world. This organization is enforced through the panoptical and coercive function of racialized space and through the metaphor of the color line, "always more than a metaphor," according to Samira Kawash, and "operating to enable and justify the social and spatial distribution of power, wealth, access, and privilege" (12–13). Wright's representation of racialized space yields, further, a rhetoric of doubleness, whether through an articulation of double-consciousness or an identificatory process of subject formation, to which the dynamics of (self-) recognition through the racialized gaze of another is central.

Notes

This essay is a substantially longer version of the article that appeared in *The Black Scholar* 39.1–2 (Spring-Summer 2009): 23–26.

1. Smith 67.
2. Here I subscribe to Yi Fu-Tuan's idea that "in experience the meaning of space often merges with that of place" (qtd. by Baker 85).
3. "Wright assert[s] that the color line [...] was both an intractable fact and an unstable artifact, its borders permeable and elastic" (Jurca 102). Permeability and elasticity are precisely the qualities of the color line that place Bigger in mortal danger.
4. William J. Maxwell's observation regarding the theme of "black folk wisdom" and its possible compatibility with "Communist strategy" in Wright's 1939 short story "Bright and Morning Star" (*New Negro, Old Left* 182). Cf. "*Native Son* presents a new social archetype of American hunger, one that attempts to view the distorted strength of the black folk hero through the lens of a communist defense. Yet the merger between the red and the black is as problematic in the novel as it came to be for Richard Wright in his life" (Johnson 62).
5. "The prior experience of 'living in jail' portends and is conflated with Bigger's eventual relocation to prison" (Jurca 101).
6. In "How 'Bigger' was Born," Wright confesses that after the publication of *Uncle Tom's Children* (1938), "I realized that I had made an awfully naïve mistake. I found that I had written a book which even bankers' daughters could read and weep over and feel good about." Wright "swore [...] that if I ever wrote another book, no one would weep over it; that it would be so hard and deep that they would have to face it without the consolation of tears" (874).
7. The orthographic, phonetic, and trochaic specularity among the names Bigger/Britten/Buckley/Bessie perhaps deserves scrutiny as reinforcement of other levels of specularity in the novel.
8. Slavoj Žižek (qtd. in JanMohamed 307n7, emphasis in original).
9. Cf. "Bigger's desire [for Mary] is [...] equally racial and sexual: he wants to be recognized as being equal to *white* men as well as to white *men*" (JanMohamed 114).
10. Johnson's strongly psychoanalytical interpretation of *Native Son* also attributes an enabling function to Bessie, whom she invests with the ability accurately to "read" Bigger after he has written the ransom note demanding money in exchange for Mary's safe return. Johnson

interprets Bessie's flash of insight—she guesses the truth—in racial and gendered terms: "The black woman, then, is a reader whose reading is both accurate and threatening" (69). Bessie's perceptiveness is her downfall, according to Johnson: "Bigger first rapes, then kills Bessie in order to prevent her from talking, in order to gain control over a story that has been out of his control from the beginning" (69).

BIBLIOGRAPHY

Baker, Houston A., Jr. "Native Son and the Dynamics of Place in Afro-American Literature." *New Essays on Native Son*. Ed. Keneth Kinnamon. Cambridge: Cambridge UP, 1990. 85–116. Print.

Bassard, Katherine Clay. "Crossing Over: Free Space, Sacred Place and Intertextual Geographies in Peter Randolph's *Sketches of Slave Life*." *Religion and Literature* 35. 2–3 (2003): 113–41. Print.

Douglass, Frederick. *The Narrative of the Life of Frederick Douglass, an American Slave*. Harmondsworth: Penguin, 1986. Print.

Drake, St. Clair, and Horace R. Cayton. *Black Metropolis: A Study of Negro Life in a Northern City*. 1945. Chicago: U of Chicago P, 1993. Print.

Du Bois, W. E. B. *The Souls of Black Folk*. 1903. Eds. Henry Louis Gates, Jr. and Terri Hume Oliver. New York: Norton, 1999. Print.

Foucault, Michel. "Of Other Spaces, Heterotopias." 1967. Web. 29 Dec. 2005.

JanMohamed, Abdul. *The Death-Bound Subject: Richard Wright's Archeology of Death*. Durham, NC: Duke UP, 2005. Print.

Johnson, Barbara. *The Feminist Difference: Literature, Psychoanalysis, Race, and Gender*. Cambridge, MA: Harvard UP, 1998. Print.

Jurca, Catherine. *White Diaspora: The Suburb and the Twentieth-Century American Novel*. Princeton, NJ: Princeton UP, 2001. Print.

Kawash, Samira. *Dislocating the Color Line: Identity, Hybridity, and Singularity in African-American Literatures*. Stanford: Stanford UP, 1997. Print.

Kinnamon, Keneth, ed. *New Essays on Native Son*. Cambridge: Cambridge UP, 1990. Print.

Maxwell, William J. *New Negro, Old Left*. New York: Columbia UP, 1999. Print.

Morrison, Toni. *Beloved*. 1987. London: Vintage, 1997. Print.

Pratt, Mary Louise. *Imperial Eyes: Travel Writing and Transculturation*. London: Routledge, 1995. Print.

Smith, Valerie. *Self-Discovery and Authority in Afro-American Narrative*. Cambridge, MA: Harvard UP, 1987. Print.

Wright, Richard. *Early Works: Lawd Today! Uncle Tom's Children. Native Son*. New York: Literary Classics of the United States, 1991. Print.

6

BECOMING RICHARD WRIGHT: SPACE AND THE WPA

Thadious M. Davis

The national, international, and transnational spaces ever apparent in Richard Wright's search for a space to be a black man in the twentieth century are touchstones for the consideration of the intersection between race and place manifested in the power struggle that he undertook to create a mature, masculine subjectivity in times both of decreasing economic and class resources and of challenging social and regional locations that functioned to diminish the possibilities for individual self-awareness, racial actualization, and social agency. The physical and psychological space associated with the South/North axis and with the liberatory northern migration is typically figured as central to Wright's becoming a writer and his development as a writer; however, one aspect of his early years in Chicago and New York has received noticeably less attention. Wright's own drive to find a space not simply for an expressive black masculinity but for becoming a modern writer finds a counter-drive in the formation of the Federal Writers' Project (FWP) of the Works Progress Administration (WPA) to foster and employ writers during the Great Depression. The Writers' Project became a way for Wright and other black writers to imagine their own lives as professionals, as practitioners of a vocation, despite their dislocation from the South and concomitant dispersal throughout the national landscape and the foreign places more hospitable to racialized subjects. In the WPA, a long list of individuals racialized as black, for example, Wright, Margaret Walker, Shirley Graham, Ralph Ellison, Frank Yerby, Theodore Ward, Frank Marshall Davis, Arna Bontemps, and Sterling Brown, could imagine themselves as writers and develop their craft within a cadre of practicing professional writers. The social, intellectual, artistic, and political space provided by the WPA enabled a young southern black man to become the writer Richard Wright and to inhabit the space he envisioned for himself in a writing career.

Experience occurs within a place, yet social theory has often lacked the inclusion of space. In the last decades of the twentieth century, however, new geographers such as Edward Soja have advocated strongly for integrating space into the formulation of social theories because separating spatial processes from social processes defies the logic of understanding that phenomena occur in a specified or given place. Daphne Spain, for instance, has pointed out, "Space is essential to social science; spatial relations exist only because social processes exists. The spatial and social aspects of a phenomenon are inseparable" (5).[1] In recognizing the impact of people and social communities on landscape, cultural geographers have delineated forms that demonstrate the inextricable interaction of the spatial and the social.[2] One now-familiar example that has had an impact across disciplinary boundaries is the work of social scientist Paul Gilroy who, in conceptualizing the "Black Atlantic" as a social space, focused attention squarely on the interlocked social and spatial relations manifested in black migration and diasporic practices.

Similarly, literary theorists and cultural critics also articulated space into their late-twentieth-century analyses of texts and social phenomena. In 1995, the Black Public Sphere Collective defined its subject as "a transnational space whose violent birth and diasporic conditions of life provide a counternarrative to the exclusionary national narratives of Europe, the United States, the Caribbean, and Africa. Thus the black public sphere is one critical space where new democratic forms and emergent diasporic movements can enrich and question one another" (The Black Public Sphere Collective 1).[3] Within this "critical social imaginary," as the Black Public Sphere Collective identified itself, was a significant awareness of politics, a "visionary politics" intersecting with critical practice, or put another way, the political taking shape and direction from vernacular practices within a shared social space (The Black Public Sphere Collective 3). In calling attention to the Black Public Sphere as political counternarrative, the Collective not only responded to Jurgen Habermas and *The Structural Transformation of the Public Sphere* but also understood space as interactive and constitutive.

Spatial parameters or boundaries of experience are increasingly mapped by scholars whose theoretical concerns range from postmodernism and global feminism to the body and prisons. Henri Lefebvre,

Michel Foucault, David Harvey, Doreen Massey, Yi-Fu Tuan, and John Berger, for example, constitute a partial list of those who have argued for a spatial hermeneutic.[4] The feminist geographers writing in Nancy Duncan's *Bodyspace,* for instance, have insisted on including the human body as the subject of geographical knowledge, and the body has become one of the key spaces in postmodern readings of place. Feminist scholars working in a wide range of disciplinary fields have been both noticeable and persistent in interrogating the relationships between women, women's conditions, and space, whether bodily, global, or textual.[5] Susan Stanford Friedman, for instance, in *Mappings,* assumes a locational epistemology based on changing geographical and historical specificities in her discourse on the future of feminism (3–13).[6]

Space from the perspective of literary scholars is now frequently aligned with the production of narrative, particularly in postmodern discourse. Brian Jarvis in *Postmodern Cartographies* suggests from his examination of American fiction that geography is infused with narrative: "Given the structural inseparability of space/place/landscape and social relations there can be no geographical knowledge without historical narrative. In other words, all spaces contain stories and must be recognized as the site of an ongoing struggle over meaning and value" (7). Approaching space as a site of struggle over value and meaning necessarily involves engagement with the structures underpinning and driving narration itself. In positing narration alongside space in postmodern studies, Patricia Yaeger raises a series of interconnected issues: "If ordinary space can be scripted as heterogeneous and multidimensional, refusing the simplicity of linear narrative, if local politics can be concealed or immersed in tropes of tragedy and romance…, space has an additional political-psychological dimension. The physical world is also a site where unrequited desires, bizarre ideologies, and hidden productivities are encrypted, so that any narration of space must confront the dilemma of geographic enigmas head on, including the enigma of what gets forgotten or hidden, or lost in the comforts of ordinary space" (4). The forgotten or the hidden, repressed or disguised, all too often will turn on issues of power. Within sites of power where there is a lack of obscuring camouflage, imbalances and abuses make justice a formidable subject. Importantly, as David Harvey's interpretations have underscored, justice is as much a constitutive element of geography as is place and space.[7]

Power and privilege follow from the creation of spaces within the American South of Richard Wright's youth to mark social relations and to segregate by racial difference. The historical South as a region and as a space allowed for the production of structures of power based on its slave economy and white racial hegemony. It is from this constrictive spatial reality that Wright migrated to Chicago and eventually found himself not only within a new geographical configuration but also within a new spatial imaginary—the FWP of the WPA, an institution lacking the most obvious racial hierarchy and oppressions found in Wright's homeplace, Mississippi.

In a speech presented on June 2, 1939, Langston Hughes told the Third Annual Writers' Congress: "It is hard for a Negro to become a professional writer. Magazine offices, daily newspapers, publishers' offices are tightly closed to us in America." This assessment by the major black writer in America at the end of the 1930s came as no surprise to other black writers who, inspired by the cultural awakening of the New Negro Renaissance in the mid-1920s, had attempted to support themselves by writing. Arna Bontemps, Zora Neale Hurston, Jessie Fauset, Countee Cullen, Claude McKay, Hughes himself, and their compatriots soon had discovered not only that the "vogue" for racial materials was amazingly brief but also that the opportunities for black employment in the world of letters were largely absent. The writers understood that their exclusion was due to racism; for example, in an effort to erase the difficulty of a black presence in a white office setting, Fauset offered an out for any publisher interested in hiring her: "If the question of color should come up I could of course work at home."

Hughes made his observation about the difficulty of becoming a professional writer at a critical juncture in the nation's cultural history when the decade-long economic pressures precipitated by the Stock Market Crash of 1929 had nearly decimated the developing ranks of black writers, yet when the institutional process for assisting writers, the FWP of the WPA, had already been initiated. Though Hughes never participated in the Writers' Project, he delivered his speech to a Carnegie Hall audience that included a young black writer who did: Richard Nathaniel Wright.

Wright in recounting his early life in Mississippi would write, "I had no hope of becoming a professional man" (*Black Boy* 227). Mississippi was the geographical no-man's land for black men of Wright's generation. In addressing the FWP and its ability to alter the hopes of a black man from Mississippi, I call attention to the way in which institutional space intersects with geographical space to reconfigure, modify, or create social conditions that in turn make possible new social, political, or cultural action. What the FWP as an institution enabled was the circumstances within a reconfigured spatial location by which Wright and others who were raced "Negro" in the 1930s could develop vocational ambitions and personal desires and become members of the writing profession. For Wright and those others, the FWP provided a movement into a public sphere that might otherwise have remained closed to them.

Two years before the Writers' Congress, Wright had arrived in New York from Chicago, where he had begun his writing career with the encouragement of the John Reed Club and, importantly, in 1936 with employment in the Federal Theater Project's Negro Unit and, within the year, in the Illinois Writers' Project. Ralph Ellison, whom Wright mentored at the end of the 1930s, has observed that "[t] hrough his cultural and political activities in Chicago [Wright] made a dialectical leap into a sense of his broadest possibilities, as a man and as artist" ("Remembering" 208). Margaret Walker, who worked with Wright on the Illinois Writers' Project and in the Southside Writers' group, has recalled that Wright's employment allowed him to move through his "various stages of conception, organization, and real-ization" and his "first scissors and paste job" (48). Essentially, the project allowed Wright to conceive of himself as a professional writer, or as Nelson Algren, another FWP writer, has put it: Wright was the "writer whom the Illinois Project helped the most.... He was alert to its advantages and more diligent than most of us. It gave him the time to write" (qtd. in Mangione 121). Not only did Wright complete his first novel, published after his death as *Lawd Today*, but he also wrote the stories for his first book, *Uncle Tom's Children*, and his first major essay, "A Blueprint for Negro Writing," which assumes as part of its premise that blacks can be both artists and professionals. "Writing has its professional autonomy," he concluded in that essay, "it should complement other professions" (48).

The segregated world of Mississippi in particular and the South in general could not accommodate a black youth like Richard Wright with ambitions to become a writer. The divided social space that blacks lived within fractured their visions of potential and functioned to delimit their desires. While the very cultural geography of Mississippi dictated a narrow social sphere for blacks, the lack of any conception of blacks earning a living by writing exacerbated the situation for someone of Wright's talents. Despite his poverty-ridden childhood, Wright was a precocious Deep South youth, who had been spinning yarns to entertain his schoolmates and crafting stories to read aloud to them. "Hell's Voodoo Half Acre" was his first story, but there would have been no public outlet for it in the brutal circumstances in which he lived. While within the private sphere of his race-defined social world, Wright might well have continued to write creatively, he would have been unable to pursue writing as his vocation. His departure for Memphis and from there for Chicago enabled him to experience a place with institutions (libraries, writing classes, writers' clubs, and publishing outlets) that both fostered and sustained writers. While much attention has been paid to the role of the urban Chicago Communist Party and its various organs in developing Wright's creative ability, less notice has been given to the FWP in Chicago and its nurturing of his ambition to write. In fact, his decision to forego the safety of a job in the U.S. Postal Service was informed by his broader understanding of the possibilities for earning a living by writing developed during his tenure with the Writers' Project. Importantly, in May 1937, when Wright left Chicago for New York, he was not only already committed to writing as more than an avocation pursued in his spare time, but he also anticipated the continuation of his association with the New York WPA as a writer.

When the Writers' Congress met in 1939, Wright was affiliated with the New York Writers' Project and its *American Stuff* collection even though he had already achieved the publishing success that had eluded him in Chicago. The first of his books, *Uncle Tom's Children*, a 1938 collection of four novellas, had resulted from his winning the 1938 *Story* magazine contest for WPA writers. The Writers' Project had worked for him and, as Ellison has maintained, for other blacks as well, by allowing them "to achieve their identities as artists" ("Remembering" 205). Wright's prize-winning story, "Fire and Cloud," earned him a contract from Harpers' for the publication of *Uncle Tom's Children,* and that book in turn brought him recognition as a serious, talented author. Though he found initial success within a year of his arrival in New York, Wright continued with the Writers' Project through the writing and publication of *Native Son.* By then, he viewed the project as an access route to the literary and publishing world in New York.

Native Son, the 1940 novel that was to ensure Wright's place as a major black author, brought him immediate financial success because of its selection by the Book-of-the-Month Club. The powerful novel of a black youth in Chicago's ghetto eclipsed even the work of the acknowledged dean of black writers, Langston Hughes, whose autobiography, *The Big Sea,* appeared with less fanfare that same year. Wright's publisher, recognizing that the critical reception accorded to *Native Son* gave its author national visibility and marketability, brought out a new edition of *Uncle Tom's Children* with an added story, "Bright and Morning Star," and an introductory autobiographical essay, "The Ethics of Living Jim Crow," which was, according to Sterling Brown, who served as the WPA National Editor for Negro Affairs from1936 to1940, "one of the finest pieces in *American Stuff*," the FWP's anthology of creative writings. These interconnections between the WPA's Writers' Project and the phenomenal development of Wright's career, while not unknown have not been linked directly to the progress that Wright made as a writer. "The Ethics of Living Jim Crow" from *American Stuff*, for example, was also the kernel of Wright's autobiographical work, *American Hunger*, the first part of which was published five years later as *Black Boy*, a title Wright arrived at after his editors and publishers divided his "Record of Childhood and Youth" from the longer work. The essay's publication in the Writers' Project collection signaled the process of bridging, or of building, as Wright put it, "a bridge of words between me and that world outside" (*American Hunger* 135). The architecture of the bridge is one of the ways of approaching Wright's construction of his fiction, and the span in the building process may be read as the WPA.

At the same time, an interrogation of the texts Wright produced during this phase of his career also reveals the relationships between race, racial conditions, and space (whether bodily, global, or textual). He focused specifically on the social geography in his native Mississippi that made exclusion and containment acceptable. In effect, Wright pointed to a normalizing of restrictive legal practices and social controls that produced a specific system of race-based identity and social relations in the United States, in particular in the American South, and in an exacerbated and cruelly exaggerated form in Wright's Mississippi. What he demonstrated in those texts produced during his tenure with the WPA was how regulatory boundaries delimit not merely access to space, but also subject formation and agency. Geographical and spatial claims are implicit in the transgression of legal and social attempts at racial exclusion and similar practices of power and privilege evidenced in *Native Son* and his short stories set in Mississippi as well as in his autobiographical texts, *Black Boy* and *American Hunger*.

"The WFP had limited value for professional writers," Monty Noam Penkower observes in his thoughtful study, *The Federal Writers' Project: A Study in Government Patronage of the Arts* (179). Penkower may well be right in drawing his conclusion about white creative writers because, as he points out, few of the literary projects came to fruition and no permanent writers' bureau resulted. However, with regard to black writers, Penkower's observation misses the mark, even though it contains the term that perhaps best characterizes the main and lasting value of the WFP for the black writer: "professional." A generation of blacks became "professional" writers largely due to their work experiences with the FWP and their social experiences with writers involved in the project.

Although the label "professional writer" applied to a few black writers before the decade of the 1930s, not until then did it have a literal meaning for many aspiring black writers. Both survivors and heirs of the Harlem or "New Negro" Renaissance of the 1920s came to the Writers' Project from diverse and varied backgrounds; some, such as Sterling A. Brown, Zora Neale Hurston, Claude McKay, and Arna Bontemps, were already published authors who had earned reputations as participants in the Renaissance, while others, such as Ralph Ellison, Margaret Walker, Willard Motley, Richard Wright, Frank Yerby, and Ted Poston, began virtually literary careers during their tenure with the FWP. All of them, however, expanded their vision of the possibilities for earning a living by writing, for reaching wider audiences with their work, for practicing their crafts, for researching their subject matter, particularly folk sources, and for interacting with other writers.

It may seem odd to designate these black writers of the 1930s as an initial group of black professional writers, especially when the Harlem Renaissance writers of the 1920s actually achieved greater popularity and visibility than any black writers before them. Indeed, the Renaissance writers enjoyed a wider access to more varied publishing outlets both within and outside the black community as well as in small private and large commercial ventures; they published in *The Crisis, The Messenger,* and *Opportunity,* the official organs of the NAACP, the Brotherhood of Sleeping Car Porters, and the Urban League, respectively; in *Fire* and *Harlem,* short-lived independent magazines; and in *Survey Graphic, The Atlantic Monthly,* and *Forum.* Many shared the dream and enthusiasm of Arna Bontemps, who arrived in New York from Los Angeles, as he said, "to find the job I wanted, to hear the music of my taste, to see serious plays, and to become a writer" (4) Few, however, considered writing their profession. Countee Cullen, for example, was a school teacher, as were Bontemps and Jessie Fauset. Claude McKay and Wallace Thurman did manage to work as editors, but Rudolph Fisher was a medical doctor, Georgia Douglas Johnson a government worker, and Nella Larsen a librarian. Others, such as Hughes and Hurston, were primarily students who earned a living by performing a variety of short-term jobs.

When the Depression hit and, as Hughes put it, "the Negro was no longer in vogue," most of the surviving Renaissance writers retreated from Harlem into whatever regions where they could find employment. Georgia Douglas Johnson, who participated in the Renaissance from her home base in Washington, had eloquently articulated their common plight in 1927 when she wrote an autobiographical sketch for *Opportunity* magazine's "Contest Spotlight":

> I write because I love to write…. If I might ask of some fairy god-mother special favors, one would sure to be for a clearing space, elbow room in which to think and write and live beyond the reach of the Wolf's fingers…. much that we do and write about comes just because of the daily struggle for bread and breath….

By the mid-1930s when, out of economic necessity, the coterie of Renaissance writers had scattered, Johnson's assessment had even more meaning for blacks who wanted to write, who dreamed of writing.

In Chicago, Richard Wright and others from his South Side Writers' Workshop became affiliated with the WPA. Although Wright wanted to write and had begun writing stories and poems before he left the South in 1927, his ambition was to get a position with the Chicago Post Office as the start of a secure career as a civil servant. His literary activity with the John Reed Club in 1932–33 and with the Communist Party had, of course, fueled his desire to write and to publish; nevertheless, before his first appointment with the FWP, he had seriously considered neither the possibility of writing full-time nor the idea of writing as a primary vocation. The urban space in which he found himself functioned in many social ways as an extension of the South; however, community interdependence fostered by the WPA represented an answer to the southern landscape of segregation and an access route to social justice within a new structure of power. One of the points Phoebe Cutler makes in *The Public Landscape of the New Deal* speaks to the overarching conception of American society that informed the WPA and the FWP: "A cohesive, integrated society was sought, in which land patterns could promote a wholesome combination of work, play, and education. In the 1930s Americans still viewed the landscape, along with church and family, as a force in character formation. Recreation enjoyed the moral hegemony that conservation still retains. This idealism imbued the landscape" (4). Importantly, for writers and artists, "the era romanticized not the place but the purpose of the place" (Cutler 19). Art became linked to recreation in the work of character formation.

Wright was not alone among the black Chicago writers in viewing writing as therapeutic, perhaps even a psychological necessity, though not as an occupation. Margaret Walker Alexander recalls that when she was first introduced to Wright by Langston Hughes on February 16, 1936, neither she nor he had "published one significant piece of imaginative prose" (48). His work on the Illinois Writers' Project directed by Louis Wirth soon changed that. Walker, who had graduated from Northwestern in 1935, found herself still unemployed in the early months of 1936, but like Wright, she was searching for a way to remain in Chicago, where, as she says, she "hoped to meet other writers, learn something more about writing, and perhaps publish some of [her] poetry" (49). Her opportunity came on March 13, 1936, when she received a notice to report to the Wells Street office of the WPA Writers' Project; her salary was $85 a month, though a year later it was increased to $94. As a junior writer, Walker reported to the Project office for semiweekly assignments, and there she continued her friendship with Wright, who introduced her to Arna Bontemps and Sterling Brown, and brought her into the South Side Writers Group. This period marked the beginning of Walker's sense of herself as a professional writer, though her career was in its apprenticeship stage and none of her work had been published.[8]

Although Wright's employment with the WPA began before Walker's, his term initiated with the Theater Project. When he relocated to the Writers' Project, his position was that of a supervisor with a salary of $215 a month because he had not only himself but also his mother and brother to support, and he had already published poems in *Left Front, The Anvil,* and *New Masses.* Though not free of either segregation or racism, Chicago as a major metropolis, then the second largest U.S. city, provided opportunities unimaginable in Mississippi, even in its quasi-urban areas, Jackson and Natchez.

Wright, Walker, Katherine Dunham, Frank Marshall Davis, Theodore Ward, Frank Yerby, and Arna Bontemps were only a few of the black writers who were on the WPA and who worked on the Illinois Writers' Project. All of them had connections to the South. It is important, however, to keep in perspective the relatively small number of blacks who were enrolled in the Project nationwide. In February 1937, Sterling Brown's office reported that the number was 106, or a mere 2 percent of the total number of writers on the Project; during the duration of the FWP, the number of blacks had been as low as 80 and never rose above 150 (Gabbin 70). Fortunately, Wright was among the 2 percent, and indeed he went on to become the most successful black writer of his generation. But in Chicago, he had been like the others, struggling to earn a living, and affirmed in his vocation by the very existence of the FWP.

In 1936, Sterling Brown's appointment as national editor of Negro affairs for the FWP marked a major turning point not only in the usually acknowledged impact that the project would have on studies of blacks in America but also on the professional careers of black creative writers. Brown's editorial position came about as the direct result of Director Henry Alsberg's decision to promote both the hiring of blacks and the inclusion of black sociocultural history in the state projects. Alsberg, however, was responding to influential blacks such as Ralph Bunche, Walter White, Robert Weaver, William Hastie, and John P. Davis, who individually and collectively through their organizations recognized that a knowledgeable black person should be appointed to the national FWP office in order to ensure that black history, culture, and literature would be included in the Project's undertakings. Brown himself was a poet and critic, educated at Williams College and Harvard, but completely grounded in the folklore and folk traditions of black America. Under his creative leadership from 1936 to 1940, the Project began a massive program of researching and writing the history of blacks in America, which was Brown's idea for redressing the sparse treatment of blacks in individual state guides. It was a realignment of the American narrative and a struggle to assert power as part of racial equity and justice.

Brown, along with his editorial staff, had managed to prevent the state guides in progress from neglecting or excluding black material as had the six New England guidebooks that were completed before his tenure with the Project. Although, as Jerre Mangione observes in *The Dream and the Deal: The Federal Writers' Project, 1935–1943,* the "honest and accurate . . . coverage given to the subject in these books represented, in effect, the first objective description of the Negro's participation in American life," that coverage still was not extensive enough (259). Brown believed that comprehensive studies could reveal the Negro "as an integral part of American life" and so instituted and directed field projects in which black writers researched black history, culture, and folklife within the contexts of their relationship to the larger American experience (Mangione 258, 259).

In terms of tangible publications resulting from Brown's research and editorial program, only *The Negro in Virginia* (1940), a study now considered a classic in the field, appeared in print. Supervised by Roscoe E. Lewis at the Hampton Institute, the Virginia project was an all-black unit of the Virginia Writers' Project whose state director, Eudora Ramsay Richardson, followed the lead of Brown and Alsberg in encouraging the research and production of what they hoped would be, and indeed it became, a model book. Despite the fact that other comparable publications did not materialize, the program was crucial to the development of black professional writers, because two of its major research collection projects were in Illinois and New York where large concentrations of blacks lived and where a number of young blacks found employment through the WPA.

Because of Henry Alsberg's assistance, Richard Wright was able to transfer to the New York Writers' Project. His initial assignment was on the New York City Guide, but he was soon placed with Willard Maas, Claude McKay, Harry Kemp, and Maxwell Bodenheim on the *American Stuff* project, an anthology that allowed the writers "to work at home on their own material, with the sole stipulation that they report to the Project office once a week with evidence of their work" (Mangione 245). The move and the continuation with the Project proved fortuitous because, though all the fiction manuscripts he had sent out from Chicago had been turned down by publishers, his first manuscript submission in New York not only was accepted for publication but also won the 1938 *Story* magazine contest for WPA writers. The prize-winning story, "Fire and Cloud," also brought him a contract from Harpers' for *Uncle Tom's Children* (1938), along with recognition as a serious, talented writer. Importantly, Wright chose to continue on the Project after his initial success; he remained through the writing and publication of *Native Son* (1940), the novel that was to ensure his place as a major professional writer and that, as a Book-of-the-Month Club selection, brought him financial success.

The New York City that Wright encountered as part of his migration and developmental process offered the opportunity for a new subjectivity. Migration east allowed for a redefinition of self in a new space, yet at the same time it came with the security of a ready-made organizational base, which promoted writing as work and as a career. Economic and vocational choices were easier to make, given the system of support and acknowledgment institutionalized within the Writers' Project.

Ralph Ellison, in "Remembering Richard Wright," an essay about his early days in New York and the beginning of his friendship with Richard Wright, points to the FWP as "most important to the continuing development of Afro-American artists," and as providing "the possibility for a broader Afro-American freedom" (204). His statement suggests the concept that space equals freedom, an idea theorized later in the geographical work of Yi-Fu Tuan. Ellison clarifies his point by reflecting on his personal condition at the time he became involved with the FWP. He states in *Going to the Territory:*

> Wright himself worked on both the Chicago and the New York Federal Writers' Project, and I could not have become a writer at the time I began had I not been able to earn my board and keep by doing research for the New York project. Through Wright's encouragement, I had become serious about writing, but before going on the project I sometimes slept in the public park below City College because I had neither job nor money. But my personal affairs aside, the WPA provided an important surge to Afro-American cultural activity. The result was not a "renaissance," but there was a resuscitation and transformation of that very vital artistic impulse that is abiding among Afro-Americans....Afro-American cultural style is an abiding aspect of our culture, and the economic disaster which brought the WPA gave it an accelerated release and allowed many Negroes to achieve their identities as artists. ("Remembering" 204–05)

Although his perspective is quite personal, Ellison recognizes that the FWP made it possible for himself and other blacks to become writers and professionals during a bleak period in the national economy, which, for those lowest on the socioeconomic scale, was even bleaker. Ellison's own words ("the WPA...allowed many Negroes to achieve their identities as artists") help to make the main point that I have stressed: that blacks not only found employment with the FWP but also began to conceive of themselves as professional writers whose vocation could be solely that of writer. This discovery and the shift in subjectivity mark the beginning of a class of blacks labeling themselves writers/authors and earning their living as writers. Importantly, too, it is a shift to an assumption of social significance and power within a space previously closed to blacks.

By way of conclusion, I want to return briefly to two points about Sterling Brown's WPA collection and research projects on blacks in America and their relationship to Richard Wright's development as a writer. One is that the work done in Chicago, much of it still unpublished and housed in the Vivian Harsh Collection of the Chicago Public Library, formed the ideological framework for one of Wright's major essays on black writing and writers, "Blueprint for Negro Writing," which appeared in *New Challenge* in the fall of 1937 and which restates the premise that Brown had for the project: "There is a culture...of the Negro which is his and has been addressed to him; a culture which has...helped to clarify his consciousness and create emotional attitudes which are conducive to action. This culture has stemmed mainly from two sources: (1) the Negro church; and (2) the folklore of the Negro people." (54) Although Wright's "Blueprint" is more typically linked to the influence of communism on Wright, it is very much a reformulation of Brown's general tenets for the FWP's Negro studies, as the section on "Social Consciousness and Responsibility" makes clear in its opening:

> The Negro writer who seeks to function within his race as a purposeful agent has a serious responsibility. In order to do justice to his subject matter, in order to depict Negro life in all of its manifold and intricate relationships, a deep, informed, and complex consciousness is necessary; a consciousness which draws for its strength upon the fluid lore of a great people, and molds this lore with the concepts that move and direct the forces of history today. (54)

It seems doubtful that without Brown's guidance, statements, and vision, Wright would have come so early to these conclusions about the black writer and black folklife and folklore. And by extension, neither would Ellison and other black writers have come so directly at the start of their careers to so intense an appreciation of and commitment to the materials of black folklife had they not had the experience of working not simply with the FWP but specifically with the studies of blacks conceived and planned by Brown.

Wright's work in the new edition of *Uncle Tom's Children* owed a debt to Sterling Brown's *Southern Road* (1932) and to his signature poem in dialect, "Odyssey of Big Boy." Though born in Washington, D.C., Sterling Brown had spent six years living and teaching in the South during the 1920s, when he developed into a successful and well-published poet using folk forms and speech most closely associated with southern black life (Tidwell and Sanders 6–7). Brown's "Big Boy" provides a model for Wright's "Big Boy Leaves Home" and Bigger Thomas in *Native Son,* and a bridge spanning the South that Wright had left behind and the South that he could construct in fiction and expose in narrative the imbalances of power.

The second of these two final points is that for many years after the Writers' Project ended, black writers, whether or not they had been employed by it, made use of the cultural materials researched for the incomplete Negro studies projects. Examples include Gilbert Osofsky's *Harlem: The Making of a Ghetto, Negro New York 1890–1930* (1966); Roi Ottley and William J. Weatherby's *The Negro in New York: An Informal Social History, 1626–1940* (1969); and Sterling Brown, Arthur Davis, and Ulysses Lee's *Negro Caravan* (1941). And that usage continues today with researchers availing themselves of the materials at the Schomburg Collection of the New York Public Library and, to a lesser extent, those in Chicago's Harsh Collection and research collections around the United States. Among the earliest works to utilize the FWP collection projects, Horace Cayton and St. Clair Drake's *Black Metropolis: A Study of Negro Life in a Northern City* (1945) seems especially pertinent here because Richard Wright wrote the introduction in which he included yet another statement reiterating the position on the Negro in American life charted by Brown for the FWP: "Both the political Left and the political Right try to exchange the Negro problem into something they can control, thereby denying the humanity of the Negro, excluding his unique and historical position in American Life" (xxix). Thus, as Brown intimated, the WPA created a political and social space that allowed a racially restricted group of individuals an opportunity to step out into a public life, a public sphere, free to declare themselves without apology as writers.

While it is quite apparent that Wright's unprecedented success as an author, a black author from the South involved in the FWP, initiated the telling of his life's story, it has been less clear that *Black Boy* and its sequel, *American Hunger,* were intimately connected with Wright's decision to become a professional author, to make a living as few blacks had done by writing. The two books narrate, develop, and may be read as a cultural story of the creation of the black professional writer in a field long unavailable to even the most serious black authors. Wright portrays in these narratives how his inclinations, temperament, and intelligence all combined to make him suited for no other role in life.

In her introductory note to *Black Boy,* Dorothy Canfield Fisher called Wright, "that rarely gifted American author." Those concluding words may well have been the most significant marker of Wright's achievement in the autobiographical work: his acceptance as author, an American author. Though Fisher was, no doubt, responding to Wright's style and technique in *Black Boy,* she may have also recognized in the text, a site of power over the creation of a unique black self as artist and the quest for authorship as profession.

NOTES

1. Spain relies on the work of feminist geographers who pioneered theories about space and gender. She hypothesizes that "initial status differences between women and men create certain types of gendered spaces and

that institutionalized spatial segregation then reinforces prevailing male advantages" (6). Her point, in language and in conception, is dependent upon a knowledge of racial segregation and white social advantages stemming from that practice.

2. William E. Mallory and Paul Simpson-Housley, in recognition of the interconnection of the spatial and the social, organized an interdisciplinary project in which they brought together geographers, creative writers, and literary critics in the work of what they term, "giving the world...a more unified shape" (xi–xii).

3. The Collective responded to Jurgen Habermas's *The Structural Transformation of the Public Sphere: An Inquiry into a Category of Bourgeois Society,* trans. Thomas Burger with Frederick Lawrence (Cambridge, MA: MIT Press, 1993).

4. See, for example, Lefebvre and Massey.

5. See, for instance, Ainley; Blunt and Rose; Higonnet and Templeton; Columina; Anzaldua; and Fryer.

6. See also Caren Kaplan's chapter "Postmodern Geographies: Feminist Politics of Location" in her *Questions of Travel: Postmodern Discourses of Displacement.*

7. See Harvey, *Justice, Nature and the Geography of Difference.* Harvey's chapter, "City and Justice: Social Movements in the City" in his *Spaces of Capital: Towards a Critical Geography,* links urban organization and environment with Marxism and the production of space and uneven geographical development.

8. Margaret Walker became a full-fledged writer in Chicago. Her poetry would later win the Yale Younger Poets Award, and the book *For My People* would become one of the signature texts of modern American and African American poetry. Walker spent long years living, writing, and teaching at Jackson State University in Jackson, Mississippi, an almost ironical connection back to her relationship with Richard Wright and their WPA days in Chicago, about which she would write in *Daemonic Genius,* her study of Wright's life and career.

BIBLIOGRAPHY

Ainley, Rose, ed. *New Frontiers of Space, Bodies, and Gender.* London: Routledge, 1998. Print.

Alexander, Margaret Walker. "Richard Wright." *Richard Wright: Impressions and Perspectives.* Eds. David Ray and Robert Farnsworth. Ann Arbor: U of Michigan P, 1973. 47–67. Print.

Anzaldua, Gloria. *Borderlands/La Frontera: The New Mestiza.* San Francisco, CA: Aunte Lute, 1987. Print.

The Black Public Sphere Collective, ed. *The Black Public Sphere: A Public Culture Book.* Chicago: U of Chicago P, 1995. Print.

Blunt, Alison, and Gillian Rose, eds. *Writing Women and Space: Colonial and Postcolonial Geographies.* New York: Guilford, 1994. Print.

Bontemps, Arna. Preface. *Personals.* By Arna Bontemps. 1963. London: Paul Breman, 1973. Print.

Brown, Sterling. "Negro Studies." Federal Writers' Project, National Archives, Record Group 69.

Columina, Beatriz, ed. *Sexuality and Space.* New York: Princeton Architectural, 1992. Print.

Cutler, Phoebe. *The Public Landscape of the New Deal.* New Haven, CT: Yale UP, 1986. Print.

Duncan, Nancy, ed. *Bodyspace: Destabilizing Geographies of Gender and Sexuality.* London: Routledge, 1996. Print.

Ellison, Ralph. "Hidden Name and Complex Fate: A Writer's Experience in the U.S." *The Writer's Experience: Ralph Ellison and Karl Shapiro.* Washington, D.C.: Library of Congress, 1964. 1–15. Print.

———. "Remembering Richard Wright." *Going to the Territory.* New York: Random House, 1986. 198–216. Print.

Fauset, Jessie. Letter to Joel Spingarn. 26 Jan. 1926. Schomburg Center for Research in Black Culture, New York Public Library. Print.

Fisher, Dorothy Canfield. "Introductory Note." *Black Boy: A Record of Childhood and Youth.* By Richard Wright. New York: Harper, 1945. Print.

Friedman, Susan Stanford. *Mappings: Feminism and the Cultural Geographies of Encounter.* Princeton, NJ: Princeton UP, 1998. Print.

Fryer, Judith. *Felicitous Space: The Imaginative Structures of Edith Wharton and Willa Cather.* Chapel Hill: U of North Carolina P, 1986. Print.

Gabbin, Joanne V. *Sterling A. Brown: Building the Black Aesthetic Tradition.* Westport, CT: Greenwood, 1985. Print.

Gayle, Addison. *Richard Wright: Ordeal of a Native Son.* Garden City, NY: Anchor Press/Doubleday, 1980. Print.

Gilroy, Paul *The Black Atlantic: Modernity and Double Consciousness.* Cambridge, MA: Harvard UP, 1993. Print.

Harvey, David. "City and Justice: Social Movements in the City." *Spaces of Capital: Towards a Critical Geography.* New York: Routledge, 2001. Print.

———. *Justice, Nature and the Geography of Difference.* Oxford: Basil Blackwell, 1996. Print.

Higonnet, Margaret, and Joan Templeton, eds. *Reconfigured Spheres: Feminist Explorations of Literary Space.* Amherst: U of Massachusetts P, 1994. Print.

Hughes, Langston. Third Annual Writers' Congress. June 2, 1939. Speech.

Jarvis, Brian. *Postmodern Cartographies: The Geographical Imagination in Contemporary American Culture.* New York: St Martin's, 1998. Print.

Johnson, Georgia Douglas. "The Contest Spotlight." *Opportunity.* June 1927. Print.

Kaplan, Caren. "Postmodern Geographies: Feminist Politics of Location." *Questions of Travel: Postmodern Discourses of Displacement.* Durham, NC: Duke UP, 1996. Print.

Lefebvre, Henri. *The Production of Space*. Trans. Donald Nicholson-Smith. Cambridge, MA: Basil Blackwell, 1991. Print.

List, Robert N. *Dedalus in Harlem: The Joyce-Ellison Connection*. Washington, D.C.: UP of America, 1982. Print.

Mallory, William E., and Paul Simpson-Housley. Preface. *Geography and Literature: A Meeting of the Disciplines*. Syracuse, NY: Syracuse UP, 1987. xi–xv. Print.

Mangione, Jerre. *The Dream and the Deal: The Federal Writers' Project, 1935–1943*. Boston: Little, 1972. Print.

Massey, Doreen. *Space, Place, and Gender*. Minneapolis: U of Minnesota P, 1994. Print.

Penkower, Monty Noam. *The Federal Writers' Project: A Study in Government Patronage of the Arts*. Urbana: U of Illinois P, 1977. Print.

Soja, Edward. *Postmodern Geographies: The Reassertion of Space in Critical Social Theory*. London: Verso, 1989. Print.

Spain, Daphne. *Gendered Spaces*. Chapel Hill: U of North Carolina P, 1992. Print.

Tidwell, John Edgar, and Mark A. Sanders, eds. *Sterling A. Brown's* A Negro Looks at the South. New York: Oxford UP, 2007. Print.

Walker, Margaret. "Richard Wright." *Richard Wright: Impressions and Perspectives*. Eds. David Ray and Robert Farnsworth. Ann Arbor: U of Michigan P, 1973. 47–67. Print.

Webb, Constance. *Richard Wright, A Biography*. New York: Putnam, 1968. Print.

Wright, Richard. *American Hunger*. 1945. New York: Harper Collins, 1993. Print.

———. *Black Boy: A Record of Childhood and Youth*. New York: Harper, 1945. Print.

———. "Blueprint for Negro Writing." *New Challenge* II (1937): 53–63. Print.

———. "Introduction." *Black Metropolis: A Study of Negro Life in a Northern City*. 1945. Eds. Horace Cayton and St. Clair Drake. Chicago: U of Chicago P, 1993. xvii–xxxiv. Print.

Yaeger, Patricia. "Introduction: Narrating Space." *The Geography of Identity*. Ed. Patricia Yaeger. Ann Arbor: U of Michigan P, 2001. Print.

PART III

WRIGHT: PULP AND MEDIA, REALITY AND FICTION

The three essays in this section examine the relationship of Wright's art to documentary fiction, criminal profiling, and the postwar crime story. They emphasize Wright's place as an essential writer and thinker on modernity. Taken together, they reveal the importance of including both Wright's work and influence in the discursive histories of contemporary modernist cultural theory. Paula Rabinowitz's "Savage Holiday: Documentary Noir and True Crime in *12 Million Black Voices*" focuses on the spaces for critique provided by popular cultural forms. "Wright understood the particular mode of American modernist thinking," she argues, "that wedged critique into popular forms as these very debased genres 'instilled restlessness.'" Rabinowitz demonstrates how Wright's and Edwin Rosskam's phototextual book, *12 Million Black Voices*, supplements and inverts the crime narrative to retell a "true" crime story that begins with slavery and traverses through the Jim Crow South and its concomitant racist culture. Working within recent trends that have extended "high" modernism downward to popular forms such as "true stories," sensationalism, pulp, and melodrama, Rabinowitz calls for a revisionary modernism to clarify the works of Wright that "slid[e] among case study, autobiography, choral poetry, and fiction." Rabinowitz's chapter makes the first in a series of gestures in this volume toward understanding how Wright's work expands beyond the territories of the purely literary text. In addition, her chapter provides a base for understanding Wright's *A Father's Law*, the subject of the other two essays in this section.

Joyce Ann Joyce's chapter shares the logic initiated by Rabinowitz and takes the modernist analysis of Wright's works into a new direction. Joyce argues that *A Father's Law*, as "a twenty-first century novel," encapsulates "criminal profiling as its structural vehicle." She locates in Wright's 1945 introduction to St. Clair Drake and Horace C. Cayton's *Black Metropolis* the destruction of a black character who seemingly has achieved the degree of economic and political freedom, which could only be dreamt about by earlier Wright characters. Echoing the importance that Miller gives to Chicago as an "ancestral locus of modern memory," Chicago is, for Joyce, Wright's modernist palimpsest for the ideas expressed in *Black Metropolis*. Arguably the first of Wright's books to give equal importance to the effects of race and class on "the black psyche," *A Father's Law* is both a psychological thriller and a careful study of familial and cultural determinism. The novel represents Wright's prescience—in this case, his use of profiling a black man (and a black family) who indiscriminately accepts the values of Western society—a prescience that both signals the diversity of Wright's canon and tests our critical "intellectual vulnerabilities" as well, as Joyce points out. In the final analysis, Joyce asserts that the true critic of Richard Wright's work is an evolving entity, and accordingly, critical perspectives on his work are beginning to catch up with his intellectual vision here in the twenty-first century.

John C. Charles's "A Queer Finale: Sympathy and Privacy in Wright's *A Father's Law*" likewise insists upon the need to examine Wright's literary ties to popular forms. *A Father's Law* is a "crime story genre marked by sentimentalism and idealized versions of male fellowship." As stressed by several of our contributors, what Wright chose to *read*, whether canonical works or pulp fiction, profoundly affected the development of his fictional and nonfictional works. Charles suggests that Wright, as evidenced in the "inter-racial male sympathy" of *A Father's Law* and in his personal reading history, was at the time of his death moving beyond the limitations presented to black writers by their supposed need to write only about the "Negro problem." Wright twists the crime novel genre into "a sentimental secular narrative" infused with a modernist sensibility of "interracial fraternity" and provocative philosophical postulations, and Charles contends that Wright's prescient claim for an "expansive moral authority" was not only a counterclaim that foreshadowed the rejection of "Negro writer" as a mere writer of protest fiction but also served as a compelling response to the conditions of modernity.

All of the chapters in this section coalesce around the crucial arguments made by Rabinowitz in her reading of *12 Million Black Voices*, namely that Wright's modernism forged an urban idiom and mythologized a realism that proved continually inadequate to his political and artistic intentions when he depicted the traumas associated with racialized worlds. Wright's voice may have been born in the realism that he inherited from his youthful reading, but he was one of the crucial American authors of his time to make a strong impact on the modernist aesthetic, an impact shaped from his early life experiences. His life of exile was his avenue toward an affirmation of the risks he had taken in distancing himself from the generic registers to which he was confined in early and—as evidenced by several of the recent reviews of *A Father's Law*—late phases of his career.

7

SAVAGE HOLIDAY: DOCUMENTARY NOIR AND TRUE CRIME IN *12 MILLION BLACK VOICES*

Paula Rabinowitz

Negro writers face a new landscape of subject matter…the battled thoughts of that Negro woman social worker who works in the slum areas of her race; and that sixteen-year-old Negro girl reading the *True Story Magazine*; all constitute a landscape teeming with questions and meaning.

—Richard Wright, "Blueprint for Negro Writing"[1]

For the corpse is not dead! It still lives! It has made itself a home in the wild forest of our great cities, amid the rank and choking vegetation of slums! It has forgotten our language!

—Richard Wright, *Native Son*

The revolution that calls itself the Investigation had its rise in the theaters of communication, and now regularly parades its images across them, reiterates its gospel from them, daily and hourly marches through the corridors of every office, files into the living-room of every home. These avenues of communication are television, radio, picture magazines, motion pictures, magazines of news interpretation, digests of news digests, newspaper chains, syndicated features, the house journals of chair industries.

—Kenneth Fearing, "Reading, Writing, and the Rackets," *New and Selected Poems*

"Americans don't like being lied to by their leaders," declared Frank Rich in a *New York Times* op-ed column, referring to the brouhaha over former president George W. Bush's press secretary Scott

McClellan's 2008 memoir, "especially if there are casualties involved and especially if there's no accountability. We view it as *a crime story*, and we won't be satisfied until there's a resolution" (Rich 12, emphasis added). Frank Rich, who began his career at the *Times* as a theater critic, taps into a pervasive tendency within modern(ist) American culture: an enduring fascination with sensational crimes and melodramatic endings. Crime, no matter how pervasive, in this form of thinking, is always a singular event perpetrated against an innocent victim by a corrupt or deranged individual, a grotesque figure who often appears as normal as one's next-door neighbor, and who, once identified, is subject to justice carried out through methodical detective work. Despite the systemic nature of criminality—both as an enterprise involving corporate or state structures and within a justice system targeting certain populations and not others—crime is narrativized in America as local, random and unique—scintillating because of its very discreetness yet capable of endless resuscitation as a coded language for the deeper violence and criminality it both mimics and shrouds.

I have titled this essay after Richard Wright's 1954 novel, *Savage Holiday*, a study in just the kind of criminality Rich is talking about: one day, a seemingly normal guy—one who works, incidentally or did so until the day before, in a business concerned with crime, insurance—inadvertently causes a death that leads him to commit a venal murder that ends up headlining the news. Wright was fascinated by crime—from observing the "bad black boys," as he calls them, who went down to white supremacist violence in a flame a glory while a youth in Mississippi, to his use of the Robert Nixon case as the basis for *Native Son,* to his investigations of Cross Damon's Nietzschean reasoning for murder in *The Outsider.* Crime narratives offer a means—as they have in Western culture at least since Oedipus or Cain and Abel—to understand violence, rage, mortality, family, nation, you name it.

Counterintuitively, Wright understood that when African Americans read "True Story magazines"—those bastions of excess and incredulity—they opened "a landscape teeming with questions and meaning," which I take to mean an incisive, and in Jim Crow America, seemingly improbable, idea that black people could pursue their dreams and desires, could believe—in themselves not America's lies—by posing questions and seeking meaning. In the words of the editors of *New Challenge: A Literary Quarterly*, that is, in associate editor Wright's words, they help "plac[e] his [sic, the writer's] material in the proper perspective with regard to the life of the Negro masses"

(Vol. 11, no. 1, Spring 1937: 3). Wright's comment on "True Story" magazines reflects a deeper understanding of the role of the word *True* in the title of these pulp magazines than Theodor W. Adorno had when he read "True Astrology" magazines a few decades later: "They fall in line with the pattern of modern mass culture which protest the more fanatically about the tenets of individualism and the freedom of the will, the more actual freedom of action vanishes" (Adorno 44). Wright's insight is mirrored in the findings of E. Franklin Frazier that young black girls were reading "True Romance" magazines and other pulp melodramas to forge identities that contrasted with their parents' message of racial uplift (Heard). Like Kenneth Fearing, whose entire opus of poems reads like the text of a "True Crime" magazine, Wright sensed that "True Story" magazines could be read against the grain and as such could uncover American lies.[2] In this, Wright understood the particular mode of American modernist thinking that wedged critique into popular forms as these very debased genres which appealed to the "longing and restlessness" instilled by the city and its cramped kitchenettes and hard pavement (*12 Million* 111).

In modern America, as Frank Rich suggests, the crime story holds a particular sway for its pervasiveness—we live in a nation founded over and over again on violence and war and its invasion of daily life through popular media—and for its undercover nature. Foundational violence gets forgotten; even as murder, or at least its narration, becomes a form of relaxation. In this form, it is also a commodity circulating within an economy that trades on desire and exhaustion. It also serves, in Nicholas Abraham and Maria Torok's terms,[3] as a crypt—a repository, at once ever-present yet inaccessible, of that which fundamentally determines subjectivity. A forgotten language untranslatable, encysted, its presence within a substratum of identity exudes ongoing and intense pressures—restlessness, if you will—shaping consciousness, which cannot be named or even felt directly; its access is circuitous, found in traces of materials gleaned elsewhere.

Wright plumbed America's history of crime as a crypt; he understood its use for containing and also conveying—telescoping ideas about class, money, sex, love, race—social forces. A close reader of trash, from his earliest exposure to pulp magazines, he deployed what he'd learned in his novels and essays: "I read tattered, second-hand copies of *Flynn's Detective Weekly* or the *Argosy All-Story Magazine* or dreamed, weaving fantasies about cities I had never seen...." (*Black Boy* 156). Crime, as a narrative device, enabled—as it had for two of his inspirations, Theodore Dreiser and Fyodor Dostoevsky—his explorations of psychological and economic forces, showing how the two collide in an individual. But it did more for Wright—or rather he did more with it—and this is the subject of my essay: How Richard Wright's and Edwin Rosskam's phototextual book, *12 Million Black Voices,* supplements the crime narrative—or, better, inverts it—to make clear that *the* crime, that which the American people, or at least white Americans, had been lied to and been lying to themselves about, was the crime of slavery and its attendant Jim Crow laws and culture of racism. This was *the true crime story* that Wright was exploding/exposing: America's crypt encrypted: Thoroughly evident yet utterly unrecognized, its corpse not dead but haunting us still. Using the format of the "True Story" magazine—its typography and layout, an iconography of documentary noir that sensationalizes facts, inherited from Jacob Riis's 1890 *How the Other Half Lives* (Weinstein)—Wright and Rosskam pried open America's uncanny crypt to listen to its voices. Jeffrey Allred argues for the "pedagogical stance" of the text whose collective "we" does not encompass everyone, but "figures readers as pupils...and divides groups along lines of class, race, and region," (though it does not demonstrate an equal attentiveness to sex and gender, I might add) in order to instruct them (550). In this, *12 Million Black Voices* fulfils the basic requirements of the ideological novel as a genre, according to Susan Rubin Suleiman: to entertain and to instruct. "True Story" magazines were consummately novelistic as well, ensuring that lessons were learned as excitement was sensed. Moreover, by accessing that which cannot be readily seen—Riis's mercury flashes or, later, Weegee's midnight shots of perp walks come to mind, as does Freud's interpretations of dreams—"True Story" magazines popularized the "case" and its study. Wright mined the magazine culture of the mid-twentieth century and put its residue to use, as did Edwin Rosskam, whose career took him to Paris in the 1920s as an expatriate painter where he ended up working on a Surrealist magazine. Then, after traveling to French Polynesia as a photographer for the government, he returned to the United States in the 1930s and got a job on a new tabloid Philadelphia paper, a Democratic rival to the *Inquirer,* where he became what he characterized as, forgetting Riis's work in New York, the first photographer/journalist, both making pictures and writing stories. From there, he did a stint at Henry Luce's picture magazine, *Life,* before being hired by Roy Stryker to supervise the distribution of the Farm Security Administration (FSA) photographs.

In their collaboration and in their attention to popular magazine culture, Wright and Rosskam were not necessarily unique. James Agee and Walker Evans, who worked respectively for Luce's *Fortune* and

Figure 1   Page layout from Jacob Riis, HOW THE OTHER HALF LIVES New York: Charles Scribner, 1890.

Stryker's FSA during the 1930s, conceived of a plan to start a magazine and book series that would cancel Time Inc.'s magazine empire through its use of photography and journalism to explore the perverse nature of modern America. This series, according to Agee's journals, would include "general content: some text, some pictures. Records, symbols, science, analysis, discussion & criticism…Characteristics: absolute absence of ingratiation; excellence of reproductions; plainness; the utmost cheapness wherever possible: a steady correction of every fashion" (qtd. in Davis and Lofaro 158).[4] One volume might be dedicated to "A sampling of news clips…poems: composed of advertisements, news photographs, and photographs, and photographs personally made…An analysis of misinterpretation (or worse) of crime and of excellence, as found in newspapers, magazines, courts & speeches" (158–59). It never got off the ground, though Evans's scrapbooks of juxtaposed images provide a glimpse of how it might have been laid out.[5] Remnants of their project remain in their 1941 phototextual extravaganza *Let Us Now Praise Famous Men.*[6] But *12 Million Black Voices* features a closer resemblance to the tabloid aesthetics so formative for Wright and Rosskam. The two volumes, published within months of each other (April and November 1941), coming too late, after the fact, and for very different reasons, speak across various divides—white/black, textual/visual, poetic/factual, and middle-class readers/impoverished subjects.[7] As many contemporary reviewers noted, they spoke to each other and to "mass" culture and its politics as well.[8]

Agee, born to an upper-middle-class white family in Tennessee a year after Wright was born in Mississippi, undertook his project to record three Southern white tenant farmers under many of the same conditions as Wright's project on black folk—a deep understanding of American popular cultures of North and South, a love of photography, a skepticism about literature, and a love of movies. When Agee was taking a break from the three weeks he and Walker Evans spent sleeping on the porch and in the front room of the Burroughs's house in Hale County, Alabama, in July 1936, he skipped out of Mills Hill into town—found a prostitute and a drink and let us know about it. Two years later, as he began working on "the book," as he referred to *Let Us Now Praise Famous Men* to his mentor Father Flye, he picked up some magazines as a diversion while in Atlantic City.[9] Ten or so pages of detailed description follow the layout of the pages, creating a mini-screenplay for a film noir detective story in his intimate journal.

Monday 10. [January 1938]

Friday afternoon-evening-night. Saturday morning frustration

Atlantic City. Sunday night. Picture Detective.

Two magazines: Picture Detective and another. They have revived the old gangster pamphlet ideas of police photographs and taken it into more general crime. The other devotes itself to women in crime. I brought this instead (lacking money for both) for the picture on the cover. As Walker says they must be thoroughly aware of the pathological public they feed + count on. From circulation it might be possible to intimate sadistic population but not really: big (buy) enough stores (stares?) of it so that a huge number—one issue in these (three). Part of my own interest in that. I'm not made sick by work of these as Via is. It is of greatest good for the sets and properties surrounding the murders and crimes,—and for various faces. The lunch room street scene dominated by Indian Simmons; and inside...The bathroom linoleum and sink where the cop dies. The desk, radiator and shirt. Even the dark paint around the latch and handle of the door...the 2 cars. The lunchroom mirror the corpse, and dawn outside. The bare hallway to Weir's room and the carpet on it. The room where all that DESPERATE, CRAMPED AND LONELY FEEL(UCK)ING TOOK PLACE. The wallpaper. The Kentucky road. All the Kentuckian faces. The Armstrong Hotel...The cover picture disembodied from any context is one of the most frightening I know. The completely savage world. The hard flash does a great deal. 2 kinds of idiot cruel laughter. None of them look like cops. They look like special appointees of a Kafka but American second world disguised as cops....I like the reversed 5¢ and the 5 across the street, the neon hamburger, to ogle and again the 2 faces looking at the camera. Unposed faces looking at a camera have a special human expression nearly unprecedented (Not quite; some paintings show these faces). Of this in its varieties + of its uses there must be investigation analysis and study.

> Rain in all these pictures...... ."

He goes on for pages until " ...I wrote till 3. a new start on the Alabama book... "[10]

At the same time as Agee was deconstructing the pages of *Actual Detective*, Wright was jotting notes to himself, which would become the source materials for *12 Million Black Voices*. Despite Rosskam's protest to the contrary (and it is true that the first typed complete draft of the text is dated January 1941), Wright had been preparing for this study at least since 1938 when he began collecting documentary materials on Chicago housing and notes on African American history and folk culture; in fact, if one does a close comparison of *12 Million Black Voices* and *Lawd Today!* his material for the phototext actually dates from 1934. Wright's notes include a thirteen-point outline, which moves from escaping home to traveling the nation to developing a new sense of the contemporary world and the masses.[11] Essentially, this trajectory in thirteen steps traces the path of *12 Million Black Voices,* but might also be said to outline the distribution routes of pulp magazines across America, as each town's magazine racks connected small villages to the massive nation. And while it is clear that his outlined path from separation from home to connection with the masses refers to the Communist Party of the United States of America (CPUSA)'s Popular Front, it is imperative to remember, as Michael Denning has demonstrated, that the political "mass" of the "Cultural Front" was deeply attached to popular or mass culture, too.[12]

"True Story" magazines, with names such as *True Crime, Detective Annals, Actual Detective, and Picture Detective,* were ubiquitous during the 1930s and 1940s at newsstands, bus depots, train stations, drugstores, and kiosks across small-town and big-city America. Magazines, as a collective form, were everywhere, and wherever they were, they invited readers into America's crypt. If sensational crimes dominated the U.S. magazine culture, Spanish Loyalist culture was permeated by the phototextual layout revealing the crimes of Fascists against the people.[13] FSA photographers John Vachon and Russell Lee, especially, were drawn to the newsstands of America as locations themselves drawing readers to peruse the hidden recesses of desire—criminal, erotic, economic, mobile—locked within the pages of *True Romance, Better Homes and Gardens, Popular Locomotion*—some more wholesome: economy and mobility; others more lurid: murder and sex. It was at the newsstand in a Memphis bank lobby where Wright first encountered H. L. Mencken's name as he was skimming the papers: "One morning I arrived early at work and went into the bank lobby where the Negro porter was mopping, I stood at a counter and picked up the Memphis *Commercial Appeal* and began my free reading of the press" (*Black Boy* 288).

Even more than newspapers on display, magazines beckoned: "The cover picture disembodied from any context is one of the most frightening I know," wrote Agee in a notebook he kept for *Let Us Now Praise Famous Men* of the December 1938 issue of *Actual Detective*. "The completely savage world. The hard flash does a great deal...for the sets and properties surrounding the murders and crimes—and for various faces." He bought the magazine "for the picture on the cover."[14] This "savage world" encapsulated by this "frightening" picture stirred Agee, as it did many others, to buy the magazine, as he himself lolled in a hotel in Atlantic City, reading and masturbating and thinking about how to proceed with his new love and his new work—on a "savage holiday" of sorts from his job at *Fortune.* The cover of *Actual Detective,* like dozens of others, was meant to attract buyers, not merely readers. Wright hadn't purchased the Memphis newspaper with Mencken's column; having no money, he'd read it and replaced it. Edwin Rosskam noted this potential problem with Archibald MacLeish's phototextual book *Land of the Free,* which he argued could be browsed at the bookstore and left back on the shelf unsold. Instead, the magazines that sold well combined image with enough text to draw in the customer—who needed time, much more time than was available at a street-corner kiosk, even if browsing was encouraged—to thoroughly absorb the textual desire and depravity without being caught.[15] The covers served as "dark mirrors" into contemporary culture; they relentlessly point into the crypt.

12 Million Black Voices begins with a misrecognition—"and we are not what we seem" (10), playing as it does with the book's first image by Dorothea Lange of a sharecropper's hands cradling a hoe; his racial identity cannot easily be determined. It ends 30,000 words later with the insistence "Look at us and know us and you will know yourselves, for *we* are *you,* looking back at you from the dark mirror of our lives!" (146). Seeing in the "dark mirror," one peers into the crypt, a *mise en abyme* without reflection, a black hole.[16] Wright's words, unlike MacLeish's "shooting script," needed to be read in one long sitting— but they also could be extracted into captions that would link image to image. Acutely attuned to film and to pulp as serialized narrative

Figure 2 Front Cover ACTUAL DETECTIVE STORIES OF WOMEN IN CRIME, December 1938 (author's collection).

modes, writer Wright and photo-director Rosskam knew how to draw in the audience.

Agee bought *Actual Detective* and studied it as a "document," in Walter Benjamin's sense. Mining the one-way streets of 1920s Berlin, Benjamin analyzed the imperatives, handbills, leaflets, and other "primitive" writing in his meandering series of vignettes,

"Post No Bills": "The document serves to instruct. With documents, a public is educated. All documents communicate through their subject matter. In documents the subject matter is wholly dominant. Subject matter is the outcome of dreams. The more one loses oneself in a document, the denser the subject matter grows. Forms are merely dispersed in documents. The fertility of the document demands: analysis. A document overpowers only through surprise" (459). The "savage" covers of *Actual Detective* represented the more popular forms (and Surrealist versions) of what Benjamin referred to as "documents," which "serve to instruct...through...their subject matter...the outcome of dreams." Its more respectable modes he linked to the journalistic "New Objectivity," referencing its many forms prevalent in Weimar Germany that "fashionabl[y] appeal[led] to facts—hostile to fictions removed from reality...it attacks theory" ("Critique" 417). For Benjamin, facts' "political significance was exhausted by the transposition of revolutionary reflexes (insofar as they arose in the bourgeoisie) into objects of distraction, of amusement, which can be supplied for consumption" ("Left-Wing" 424). "Its stock in trade was reportage," he later explained. Both its photographic and literary forms "owe the extraordinary increase in their popularity to the technology of publication: radio and illustrated press" ("Author" 774). The New Objectivity, Benjamin further complained, "has made the *struggle against poverty* an object of consumption" ("Author" 776).

This consumerist sentimentality could only be overcome "when we—the writers—take up photography." In so doing, the photograph will be augmented with "a caption that wrenches it from modish commerce and gives it a revolutionary use value" (Benjamin, "Author" 775). Wright would surely agree.[17] His own photography and his intimate participation in the February 1941 Southside shoot with Edwin Rosskam and Russell Lee, from which most of the images for Parts 3 and 4 of *12 Million Black Voices* derived, connect Wright's work to another "sensational modernist," in Joseph Entin's phrase. Like Bertolt Brecht, who was the hero of Benjamin's 1934 address to the Institute for the Study of Fascism in Paris, Wright was taking advantage of every "trick of the (epic) trade"—foremost among them montage, in which "the superimposed element disrupts the context in which it is inserted." By bringing together songs, sermons, sociology, case study, biography, fiction, and poetry with photography, the "principle of interruption" (Benjamin, "Author" 778) forced audiences to see the underworld of "folk history," as Wright originally subtitled the book.

There are no black criminals sensationalized in "True Story" magazines, which depict crimes across class boundaries within white America; instead, black criminals appeared in the pages of daily tabloid newspapers that Wright clipped for his records as he compiled an archive on the Robert Nixon case. His extensive tear sheets also included details about a black nurse who bludgeons a white nurse to death in Tennessee and other sordid descriptions of black-on-white crime. In addition to a copy of the tabloid, *Hollywood Crime,* Wright's newspaper morgue archives the serialized 1938 exposé of slum housing—many of the photographs (which are unattributed) perhaps coming from the FSA—entitled "Misery." Like Jacob Riis's earlier newspaper exposés of New York tenements, which became the images for the first phototextual volume, *How the Other Half Lives* (1890), these pictures traded on scandal and bordered on stereotype, as did the emerging form of the case study to which this series and Riis's reports nod (after all it is Chicago, with its School of Sociology) (Cappetti; Weinstein). The page layout indicates how easily assimilated the medium of urban squalor exposé, the case study, is with such dubiously newsworthy items as Dorothy Lamour's divorce and Shirley Temple's tenth birthday. As Benjamin described it in 1934: "The scene of this literary confusion is the newspaper; its content, 'subject matter' that denies itself any other form of organization than that imposed on it by the reader's impatience" ("Newspaper" 741).

Despite potential drawbacks, the case study was a central device for Wright borrowed from Robert Parks, Louis Wirth, and Horace Cayton and from his reading of Freud and Dostoevsky.[18] Like almost every other modern(ist) author, Wright discerned in the case study a literary form capable of charging the document with the energy of the dream, as Benjamin noted and of course as Freud recorded. The entire premise of the case study rests on unpeeling the onion, but to what? Nicholas Abraham and Maria Torok describe this space that cannot be plumbed as an emptiness, the recess emanating effects seemingly without cause. *12 Million Black Voices* unearths the crypt of America, a bizarre series of demons and desires, lurking throughout America's racial and sexual history gleaned from the methodology of slavery and racism, not because it was hidden—it was an open sore at work in the present—but because this very availability was deferred, located in the sensational journalism crowding street corners. America's True Crime Story is the crypt holding the corpse haunting the recesses of every space of America—its "we" and its "you," both wanting. Like the Wolf Man's magic word, discovery needed an adept caseworker, one attuned to voices, to (un)cover it, one who could speak as "we"

Figure 3   Page layout from Sunday, Chicago Times, April 23, 1938 (in Richard Wright papers Yale Collection of American Literature, Beinecke Rare Book and Manuscript Library, Yale University).

Image credit: Yale Collection of American Literature, Beinecke Rare Book and Manuscript Library, Yale University.

to "you." Wright first depicts it in Bigger but has Max read him, or speak him, for us; then, a year later, "we" shows and tells "you"—like a how-to manual—in *12 Million Black Voices* exactly as the detectives uncovering True Crime reenact the scene, lurid yet matter-of-fact. Collective crime demands a plural narrator.

Wright's attention to media was a recognition of their power as a force at once of coercion and liberation for black Americans: "To paint the picture of how we live on the tobacco, cane, rice and cotton plantations is to compete against mighty artists: the movies, the radio, the newspaper, the magazines, and even the Church. They have painted one picture: charming, idyllic, romantic; but we live another; full of fear..." (35). However, as the epigraph I begin with indicates, he sensed how much the mobilization of desire through religion, advertisements, Hollywood movies, radio broadcasts, and screaming tabloid headlines describing the "Python Killer" who "killed six men...drugged 'em and then smothered 'em to death with pillows when they was sleeping" or "Tiger Woman," or "the Cat Killer," or "the Canary Girl, the one who had the sweet voice and killed all her babies," served to forge modern meaning (*Lawd Today!* 117–19).

These dangerous women, like the "thrill guys, Loeb and Leopold," offered a violent vision of betrayal and defiance, perverse though it may be, to norms of behavior by pretty women, sweet-voiced mothers, or well-heeled college students. These stories were steps on the road (or "pathway" as Wright says in his 1938 notes) linking folk culture to popular culture, the popular to the political. If all of these middle-class white people could go berserk, committing ghastly crimes, certainly it was possible, even logical, that impoverished black men and women might, too.

This was precisely the lesson the reviewer for *Harper's* took from *12 Million Black Voices*: "After reading and looking at this short history of the Negro race in America, in prose and remarkable photographs, one does not wonder that there are occasional crimes committed in Harlem. One wonders why there aren't more, in the face of the crimes which our society has committed against the black man."[19] But if sensational criminality—and its vengeful assault on black women—is ever present in Wright's fiction, it is not evident in *12 Million Black Voices*, which offers a dialogue with its white readers as it expressly ignores the "talented tenth" in favor of a story of a segment, "a debased feudal folk," only recently become visible because of "urbanization," in part through tabloids, in part through the FSA (*12 Million* xx).

This book, conceived as a "shooting script," reads like a novel in which the reader/viewer—"you"—becomes a participant in the underlying crime, the one that is unremarkable because ubiquitous. For Ann Petry, "the novel as social criticism" was a necessity in the United States because "the arguments used to justify slavery still influence American attitudes toward the Negro. If I use the words intermarriage, mixed marriage, miscegenation," she explains, "there are few Americans who would not react to those words emotionally. Part of that emotion can be traced directly to the days of slavery. And if emotion is aroused merely by the use of certain words, and the emotion is violent, apoplectic, then it seems fairly logical that novels which deal with race relations should reflect some of this violence" (37–38). "You" don't just "see their faces," as Erskine Caldwell and Margaret Bourke-White would have it in their phototextual reportage; instead "you" are indicted by and inducted into the narrative precisely for *not* seeing, *not* hearing, *not* knowing this story, these people, these kitchenettes, this (folk) history. "This is the black 'J'Accuse,'" notes Richard F. Crandell, critic for the *Herald Tribune*.

Contemporary reviewers, black and white, read the text to *12 Million Black Voices* as at once a "cartoon," a "novel," an "autobiography," "stereotype," as "pamphleteering." For those writing in the

black press, the volume performs "the cardinal literary sin: oversim-
plification." "Biased and depressing," its content presents "a betrayal
of facts," in its "resort to melodrama." As a polemic, its novelistic
traits seemed to undercut its sociological purpose. Most saw the pictures differently. The anonymous (and presumably white) reviewer
for *U.S. Week: A National Journal of News and Opinion* declared that
the photographs

> clinch the argument. They are magnificent. Apparently there never
> was a Negro who was not (to use a hackneyed word) photogenic.
> Culled chiefly from the files of the Farm Security Administration, U.
> S. Department of Agriculture, these pictures are unforgettable—black
> bodies caught in postures of resignation, despair or joy, hands eloquent
> of toil, eyes searching, questioning in a way that we cannot evade.[20]

These reviewers recognized the interplay between voice/text and
vision/photograph as a dynamic and dialogic one even if they sometimes found the text lacking.

It is obvious from the typed manuscript that Wright wrote the
original 50,000 words comprising the text in practically one sitting.
This was material intimately known to him, as life story, as research,
through observation and analysis, from his earlier fiction,[21] from his
journalism about Harlem, from his clipping collection on housing
in the Southside and on media hysteria about black criminality. He's
telling his story to be sure—but he's telling 12 million stories too,
a figure Max also cites in *Native Son* (333). Likewise, Rosskam, the
"photo-director," as Viking called him, gathered together images
produced under government aegis (and in two cases news media and
in one case Richard Wright's own camera work) by many different
artists, freely cropped the pictures and put them into dialogue with
each other, and with Wright's prose, culling captions from the text
to dramatize image and choosing photographs to reinforce text. John
M. Reilly calls the book a "simulated sermon" indebted to the "oral
utterance derived from the spontaneous arts that shape the orations
of the preacher; it is a secularization of the sacred moral voice of the
folk." Wright becomes a "vernacular orator"—and as such, through
his incorporation of the "shared 12 million subjects"—he achieves
"a uniquely modern personality" (117). Because, I would add, of the
uniquely modern form of the book—its attention to mass media as
well as to collective orality.

Claiming that the book reflects Rosskam's signature style of layout
and typography and captioning, Maren Stange argues for his "invoking

houses for us to live in, because we have been used to sleeping several in a room on the plantations in the South, we rent these kitchenettes and are glad to get them. These kitchenettes are our havens from the plantations in the South. We have fled the wrath of Queen Cotton and we are tired.

Sometimes five or six of us live in a one-room kitchenette, a place where simple folk such as we should never be held captive. A war sets up in our emotions: one part of our feelings tells us that it is good to be in the city, that we have a chance at life here, that we need but turn a corner to become a stranger, that we no longer need bow and dodge at the sight of the Lords of the Land. Another part of our feelings tells us that, in terms of worry and strain, the cost of living in the kitchenettes is too high, that the city heaps too much responsibility upon us and gives too little security in return.

The kitchenette is the author of the glad tidings that new suckers are in town, ready to be cheated, plundered, and put in their places.

Figure 4 Page Layout from Richard Wright and Edwin Rosskam, 12 MILLION BLACK VOICES, Viking 1941, photograph Edwin Rosskam "Children in front of 'kitchenette' apartment," Black Belt, Chicago, Illinois, April 1941. Library of Congress, Prints & Photographs Division, FSA/OWI Collection LC-USF 33-005183-M4.

Image credit: Library of Congress, Prints & Photographs Division, FSA/OWI Collection LC-USF 33-005183-M4.

in its arty informality the medium's expressive and symbolic possibilities,"
a recognition of its immersion in modernist aesthetics. The full-page
bleeds and closely cropped images contribute, she goes on to suggest, a
sense of the complicated "placelessness and boundedness posited in the
text" (183–84). Rosskam's design advances Wright's textual argument,
even or especially, when it is out of sync with it. But Wright himself clearly
understood the "double-voiced," polyphonic conversation between text
and image found in this modernist novel format as coming directly from
True Story and other popular publications. As Rosskam recalled:

> Dick Wright really knew that stuff cold; he knew where everybody
> was, and he knew everybody in the Negro world of Chicago. And I
> don't know if many white men had the opportunity to see it the way
> we saw it. Man, that was an experience. We did everything from the
> undertaker to the gangster…I was not on the staff then, I went out
> with Russell Lee to finish the coverage, was in Chicago and that was
> used later on in The Voices, Twelve Million Black Voices, because he
> couldn't do migration without showing, finally where migration went
> to. Migration went to the city. (Doud, "Interview")

Again, like contemporary critics Walter Benjamin and Mikhail
Bakhtin, Wright understood from the novelists he loved, Dostoevsky
and Dreiser and Dos Passos, that newspapers and the ephemera of
the city provided key elements of modern consciousness and that the
novel offered a venue for its vocalization, "migration went to the city"
and spoke in many dialects. In *Lawd Today!* Wright recounts verba-
tim, complete with all diacritical marks, the entire text of a religious
flyer sent in the mail by "St. Paul." Side one asked:

> WHICH RAILROAD WILL YOU TAKE?????????????????? ALL
> HOURS OF THE DAY AND NIGHT SPECIAL TRAINS ARE
> RUNNING FROM: Thomas Paine Avenue, Dime Novel Park, Theatre
> Lane, Dopedel, Blasphemers' Hall, Smokers' Furnace, Masturbation
> Alley, Prostitution Boulevard, Dancehall Station, Highball Lagoon,
> Adultery Depot, Greed Mountain, Gambling Pause, Ingersoll Canyon,
> Evolution Grounds, and Communist Junction." Signed by Prince
> Lucifer, President!!!!!!!!!!!,##############, *****************
> ****_____………… ''''''''''''''''''??????
> ???????] (*Lawd Today!* 140–41)

The flip side revealed salvation.
He knew from his attention to the "way we saw it," that the novel
must be a visual form. An accomplished amateur photographer who

studied how-to manuals to improve his photographic skills, Wright, before Marshall McLuhan, understood the importance of a visual text, one that mimicked the onslaught of words and images found everywhere as instilling "restlessness" within "the modern personality." His photograph of the sign in the Brooklyn apartment used in the first edition of *12 Million Black Voices* recalls others by FSA photographers attentive to signage—Walker Evans, Dorothea Lange, and Esther Bubley (whose 1943 photograph replaces his in later editions), in particular. Rosskam, too, learned "…an understanding of the use of photographs as a language. From there it was only a short step to photographs with captions as a language, and then only another short step further to photographs with text so combined, that they complimented (sic) each other at all times" (Doud). It was a lesson Wright had imbibed through his early reading and his sensational experiences as a city dweller. America's cities, with their open crypts, were an urban modernist's dreamscape. Wright viscerally embraced his status as "a city boy," in Robert Sklar's words for the ethnic gangsters of 1930s Hollywood; and so, he understood text as texture.

Seeing and knowing ["when you see us…and think you know us…we are not what we seem" (*12 Million* 10)] the spectral crypt of "our strange history" requires attending to that which appears invisible; but it also means reading every visible sign as if it were a clue destined to solve a ghastly crime. Recreating the feel of detection, tracing signs and symbols and clues, was part of Wright's project as a mythologizing, that is to say modernist, realist. *Lawd Today!* maps out the bridge hands the four postal workers play as a newspaper bridge column would, substituting north, south, east, west with their names. *12 Million Black Voices* is laid out like the city pages of a metropolitan tabloid paper. Anticipating Theodor W. Adorno, who would find precursors to the Authoritarian Personality in popular astrology columns,[22] Wright details how pictures were read as vehicles to establish psychological evidence central to "True Story" magazines:

"Her eyes is close together, meaning she's mean."

"And her bottom lip pokes out, meaning she's deceitful. She fooled folks."

"And that thick neck? What it say about it?"

"That means," read Al: "Uncontrollable passions, masculine feelings." (118)

Wright claimed that "the huge mountains of fact piled up by the Department of Sociology at the University of Chicago gave me my first concrete vision of forces that molded the urban Negro's body and soul." And through them he was able to "tell my story. But I did not know what my story was, and it was not until I stumbled upon science that I discovered some of the meanings of the environment that battered and taunted me" (Wright, Introduction xvi). Sociology and Marxism offered insights, but so too the tabloids and "True Crime" magazines were, in their own degraded way, "documents," "science," and "meanings." This multiply constructed "modern personality," as John M. Reilly calls it—at once individuated and collective—is akin to the invention of the dialogic characters/ narrators in Dostoevsky's novels, according to Bakhtin. In fact, the double-voicing and the polyphonic qualities of modern novels here augmented by multifaceted images—taken for purposes not precisely aligned with Wright's narrative—make this book into an example of a modern novel, according to Bakhtin's definitions, especially when one thinks of the reader as the second term (which for Bakhtin happened through the author/narrator dyad) between collective narrator "we" and the addressee, "you."

The novel: a "double-voiced" form, Bakhtin echoing W. E. B. Du Bois's term, "a twoness" that can both observe and participate. Thus Carla Cappetti's insistence that modernism be understood as an ethnographic project, and, in Walter Benjamin's understanding, a visual one and from Mikhail Bakhtin's, a vocal one. Much of Wright's work slides among case study, autobiography, choral poetry, and fiction; this text does it explicitly in an effort to invent a new mode of decryption. He had absorbed Dostoevsky's method. Bakhtin, writing of "Discourse in the Novel" and often citing Dostoevsky as a prime example of how discourse operates in fiction, notes that "the novel is the realm in which biography, consciousness and social convention come into immediate dialogic field of vision." They do so through the incorporation of texts extraneous to narration—poems, songs, newspaper headlines, etc. The novel's true subject is the "speaking voice," which becomes multiply polyphonic and double-voiced as author's, narrators', and characters' voices intermingle, contradict, and come into "contact zones" with each other across "thresholds."[23] That contact zone encompassed the "dusty land" and the "hard pavement," "we" and "you," where "True Story" magazines, themselves novels of America, crossed the thresholds from newsstands to bedrooms—bringing public and private into contact with the corpses buried but still speaking, through the 12 million and more black voices.

NOTES

1. A shorter version of this essay appeared in the Fall 1937 issue of *New Challenge*. This version is a much longer development of the original one and was published for the first time in *Amistad 2: Writings on Black History and Culture*. Eds. John A. Williams and Charles F. Harris (New York: Vintage Books, 1971) (accessed November 21, 2010, http://www.nathanielturner.com/blueprintfornegroliterature.htm).

2. One could read almost any of Kenneth Fearing's poems as spoofs of/homages to True Crime prose: See for instance, this excerpt from "Longshot Blues":

> Whose whole life falls between roto-press wheels moving
>   quicker than light, to reappear, gorgeous and
> calm, on page eighteen,
> Who reads all about it: Prize-winning beauty trapped,
>   accused,
> Who rides, and rides, and rides the big bright limited south, or
>   is found, instead, on the bedroom floor with
> a stranger's bullet through the middle of his heart,
> Clutching at a railroad table to the south while the curtains
>   blow wild and the radio plays the sun
> shines on, and on, and on, and on, (87)

> Or from "Aphrodite Metropolis (2)":
> On Sunday, when they picnic in emerald meadows they look at
>   the Sunday paper:
> GIRL SLAYS BANKER BETRAYER
> They spread it around the grass
> BATH-TUB STIRS JERSEY ROW
> And then they sit down on it, nice. (14) *Collected Poems* (New
>   York: AMS Press, 1977).

   So, too, Nelson Algren's *Chicago: City on the Make* (1951) or Horace McCoy's *I Should Have Stayed Home* (1938). Both books have been reprinted: Algren (Chicago: University of Chicago Press, 2001); McCoy (London: Serpent's Tail Press, 1996).

3. They define the process as "a precocious traumatic scene, removed, sent to a crypt, encrypted" (lxxi).

4. James Agee, Journal, Folder 17, Box 1, Series I, MS 1500, James Agee Papers, Special Collections Library, University of Tennessee. This journal is reprinted in Davis and Lofaro, though I decipher Agee's handwriting a bit differently in some places (I note them parenthetically). Thanks to Jeffry Allred, "Boring from Within: Luce, *Life* and the Avant-Garde (1941)," Seventh International Conference on Word and Image, Philadelphia, September 2005, for bringing this volume to my attention.

5. Again, thanks to Jeffry Allred for alerting me to the Evans scrapbooks.

6. Not necessarily in the overt way. I argue one finds magazine culture in *12 Million Black Voices,* but there nevertheless—in Evans's photographs of the decoration they provided the tenants' walls, in Agee's careful rendering of the texts found in the newspaper doilies saved in their trunks or, most spectacularly, his mocking inclusion of the *New York Post* fluff piece on Margaret Bourke-White's career. See Agee and Evans, 450–54. For more on this, see Rabinowitz.

   John T. Frederick in his conversation with Arna Bontemps broadcast from *Northwestern University on the Air* radio show "Of Men and Books" (Evanston, Illinois, November 18, 1941), and more definitively in a corollary text also mentioned in the show (on black poetry) *12 Million Black Voices* (Folder 741, Box 63, Richard Wright Papers, Yale Collection of American Literature, Beinecke Rare Book and Manuscript Library).

7. *Let Us Now Praise Famous Men* sold only about 600 copies upon its first publication in April 1941; however, as a royalty statement from Viking shows *12 Million Black Voices* was considerably more popular despite its appearance just weeks before Pearl Harbor was attacked. For instance, it was assigned in Dartmouth sociology classes and was widely available thanks to a campaign by Viking and the FSA to distribute it to leading New Deal jurists and politicians (Edwin Rosskam, letter to Robert Hatch, 1941, Folder 1585, Box 105, Richard Wright Papers, Yale Collection of American Literature, Beinecke Rare Book and Manuscript Library). In 1942, about 1,600 copies of the book were distributed through sales and previews.

8. See the radio interview by John T. Frederick of Arna Bontemps on Negro Writers in the series, "Of Men and Books," November 18, 1941, from Northwestern University (in Folder 742, Box 63, Richard Wright Papers, Yale Collection of American Literature, Beinecke Rare Book and Manuscript Library).

9. See Agee.

10. James Agee Papers, Folder 17, Box 1, Series I, MS 1500, Special Collections Library, University of Tennessee.

11. This analysis is based on my perusal of Richard Wright's papers at the Yale Collection of American Literature at the Beinecke Library.

12. Richard Wright Papers, Holograph, 1938, Folder 734, Box 63, Yale Collection of American Literature, Beinecke Rare Book and Manuscript Library.

13. See *Revistas y Guerra, 1936–39,* the University of Illinois website of Spanish Civil War posters and magazine covers, and Mendelson.

14. James Agee Papers, Notebook p 20, Monday [January 10, 1938], Folder 17, Box 1, Series I, MS 1500, Special Collections Library, University of Tennessee.

15. In *Hud,* the seventeen-year-old boy, Lon, leafs through pulp paperbacks in the local drugstore of his Texas town as he waits for his uncle to finish

drinking at the bar. When the druggist starts talking to him about the racy parts—knowing precisely on which pages they can be found—Lon replaces the book and moves on.

16. Joseph Entin's reading of the first two images—the headless white man holding a hoe and bodiless black face haloed by white hair—remarks on them as a "bizarre biracial Frankenstein" cobbling together two parts of the racial makeup of Southern rural sharecropper culture (222).

17. See Sara Blair's *Harlem Crossroads: Black Writers and Photography in the Twentieth Century*, which offers the most comprehensive reading of Wright's photographic investment to date; she sees his photography as intimately linked to writing as a practice.

18. Carla Cappetti has argued persuasively for reading Wright's autobiography as "the conjunction between literary autobiography and sociological life history," a methodology Wright borrowed from the Chicago school sociologists with whom he worked closely and to whom he owed his "story," as he noted in the introduction to St. Clair Drake and Horace R. Cayton's *Black Metropolis: A Study of Negro Life in a Northern City*. Chicago School sociology—with its interest in caste and class, and the movement of rural folk to urban proletariat as marginal men, which as Carla Cappetti argues, dovetailed with the CPUSA's interpretation of Stalin's ideas (dimly acknowledged in early drafts of *12 Million Black Voices*) about the national question—offered an overview for a story of self (198). Actually, all his fiction and nonfiction owe the same rendering of life-course case study through journalistic anecdote, ethnography, and personal reminiscence, as John M. Reilly notes.

19. June 1942. This and all other reviews come from Richard Wright's scrapbook, with clippings and other ephemera related to *12 Million Black Voices*, Richard Wright Papers, Folder 741, Box 63, Yale Collection of American Literature, Beinecke Rare Book and Manuscript Library.

20. This and all the quotations come from Richard Wright Papers, clippings file on *12 Million Black Voices*, Folder 741, Box 63.

21. For instance, pages 152–53 in *Lawd Today!* are rendered as choral dialogue, what became almost word for word a prose poem in *12 Million Black Voices* on pages 32–33.

22. For more on America's irrational culture, see Adorno. I am arguing that it is precisely this irrationality, in the form of the haunted American landscape full of ghosts unacknowledged, that comprises American literary history and politics. See Gordon, who sees the ghostly as "a paradigmatic way in which life is more complicated than those of us who study it have usually granted" (7).

23. The quotations come from Mikhail Bakhtin, *Problems of Dostoevsky's Poetics*, ed. and trans. Caryl Emerson (Minneapolis: University of Minnesota Press, 1984) 70–73, and the second from "Discourse in the Novel," *The Dialogic Imagination: Four Essays*, trans. Michael Holquist and Caryl Emerson (Austin: University of Texas Press, 1981) 73.

BIBLIOGRAPHY

Abraham, Nicolas, and Maria Torok. *The Wolf Man's Magic Word*. Trans. Nicholas Rand. Foreword by Jacques Derrida. Minneapolis: U of Minnesota P, 1986. Print.

Adorno, Theodor W. *The Stars Down to Earth and Other Essays on the Irrational Culture*. Ed. Stephen Crook. New York: Routledge, 2001. Print.

Agee, James. *Letters of James Agee to Father Flye*. New York: Braziller, 1962. Print.

Agee, James, and Walker Evans. *Let Us Now Praise Famous Men*. Boston: Houghton Mifflin, 1941. Print.

Algren, Nelson. *Chicago: City on the Make*. 1951. Chicago: U of Chicago P, 2001. Print.

Allred, Jeffrey. "From Eye to We: Richard Wright's *12 Million Black Voices*, Documentary, and Pedagogy." *American Literature* 78.3 (2006): 549–83. Print.

Bakhtin, Mikhail. "Discourse in the Novel." *The Dialogic Imagination: Four Essays*. Trans. Michael Holquist and Caryl Emerson. Austin: U of Texas P, 1981. Print.

———. *Problems of Dostoevsky's Poetics*. Ed. and trans. Caryl Emerson. Minneapolis: U of Minnesota P, 1984. Print.

Benjamin, Walter. "The Author as Producer." *Selected Works*. Eds. Michael Jennings and Howard Eiland. Vol. 2. Cambridge, MA: Belknap, 1998. Print.

———. "Critique of the New Objectivity." *Selected Writings*. Ed. Michael Jennings and Howard Eiland. Vol. 2. Cambridge, MA: Belknap, 1998. Print.

———. "Left-Wing Melancholy." *Selected Writings*. Ed. Michael Jennings and Howard Eiland. Vol. 2. Cambridge, MA: Belknap, 1998. Print.

———. "The Newspaper." *Selected Writings*. Ed. Michael Jennings and Howard Eiland. Vol. 2. Cambridge, MA: Belknap, 1998. Print.

———. "Post No Bills." *Selected Writings*. Ed. Marcus Bullock and Michael Jennings. Vol. 1. Cambridge, MA: Belknap, 1996. Print.

Blair, Sara. *Harlem Crossroads: Black Writers and Photography in the Twentieth Century*. Princeton, NJ: Princeton UP, 2007. Print.

Cappetti, Carla. *Writing Chicago: Modernism, Ethnography and the Novel*. New York: Columbia UP, 1993. Print.

Crandell, Richard F. "Dark Thoughts on Dark Citizens." *New York Herald Tribune* 23 Nov. 1941. Print.

Davis, Hugh, and Michael Lofaro, eds. *James Agee Rediscovered: The Journals of* Let Us Now Praise Famous Men *and Other New Manuscripts*. Knoxville: U of Tennessee P, 2005. Print.

Fearing, Kenneth. *Collected Poems of Kenneth Fearing*. New York: AMS, 1977. Print.

Gordon, Avery F. *Ghostly Matters: Haunting and the Sociological Imagination.* Minneapolis: U of Minnesota P, 1997. Print.

Heard, Sandra Rena. "Washington, DC's 'Negro' Press: The Unmaking of a Cooperative Black Society." American Studies Association Annual Meeting. Albuquerque, New Mexico. October 2008. Speech.

McCoy, Horace. *I Should Have Stayed Home.* 1938. London: Serpent's Tail, 1996. Print.

Mendelson, Jordana. *Documenting Spain: Artists, Exhibition Culture, and the Modern Nation, 1929–1939.* University Park: Pennsylvania State UP, 2005. Print.

Petry, Ann. "The Novel as Social Criticism." *The Writer's Book.* Ed. Helen Hull. New York: Barnes and Noble, 1956. Print.

Rabinowitz, Paula. *They Must Be Represented: The Politics of Documentary.* London: Verso, 1994. Print.

Reilly, John M. "Richard Wright Preaches the Nation: *12 Million Black Voices.*" *Black American Literature Forum* 16.3 (1982): 116–19. Print.

Revistas y Guerra, 1936–39. Museo Nacional Centro de Arte Reina Sofía, 2007. Print.

Rich, Frank. "McCain's McClellan Nightmare." *New York Times* 1 June 2008, natl. ed., sec. 4: 12. Print.

Rosskam, Edwin, and Louise Rosskam. Interview with Richard Doud. Archives of American Art, Smithsonian Institution. Rosskam Residence, Roosevelt, New Jersey. 3 Aug. 1965. Web. 10 June 2008.

Stange, Maren. "'Not What We Seem': Image and Text in *12 Million Black Voices.*" *Iconographies of Power: The Politics and Poetics of Visual Representation.* Eds. Ulla Haselstein, Berndt Ostendorf, and Peter Sneck. Heidelberg: Winter, 2003. 173–86. Print.

Suleiman, Susan Rubin. *Authoritarian Fictions: The Ideological Novel as a Literary Genre.* New York: Columbia UP, 1983. Print.

U.S. Week: A National Journal of News and Opinion 1.41 (1941). Print.

Weinstein, Margie. "Reframing Law and Lens: Jacob Riis's Documentary Photography and Legal Discourse during the Progressive Era." Diss. U of Minneapolis, 2008. Print.

Wright, Richard. *12 Million Black Voices.* New York: Viking, 1941. Print.

———. *Black Boy.* New York: Harper Perennial, 1993. Print.

———. Introduction. *Black Metropolis: A Study of Negro Life in a Northern City.* Eds. St. Clair Drake and Horace R. Cayton. New York: Harcourt, 1945. Print.

———. *Lawd Today!* Foreword. By Arnold Rampersad. Evanston, IL: Northwestern UP. Print.

———. *Native Son.* New York: Viking, 1940. Print.

8

Richard Wright's *A Father's Law* and *Black Metropolis*: Intellectual Growth and Literary Vision

Joyce Ann Joyce

Reaching Richard Wright's readers during the year of his centennial birthday and forty-eight years after his death in 1960, the publication of his very rarely mentioned unfinished novel, *A Father's Law,* will certainly prove to provoke the literary community. Though the novel held me captive as I read, thinking of Wright's diversity as a craftsman and of his profoundly deeply seeded obsession with the complexity of human nature, I am aware of the initial and final questions that will plague the thoughts of numerous scholars. These problems may, perhaps, begin with the introduction to this latest gift from the Richard Wright Estate. Julia Wright, Wright's eldest daughter and executrix of his estate, writes the introduction to the novel. She explains that after her father's funeral, she found the 306-page manuscript in her father's studio. Her two other factual descriptions of the novel are that it was a "draft—so peculiar, so unwieldy, like a patch work quilt of psychological horror with some pieces not quite fitting" (vii) and that the novel is "faulty, sketchy, [and] sometimes [a] repetitive draft" (viii).

Interestingly, at the same time that teachers and scholars are quite comfortable suggesting to others what to think about a literary piece, they also submit themselves to the dictum that primarily only completed novels, submitted to the publisher by the author, acquire status in an author's canon. Editing and completing Ralph Ellison's unfinished novel, literary critic John F. Callahan in his introduction to

Juneteenth, cautiously includes at the end of his edition of the novel a section titled "Afterword: A Note to Scholars," in which he carefully explains the voluminous sections of the manuscript and the steps involved in how he brought the manuscript to a unified whole. He adds that he plans to submit for publication a scholar's edition that will detail his corrections and "include sufficient manuscripts and drafts of the second novel to enable scholars and readers alike to follow Ellison's some forty years of work on his novel-in-progress" (368).

In contrast, Julia Wright's introduction to her father's work is more personal. She concentrates briefly on how her father wrote consistently, despite problems with his health; on how her father's manuscript is suggestive of his thoughts about his relationship with his family, particularly his children; and on his fascination with "the psychology of murder, i.e., the sociological, racial, political, cultural and historical forces that, given a certain context, opportunity and lack of communication, can lead to the act of murder in most of us" (viii). With this insight, Julia Wright captures the essence of her father's fiction and of his own well-documented comments about why he writes in *American Hunger* and in his many interviews.

Though Wright died in 1960 and though *Native Son* was published in 1940, the publication of *A Father's Law* evinces a polarity in the reviews of Wright's novel, not unlike the reviews and diversity of the criticism that describe his previous work. While the *Chicago Tribune, Washington Post,* the *Milwaukee Journal Sentinel, The Seattle Times, The Boston Globe,* the *Los Angeles Times,* and *The New York Times Book Review* all carry reviews of this new novel, veteran Wright scholar Jerry Ward's review and Ron Powers's review from the *New York Times Book Review* reveal the contemporaneity of discord when Richard Wright is the subject. Ward places *A Father's Law* in the context of Wright's other five novels, asserting that "the novel is a summation of Wright's aesthetic, his hardboiled vision of a future for which the Cold War was preparing us and the worlds we inhabit." He ends, "Even in its unfinished state, *A Father's Law* succeeds in reading mankind's dirty laundry and in leaving us with the option of reading against the patriarchal grain" ("Weight and Substance"). Ron Powers is not so magnanimous. He says of the novel, "Its flaws are so many and so foregrounded that they all but dare the reader to work through them and engage the ideas with which Wright was grappling. Without having first read his thunderous classics, we might plausibly dismiss the author as a tendentious, technically naïve amateur and disdain the works that made him indispensable in American letters" ("Ambiguities"). Powers demonstrates that he reads Wright's novel only in contrast to Wright's previous works rather than like Jerry Ward who reads *A Father's Law* in the context of Wright's previous works. Ward understands that Wright was constantly in search of new ways to structure his understanding of the human condition.

I propose that Wright's introduction to St. Clair Drake and Horace R. Cayton's *Black Metropolis: A Study of Negro Life in a Northern City* provides the intellectual framework for an exploration of what we learn about the consistency of Wright's thoughts and about how he persistently searched for new structures to encapsulate those ideas. Published originally in 1945, Wright's introduction to *Black Metropolis* culls his individual philosophy regarding how growing industrialization reflects the anxiety and immorality of dominant cultures. I cite here a necessarily lengthy passage from this introduction that explains the core of Wright's position, a position reflected, to varying degrees, in *Native Son*, in the rest of his novels, in *White Man! Listen*, in *Black Power*, in *Pagan Spain*, and finally in *A Father's Law*. He explains:

> But another and deeper dilemma rose out of the white man's break with the feudal order, a dilemma more acidly corroding than even that of slavery [which he addresses in the previous two paragraphs], one which colored and toned every moment of his life, creating an anxiety that was never to leave him. The advent of machine production altered his relationship to the earth, to his family, to his fellow men, and even to himself. Under feudalism the family had been the unit of production, the nexus of emotional relations, a symbol of the moral order of the universe. The father was the head of the family, the king the father of the state, and God the ruler of the world, and God's priests represented Him in the mundane affairs of man. The eternal and temporal orders of existence coalesced and formed one vivid, timeless moment of meaning, justification, and redemption. Man and earth and heaven formed a unit. (xxii)

Wright continues to explain that despite the intervention of "rationalizations," made by scientists and thinkers, the "jumps" between wars and peace only confused man's mind. At the same time that man attempted to hold on to feudal order, his consciousness is torn apart, tensions enhanced, anxiety increased by "every turn of wheel, throb of engine, and conquest of space" (xxii). Wright's introduction sets up Chicago as a model for the northern city in which both the black and white man suffer as a result of a denial of failure, a throbbing insecurity, an impassioned fear, and a greedy competitive drive that motivate the power of white dominance.

Wright locates *A Father's Law* in Chicago, and such a location calls attention to his ideas in *Black Metropolis*, whose introduction appears five years after the publication of *Native Son*. Readers, like Ron Powell, who anticipate seeing the Wright of *Native Son* or *The Long Dream* will surely encounter disappointment and frustration when reading *A Father's Law*. We must understand that this Richard Wright is not the same man who moved from the United States to live in Paris in 1947. The Richard Wright who traveled to Italy, Belgium, Switzerland, Germany, Spain, Ghana, and England has survived many personal and professional disappointments, read prolifically, and exchanged ideas with a wide range of ethnically diverse intellectuals.

I deduce from Michel Fabre's *The Unfinished Quest of Richard Wright* that a culmination of events stimulated Wright's work on *A Father's Law*. In the 1950s, not only was Wright suffering from amoebic dysentery, but he also experienced many challenges with his publisher Harper & Row. He knew that Paul Reynolds, his agent, felt that he had lost touch with his southern roots and thus the source of his creativity. Reynolds did not like *The Long Dream*, and too many of the reviews of *The Long Dream* and the previously published *The Outsider* were not favorable (468). Another disturbing incident with tremendous affect on Wright is far too entangled to detail here. In brief, the incident involves Richard Gibson and Ollie Harrington, who rented Gibson his apartment in Paris. Gibson not only refused to move when Harrington returned, but he also claimed he owned Harrington's possessions. In this dilemma, Wright took the side of his close friend, Harrington. The situation ballooned into internecine issues within the already fragmented black expatriate community in Paris. At one point, the story spread that Wright was a CIA agent, and Wright thought the CIA was responsible for the story (*Unfinished Quest* 461–63).

Following numerous other incidents that fueled his fears, Wright convinced his dear friend, Ollie Harrington, to leave France for his emotional and physical safety (*Unfinished Quest* 510–11). On July 23, 1960, he writes to Margrit de Sabloniére, "What a stupid thing life is. At the time when I ought to work hard to keep up my income, I feel absolutely no energy to work. Yet I know I must. So I sit and fret through the days" (*Unfinished Quest* 512). Before the publication of *A Father's Law*, we were able to elide the significance of Michel Fabre's discussion of the letter Wright sent to de Sabloniére and the fact that Fabre tells us that Wright in August 1960 decided not to write a new preface to *Black Metropolis*. Instead, we are told, "he took Margrit's suggestion of writing a story very different from his usual style, a break which might liberate him" (*Unfinished Quest* 512). On August 2, Wright responds to de Sablonière:

> I started a brand new piece of prose, the idea of which had been simmering in my mind for a long, long time. I'm pounding on the machine morning and night. It makes me feel much better. You know I think that writing with me must be a kind of therapeutic measure....Now I'm free, with white sheets of paper before me, and a head full of wild ideas, ideas that excite me. Maybe writing with me is like being psychoanalyzed. I feel all the poison being drained out. I'll tell you in another letter about the theme that has me by the throat. (*Unfinished Quest* 512)

By August 18, Wright had completed 300 pages of a manuscript he initially titled "The Law of the Father" and whose value he did not doubt (*Unfinished Quest* 512).

It is highly significant that thoughts of *Black Metropolis* were living in Wright's mind at the same time that thoughts of his "brand new piece of prose" had also been "simmering in [his] mind for a long, long time." In the early 1960s, Harper asked Wright to write a new preface to *Black Metropolis* that would detail the changes having occurred in Chicago's black community since 1945. After writing a "long rough draft," Wright decided to write Drake and Cayton to get a sense of their wishes. When they did not respond, he "temporarily abandoned" the preface. In March, Wright abandoned the preface altogether (*Unfinished Quest* 504, 509). Moreover, with a long memory and very sensitive about the reception of his work, Wright, during the late 1950s was quite troubled regarding the reactions to *The Outsider* and particularly to *The Long Dream*. White critics challenged his ignoring the progress made toward desegregation and the resulting "improved standard of living and the civil rights" blacks enjoyed (*Unfinished Quest* 466). These details provide an entrée into understanding why *A Father's Law* emerges as consciously and dramatically different from all of Wright's previous fiction. Perhaps, using what he learned about Chicago in preparation to write the revised introduction to *Black Metropolis*, Wright responds to his critics in *A Father's Law*. I propose then that we can read *A Father's Law* as a creative manifestation of Wright's critique of Western society.

Thus set in Chicago, like *Native Son*, *A Father's Law* emerges as far more than the story of a black police chief, Ruddy (Rudolph) Turner, and his failing relationship with his son. *Washington Post* reviewer

Ralph Eubanks may be correct when he says that a black "police chief in suburban Chicago would have been a stretch in 1960" ("Fathers and Sons"). However, I propose that Wright was not only aware that there were indeed a very few black policemen on the Chicago Police force in the 1950s, but that he also knew that Rudy Nimocks joined the Chicago Police Department in 1956. Twenty-nine years after Wright's death, in 1989, Nimocks became chief of the University of Chicago Police Department from which he retired in 2009. Therefore, I am suggesting that it is not fortuitous that the first name of the father in *A Father's Law* is *Rudy*. Just as Wright used, to some degree, the reality of Robert Nixon's life to shape his fictionalized version of Bigger Thomas, I assert that Rudy Nimocks becomes Rudy Turner in Wright's unfinished manuscript.

A Father's Law significantly evinces Wright's prescience, his ability to predict both the future development of Chicago, the Black Metropolis, and its effect on the lives of its inhabitants, in this case a middle-class black father and his middle-class black son, Tommy. Although *Black Metropolis* details the ethnical and emotional weaknesses of a white society responsible for what Wright calls the "estrangement" of blacks in the urban city of Chicago, *A Father's Law* fictionalizes what can happen to an educated black man who accepts the political, cultural, and economic mores of Western society. Both Rudy and his son have fallen victim to the anxiety, insecurity, and fear, which Wright says characterized modern man's emotional life, following the dissolution of the feudal order. In *Black Metropolis*, Wright says that the conflict of cultures (one black and subjugated and the other white and dominant) will inevitably lead to violence. Yet, he explains that the most "tell-tale" signs of modern man's destiny seethe in the heart of the middle-class white man. Wright's description of this human condition analogously examines why Tommy's world falls apart in *A Father's Law*:

> Social discontent assumes many subtle guises, and a society that recognizes only those forms of social maladjustment which are recorded in courts, prisons, clinics, hospitals, newspapers, and bureaus of vital statistics will be missing some of the most fateful of the tell-tale clues to its destiny. What I mean is this: It is distinctly possible to know, *before it happens*, that certain forms of violence will occur. It can be known that a native-born white man, the end product of all our strivings, educated, healthy, apparently mentally normal, having the stability of a wife and family, possessing the security of a good job with high wages, enjoying more freedom than any other country on earth accords its citizens, *but devoid of the most elementary satisfactions*, will

seize upon an adolescent, zoot-suited Mexican and derive deep feelings of pleasure from stomping his hopeless guts out upon the pavements of Los Angeles. (xxvi–xxvii)

Wright's reference here is to the Los Angeles zoot-suit riots in which white World War II soldiers in 1943 mercilessly attacked Latino adolescents who wore zoot suits, made of woolen fabric that was rationed by the War Production Board. Racial bigotry motivated the soldiers and policemen to stereotype the Mexican American youths as violent criminals unsympathetic to the war (Pagán 1–2). Despite Saunders Reddings's contention that Wright's living abroad had caused the cutting of the "emotional umbilical cord through which art was fed" (60), Wright reveals that he not only remained tied to the sociological and political complexity of black lives in Chicago, but he was also aware of the terror experienced by Mexican Americans in Los Angeles. And most strikingly, Wright roots the cause of the anger in whites in Los Angeles to the anxiety and fear the hegemony experiences because of the diminishing of "the nexus of emotional relations" in an industrialized society. Tommy, too, embodies the emotional malaise exemplified in the soldiers' attack of Mexican American youths. Tommy's actions are stimulated by the failures of his middle-class upbringing and the dissolution of the moral order that accompanied that upbringing. Following Margrit de Sablonière's suggestion that he write something stylistically very different, Wright frames his new ideas regarding the Black Metropolis in the shape of a mystery novel, thus challenging the expectations of his readers on two different levels. What follows is an exposition of how Wright encapsulates his presentation of the dissolution of a middle-class black character in a mystery novel with criminal profiling as its structural vehicle.

The early scenes excitingly prepare the reader for the denouement when Ruddy becomes sure that his son is a serial murderer. Hazel Rowley misleads the reader unfamiliar with the novel in its current form when she insists that the Turners live on the Southside of Chicago (149). If the Turners live on the Southside, it is not the neighborhood on the Southside of Chicago in which Bigger lived. The first paragraph of chapter 2 answers all questions regarding the Turners' class status and living conditions:

"Quiet neighborhood," [Ruddy] appraised the quarter in which his two-story stucco house stood in keeping with his officer's rank. Catholic—had made it. His neighbors were white; he did not have to fear hoodlums loitering about his premises. He had at once, as soon as he had purchased his property, joined the neighborhood protective

association to guard the interests of all who owned property in the
area, and he had been accepted with enthusiasm. (15)

Ruddy's neighbor is vice president of the Greenlawn Bank and
Loan Association; his son is a student in sociology at The University of
Chicago; his police comrades are white, and the intellectual among his
squad is Ed Seigel [sic], a Jew, whom Ruddy likes and highly respects;
"yet he feared that if he had too much to do with him, people would
think that he was too intimate with an unpopular minority. And
Ruddy loved being with the majority..." (26). Ruddy's comfortable
home, his integration into the white community, and his craving to be
accepted by his white "peers" manifest what Wright sees as changes for
some in Chicago's Black Metropolis as early as the late 1950s.

Wright uses the Turner family as the focal point of his exploration of how few differences exist between the striving middle-class
black family and the dominant white society with whom the Turners
identify. At the beginning of the novel, Ruddy worries consistently
about the distance between him and his son. This worrying finally
reaches its peak when Ruddy decides to have a heart-to-heart talk
with Tommy, who has changed significantly in the last year, becoming quite withdrawn. It is during this conversation that Ruddy learns
of Marie's syphilis and promises to keep Tommy's secret. Though
Ruddy understands Tommy's decision not to marry Marie, he feels
strongly that his son should have tried to comfort Marie and to maintain communication with her. In this initial discussion with Tommy,
Ruddy concludes that his son is strange when they discuss a man who
was convicted of a crime that Tommy is convinced the man did not
commit. It is during this discussion that the reader gets more than
a glimpse of Tommy's disrespect for authority and doubts of police
intelligence. When Ruddy tells his son that all the criminals he has
met feel guilty, Tommy says that it is hard to catch a criminal who
feels no guilt and that most of the criminals in Brentwood Park feel
no guilt. The reader has already learned of the revenge murder of the
former chief of police of Brentwood, of housemaid pregnancy, of the
sexual abuse of children, and that the white elite of Brentwood, with
their political power, manage to keep their transgressions out of the
newspapers.

As Tommy stays two steps ahead of his father—who has consistently discussed the three murders with his son—Ed Siegel profiles
the killer:

> "Well, in the light of what we got to go on," Ed began, "it's a kind
> of psychological guess....A preacher is killed with a woman. Then a

priest is killed with a nun. Then the detective's son is killed—alone.
Now Ruddy, I've been sitting here trying to put myself in the murderer's place. It's hard. Now, that preacher, that priest, and the detective's son represented something to that killer. Ruddy, a woman is an
earthly kind of creature. If she hates you, she kills you. And there is
always an understandable reason. But a man kills in a funny kind of
way. First of all, those whom he kills have to be kind of transfigured
in his mind...." (137)

When Ruddy responds confoundedly, Ed adds, "That priest was not
just a priest. That preacher was more than a man of the cloth. And
that detective's son was more than merely some man's son" (137).
Ed explains that the preacher, the priest, and the detective's son were
"symbols of something hated" (137).

Ed is unaware that each step in his teaching Ruddy the profiles of
the killer augments further in Ruddy's mind that his son is the killer.
Ed presents Ruddy with three analogies or scenarios—too lengthy to
detail here—that all have in common a deeply confused mind that is
intelligent and feels betrayal, anger, and hatred. Ed's abstract description of the killer, his deductive reasoning, the cement Ruddy finds
on his son's tennis shoes, the fact that a .38 was used for all the murders, the fact that the cement on Tommy's shoes matched the cement
found in the factory where Tommy had broken up pieces of the gun
and thrown them into the cement, Ruddy's order to break up the
cement in the factory and carry it to the police yard to be broken with
hammers—all bring Wright's mystery novel into twenty-first-century
popular culture.

Any reader familiar with recent popular television shows such
as "CSI: Crime Scene Investigation," "Criminal Minds," "CSI:
Miami," and "CSI: NY" will recognize that computer technology
has taken crime solving investigation far ahead of previous televi-
sion mysteries such as "Murder, She Wrote" and "Perry Mason."
Wright's library substantiates his interest in criminal profiling.
Some of the books that would replace modern technology are Ben
Karpman's *Case Studies of the Psychopathology of Crime*, Henry T.
Rhodes's *The Criminals We Deserve: A Survey of Some Aspects of
Crime in the Modern World*, Paul Reiwald's *Society and Its Criminals*,
Frederic Wertham's *Dark Legend: A Study in Murder* and *The Show
of Violence*, and Theodor Reik's *The Unknown Murderer*. Without
the assistance of contemporary technology that describes forensic
science, Wright uses the resources on the shelves of his library. In
"Criminal Minds"—a current television crime drama—the agents

of the FBI Behavioral Unit solve crimes exclusively by determining the "unsub's" (the unknown subject's) behavioral personality, using that profile to predict the unsub's subsequent victims, and then capture the criminal.

In "Criminal Minds," the behavioral agents search for an emotional trauma or stressor that is the direct cause of the unsub's criminal actions. The Behavioral Unit identifies the unsub's stressor as the original emotional response to a devastatingly humiliating and/or painful experience that becomes the focal point for the unsub's self-concept and response to others. Though the word *stressor* was not in Wright's lexicon, his disciplined reading knowledge of criminal psychology was seriously deepened by his close friendship with psychiatrist Frederic Wertham. While Wright's relationship with Wertham is well documented, it is essential for my purposes to note that after reading Wertham's *Dark Legend: A Study in Murder*, Wright on October 24, 1941 (after the publication of *Native Son*), wrote to Wertham, asking him to discuss the "factors, motives or psychological abnormality [that] made [Clinton Brewer's] second murder possible" (Fabre 236). Working together, at Wright's suggestion, Wright and Wertham with Wertham's testifying at Brewer's second trial for murdering his second woman, Wertham convinced the court to give Brewer a life sentence, believably asserting that Brewer had a pathological obsession (Fabre 236), his violence a response to what he perceives as the rejection of women.

Wright's use of the stressor poignantly separates his mystery novel from Chester Himes's work. In *Richard Wright: Books & Writers*, Fabre includes a comment in which Wright makes an invaluable distinction between his work and that of his friend Chester Himes. Wright explains, "Now Chester Himes and I are of a different stamp. Himes is a naturalist and I'm something, no matter how crudely, of a psychologist" (9). Wright's explanation of how his work differs from that of the masterful Chester Himes proves quite useful. While Wright suggests that Himes's focus is the effect of environment on character, he identifies his concentration on the emotional aspects of human nature.

The voluminous books that Fabre lists as part of Wright's library more than substantiate Wright's description of his work. Some of the books that illuminate the psychological focus of Wright's work are Helen Deutch's *Psycho-analysis of the Neuroses*, *Encyclopaedia* [sic] *of the Social Sciences*, Edna Heidbreder's *Seven Psychologies*, David Hume's *An Abstract of a Treatise of Human Nature, 1740, a Pamphlet Hitherto Unknown*, Karl Jasper's *The Perennial Scope of Philosophy*, Carl

G. Jung's *Psychology of the Unconscious: A Study of the Transformation and Symbolisms of the Libido*, seven books written by Nietzsche, sixteen by Sartre, fifteen by Kierkegaard, and eight by Dostoevsky. With these resources in addition to his keen and in-depth understanding of human nature, Wright gives us a psychological thriller that differs from Himes's work in other important ways: Himes's detective fiction, especially novels such as *Cotton Comes to Harlem* and *Blind Man with a Pistol*, does not probe human consciousness, and these novels do not unfold using behavioral profiling exclusively. Moreover, Wright's *A Father's Law* has little of the humor that describes Himes's detective fiction.

Wright's comments, in reference to his appreciation of Dostoevsky's work, by implication, further support a reading of *A Father's Law* as a fictional, psychological look at the risk the black middle class takes when it blindly accepts the moral entrapments of urbanization. Wright says, "There is one thing it [the petty bourgeoisie] has in abundance—emotional consciousness, intense emotional consciousness. Its life can be linked to a man standing with his back to the wall, cowed, or a man holding above his head a great weight which he dares not turn loose, lest it should crush him.... His emotional intensity can be weighed in the works of Dostoevsky, Hemingway, etc." (*Richard Wright: Books & Writers* 40). Wright follows this same line of thinking in his characterization of the bourgeoisie in *Black Metropolis*. He writes, "Capitalists today hate Hitler for his wholesale, gratuitous murders; but they hate him for another and subtler reason: They hate him for revealing the shaky, class foundation of their society, for reminding them of their sundered consciousness, for flaunting their hypocrisy...." (xxiv). In his presentation of Tommy, Wright gives us a character whose emotional consciousness, shaped by his class status, his race, and his religion, and whose severed consciousness break down in the face of what he sees as the hypocrisy imbedded in all that he has been taught to believe.

When Tommy explains to his father why he moved his research from the Black Belt to Brentwood after he learned of Marie's syphilis, the interconnection among race, class, and religion reaches a peak as all elements of the novel coalesce. Tommy explains that the Black Belt (where Marie lives) is contaminated and poisoned. He continues, "I've never been in the Black Belt since [he learned of Marie's condition]. What kind of a world is that? How could a thing like that happen? I ride past the Black Belt now. Whenever I walk the streets there, I feel like I'm going to faint, fall down" (91).

When Ruddy and Tommy discuss Ruddy's visit with Marie, Tommy's response echoes Ed's profiling of the murders as symbolic. Tommy explains, "You see, I was told in school and church that love was the greatest thing on earth, that it could conquer all.... Hell, it didn't and it can't. What can and will conquer are fear and hate. You can be fearful before you know it; you can hate without knowing it" (176). Because his father has spent most of his time pursuing a career as a policeman, because Tommy has had all material advantages without the supervision and advice of parents, because his parents were told he is a genius, because the Catholic church has been the primary shaper of his moral values, and because he has never experienced the deep suffering that would characterize the lives of many blacks in the Black Belt, Tommy has no training in emotional strength and is totally decentered by Marie's reality. Thus, as Ed predicted, Tommy's murders emerge as symbols of his estrangement from his blackness as well as his hatred of both his father's laws: those of his spiritual and his biological father. Wright's choice of Catholicism as the Turner family's religion indicates their perception of their class affiliation. Most blacks in the Black Belt would be lured to the Baptist faith like Reverend Hammond in *Native Son*. Though all traditional religions in the West view marriage as both a religious and civil arrangement, Catholicism has strict rules regarding intercourse and "purity." Two other books in Wright's library, Oliver Cox's *Caste, Class, and Race: A Study in Social Dynamics* and Richard R. Miller's *Slavery and Catholicism,* suggest Wright's intellectual investigation of how the interconnection of class, race, and religion influence the individual's perception of self and the relation of that self to others.

Tommy's training regarding "purity" provides the clue to his "signature" as a serial killer. In his portrayal of Tommy in his unfinished manuscript and in his depiction of Cross Damon in 1953[1], Wright presages what is referred to as the "signature" of the serial killer, whose identity is largely determined by criminal profiling. In "Criminal Minds" and "NCIS," this profiling involves physical/material and psychological evidence. While the material signature may be the repeated, consistent cutting off of a specific and always the same body part of the victim, a psychological signature makes a serial killer far more difficult to identify. Though Damon and Tommy are motivated by psychological factors, Damon, unlike Tommy, is careful not to leave material evidence, and his psychological profile is far more complicated than Tommy's. Ely Houston, the district attorney whom Damon met on his train ride from Chicago to New York and who identifies emotionally and intellectually with Damon, views world history, religion, and politics from an individualistic perspective. Houston's questions to Damon, before Houston realizes that Damon has killed at least three people, have answers that illuminate how Tommy differs from Damon:

> Could there be a man in whose mind and consciousness all the hopes and inhibitions of the last two thousand years have died? A man whose consciousness has not been conditioned by our culture? A man speaking our language, dressing and behaving as we do, and yet living on a completely different plan? A man who would be the return of ancient man, pre-Christian man?
>
> […] He's a man living in our modern industrial cities, but devoid of all the moral influences of Christianity.…(316)

Though anger motivates both Tommy's and Damon's murderous acts, Tommy's murders are planned reactions to trauma: his stressor is Marie's congenital syphilis. Damon's actions are spontaneous reactions of outrage. Tommy, unlike Damon, kills because he feels totally deceived/betrayed by moral and legal laws. As Houston notes, Damon has always lived outside those laws.

Unlike the women in Wright's previous novels, Tommy's mother, Agnes, evidences a balanced compassion and logic that challenge stereotypical male moral law. When Rudy tells her about Marie's congenital syphilis and Tommy's complete repulsion and desertion of Marie, Agnes asks if there is any chance that Tommy and Marie can get together. Ruddy explains that Tommy does not want it and that Marie has to accept Tommy's decision. In response, Agnes "whispered in a barely audible breath: 'Men…'" (254). Agnes does not give up easily. She says that she thinks Tommy and Marie could have a life because Marie's syphilis is being cured. Though Ruddy logically exclaims that after marriage the syphilis could always exacerbate Tommy's emotions in any argument and that Marie may always feel "damaged," Agnes, "speaking in a voice that came from her heart: 'Men are strange, Hummnnn. They look for fireworks, neon lights, rainbows, and shooting rockets in love. They're always making women something they are not…" (255). Unwittingly, Agnes's response here echoes Ed Seigel's comments to Ruddy when Seigel says that the killings of the priest and the preacher are symbolic of something in the murderer's mind. Agnes emerges then as a more balanced, less stereotypical character than the women in Wright's previous fiction.

While Agnes's relationship with her husband and with her son makes her a typical, middle-class black woman of her era, at the same time, Wright's portrayal of Agnes raises certain questions. Biographers Michel Fabre and Hazel Rowley tell us that Wright was set to marry Marion Sawyer when he learned that she had congenital syphilis. According to Fabre, Wright "broke completely with Marion, although her illness was congenital and not communicable. His physical or moral revulsion, no doubt, was due to his puritanical upbringing, in which shameful diseases were associated with 'bad women.' [...] This episode left only a faint literary trace in Wright's work" (196–97). Rowley contends, "In the last summer of his life, Richard Wright was haunted by his cruelty toward Marion Sawyer. At his desk in Normandy, he wrote a whole novel within six weeks. *A Father's Law*, unpublished to this day..." (148). It is clear from Fabre's biography that Wright had numerous affairs with both married and unmarried women (195) and that given his first short marriage, his personal relationship with women is at best a conundrum. What we know with confidence about Wright's literary habits is that he channeled real-life events though his imagination. Therefore, the only certainty we have is that Marie emerges as a fictional, empathetic conceptualization of Marion Sawyer.

The value of Wright's more balanced portrayal of a black woman, such as Agnes, is that it suggests that Wright grew beyond his depiction of the women discussed in some brilliant classic feminist essays that focus on the women in his work, such as Sherley Anne Williams's "Papa Dick and Sister-Woman: Reflections on Women in the Fiction of Richard Wright," Sylvia Keady's "Richard Wright's Women Characters and Inequality," and Trudier Harris's "Native Sons and Foreign Daughters." Though we are not sure what provoked Wright's broader and more emphatic view of women, it is not difficult to understand what Agnes means when she merely says "Men" in her conversation with Ruddy. She further clarifies this when she implies that men and women do not think alike. Agnes identifies with the terror and horror that Marie experiences on a level that evades male perception. Though he is stronger and has more compassion than his son, Ruddy recognizes that his wife is stronger than he: "Yeah, women were strong. Here he was trembling in the face of one of his best friends [Ed], and Agnes had taken what now was troubling him in her heart's stride" (264).

Agnes is clearly neither Bessie nor Bigger's mother in *Native Son*; she is not Aunt Sue, nor the more complex Sarah, both from two different stories in *Uncle Tom's Children*. *A Father's Law* analogously evidences that the Richard Wright who wrote novels in the late 1930s, 1940s, and 1950s was growing emotionally, intellectually, and creatively.

With his representations of Agnes, Ruddy, and Tommy, a complex middle-class black family, Wright overcomes an obstacle, addressed quite poignantly in Hurston's essay, "What White Publishers Won't Print." She says that because white publishers prefer uncomplicated, stereotypical portraits of "quaint" blacks, they are not interested in books about the black middle class (170).

Regardless of the fact that Wright died before he finished his manuscript and despite the fact that the novel was published forty-eight years after his death, the novel merits serious attention because of what we learn about the consistency and evolution of Wright's exploration of the human subject and about his shaping of that investigation. It seems almost an act of destiny that Ella Winter sent Wright a copy of Wertham's *Dark Legend* that led to a friendship and intellectual collaboration of almost twenty years. Though *Native Son* was in print for approximately a year before Wright began his camaraderie with Wertham, Wright's characterization of Bigger Thomas reflects Wertham's investigation of the interconnection between sex and crime. Fabre explains that Wright admitted to Wertham that his having walked in the home of Mrs. Walls, for whom he was working, and finding her undressing emerges as a "psychological determinant" in his emotional development, in part, because of the taboos governing the interaction between black men and white women (47). Moreover, we can expect that the suppression of all that is sensually natural by Wright's rigid, socially restricted, and religiously sexually repressed Seventh-day Adventist grandmother could have easily made an indelible scratch on the wall of Wright's psyche. Usually represented in the mother figure in Wright's novels, this connection between repressed sexual desires and contact, the incongruity between sexual desire and arbitrary moral codes, a rejection of religion connected to the mother figure, and the violence that accompanies this trilogy all link *Native Son*, *The Outsider*, *Savage Holiday*, *The Long Dream* to *A Father's Law*. Responding to environmental determinants, Bigger Thomas feels shame and self-loathing, fear of whites, and is contemptuous of his mother's religion; Erskine Caldwell has repressed anger and sexual desire, both interconnected and rooted in his perception of his mother's rejection of him; Cross Damon violently reacts to self-appointed demigods of communism and fascism, and he, too, sees his mother's religion as submissive and passive; Rex Tucker, Fishbelly, "loses" his given name as his fear of fish becomes conflated with his fear of the white world, represented by Chris's lynching because of his sexual relationship with a white woman (Joyce 170). Fishbelly grows to hate his mother's religion as much as he loathes his father's "feigned" submissiveness and consistent passivity to whites.

A very financially comfortable middle-class intellectual, Tommy Turner, son of initially Captain and later Chief of Police, Rudolph (Ruddy) Turner, responds violently with anger and hatred, the symbols reflected in God's and his earthly father's betrayal as well as in the failure of moral law. In *A Father's Law*, Wright's "brand new piece of prose," he explores for the first time the dilemma of a black psyche that achieves the political and economic freedom sought by the black characters in much of his earlier fiction. *Black Metropolis* provides the paradigm for what these characters can expect in a morally bereft urban society.

It is indeed a contemporary novel. I wonder how Wright's reviewers and scholars would receive *A Father's Law* if the novel were perceived through the same lens as the crime fiction of John Grisham, a twentieth- and twenty-first-century successful author of crime thrillers, who does not share Wright's history as a "serious" intellectual novelist, studied almost exclusively in the academy. Though Grisham was born in Jonesboro, Arkansas, he was raised in DeSoto County, Mississippi. It is interesting that both Grisham and Wright share an Arkansas and a Mississippi history. Grisham's first novel *A Time to Kill* is now well known, having been made into a successful film with Samuel L. Jackson playing the role of the father who killed the white assailants who raped his daughter. If we view Wright's novel within this contemporary context, what becomes most important is not that the novel comes to us without Wright's precision, with flaws, and without his final touches, but that what surfaces as most important for the future study of Richard Wright is what we learn from his willingness to grow, from his ability to sustain his intellectual and political thoughts, and from his flexibility in shaping these ideas in new form. Amazingly, the diversity of Richard Wright's canon continues to confuse us, to educate us, to awaken us to our own intellectual vulnerabilities, and to stimulate our curiosity to vary our approach in studying his craft.

I am fascinated by the possibility that Wright's characterization of Tommy in *A Father's Law* emerges as Wright's continuing, shrewd exploration of the effect of urbanization on human character. In his pursuit of this concern, Wright accomplishes three things: he remains consistent in his probing of the human soul, the human consciousness as it is influenced by modernization; he demonstrates how the achievement of riches easily has the same deteriorating effect on the soul of both the black and white Western man; and he enhances his creative skills by pursuing what is for him a previously uncharted structural terrain.

Those critics and readers who leave the novel with uneasiness and skepticism might want to read Michel Fabre's summary of the 300 pages of the manuscript Wright wrote by August 18, 1960, appropriately three months before his sudden death. Fabre's account of the manuscript, which he read before 1973, validates much of Wright's authenticity. Though we do not know how Wright would have ended his novel, I find the ending quite plausibly conceived. The editor for the manuscript, Julia Wright, was a student of sociology and spent time with her father during the last months of his life. She does not tell us in the introduction if her father talked to her about his work and specifically his work on *A Father's Law* before his death. Yet, what we do get from our reading of the novel—in comparison to and in contract with Wright's previous novels—is that *A Father's Law* is our most recent experience with Wright's trajectory of the depth of the psychological commingling of sex and crime. We also know that *A Father's Law* indeed presages our current widespread "obsession" with profiling criminals and prophesizes the middle-class comfort zone of an elite black middle class family in twenty-first-century Chicago. Perhaps, today this middle class would replace those sooty bones as symbols that lie between Wright's creative vision and psychological probing of human vulnerability in his poem "Between the World and Me."

Note

1. At the International Richard Wright Centennial Conference in Paris in June 2008, I read an earlier version of this essay, then recently published in *Drumvoices Revue* 16, (Spring-Summer-Fall 2008). On November 29, 2008, an inspiring young scholar from University of Chicago, Vaughn Rasberry, delivered a presentation titled "On Cosmopolitanism and the Postcolony: Rethinking Richard Wright on Culture" at the Richard Wright at 100 International Conference at the Universidade da Beira Interior in Covilha, Portugal. Though Professor Rasberry's presentation did not address the concept of criminal profiling in *The Outsider* and though he did not mention *A Father's Law* at all, hearing his paper is directly responsible for my observing that *The Outsider* was the first of Wright's novels to use criminal profiling, despite the remarkable differences between the two novels.

Bibliography

Callahan, John F. "Afterword: A Note to Scholars." *Juneteenth*. Ed. John F. Callahan. New York: Random House, 1999. 366–68. Print.

Eubanks, Ralph. "Fathers and Sons." *Washington Post* 13 Jan. 2008. Web. 7 Feb. 2010.

Fabre, Michel. *The Unfinished Quest of Richard Wright.* New York: Morrow, 1973. Print.

Gigerenzer, Thalia. "Leaving the Force." *Chicago Maroon* 1 June 2009. Web. 7 Feb. 2010.

Hurston, Zora Neale. "What White Publishers Won't Print." 1950. *I Love Myself When I Am Laughing.* Ed. Alice Walker. Old Westbury, NY: Feminist. 169–73. Print.

Joyce, Joyce A. "Richard Wright's *The Long Dream*: An Aesthetic Extension of *Native Son.*" Diss. U of Georgia, 1979. Print.

Pagán, Eduardo Obregón. "Los Angeles Geopolitics and the Zoot Suit Riot, 1943." *Social Science History* 24.1 (Spring 2000): 223–56. Print.

Powers, Ron. "Ambiguities." *New York Times* 24 Feb. 2008. Web. 7 Feb. 2010.

Redding, Saunders. Rev. of *The Long Dream.* By Richard Wright. *Richard Wright: Critical Perspectives Past and Present.* Eds. Henry Louis Gates, Jr. and K. A. Appiah. New York: Amistad, 1993. 60–61. Print.

Rowley, Hazel. *Richard Wright: The Life and Times.* New York: Holt, 2001. Print.

Ward, Jerry. "The Weight and Substance of *A Father's Law.*" Rev. of *A Father's Law,* by Richard Wright. *Chicken Bones: A Journal for Literary & Artistic African-American Themes.* 18 Nov. 2007. Web. 7 Feb. 2010.

Wright, Julia. "Introduction" in *A Father's Law.* By Richard Wright. New York: HarperCollins, 2008. v–xiii. Print.

Wright, Richard. *A Father's Law.* New York: HarperCollins, 2008. Print.

———. Introduction. *Black Metropolis: A Study of Negro Life in a Northern City.* By St. Clair Drake and Horace R. Cayton. Chicago: U of Chicago P, 1993. xvii–xxiv. Print.

———. *The Outsider.* New York: Harper, 1953. New York: Perennial Library, 1965. Print.

———. "Personalism." *Richard Wright: Books and Writers.* Ed. Michel Fabre. Jackson: UP of Mississippi, 1990. 40. Print.

9

A Queer Finale: Sympathy and Privacy in Wright's *A Father's Law*

John C. Charles

Richard Wright's posthumously published fragment, *A Father's Law*, is, in many respects, a queer work. Tommy Turner, the protagonist's son, is the text's most queer figure; his father, Ruddy Turner, repeatedly thinks to himself that his son is "queer" because of his perplexing philosophical ideas and his carefully guarded personal privacy, and when Tommy becomes the primary suspect for a series of killings, the question of whether he might be sexually queer arises as well. Queerer still, in terms of Wright's oeuvre, is the life and career of Ruddy Turner, a veteran black police officer who has risen in the ranks of the Chicago police force to his latest assignment, chief of police of the affluent white municipality, Brentwood Park. Wright's treatment of the police department is unlike any other in his body of writing. There is no corruption, no police brutality, and most strange of all, no mention of anti-black racism. Quite the contrary, Ruddy is treated with unqualified respect at every level, from fellow cops who repeatedly say they are happy to "serve" him, all the way to the mayor, a white man, who invites him to dine with his family at his home.[1] Respect and sympathy flow among the officers to such an extent that it can only be called sentimental. When the police commissioner offers Ruddy his new position, a crowning professional achievement and symbolic triumph over Chicago's historical racism, Ruddy cries unreservedly before "whisper[ing] fervently: 'Bill, I'll do it for you or die trying.'" Critic Ron Powers singles out this tearful scene of intimate fraternity in his dismissive review as evidence that *A Father's Law* shouldn't have been published at all, and that "to present it to the public at this embryonic stage violates [Wright's] writerly privacy and does him a disservice." Powers's critique unwittingly hits on a key issue—writerly privacy—and I argue that the peculiar (or queer) sympathy that Ruddy experiences among the idealized fraternity of the police force works in tandem with the queer privacy of his son, Tommy. Both function to provide Wright the "writerly privacy" he was denied as the most widely known "Negro writer" of his era.

A Father's Law is of a piece with Wright's post-expatriation attempt to break away from what many critics considered his obligatory theme, "the Negro problem," and to move toward an interrogation of what he called "the big problem—the meaning of western civilization as a whole and the relation of Negroes and other minority groups to it" (Fabre 366). I contend that the marked sentimentality of Wright's final novel facilitates this shift in critical focus. The precise function of sympathy and sentimentality in Wright's larger project becomes legible, I argue, by attending to his appropriation of the crime story genre. Postwar era American crime fiction was increasingly structured by sentimentality and idealized visions of masculine fellowship, a tendency that lent itself to Wright's own penchant for scenes of interracial male sympathy, an understudied motif in his work.[2] The crime story genre appealed to Wright both because of his lifelong interest in crime and criminology as well as the crime story's sentimental investments, which served two primary purposes.[3] The sentimental bonds within the law enforcement community forestall racially prescriptive readings that would reduce the work's larger intellectual project to racial protest. At the same time, however, the protagonist's sentimental faith in law, both legal and religious, (i.e., "the father's law") is the object of Wright's critique. This critique is voiced by Ruddy's "queer" intellectual son, who, like Wright, studied Chicago School Sociology and Freud. *A Father's Law* is, somewhat paradoxically, a sentimental "anti-sentimental" novel. I frame my reading of *A Father's Law* with a brief discussion of Wright's first two novels after expatriation, *The Outsider* (1953) and *Savage Holiday* (1954), to highlight the extent to which Wright had been wrestling with the same concerns, thematic and authorial, at least since moving to Europe. *A Father's Law*'s return to these concerns reinforces our understanding of Wright's reorientation in the second half of his career, an enormously productive period that has yet to receive the critical attention that it deserves.

In brief, *A Father's Law* focuses primarily on Ruddy Turner, a black Catholic, family man, and decorated Chicago police officer, who is prevented from retiring when he is chosen to be the chief of police of Brentwood Park—a wealthy, all-white suburb—after the former chief is killed. His top priorities are to stop the rampant "perversion" in the area and to investigate a series of mysterious unsolved murders—the victims are primarily figures associated with forms of "law," including a preacher, a priest, a nun, and the son of a detective. Ruddy turns to his son, Tommy, for information, as he has been conducting sociological research of the area as part of his studies at the University of Chicago. Tommy is a brilliant student, though he has become increasingly distant from his family, his father in particular, after suddenly ending his engagement with his fiancée, Marie Wiggins. At Ruddy's prompting, Tommy confesses that he ended the relationship after learning that Wiggins has advanced syphilis, which she inherited from her father. Tommy is devastated and refuses to communicate with Wiggins, and Ruddy resolves to support both Tommy and Wiggins unconditionally. Conversations with Tommy and Wiggins lead Ruddy to begin making connections between the unsolved murders and his son, much to his discomfort. Tommy holds radically skeptical views toward all forms of law, legal and religious, which Ruddy finds offensive and disturbing. As Ruddy is forced to begin investigating his own home, he becomes aware of his own repressed feelings of guilt for having once been "seethingly race conscious" and plagued by "wild daydreams" of taking a "smashing potshot at society" (36). Another murder takes place in Brentwood Park, and Tommy's sense of guilt intensifies until he confesses to the killings—an act that symbolically kills Ruddy, as his career and personal life are effectively destroyed.

The reviews of Wright's unfinished novel have been notably mixed, and somewhat predictably the urge to restrict Wright's vision to the realm of racial protest has surfaced again. Amanda Heller observed:

> By 1960 Wright had spent over a decade in self-imposed exile, out of touch with the American idiom and American reality, a problem all too evident here. The language is stilted, and unlike Wright's classics of racial identity, this sketchy novel has virtually nothing to say about race, treating as literally unremarkable the appointment of a black police chief in the Jim Crow America that Wright himself had fled. (Heller)

These remarks echo the sorts of reviews Wright's other postexpatriation novels, *The Outsider* and *The Long Dream*,[4] received. Saunders Redding observed, "'The Long Dream' proves that Wright has been away too long…He has cut the emotional umbilical cord through which his art was fed" (61). Paul Gilroy succinctly captures the critical responses to this phase of Wright's work: "As far as his art was concerned, the move to Europe was disastrous" (156). Heller follows her critical predecessors by implying that Wright's absence from American soil has impaired his ability to adequately address his primary theme: racism.

A Father's Law does in fact have plenty to say about race, but not what we might expect. Ruddy is not only not discriminated against on the force, but his career is also actively advanced by other white officers. The commissioner calls him "one of the finest officers we ever had on our staff," and then toasts him, "Here's to friendship among true men" (39). Ruddy's ranking officer in Brentwood Park tells him, "We're all very happy that you're going to be with us, going to be our chief. I came up through the ranks myself, and I want you to know that I'll be personally proud to serve under you, sir." This pleases Ruddy, especially the "manner in which the captain readily surmounted all jealousies and racial feelings and put police work utmost." These are just two of many examples in which Wright represents the police force as a perfectly harmonious and democratic institution, a masculine meritocracy virtually untouched by racism. Outside of work, when Ruddy moved into a predominantly white neighborhood, he is welcomed, not shunned or harassed: "To his neighbor, Mr. Stonewell Britten, vice-president of the Greenlawn Bank and Loan Association, who had greeted him the morning he had moved in with 'We're damned particular about who lives around here.' Ruddy had said heartily: 'I'm glad to hear that. Now that I'm here, I'm particular *too*.' Yes, things were all right with him" (15, emphasis in original). This exchange is all the more striking in light of Chicago's history of violent conflict around neighborhood integration, which Wright knew all too well.[5]

Moreover, Wright presents Tommy's life as unaffected by racism and, like his father, he garners praise from all around. The police commissioner, for example, congratulates Ruddy on his son's accomplishments, "I've been hearing some wonderful things about that son of yours. Seems like he's burning up those classrooms at the University of Chicago" (40). Tommy has grown up in a financially stable household, with two loving parents, and he has distinguished himself at one of the nation's top universities—he is, in short, a highly privileged young man. And though he comments on socioeconomic concerns over the course of the novel, he makes no mention of ever having experienced any form of racial prejudice, or of harboring any racial resentments of his own. In earlier works, such as *Native Son, Black Boy,* and *The Long Dream,* to name only three of Wright's better-known major texts, the police, schools, and neighborhood associations are instruments of white supremacy, not institutions of democratic inclusion. In his final work, Wright quite conspicuously raises erstwhile scenes of racial subjection in order to recast them outside the protocols of "racial protest."

"Writing is for me a means of being free," Wright observed once, "[it is] a means of defining my relationship with the world and with the society in which I live or which I am observing...." (Kinnamon and Fabre 166). In the mid-twentieth century, however, this was more of an aspiration than a reality, as readers, critics, and publishers insisted on defining his relationship with the world within the narrow confines of "Negro writer." Wright had been privately voicing his frustration at these limitations as early as 1945, when he wrote in his diary:

> This gloomy but sunlit afternoon I've been wondering how I can ditch the literary life and start anew at something else. I've had this yearning many times.... *I know that as long as I live in the United States, I can never change my profession, for I'm regarded fatally as a Negro writer, that is, as a writer whose ancestors were Negroes and therefore the Negro is my special field.* (qtd. in Rowley 307, emphasis added)

Wright was painfully aware that "Negro writer" was a dominant culture construct that violated his writerly privacy by excluding him from the right to creative autonomy that at least in theory is accorded the unmodified title of "writer." Although white authors certainly had to negotiate the compromises demanded by the marketplace, contemporary black writers knew perfectly well that white writers were not restricted a priori to addressing the "problems of white America"; white writers, particularly men, possessed the epistemological authority to analyze any cultural group and theme they chose. Wright's sense that being interpellated as a "Negro writer" constitutes a sort of fatality demonstrates unambiguously the extent to which the category constricted his agency as an author and an individual.

Wright moved to France with his family in 1947 in search of both political and creative freedom. In an interview with novelist William Gardner Smith, Wright pointed out, "My break from the U.S. was more than a geographical change. It was a break with my former attitudes as a Negro and a Communist—an attempt to think over and re-define my attitudes and my thinking" (Fabre 366). His first novel following expatriation, *The Outsider* (1953), indirectly yet insistently addresses the intellectual limitations inherent in the phrase "Negro writer." In a French radio broadcast, Wright commented that "in my novel *The Outsider*, the hero of which was a Negro, I had already abandoned the black hero proper. That novel is anchored mainly in reflection and is concerned with problems that would beset anyone, black or white" (Kinnamon and Fabre 167). Wright told a Dutch interviewer that the main theme of *The Outsider* was "Man without a home, without rest, without peace, in an industrial culture. The main character is a Negro, but he, in contrast to Bigger Thomas in *Native Son,* does not react as a colored person in a dominating white world, but as a human victim of social circumstances" (Kinnamon and Fabre 158).

The Outsider broaches several themes that Wright reintroduces in *A Father's Law,* providing a valuable key to grasping his final work's critical project. I will discuss these themes at more length below, but for the moment I want to address how Wright represents Cross in such a way that attempts to manage reader's expectations regarding "a black hero proper." The narrator tells us that

> Cross's opportunistic rejection of his former life had been spurred by his shame at what a paltry man he had made of himself....His consciousness of the color of his skin had played no role in it. Militating against racial consciousness in him were the general circumstances of his upbringing which had shielded him from the more barbaric forms of white racism; also the insistent claims of his own inner life had made him too concerned with himself to cast his lot wholeheartedly with Negroes in terms of racial struggle....What really obsessed him was his nonidentity, which negated his ability to relate himself to others. (194–95)

In short, in addition to being highly contemplative, Cross's psyche (or sense of self) has suffered no significant racial injury; he is unconcerned with racial struggle, and is "obsessed" not with what it means to be "a black man in a white man's world," but rather with a sense that he has no identity at all, racial or otherwise. The narrator intrudes repeatedly to remind the reader that Cross is not "the black hero proper"—that is, a victim of racial prejudice who can think of nothing beyond his racial traumas. The narrator's repeated insistence on this point conveys a sense that Wright assumes that his audience will be unwilling, or possibly incapable, of believing that Cross could have any motivations, perspectives, attitudes, or desires that were not fundamentally racial—that is, fundamentally "black." "There was no racial tone to his reactions," the narrator tells us, "he was just a man, *any* man who had had an opportunity to flee and had seized upon it" (109, emphasis in original). One of Cross's many ethical dilemmas is when a white woman, Eva, falls in love with him because she imagines him a racially persecuted black man; he wonders, "Could he allow her to love him for his Negritude when being a Negro was the least important thing in his life?…She wanted to love him for his being black because she thought he was an innocent victim" (385–86). These remarks are all attempts by Wright to anticipate and redirect racially reductive readings of his protagonist, and by extension his novel, which considers (alongside racial concerns) such "universal" subjects as whether "man's heart, his spirit, is the deadliest thing in creation" (171).

Notwithstanding these efforts, *The Outsider* was read by early reviewers and critics primarily from a racial lens and the work was faulted for deviating too far from protest into philosophical concerns. Wright went to even greater lengths to avoid these reductionist reading modes in his follow-up novel, *Savage Holiday*, which featured only one minor black character and centered on the emotional chaos experienced by white insurance executive Erskine Fowler when he is forced into early retirement. *Savage Holiday*, like *The Outsider*, anticipates *A Father's Law* in many ways, but most notably through Erskine Fowler who clearly foreshadows Ruddy Turner. Fowler, like Ruddy, is a religious and successful "organization man" deeply committed to his work and exceptionally good at capturing law breakers due to his own repressed feelings of guilty rage. Fowler's feelings stem from his experiences of maternal abandonment, which he compulsively acts out by killing a woman he considers a "bad mother" like his own. Ruddy's guilty rage stems from social causes, racism in particular, which I will discuss below.

Wright may have felt free to recast this character in *A Father's Law* because evidently few people read *Savage Holiday*. Released as a paperback original, *Savage Holiday* sold poorly and received no American reviews.[6] As the response to *The Outsider* and *Savage Holiday* suggest, the critical establishment was quite resistant to Wright's attempts to claim a form of "writerly privacy" by moving beyond an exclusive concern with racial protest. Nevertheless, *The Outsider* and *Savage Holiday* can be seen as rejecting the racist reader's skepticism about a black subject's capacity for philosophical and psychological inquiry as well as the racial liberal reader's desire to feel sympathy for the suffering black other. *A Father's Law* extends the primary concerns of these works, including the interrelationship of family relations, guilt, and crime in the modern West. Wright embeds these themes within the crime story genre, mobilizing its sentimental perspective as a strategy for, once again, managing his readers' search for racial protest to the exclusion of all other topics.

Leonard Cassuto has shown that, despite all appearances, "inside every crime story is a sentimental narrative that's trying to come out" (7). Hard-boiled crime stories convey a sentimental investment in family-oriented ideals of community that can be traced directly to nineteenth-century domestic fiction. Sympathy is at the center of the sentimental worldview, which stresses human connection through "family, community, society, and shared faith—faith in other people and in Christian salvation" (68). The self-sacrificing, women-centered domestic vision of sentimentality functions as a moral bulwark against the destructive influence of market-driven individualism. In contrast, the typical hard-boiled crime story centers on male agency, the failure of communal, domestic ties, and is almost always resolutely secular in its perspective. Even so, according to Cassuto, the genre is no less invested in community and domesticity: "it identifies, embraces, reifies, dances around, or actively opposes the family (or the empty space it once occupied) and the values associated with the family. Crime is a social matter, of course, [but] the social effects of crime start at home" (93). Cassuto, alongside other critics such as Sean McCann, have noted how in post-WWII crime fiction, the heroes become increasingly emotionally involved not merely in their clients' personal lives, but in restoring traditional domestic arrangements as well.[7] The recuperation of the broken family often takes precedence over the murders themselves. The postwar crime story hero steps into "the role once played by the sentimental mother in fiction of the previous century: he actively defends the sentimental worldview based on faith, family, home, and community" (98).

A Father's Law reproduces many of the conventions that shaped the postwar crime story, especially the image of the sentimental law man fighting to protect the endangered family. Along the way, however, Wright critiques the traditional forms of faith that underpin the genre and offers his own sentimental secular alternative, one based on psychological, interracial fraternity. When the self-identified "Micky Irish" police commissioner, Bill King, offers Ruddy the job, he tells him, "I'm trusting you as though you were my own son" (41), establishing unambiguously the sentimental, family-like nature of the bond among the police officers. King charges Ruddy with an explicitly sentimental task, replete with sentimental imagery:

> I want this kidnapping wave stopped. I want all this molesting of young children by perverts stamped out. I want housebreaking cleaned up. I want the streets of Brentwood Park so calm that a six-year-old girl can roll her hoop down the main street without fear, singing her little nursery song. (41)

Moral corruption is rampant, but "the big crime in Brentwood is the sexual molestation of children" (45). Cassuto reminds us that "if the family—or more precisely, the idealized image of the family—became a major Cold War battlefront, the fate of children became its key battleground" (96). Wright's focus on sentimental anxieties about imperiled children in an *affluent* neighborhood allows him to foreground far-ranging psychological and sociological discourses in his investigation of "the meaning of western civilization," beyond the confines of racial protest and social realism. King observes that "if there was ever a locale where emotional factors rather than pure greed figured in crime, it is in Brentwood Park. There are no poor folks in Brentwood, and therefore no so-called class struggle" (56). King concedes that Brentwood Park's high-powered lawyers might prevent Ruddy from making many convictions, yet he insists that he must pursue a higher (and paradigmatically sentimental) objective: "You can harass 'em…you can let 'em know that they are corrupting youth. *You can make 'em feel wrong*" (47, emphasis added). King essentially updates the moral imperative laid down by Harriet Beecher Stowe one century earlier: "There is one thing that every individual can do,—they can see to it that *they feel right*" (385).

Wright's sentimental protagonist stands out in his oeuvre for several reasons. He is universally recognized by other men as an ethical and brave officer not susceptible to corruption, and he is a conscientious and indulgent husband and father. As Ruddy says, "Everything in [his] life is straight, except" his relationship with his "queer" son (6). Ruddy repeatedly associates his son's privacy and intellectual nature with "queer" criminality. He thinks to himself that his son's evasive manner of speaking reminded him of "some of the queer characters he had had to handle at the city jail. Why wasn't Tommy more straightforward?" (6). He chastises himself for being unable to avoid "regard[ing] his son somewhat in the same light that he held the criminals he questioned each day.…There was that withholding of something vital from the outside world that Tommy shared with the lawbreakers Ruddy dealt with day in and day out" (7). Wright reinforces Tommy's "queer" intellectual criminality by having Ruddy think of his son in connection with Cappy Nelson, the paroled convict who killed the former chief of police of Brentwood Park. Nelson was "a university man who had gone wrong" (31). In particular, Ruddy remembers that "he looked like a matinee idol. Quiet, too quiet. Almost sweet. Spoke beautiful English." Nelson "grew up with everything" and was "engaged to marry the daughter of a well-known something-or-other when he was caught robbing his first bank. Was let off through high influence, let off on parole. Then he started his terror" (31). Nelson, like Tommy, is a quiet, privileged, intellectual who attended the University of Chicago. Nelson parallels Tommy in two other important respects; they both "started [their] terror" after breaking off a marital engagement and they both kill the Brentwood Park chief of police—Nelson literally, Tommy symbolically. Nelson's inscrutability and failed relationship acquire a sexual valence when seen in connection with his physical beauty, "sweet" demeanor, and "beautiful English." Moreover, after recalling Nelson, "the image of his own quiet Tommy came compulsively into his mind," but Ruddy reassures himself that "Tommy's not that kind." Ruddy's memory of Nelson's physical and behavioral characteristics conform to mid-twentieth century discourses of homosexuality, including the idea of the "homosexual" as specific "kind" or pathological sexual species.[8]

It is not long after this recollection that Ruddy learns why Tommy ended his engagement with Marie Wiggins. After Ruddy's insistent urging, Tommy admits that the discovery of his fiancée's disease shocks and horrified him to such an extent that he would no longer communicate with her and that it caused him to "[change his] outlook on everything" (91). Tommy and Ruddy "sob" and "weep," and Ruddy then commits to a sentimental solution: "Now, more than ever, he had to be near that boy." Although saddened by Tommy's grief, Ruddy is also particularly worried about the effect that Tommy's "moral" revulsion will have on his relationships with women. "Jesus, I must get that kid a gal," Ruddy thinks, "for I don't want 'im to develop any crazy complexes. Just because one gal is contaminated does not mean that they all are, he reasoned" (93–94). Ruddy's wife, Agnes, expresses the same fear: "He mustn't let this throw 'im, turn him against things in life—like marriage, girls—" (254). Finally, as more concrete evidence starts to emerge connecting Tommy to the murders, Ed Siegel, a fellow officer, asks Ruddy about Tommy's relationship with Charlie Heard, the murdered detective's son:

> "...I'm thinking of a homosexual linkup."
>
> "Oh!" Ruddy was flabbergasted. "No."
>
> "You're sure?"
>
> "Positive. Nothing like that in Tommy."
>
> Yet he was afraid. What did he really know of Tommy?...Ruddy was emotionally inclined to believe that maybe many other things had happened, that the worst could be true. (264)

Although Wright includes considerable evidence connecting Tommy to the murders, he provides no evidence to suggest that Tommy is in fact sexually queer. Questions about Tommy's sexual orientation as well as his queer intellect provide insight mainly into Ruddy's fraught psyche. Above all, Ruddy is anxious about *Tommy's resistance to being incorporated within the coordinates of sentimentality*—family, home, and especially forms of community structured around faith in God, man, and their representative institutions. Tommy's thoughts and behaviors function as a critique of Ruddy's sentimental investments as well as those of the crime story genre. The plots of postwar crime fiction are ultimately centered on protecting the idea of the family. When Ruddy takes on his new position, he believes he will be protecting and restoring families in Brentwood Park, but he literally and figuratively must turn to his own home to conduct his duties. Unlike most of Wright's work, and unlike most postwar crime fiction, there is very little external action and there are no direct representations of violence. *A Father's Law* is propelled by the emotional tension that derives from Ruddy's conflicting sentimental objectives. Ruddy does what the sentimental cop and father are supposed to do—fight to protect the family. But these sentimental objectives are at odds in *A Father's Law*. Ruddy hopes that by getting to know his son, he can establish the "healthy father-and-son relationship he had always wanted and dreamed of" and also learn how to better protect the families of Brentwood Park (6). These sentimental desires lead him unexpectedly to "know" himself, however, and his self-knowledge as well as the knowledge that he gains of and from his son constitute a direct challenge to the epistemological underpinnings of the traditional sentimental crime narrative.

During one of the first conversations that Ruddy has with Tommy about his research in Brentwood Park, he asks Tommy if he knows of any reason that anyone would have wanted to kill Charles Heard, the detective's son. Tommy laughs, and responds that in his studies they ask instead "Why is Charles not being killed? ... *What is it that keeps people from killing Charles?* That takes us into history, into law, into the ideals by which we live" (71–72, emphasis in original). Tommy believes that laws are not predicated on objective notions of truth or justice, but historically specific belief systems.

Every now and then in history men meet, argue, fight, and finally embalm their so-called beliefs in great documents. The Bill of Rights. The Rights of Man. The Magna Carta, and so on. But history rolls on. Slowly time, usage, progress, saps the meaning of those documents.

Inventions, discoveries, etc., made those documents useless....*But the people did not know it.* So they went on living by the word of those documents while they really obeyed the living spirit of their times....Who's breaking those laws [in Brentwood Park]? Bad men? Gangsters? Thieves? NO! The men whose forebears made those laws. Why? Because they don't really believe in those laws anymore; they don't feel the need for them. The laws don't serve their interests anymore. (74, emphasis in original)

Tommy offers a notably Nietzschean perspective on law and social order, arguing that the passage of time and new forms of knowledge render laws "useless" by destroying the meanings and values embedded in those laws, and thus also rendering inoperative, at least subjectively, the norms governing social relations embedded therein. The scientific and intellectual advances produced under the conditions of Western modernity, Tommy argues, radically challenge the validity and efficacy of law, undercutting its capacity for permanently adjudicating between right and wrong, good and bad. Tommy's perspective cuts against a central idea in crime stories, that "bad men," gangsters, and thieves can be identified and punished. Criminality itself becomes a fundamentally unstable concept, which Tommy makes clear by insisting that the people breaking laws in Brentwood Park are not criminals: "No. They're just folks having a good time" (74). The Brentwood Park residents' social privilege gives them both a critical perspective on the law as well as the social and economic capital to flout it. They are "outside" the law, which to them has lost its disciplinary effect and moral authority.

Tommy's remarks are abstract, historical, and philosophical. His monologue is not a protest against racial or economic oppression—to the contrary, even though the residents of Brentwood Park are rich and white, he demonstrates that he not only understands their position as legal outsiders but also identifies with this condition, though for different reasons. Wright addresses this issue at length in *The Outsider,* in which the "outsider" detective, Ely Houston, points out that there are outsiders in society who exist because they "are so placed in life by accident of race or birth or chance that what they see is terrifying" (133). As outsiders, they become "psychological men" and "centers of *knowing,* so to speak" (129) capable of recognizing that "maybe the whole effort of man on earth to build a civilization is *simply* man's frantic attempt to hide himself from himself," especially from the awareness that "man may be just anything at all" (135, emphasis in original). Tommy is an outsider not because of his race, but because of "chance"—it is purely an accident that the woman he intended to marry inherited a disease and that his shock at the discovery of this accident "changed the way he saw everything." This shocking, accidental occurrence, coupled with his intellectual nature, places him outside sentimentality's disciplinary loci—the law, the domestic sphere, and religion—and, from Ruddy's perspective, renders him "queer."

Ruddy, in contrast, spends his life in a "frantic attempt to hide himself from himself." He started out a "colored man, poor, alone, not too well schooled; and he felt that the world in which he lived was so much better than he was" (34). The narrator describes him as having been "taken in" by the police force as a young man (much like Fowler, who was "taken in" by his employer at the age of thirteen). Ruddy was plagued by feelings of guilt and criminality, not because he had committed any serious crimes, but from "literally, [having] no life before him . . . the sheer void of his existence was a thing that made him feel more guilty than any deed he could remember" (34). Even deeper than this is the guilt he feels for having once been "seethingly race-conscious" as a young man, plagued by "wild day-dreams" of attacking the "world that excluded him . . ." (34). He learns to channel all of this guilty rage and angst, however, and is amazed to discover, as Fowler does, "that it was this hidden sense of guilt that aided him in ferreting out breakers of the law, and the more lawbreakers he caught, the calmer he became. . . . When he nabbed the guilty, he felt a deep degree of moral satisfaction" (35–36). Ruddy, unlike the "lawless" residents of Brentwood Park, not only believes in but desperately needs the laws: "He loved the laws and rules of the community with an abiding and intense passion. He lived, after all, by enforcing the laws and wishes of that community" (26). Ruddy and Fowler both are what Cross Damon would call "a moral slave, the slave who believes in the ideas that are given to him" (Wright, *The Outsider* 567). Unlike Fowler, though, Ruddy clings to and enforces the laws of the community as a way to manage his guilt for once feeling rage at "literally [having] no life," that is, for his experience of social death as a poor, uneducated black man. It is tempting to view Ruddy's psychic struggles entirely in terms of race, but the striking similarities that Ruddy shares with Fowler show that their racial differences are less important than their similarities in terms of Wright's larger investigation of how "man" adapts to the conditions of Western modernity. Ruddy and Fowler are what we might call brothers under the skin, specific types of modern Western men who despite their contrasting socioeconomic backgrounds share a similar psychic core—they are both "moral slaves" who cling to the disciplinary function of law and religion (however atavistic) because it allows them to avoid facing their own "hearts," their own guilty feelings of repressed rage.

Ruddy, "the moral slave," proudly believes that "all you had to do was *master yourself*" (36, emphasis added). Wright shatters Ruddy's self-mastery, however, in a scene that stands out precisely in terms of its failed sentimentality. Ruddy takes on the sentimental errand of finding Marie Wiggins, his son's spurned fiancée, in order to offer her solace. She is suffering alone, in a state of total despair and guilty self-loathing: "Never in all of his police work had he seen a criminal more abject than this girl, more claimed by a sense of guilt, more ready to accept all that could be said against her" (117). Even though she has done nothing wrong, both she and Ruddy "knew that the world would have sided with [Tommy in abandoning her] had all the facts been publicly known. How much could one ask of another in the act of love?" (118). Apparently, not much. Although he feels a "burning compassion for this girl... he could not still in him a raging revulsion" (120). Torn between compassion and abhorrence, Ruddy declares that "we must save you," as a "stab of pain stitched at his heart" (121–22). He gives her $200 and promises to give her $20 a week for payment of her syphilis treatment. When she protests, he insists that " 'this money is clean. It's from my heart... Oh, Marie, life is hard,' he half moaned, feeling hot tears stinging his eyes" (122). Ruddy, the socially privileged moral agent, feels the suffering other's pain in his heart, the seat of noble sentiment, and attempts to mollify her suffering with his tears and money. Wright introduces all of the classic signs of redemptive sympathy, however, only to show their inadequacy. He is unwilling to touch her hand, for example, when giving her the money, and instead places it on the bed. He is also unable to mask his disgust, prompting Wiggins to say, " 'I know that you think I'm poisoned. You're just like all the others,' she wailed. '...It is *horrible*,' she insisted. 'I saw it in Tommy's eyes. I see it in yours. And in my mother's eyes. Everybody's eyes' " (122). Syphilis trumps sympathy, as Wiggins feels rejected by the entire world, including her own mother, the archetypal figure of sympathy in the sentimental worldview.

Most striking, however, is the degree to which Ruddy himself is "abjected" when faced with Wiggins's abject condition. Julia Kristeva's notion of abjection is particularly helpful in understanding Ruddy's response. Kristeva describes abjection as the corporeal, psychological, and epistemological crisis one experiences when faced with that which "disturbs identity, system, order. What does not respect borders, positions, rules" (4). Although she cites certain kinds of "food, a piece of filth, waste, or dung" as items that induce this reaction, nothing reaches the level of "the corpse, seen without God and outside of science.... it is death infecting life." Kristeva argues that these things "show me what I permanently thrust aside in order to live." Wiggins, though not a literal corpse, is a "poisoned" and "rotten" girl who spends her days locked away in a dark room, like a prisoner, with a "greenish pallor about her skin" (115, 117, 119). Her sickness fills Ruddy with horror precisely because it "does not respect" the forms of "identity, system, and order" that Ruddy relies on "in order to live." Prior to this encounter with Wiggins, Ruddy "had always found some way to convince himself that those who were caught in the meshes of the law or who were in trouble, had only themselves to blame. But how could he blame Marie? Or Tommy? No, he could not" (124). Ruddy sees Wiggins and Tommy as "innocent victims," and what most "shatter[s]" "his traditionally rigid view of the world, a view outlined and buttressed by law" is that their suffering comes from a "higher law that overruled or could overrule the law he knew and executed" (125). Even more disturbing for Ruddy is the way in which Tommy's and Wiggins's suffering is transmitted through the act of "love": "It was that 'love' aspect that presented the problem! The hurt that had come had descended not with violence, not with assault, not with theft, but when all human defenses were down and the heart was open." This hurt is "all the more confounding because there is no one to blame or to forgive" (126). Wiggins's suffering invalidates Ruddy's sentimental tools of survival: God, law, and love. To borrow Kristeva's phrasing, Wiggins is for Ruddy "the place where meaning collapses" (2).

After his encounter with Wiggins, Ruddy feels extremely disoriented and intentionally avoids returning to his own domestic space, preferring instead the emotional shelter afforded by his professional identity: "From out of the depths of him, there flashed the vague and comforting image of an office, his office, the official home he had out there in far-off Brentwood Park" (127). Kristeva reminds us that the abjected subject becomes an "exile" or a "stray," leading the individual to ask "'*Where* am I?' instead of '*Who* am I?'" The thought of Ruddy's office, however, partially reestablishes the psychological boundaries that Wiggins's condition erased. "He was now psychologically organized again, a policeman on duty, an efficient officer upholding the law, an officer on a mission, on guard, alert" (127). Wiggins's suffering transforms his actual home from a haven to an implicitly diseased space; Ruddy shudders with horror that a "tainted stream of life had run close past his door and actually brushed itself against his own flesh and blood" (94). He prefers instead his "official home," because "he was frightened and he wanted the protection of the power of his office" (124). His office symbolizes the moral and epistemological certainty that Wiggin's condition destabilizes. In this instance, Wright makes clear that Ruddy's career of fighting crime and protecting families has been essentially compensatory, evidence of moral lack and psychological weakness, rather than virtue. Ruddy is so susceptible to Wiggins's suffering because he too formerly felt like an "innocent victim" whose life had been "poisoned" by vast, impersonal, and implacable forces (35). In Wright's crime story, it is an innocent act of *love* that "poisons" the family. Traditional, faith-based, domestic sentimentality is utterly ineffectual.

In the end, however, social order is at least partially restored—notably, within the Chicago police force, a community predicated on *secular, intellectual,* and *interracial* sympathy. This symbolic restoration occurs principally through Ruddy's relationship with the Jewish officer Ed Siegel, a member of "an unpopular minority" and "the intellectual among the cops" (26, 23). Although Ruddy has supportive, mutually sustaining bonds with officers above and below his position, he comes to rely on the friendship and insight of Siegel in particular. At least intellectually, Siegel rivals Tommy as the character whose perspectives most seem to resemble Wright's. It is Siegel who alerts Ruddy to the fact that Tommy is "onto the new idea about crime…that criminals ought not to be punished," but treated psychologically.[9] He is also the first to suggest that the Brentwood Park murders are related and that the killer has "transfigured" the victims in his mind: "It was law that the murderer struck at…When Churches and policemen are attacked, the law is attacked" (144). He and Tommy even briefly exchange ideas about guilt, crime, and the superego (209). Nothing solidifies his status as authorial surrogate more, however, than when he advocates for "more crime novels, crime movies" (200)—presumably ones like this one—in order to develop greater insight into the motives for crime.

Siegel is no cold egghead, though. He and Ruddy share more than one warm, feeling-laden exchange. After Ruddy selects him to be a part of his personal staff,

> Ed came from around the desk and stood facing Ruddy. "Ruddy, you didn't forget me, did you?"
> "Drop dead," Ruddy said, embarrassed.

"I'm grateful for the first promotion I've had in fifteen years," Ed
    said with a husky voice.
"You deserve it," Ruddy said....
"You're a straight guy, Ruddy," Ed said.
"You're straight too, Ed. You've been a friend of mine ever since you
    came on the force."
"That's natural."
"Sometimes."
"With me, friendship always comes natural." (134–35)

Later, as the evidence points more definitely toward Tommy as the
murderer, Ruddy longs to "[enlist] Ed's sympathy and wisdom," and
once he does, Siegel immediately responds, "approv[ing] of the apparent openness" (262). Unlike Ruddy, Siegel is neither compromised by
moral ambiguity nor afraid of considering "dangerous" new ideas. As
a member of an "unpopular minority," he possesses outsider knowledge, but he works within the law to protect society with compassion
and insight. As the novel abruptly closes with Tommy's confession,
"the scepter of moral leadership in the office of the chief of police
passed from Ruddy to his friend Ed; it passed without a word, without a gesture" (268). Thus, "the father's law" is redeemed through
a fairly stunning intellectual and racial reconfiguration—stunning in
light of Wright's highly critical treatment of racism and corruption
among the police in earlier narratives.[10]

There is no doubt that race matters in Wright's final work, but he
carefully employs key conventions of the crime story genre, especially
its sentimental orientation, to keep race from over-determining the
narrative's larger speculative project about guilt and crime under the
conditions of western modernity. Siegel states that the murders in
Brentwood Park "speak a kind of cryptic language" (136):

"there was something that murderer wanted to say...."
"To whom?"...
"S-suppose his audience was the w-world...m-mankind." (142)

Wright, like the black, queer intellectual Tommy, is using murder as a
language to speak to the world, not simply about African Americans as
suffering objects of racial oppression, but about the state of "man"—
black, white, and other—and "his heart" under the conditions of
modernity. Of course, the latter contains the former, as Wright made
clear in "How Bigger was Born." His readers, nevertheless, often
proved incapable of applying so capacious and weighty a category to

"Negro" subjects. It is with this readerly resistance in mind that we can appreciate how Wright's "queer" depiction of the Chicago police force (as a sentimental interracial meritocracy) was in the service of a "queer" desire—a desire for the "writerly privacy" necessary to claim an expansive moral and intellectual authority. Wright spent the second half of his career deflecting the Jim Crow biases that would deny him writerly privacy, and along the way produced a series of works that rendered him, in Robert Reid-Pharr's phrasing, "the funny father" of black American literature—simultaneously the figure most closely associated with, and yet radically skeptical of, the modern racial protest novel.[11]

NOTES

1. Because Ruddy and Tommy share a last name, I most often refer to these characters by their first names; the rest of the characters I reference by their last name.
2. One need only think of the centrality of Bigger's relationships with Jan and Max in *Native Son* (1940), and Cross Damon's relationship with Ely Houston in *The Outsider* (1953), to name only two of the most obvious examples.
3. On July 8, 1959, Wright wrote a long letter to Paul Oliver proposing the creation of an ambitious crime magazine: "At the present moment there exists a flood of material about crime, and I'm an avid reader of this material.... Since this hunger exists for crime stories, why cannot there be an intelligent crime magazine, international in scope and content, appealing frankly and in a civilized manner to intelligent readers?"
4. *Savage Holiday,* Wright's "white" novel, received no American reviews.
5. See, for example, Hirsch.
6. According to Fabre, *Savage Holiday* received positive reviews in the French press; it also received one positive Dutch review (see "Barbaarse Sabbath").
7. See McCann. Cassuto singles out works such as Raymond Chandler's *The Long Goodbye* (1953) and John D. MacDonald's *You Live Once* (1956) as displaying these notably domestic concerns.
8. Foucault has famously described the emergence of the homosexual as a specific kind, a sexual "species," as a phenomenon beginning in the nineteenth century. The idea of the hetero-homosexual binary had increasingly come under attack among experts in the mid-twentieth century, most notably in the 1948 Kinsey Report on male sexuality, which reported that male same sexuality was far more common than originally believed. The average citizen responded to these scientific critiques not by relinquishing a belief in binary notions of sexuality, but by attempting to police the differences all the more vigilantly, especially among juveniles who were purportedly more susceptible to influence and corruption.

9. Wright, of course, was a well-known supporter of Harlem's Lafargue Clinic. See, for example, Doyle.

10. White supremacy, corruption, and brutality characterize the police in Wright's last published novel, *The Long Dream* (1958), which appeared less than two years before he wrote *A Father's Law*. With the notable exception of Eli Houston in *The Outsider,* most of Wright's treatments of the police fit the mold presented in *The Long Dream.*

11. See chapter 1 of *Once You Go Black: Choice Desire, and the Black American Intellectual.*

BIBLIOGRAPHY

"Barbaarse Sabbath." Folder 718, Box 61. Richard Wright Papers. Yale Collection of American Literature, Beinecke Rare Book and Manuscript Library, Yale University Library. Print.

Cassuto, Leonard. *Hard-Boiled Sentimentality: The Secret History of American Crimes Stories.* New York: Columbia UP, 2009. Print.

Doyle, Dennis. "'A Fine New Child': The Lafargue Mental Hygiene Clinic and Harlem's African American Communities, 1946–1958." *Journal of the History of Medicine and Allied Sciences* 64.2 (2009): 173–212. Print.

Fabre, Michel. *The Unfinished Quest of Richard Wright.* Urbana: U of Illinois P, 1993. Print.

Gilroy, Paul. *The Black Atlantic: Modernity and Double Consciousness.* Cambridge, MA: Harvard UP, 1993. Print.

Heller, Amanda. "Short Takes: A Father's Law." *Boston Globe* 13 Jan. 2008. Web.

Hirsch, Arnold R. *Making the Second Ghetto: Race and Housing in Chicago, 1940–1960.* Historical Studies of Urban America. Chicago: U of Chicago P, 1998. Print.

Kinnamon, Keneth, and Michel Fabre, eds. *Conversations with Richard Wright.* Jackson: UP of Mississippi, 1993. Print.

Kristeva, Julia. *Powers of Horror: An Essay on Abjection.* Trans. Leon. S. Roudiez. New York: Columbia UP, 1982. Print.

McCann, Sean. *Gumshoe America: Hard-Boiled Fiction and the Rise and the Fall of New Deal Liberalism.* Durham, NC: Duke UP, 2000. Print.

Powers, Ron. "Ambiguities." *New York Times* 24 Feb. 2008. Web.

Redding, Saunders. Rev. of *The Long Dream,* by Richard Wright. *Richard Wright: Critical Perspectives Past and Present.* Eds. Henry Louis Gates and K. A. Appiah. New York: Amistad, 1993. Print.

Reid-Pharr, Robert. *Once You Go Black: Choice Desire, and the Black American Intellectual.* New York: New York UP, 2007. Print.

Rowley, Hazel. *Richard Wright: The Life and Times.* New York: Holt, 2001. Print.

Stowe, Harriet Beecher. *Uncle Tom's Cabin or, Life among the Lowly.* 1852. New York: Penguin Books, 1981. Print.

Wright, Richard. *A Father's Law.* New York: Harper Perennial, 2008. Print.

————. Letter to Paul Oliver. July 8, 1959. Michel Fabre Papers. Emory University. Print.

————. *The Outsider.* New York: Harper and Row, 1953. New York: Harper Perennial, 2008. Print.

————. *Savage Holiday.* New York: Avon, 1954. Ed. Gerald Early. Jackson: UP of Mississippi, 1994. Print.

PART IV

WRIGHT: NEW COMPARATIVE FRAMEWORKS, TRANSNATIONAL BOUNDARIES

Revealing the importance of censorship, critical reception, influence, and hemispheric studies in Wright's work, part 4 analyzes the genetic and intertextual dimensions of his writing. In particular, it looks anew at how the activist roots of African American literary history have enriched the ultimate value of that history. Claudine Raynaud's "Changing Texts: Censorship, 'Reality' and Fiction in *Native Son*" weds recent work on censorship and genetic criticism with her study of the censored Harper version of *Native Son* (1940) and The Library of America restored version (1991). Through a "critical genetic reading," she compares "the inscriptions of the sexual and racial body" in the two texts in order to demonstrate that Wright's truth claims differ and refract when the two texts are put side by side. Censorship in the guise of editorial practices must be reassessed, Raynaud asserts, because it affects ideas central to Wright's writing—"overdetermination, intraracial and interracial sexuality, the black male subject's psychic makeup and the traces of the sexed body in the text." Raynaud contends that Wright chartered a fresh course in his use of racialized sexuality as a metaphor for the perplexed human being trapped in circumstances beyond his or her control.

Julieann Veronica Ulin's essay, "'The Astonishing Humanity': Domestic Discourses in the Friendship and Fiction of Richard Wright and Carson McCullers," follows Raynaud and breaks ground within her own comparative framework. Ulin shows how the critical and personal relationship between Wright and Carson McCullers had a profound impact on their "mutual treatment of racial housing discrimination." Then Ulin applies their shared response to segregated housing to understanding Wright's later writing and his ultimate cultural alienation. Emphasizing their exchanges also provides important clues for understanding McCullers's "deep indebtedness" to Wright, seen especially in McCullers's *A Clock without Hands* (1961). Ulin discusses the critical silence surrounding McCullers's mixed-race protagonist and the correspondences between her text and *Native Son*. She then analyses *Clock without Hands* in light of this intertextuality. Like Davis and Soto, Ulin examines Wright's textually located revelations of America's "democratic claims," asking new questions about the relation of race to "spatial transgressions." Through Wright's literary constructions of the domestic—*via* McCullers's biography and fiction—Ulin shows us another social meaning of Wright's modernism.

Gary E. Holcomb's "When Wright Bid McKay Break Bread: Tracing Black Transnational Genealogy" makes a different kind of comparison. According to Holcomb, we should understand Wright's self-imposed exile in terms of "the genealogical relationship between Claude McKay as recuperated transnational father and Wright as self-exiled, prodigal, *transnative* son." Like Ulin, Holcomb examines vital social and racial truths about black authorship, in this case, during the interwar period. He argues that while both Wright and McKay had an impact on reshaping modernist writing, McKay's transnationalism ultimately determined the path of Wright's transatlantic, "revolutionary routes." An essential figure allowing Wright to see "the revolutionary potential in the transnational," McKay influenced Wright's later language of black transnationalism. Holcomb's essay expands the assessment of McKay's influence on Wright while providing a valuable general critique of Wright's connections to other black émigré authors.

Robert Shulman's "The Political Art of Wright's 'Fire and Cloud'" establishes that Wright constantly uses his inherited cultural roots and available literary forms in order to construct new ones. Shulman argues that in "Fire and Cloud" (1938), a prize-winning story set in the rural South, Wright provides a complex fusion of Marxist and Christian teleologies that anticipate late twentieth-century liberation theology. Wright not only shows the Popular Front's involvement in traditional Americanism then but also illustrates how political protest can be anchored in such American literary traditions as the Jeremiad. "Fire and Cloud" employs, in Wright's own words, "a Marxist analysis of society" to "create the myths and symbols that inspire faith in life." At the same time, Wright does not believe that we perceive only according to established religious or political forms grounded in national attributes. His desire to locate a single African American cultural matrix runs alongside his broader concern for racial, political, and cultural alterity and the effects of such alterity on his evolving literary aesthetic. Wright's distinctive take on Marxist analysis stayed with him his entire life, as Shulman notes, but also became a crucial part of his modernist vision.

Finally, John Lowe's "Richard Wright and the CircumCaribbean" argues for an international, hemispheric reconfiguration of Wright through a focus on his "especially strong influence on Caribbean writers." Through his comparative framework, Lowe illuminates Wright's conception of the United States, the Caribbean, and Africa as a kind of "triangular Black Atlantic." He compares Wright to the Barbadian novelist George Lamming, and specifically Wright's *Black Boy* to Lamming's *In the Castle of My Skin* (1953), which were already explicitly linked through Wright's published introduction to Lamming's novel. Lowe demonstrates that Wright and Lamming deployed their respective native settings to illuminate conditions and possibilities for American and Caribbean blacks. The rootless nature of Wright's exile allows him to posit a new hemispheric home, a new sense of belonging within a black diaspora that he finds crossing the boundaries imposed upon him by his native South. By extension, Lowe traces Wright's interest in diasporan history and his unfinished project in which he hoped to show the richness and variety of "black cultures in France." This careful scrutiny of the Wright-Lamming link helps to construct a more complicated and detailed *hemispheric* history of African American writing in the 1950s.

10

CHANGING TEXTS: CENSORSHIP, "REALITY," AND FICTION IN *NATIVE SON*

Claudine Raynaud

"Like Bigger himself, I felt a mental censor [...] standing over me, draped in white, warning me not to write [...]"

(LA 867)[1]

This paper will rely on a critical genetic reading of the censoring of *Native Son* (1940) from the point of view of the textual representation of subjectivity, race, and sexuality.[2] When the full text of *Native Son* is restored, as it is in the 1991 edition of The Library of America, the psychic makeup of Bigger Thomas—insofar as it can derived from the text—greatly differs from that generated by the expurgated version. We are reading another text. When one knows that the novel aimed at depicting young black boys' behavior with scientific precision within a deterministic framework, this erasure must be questioned, and not only in terms of a reader's reception. At the time of the publication of Arnold Rampersad's restored edition, numerous Wright scholars addressed the impact of these changes (e.g., Kinnamon, *New Essays* 1–33; Miller). When juxtaposing the moving texture of writing, one could indeed analyze the incidences of the play between the written and the censured, the "projected" and what had actually been retained. Edward Aswell's intervention for stylistic improvement, Wright's interferences with the character—the erasure of Bigger's understanding of communism to make him into a cruder, more naive black youth, for instance—and his numerous deletions in part III, have already been noted. My aim here is to focus on the cumulative effects of the changes in the grain of the text by paying close attention to the inscriptions of the sexual and racial body in both versions.

I. THE TEXT OR "HOW
'BIGGER' WAS EMASCULATED"

In his essay *How "Bigger" Was Born*, Wright directly addresses questions of genesis as he discloses how certain scenes were written into the thread of the novel after the fact.[3] Such is the case of the opening scene when Bigger battles the rat. Wright states: "[T]he rat would not leave me; he presented himself in many attractive guises. So, cautioning myself to allow the rat scene to disclose *only* Bigger, his family, their little room, and their relationships, I let the rat walk in, and he did his stuff" (LA 880). Wright also rewrote scenes that were torn out and added others: "For example, the entire guilt theme that runs through *Native Son* was woven in *after* the first draft was written" (LA 880). After explaining at great length how Bigger is a conflation of various types he had met throughout his life, he also acknowledges that his source was the news items of the *Chicago Tribune*: "Many of the newspaper items and some of the incidents in *Native Son* are but fictionalized versions of the Robert Nixon case and rewrites of news stories of the *Chicago Tribune*" (LA 875).[4] In other words, the factual basis of the story and its plot is vital to Wright, even if, in the Nixon case, the news item corroborated what was already written (see Kinnamon, "Native Son"; Fabre, *La Quête Inachevée* 127–40). Yet Wright claims that the truth of Bigger Thomas lies in the emotions produced by language, and not in verisimilitude: "That was the deep fun of the job: to feel within my body that I was pushing out to new areas of feeling, strange landmarks of emotion, tramping upon foreign soil, compounding new relationships of perceptions, making new and—until that very split second of time!—*unheard-of and unfelt effects with words*" (LA 877, emphasis mine).

Wright's posture in relation to truth and writing is de facto challenged when one reads the intended draft and the excised and rewritten versions side by side, since the effects of each text differ and at times even diverge. The omissions bear on explicitly sexual content, enlargements, the erasure of substantial portions of text, and substitutions that modify the perception of Bigger's psychology and overall, the poetics and politics of the text. Let us state Wright's position again in relation to verisimilitude and effect: "If a scene seemed improbable to me, I'd not tear it up, but ask myself: 'Does it not reveal enough of *what I feel to stand in spite of its unreality*?' If I felt it did, it stood. If I felt that it did not, I ripped it out" (LA 877, emphasis mine). Consequently, if the scene was only ripped out after the Book of the Month Club's intervention, one must assume that it had been previously deemed necessary to reflect the "truth" as Wright felt it. Wright asserts nothing less here than the radical novelty of his writing, its modernism (Fabre, "Beyond Naturalism?" 37–57).

The perceived "rawness" of certain scenes drew the censors' attention as it might have jeopardized publication. Indeed, when *Native Son* was considered for the Book of the Month Club, the editors demanded that passages deemed offending for the readership be expurgated.[5] Edward Aswell writes Wright on August 22, 1939:

> And incidentally the Book Club wants to know whether, if they do choose *Native Son*, you would be willing to make some changes in that scene early in the book where Bigger and his friends are sitting in the moving picture theatre. I think you will recognize the scene I mean and will understand why the Book Club finds it objectionable. They are not a particularly squeamish crowd, but that scene, after all, is a bit on the raw side. I daresay you could revise it in a way to suggest what happens rather than to tell it explicitly. Please let me hear about this as soon as possible so that I can convey your answer to the Book Club. (Beinecke, Box 98, Folder 1378)

The sole focus of the censors' argument on sexuality explains that the more traumatic rawness of the murder scene when Bigger decapitates Mary's body remained untouched while the sexually graphic was methodically removed. When Arnold Rampersad published the restored version for the Library of America in 1991, Ellen and Julia Wright were themselves extremely explicit:

> It is important to us that Bigger Thomas who was "castrated" because deprived of his sexual life in the edited 1940 text is made whole again— and made human—by the reinstatement of the masturbation scene at the beginning of *Native Son* and of references to his guilt-ridden desire for the rich white Mary prior to the panic which leads him to smother her accidentally. (Wright, 1992 in Butler, 1995)

Ironically, the black man's emasculation by dominant white culture, a theme central to *Native Son*, is duplicated almost literally by the excision of the novel's sexual content.[6] Yet since most cuts bear on overtly sexual notations, other than Bigger's, the other characters' sexuality is also tamed down in the process. In fact, it is the complexity of same race and interracial sexual relations that has been tampered with. Only a close analysis of the scenes brings out the full consequences of such changes and reveals "new relationships of perceptions."

II. Masturbation as "No Man's Land"

The changes made reverberate the opposition at the center of Bigger's consciousness: his double rejection. They also mirror the persisting difficulty of writing black manhood within the historical and cultural text of the American nation. According to Wright, Bigger is "unclaimed": "What made Bigger's social consciousness most complex was the fact that he was hovering unwanted between two worlds— between powerful America and his own stunted place in life—and I took upon myself the task of trying to make the reader feel this *No Man's land*" (LA 870–71, emphasis mine).[7] By crossing out mentions of masturbation, of erection, of sexual desire, Wright "stunts" his hero of his sexuality, modifies the truth of his character—and consequently of the other characters—as he bows to the Book of the Month Club's requests. As is evident, these revisions ironically play on the stereotype of the black male, his fantasized sexual potency being a threat to the white racial order; they bear on the configuration of black masculinity (Dawahare; Miller; Ross). Kinnamon speaks of a "highly sexed" Bigger, less congenial to bankers' daughters than the 1940 model (*New Essays* 15).

The first scene that offended the censors was the "masturbation scene." Bigger and Jack leave the poolroom—that scene was initially the opening scene of the book—and walk along the street. They decide to go to the movies at the Regal Theatre where *Trader Horn* (1931) is showing (LA 472). The two boys masturbate before the beginning of the show. They have planned the attack on Blum's store and share their feelings about it. Bigger's emotions are showing through at the beginning of the sequence: "He moved restlessly and his breath quickened" (LA 472). The jokes that the two youths share reverberate on the text itself. The mention of "the pipe organ [that was] playing low and soft" (LA 472) finds a development in the crude metaphor Bigger uses for his own sex: "I'm polishing my nightstick" (LA 472). The Harper version turns that mention into the following convoluted description: "The picture had not started and he slouched far down in a seat and listened to a pipe organ shudder in waves of nostalgic tone, like a voice humming hauntingly within him. He moved restlessly, looking round as though expecting to see someone sneaking upon him. The organ sang forth full, then dropped almost to silence" (LA 924).

Once the explicit sexual content has been excised, the pipe organ bears traces of the erasure of the actual sexual act, that of tumescence and deflation: it sings forth and drops. It is also linked to the "voice"/organ of the main protagonist, a voice that is ironically under assault in these excisions.[8] The 1940 version thus makes the elision explicit by internalizing Bigger's voice and by constructing his paranoid feeling as ventriloquism. The original version, on the contrary, shows the two adolescents bragging and shamelessly engaged in that sexual act. Indeed, both young men comment on their sexual prowess, "You pull off fast" (LA 473), and also conjure up their black girlfriends, Bessie for Bigger Thomas and Clara for Jack: "I wished I had Bessie here now," Bigger said. "I could make old Clara moan now." (LA 473). That the mention of Bessie disappears tilts the balance over toward interracial attraction. This first erasure of Bessie foreshadows Bessie's position vis-à-vis Mary Dalton in the text, in the attention that mimetically critics pay to her character, and in the trial scene where Mary's bare bones are proof of a rape that did not take place while Bessie's actual rape and murder are constructed solely as "evidence" of that same nonoccurrence, along with the series of objects exhibited.

Having killed Mary Dalton by mistake, Bigger goes to see Bessie and has sex with her. He later rapes her and kills her.[9] In the section when he meets Bessie just after the murder, the following sentence is omitted: "To let her know that he wanted her he allowed her to draw his tongue into her mouth" (LA 567) and changed into "To let her know that he loved her he circled her with his arm and squeezed her tightly" (LA 931). The incidence of that omission is a taming down of the reality of sex between a black man and a black woman: "want" becomes "love," the clinical mechanical description of a kiss turns into a love embrace.[10] Boris Max's later depiction of the relationship between Bigger and Bessie at the trial stresses need rather than love, and the essential aloneness of the two protagonists: "He had to have a girl, so he had Bessie. But he did not love her. Is love possible to the life of a man I've described to this Court? Let us see. Love is not based on sex alone, and this is all he had with Bessie" (LA 822). The whole question of *Native Son* is whether Max's depiction of Bigger is a plea, the reality of his experience, or/and a correct interpretation of what the reader has been given to read. Close analysis of the text shows that both Boris Max and the prosecution give their own ideologically slanted versions of Bigger's reality. That "reality" can only be accessed through the text of Bigger's thoughts and actions and they are fraught with tensions.

Images of Mary's body from the night before understandably come to Bigger as he makes love to Bessie. The following sentence, "He placed his hands on her breasts just as he had placed them on Mary's last night and *he was thinking of that* while he kissed her" (LA 569, emphasis mine), has been replaced in the 1940 edition by "He leaned over her, full of desire, and lowered his head to hers and kissed her" (LA 931).[11] Bigger is thinking of his gesture, and of the repetition of that gesture, rather than of Mary in a literalization of the compulsion to repetition that governs his actions. Globally, graphic details that make the black female body more visible, and hence more present, are erased in the transposition to make room for more abstract notions. "Love" is now replaced by "desire." The consequences of these changes parallel both Bigger's murder of Bessie and his subsequent decision to get rid of her body by throwing it down the airshaft. They also reflect on his musings that there were not one, but two Bessies, a body and a face: "One a body that he had just had and wanted badly again; the other was in Bessie's face; it asked questions; it bargained and sold the other Bessie to advantage" (LA 575). This excess of physicality of Bessie's body, of Bessie as body in the text, has been tamed down, detracting the reader from one of the tensions between Bigger and Bessie: their relation to sexuality and emotional bonding.

Two other inscriptions of the black female body are also deleted in that early sex scene: "and he slept in her body" and "he lay *looking* in the darkness *at the shadowy outline of Bessie's body*" (LA 570). In the Harper edition, the latter was typically changed into "...and he lay in the darkness, *gazing with vacant eyes* at the *shadowy ceiling*" (LA 932), a radical substitution that inscribes a void where the black female body had been.[12] Like the image of his hands on Mary's breasts that are brought back to his memory in the sex scene with Bessie, the image of Mary's body could not be erased from Bigger's memory even when he had checked the furnace: "[T]here was *no sign of the body*, even though the body's image hovered before his eyes, between his eyes and the bed of coals burning hotly. Like the oblong mound of fresh clay of a newly made grave, the red coals revealed the *bent outline of Mary's body*" (LA 554, emphasis mine).[13] Erasure of the mention of Bessie's body prevented this juxtaposition of similar wording in the reader's experience. It weakened the expression of Bigger's impossibility to eradicate the psychic imprint of Mary's "unburnt" (and unburnable) body (LA 554). It blunted his reliance on bodily proximity with Bessie. The contradiction between the "reality" of Bessie's body and the actual disappearance of Mary's, a tension between actually looking at Bessie's body and the remanence of the image of Mary's, superimposed to the event of the painstaking destruction of her body—the assault on the "outline"—disappeared in the changes. The substitution of Bessie's body to Mary's does not hold when the text is revised; the correction crosses out Bessie's body in Bigger's experience.

In sum, the earlier mention of Bessie, outside of a direct link with Mary Dalton, displaces the black-white dichotomy, while the masturbation scene complicates the male-female heterosexual norm of sexual polarity. Earlier on, when subject to pangs of hysteria and restlessness, Bigger had envisioned several outlets to his frustrations: "He longed for a stimulus powerful enough to focus his attention and drain off his energies. He wanted to run. Or listen to some swing music. Or laugh or joke. Or read a *Real Detective Story Magazine. Or go to a movie. Or visit Bessie*" (LA 471, my emphasis). The last alternative, watching a film or going to see his girlfriend, is to a certain extent jointly satisfied when he masturbates and mentions Bessie as the object of his sexual drive in the movie theater.

The two young black males' masturbation in anticipation of their common crime seals their pact. In building up the character's psychological makeup, that scene responds to the character's need for an outlet. The twin themes of criminality and sexuality woven into the novel are wrought from then on into a mirroring gesture. For the reader, this earlier mention of Bigger's sexuality reverberates on his murder of Mary Dalton. The focus of the novel on the white woman-black man relationship—the "rape" of the white woman as the most common plot of America's race relations—is thus somewhat deflated by this earlier mention of Bigger's sexual drive. The prosecutor at the end of the novel points at Bigger and Jack's perversion to explain Bigger's motive for his crime:

> This Court has already heard of the obnoxious sexual perversions practiced by these boys in darkened theaters. Though Jack Harding would not admit it outright, we got enough information out of him to know that when the shadow of Mary Dalton was moving upon that screen those boys indulged in such an act! It was *then* that the idea of rape, murder, and ransom entered the mind of this moron! There is your motive and the vile circumstances under which it was conceived! (LA 831)

Yet the prosecutor is wrong about the time of the masturbation since the two young men masturbate *before the movie* starts, not after. They are in the dark and the organ is playing. Then, they change seats and the show begins. The link that most critics make between the scene and the murder is a result of their predetermined perception of black men's sexuality in relation to white women. Thus the stereotype of the hyper-sexed black man lusting after the white woman is exposed as a construction of the racial imaginary. This is what *Native Son* both constructs and deconstructs (see Elmer). When Max questions Bigger as to whether he was sexually attracted to Mary Dalton more than he was to the women of his own race, he indeed answers: "Naw, but they say that. It ain't true, I hated her then and hate her now" (LA 774). He had admitted beforehand that had been mutually physically drawn to each other in their drunken state. However problematic his relation to Bessie, the actual truth of his attraction to Bessie rather than to Mary is written in the text.

III. THE FILMS OR
"THE SHADOW OF MARY DALTON"

In the Harper version, two films are advertised, *The Gay Woman* and *Trader Horn*. As both characters enter the theater, they make comments on the posters. In *How "Bigger" Was Born*, Wright insisted: "I wanted the reader to feel that there was nothing between him and Bigger; that the story was a special *première* given in his own private theatre" (LA 879). The "theatrical" metaphor presides over the writing of the novel. Richard Wright worked selling tickets for a movie theater, and his experience as a moviegoer may explain the choice of the films as well as the importance of the cinema theater as locale. *Trader Horn* (1931) is a film that depicts the love of Trader Horn and another white man for a white woman worshipped as a white goddess by an African "tribe." Shot in Kenya, it pictured nude African women dancing—local inhabitants were hired as extras—since it was produced before the implementation of the Hayes codes. The nakedness of the Black African men and women acted as a foil to the white woman's seductiveness. The overt racism of the film can be read as a comment on Bigger's own situation, although he is drawn to muse about the Africans' sense of belonging (LA 477).

The succession of *The Gay Woman* and *Trader Horn* in the Book of the Month version versus the documentary on Mary Dalton and *Trader Horn* in the original draft is a notable change (see also Miller 690). In the last sequence, the plot of the film ironically plays on Mary Dalton's position at the center of attention: the white heiress versus the white goddess. *The Gay Woman*, on the other hand, is a film that displaces on a fictional level the elements of the documentary. The "gay" of the title also carries over Mary's promiscuity and insouciance. The plot revolves around the betrayal of a wealthy young woman who cheats on her millionaire husband. Spotted by a communist, the lover nearly escapes being killed when the former tries to throw a bomb at him. The communist had mistaken the lover for the husband. The repentant young woman is reunited with her forgiving husband at the end of the film. The young man prefigures the character of Jan Erlone, the communist friend of Mary Dalton's, on whom Bigger later tries to shift the blame for Mary's murder. Thus, the plot and the characters of the film foreshadow the embroilment between communists and capitalists and the sexual politics of the novel's plot. Black characters are, of course, absent from that movie. They are not represented.

In the original version, the first movie is a newsreel that features Mary Dalton herself. A commentator insists on the "naughty rich" and their mores: "*Here are the daughters of the rich taking sunbaths in the sands of Florida! This little collection of debutantes represents over four billion dollars of America's wealth and over fifty of America's leading families*" (LA 474). Mary is seen at the beach with a young man, a radical who is no other than Jan Erlone. The press exposes and denounces the liberalism of the wealthy and their hypocrisy as they accommodate capitalism and left-wing leanings. The voice-over suggests that Mary and her boyfriend are having sex. At one point, one only sees their legs:

> The close-up faded and the next scene showed only the girl's legs running over the sparkling sands; they were followed by the legs of the man running in pursuit. The words droned on: *Ha! He's after her! There! He's got her! Oh boy, don't you wish you were down here in Florida?* The close-up faded and another came, showing two pairs of legs standing close together. *Oh boy!* said the voice. Slowly the girl's legs strained upward until only the tip of her toes touched the sand. *Ah, the naughty rich!* (LA 475)

The camera switches from the faces to the legs, leaving the voice-over to fill in the gap between what is shown and what stands outside the field of vision. The "disembodied" voice-over overdetermines the meaning of the scene and interpellates the viewer directly (Doane). This type of voice-over, usually found in documentaries, is attached to no visible character or designated diegetic figure (see Silverman; Sjogren). In this case, a distinctly white male voice "compensates" for what the screen does not show by underscoring with unambiguous interjections the sexual nature of Mary and Jan's banter. The voice doubles what the spectator is seeing: it speaks for him and leaves no room for any other interpretation. Bigger and Jack are the inadvertent addressees of words designed for a white audience that exclude them.

Boris Max qualifies these allurements as the "physical" aspect of "our civilization" (LA 815). To the voice's suggestion that they surely wish they were there, the young men ironically respond with their knowledge of the reality of racial relations: were they on that Florida beach, they would be lynched.

IV. REAR VIEWS OR "REAR MIRRORS"?

In the same version, Bigger catches sight of Mary Dalton and her lover in the rear mirror of the car. His "involuntary" voyeurism has been excised from the text; so has the fact that this scene gives him an erection. Like the accidental murder of Mary, this voyeurism is not willed. It is imposed on him. As such it could be construed as Mary and Jan's exhibitionism just as much as Bigger's voyeurism, the ambivalence arising from the difficulty of the subject position assigned to Bigger or conversely the location of that ambivalence as the site of that problematic subjectivity:

> He looked at the mirror; Mary was lying flat on her back in the rear seat and Jan was bent over her. He saw a faint sweep of white thigh. They plastered, all right, he thought. He pulled the car softly round the curves, looking at the road before him one second and up the mirror the next. He heard Jan whispering; then he heard them both sigh. Filled with a sense of them, his muscles grew gradually taut. He sighed and sat up straight, fighting off the stiffening feelings in his loins. (LA 518–19)

Mary exposes her liberated sexuality ("Maybe Mary Dalton was a hot kind of girl" [LA 476]) and her carefree rebelliousness to the black man without any shame: she can be construed as flaunting it. He is invisible, transparent, because she does not see him while he sees her and Jan in the "rear" mirror. This "reverberation"—a "rear view" that recalls with an inversion Hitchcock's *Rear Window*—becomes a synecdoche for the sexuality of the white woman with the white man as "spectacle" for the black man: it is the converse of the black man as spectacle for the white man. In Bigger's words:

> He felt that he had no physical existence at all right then; he was something he hated, the badge of shame which he knew was attached to a black skin. It was a shadowy region, a No Man's Land, the ground that separated the white world from the black that he stood upon. He felt naked, transparent; he felt that this white man, having helped to deform him, held him up now to look at him and be amused. (LA 508)

This apparatus of the rear mirror duplicates the voyeurism/exhibitionism induced by the film that stars Mary Dalton herself. Moreover, in the uncut version, the presence of a projectionist at the back of the room to whom Bigger and Jack turn foretells this scopic setup where the sexual scenes of the white world are projected for and onto them: "Now and then they glanced back up at the projector's room high *in the rear* of the theatre" (LA 473, emphasis mine). Two apparatus are at work: the actual projection in the movie theater and the "reels," themselves complex "*dispositifs*" produced by the white male gaze, a duplication that reinforces the complexity and the strength of the white power structure in relation to the scopic drive.

Lacan's theory of the schism between the look and the gaze may help us understand what is at stake in this particular apparatus that organizes Bigger's—and by extension black males'—field of vision. As he drives, Bigger watches Mary in the rear mirror: "She was kind of pretty, but very little. She looked like a doll in a *show window*: black eyes, white face, red lips" (LA 503, emphasis mine). Laura Mulvey (1975) has theorized that the gaze is male, yet here the objectification of the white woman is doubled up by an imposition of her image and her "looked-at-ness" on a black male whose status as "object" or "subject" is precisely what the novel investigates. While Bigger's narrative viewpoint makes the reader posit his subjecthood, power and race relations constantly turn him into an object. The white male gaze (that produces the images of the documentary) or the white male voice (that utters the commentary) project these sounds and images onto the black man with the instant message of prohibition or taboo. The irony of that scopic setup is that *Trader Horn* mythologizes, by making the Africans worship the white woman and elevate her at the level of a deity, what American society rules: do not "touch" the white woman. The imposed spectacle of their lovemaking onto the black "chauffeur," a function that Wright literalizes by making Bigger be in charge of the furnace and then burn Mary's body in it, "realizes," enacts the setup of the projection of the documentary. The change is Bigger's physical reaction: he is aroused, but fights off that reaction. That scene is a "lynchpin" between the movie theater scene complete with masturbation and the scene of the murder that certain critics have correctly analyzed as mimicking copulation (see Butler; Elmer). This scene also takes place after an awkward moment when Bigger is literally squeezed between Jan and Mary who are seated at the front of the car and he is forced to touch the "soft pressure" of Mary's thigh (LA 508).

In opposition to the documentary, *The Gay Woman* plays on the level of phantasm within a racialized and sexualized framework. The job that Bigger will take is only a possibility, a "maybe," in the expurgated text, whereas it becomes a reality with the viewing of the newsreel as he notes the coincidence. He also muses about the sign that bears the mark of the "Real" Estate Company owned by Mr. Dalton. In the documentary, the press denounces Mary Dalton's affair with a radical. The change in the expurgated version makes the text move from the specific, the real, the "autobiographical"—in relation to the "reality" depicted in the novel—to the fictional, and thus to the collective. The attraction is not that exercised by Mary Dalton, but by rich white women as a group. Mary Dalton just happens to "embody" that ensemble when Bigger meets Mary. Throughout the novel, white society is indeed an indistinct "blur," a mass, a white mountain. In the uncut version, the singularity of the situation as Bigger faces Mary—the knot of "reality"—anticipates the singularity of the murder as event when Bigger kills Mary by accident.

The depiction of what precedes the murder scene in the uncut version stresses the protagonists' mutual attraction, made all the more plausible by their drunkenness (see Butler). Yet the kisses Bigger gives Mary as he carries her were erased from the text. The only kiss that remains is the kiss that she unconsciously gives him:

> He tried to stand her on her feet and found her weak as jelly. He held her in his arms again, listening in the darkness [...] He eased his hand, the fingers spread wide, up the center of her back and her face came toward him and her lips touched his, *like something he had imagined*. He stood her on her feet and she swayed against him. [He tightened his arms as his lips pressed tightly against hers and he felt her body moving strongly. The thought and conviction that Jan had had her a lot flashed through his mind. He kissed her again and felt the sharp bones of her hips move in a hard and veritable grind. Her mouth was open and her breath came slow and deep.]
>
> He lifted her and laid her on the bed, (LA 524, emphasis mine)[14]

The progression from the newsreel to the scene reflected in the rear mirror to the physical contact that happens as if against Bigger's will is a repetition of a similar structure where the "real" is imposed from the rear. It is projected on a surface/a screen, a mirror that the black man is forced to watch. This setup reproduces Plato's allegory of the cave where the chained watchers take the shadows projected on the wall for reality. They are only shadows—here mere reflections— while the source, the "sun" of this delusion, is the power structure of the dominant white world.

This first kiss as Mary's lips first touch his is only "real" in Bigger's fantasy: it is "*like something* he had imagined" and not "*as he had imagined.*" The thought of her sexual promiscuity—that he had witnessed in the rear mirror—and the responses of her body to his embrace trigger the subsequent kisses. What is erased is not so much the kisses than the overall effect that they were given in response to white female desire *and* to the imposition of white to white sexuality as the norm for the black man. Together with Bigger, the reader also bears in mind the references to rich white women's zoophilic tendencies made by the young men at the cinema and their lewd allusions to the fact that they slept with poodles and their black chauffeurs (LA 925). Bigger responds within a configuration of mimetic desire as it is in relation to Jan that he is gradually drawn to kiss Mary. As earlier stated, when Max questions him, Bigger later admits that he had wanted Mary, but their mutual state of drunkenness also explains his lack of inhibition, as the threat of death that derives from the fact that her body is taboo is momentarily lifted.

V. "White Face," Black Rape

The appearance of Mary's blind mother leads to Bigger's sense of guilt over what has happened. Yet, in that scene, both white women have their senses impaired: one cannot see and the other is half-unconscious. Bigger does not look at them, but imagines and thinks. He has internalized the racist plot of the black rapist and now acts out, not so much the rape plot as its consequences. The disappearance of the kisses makes Bigger's action less understandable, but their erasure went together with the effacement of Mary's response, her corporality, the grinds and the groans. The deletion of the description also took away the "bones" of the body, those very bones that will be produced at the trial as evidence of Bigger's rape. As most critics have underlined, the rape did not occur. The disappearance of the corpse and its reduction to bare bones actually allowed the rape charge to subsist. To that fact must be added the rape of the black woman that justifies a posteriori the rape of the white woman. In a highly controversial passage, Bigger, for his part, redefines "rape" as the black man's look into a "white face": "Had he raped her? Yes, he had raped her. Every time he felt as he had felt that night, he raped. But rape was not what one did to women. *Rape was what one felt* when one's back was against a wall and one had to strike out, whether one wanted it or not, to keep the pack from killing one. He committed rape every time *he looked into a white face*" (LA 658, my emphasis). Bigger's formula short-circuits the scopic setup produced by the three previous scenes (the movie theater, the rear mirror, and the murder). The white face is the bearer of the gaze that pins him in the position of the lustful beast. Indeed, when Mary introduces Jan to Bigger, Bigger avoids his gaze: "Bigger held his head at an oblique angle, so that he could, by merely shifting his eyes, look at Jan and then out into the street whenever he did not wish to meet Jan's gaze" (LA 507). Earlier in the novel, Mrs. Dalton's face when he first sees her reminds him of "a dead man's face he had once seen" (LA 501). By looking at that face inhabited by the gaze, he is placed in the position of the rapist. Mrs. Dalton's blindness can thus be understood as the symbolic blinding of the white gaze: a white woman cannot not be raped by a black man in whose presence she finds herself. This double negation is enhanced by the doubling of similar positions in relation to Bigger. Mary is drunk, Mrs. Dalton is blind; both are white women. The "certainty" of rape and its actual nonoccurrence is the nexus of these mirroring female positions that refract castration. As Lacan makes plain, castration anxiety is at the core of the scopic drive: "The gaze is presented to us only in the form of a strange contingency [. . .], namely the lack that constitutes castration anxiety. The eye and the gaze this is for us the split in which the drive is manifested at the level of the scopic field" (SXI 69–70/72–73). At this level, Lacan further stresses, "we are not even forced to take into account any subjectification of the subject. The subject is an apparatus. This apparatus is something lacunary, and it is in the lacuna that the subject establishes the function of a certain object *qua* lost object" (SXI 168/185). In his careful analysis of Lacan's reading of Merleau-Ponty's *Le Visible et l'invisible*, Charles Shepherdson continues: "In short, in the experience of the gaze, it is the subject who identifies with the object that would make the Other complete, fading or vanishing in a sacrificial moment of identification" (84). Bigger's murder of Mary enacts this identification with the rapist of the white gaze with a temporal disjunction: he kills because "it is said" that he has raped.

The reality of the drive coincides with the real of death, an alternative that Bigger had earlier voiced as a choice between killing himself or killing (LA 453). Ultimately, circumstances—a specific "chain" of events—as much as the sexual makeup of black and white relations explain the murder as encounter. Elmer rightly suggests "that the scene of Mary's murder constitutes what Lacan calls in discussing trauma 'the encounter with the real'—'an appointment to which we are always called with a real that eludes us, the real as essentially the missed encounter'" (774). This encounter is prefigured by the documentary that uncannily produces Mary Dalton herself on the screen. When he hears the address and the name, Bigger exclaims: "That gal...That gal there in that guy's arms...That's the daughter of the guy I'm going to work for" (LA 474). The real-life Mary whom he meets at the Daltons' paradoxically announces the "reality" of the murder and its advent as inadvertence: its coincidence. Another knotting in the novel occurs here between the determinism of the social, sexual, and racial environment—both in terms of stereotype and "fate" insofar as it can be construed as the fulfillment of stereotype—and the "freedom" of the black subject.

Once Bigger has met Mary, the revised version glosses on the dreamlike quality of the images:

> He chewed his bacon and eggs while some remote part of his mind considered in amazement *how different this rich girl was from the one he had seen in the movies.* The woman he had watched on the screen had not seemed dangerous and his mind had been able to do with her as it liked, but this rich girl walked over everything, put herself in the way...(LA 928)

The full version also mentions the malleability of the images (even images of the real Mary Dalton) in opposition to the character's materialization when confronted with her: "*how different the girl had seemed in the movie.* On the screen she was not dangerous and his mind could do with her as it liked. But here in her home she walked over everything, put herself in the way" (LA 496, emphasis mine). Indeed, Mary puts herself *in the way* as she bosses Bigger around, responds physically to his embrace and then becomes an embarrassing corpse. It is as if Bigger constantly wished that the documentary should have remained as such: the quotation of a reality to which he did not belong, "shadows" with which his mind could play. Mary is incarnate. This physicality is both the cause of the murder and the rawness that must be transferred to the imagination through suggestion according to the censors' wishes. The references to the newsreel obviously disappear in the Harper version: "Yes; she was *the same girl* he had seen in the movie" (LA 493, emphasis mine). "At once Bigger recognized the man as *the one he had seen* in the newsreel in the movie" (LA 507, my emphasis). Once he has become part of that world that the documentary allows him to belatedly "recognize," the power relations take over and crush him. He obviously denies that when he brags among his friends: "'Jack was telling me you saw the gal in the movie you suppose to drive around. Did you?' 'Sure.' 'How is she?' 'Aw, we like that,' Bigger said, crossing his fingers" (LA 548). Yet the violence of these relations is prefigured by the mention of lynching in the masturbation scene. Bigger brings Jack back to reality when he tells him that he would be "hanging from a tree like a bunch of bananas" (LA 474) if he were in Florida. This statement was tamed down in the Harper version into the racist evocation that he would look like a gorilla with a tuxedo at a party (LA 925). In the original version then, during Britten's examination, Bigger lies when he says that he has never heard of or seen Mary Dalton or Jan before. To Bigger, the newsreel is part image part information about Mary: "No wonder they called her a Communist in the movies. She was crazy all right" (LA 494). In other words, reportage as opposed to fiction "fixes" reality, distills knowledge. Movies, Bigger owns, like magazines, provide an experience that he likens to his sense of self-destiny: "For the first time in his life he moved consciously between two sharply defined poles: he was moving away from the threatening penalty of death, from the deathlike times that brought him that tightness and hotness in his chest; and he was moving toward that *sense of fullness* he had so often but inadequately felt in magazines and *movies*" (LA 583, emphasis mine). The phantasm of wholeness provided by screen images, and the suture that filmic images produce, albeit inadequately, is thematized in the novel and made more explicit by the changes between documentary and narrative fiction when the censors operate. Suggestion (transposition, translation, metaphorization) takes over from factual reporting. "Bigger" explains here how he is reconciling a split self that prevents subjecthood:

> There was something he *knew* and something he *felt*; something the *world* gave him and something he *himself* had; something spread out in *front* of him and something spread out in *back*, and never in his life, with this black skin of his, had he the two worlds, thought and feeling, will and mind, aspiration and satisfaction, been together; never had he felt a sense of wholeness. (LA 670, emphasis Wright's)

Only in the escapism provided, among other things, by the movies, does Bigger feel what he wants, does he merge with the world. Another condition to a restored sense of self would have been the existence of a leader, another black man to show the way. He exclaims: "It was too stark, not redeemed, not made *real with the reality* that was the warm blood of life" (LA 671, emphasis mine). Bigger defines what life is in total opposition to death and murder. The warm blood of life that he has sought is objectified, among other things, in Bessie's warm body for which he craves.

VI. In Evidence: Bessie's Bloody Black Body

Like the masturbation scene, the "rape" scene had to be profoundly rewritten to make the graphic reference disappear. The original version read as follows: "His cold fingers touched her warm flesh, and sought still warmer and softer flesh. Bessie was still, unresisting, without response. His icy fingers touched inside of her and at once she spoke, not a word, but a sound that gave forth a meaning of horror accepted" (LA 664). The corrected version eliminates the physicality of the act, the body as flesh, the desire for warmth: "He was swept by a sudden gust of passion and his arms tightened about her. Bessie was still, inert, unresisting, without response. He kissed her again and at once she spoke, not a word, but a resigned and prolonged sound that gave forth a meaning of horror accepted" (LA 933). Bessie undoubtedly appears all the more unresponsive as the addition of numerous adjectives stresses her motionlessness. The warmth and softness of her body, a trace of their previous sexual encounter, has been erased. Whereas Bigger had smothered Mary so that she would not talk, Bessie's rape is written as the transformation of a voice (of refusal) into a sound. The metaphor of horse riding that was substituted to a more radical writing of the violence and the contradictions of emotions deprived the text of an intensity rarely achieved in favor of the banal. Here is the corrected version:

> Imperiously driven, he rode roughshod over her whimpering protests, feeling acutely sorry for her as he galloped a frenzied horse down a steep hill in the face of a resisting wind. *don't don't don't Bigger*. And then the wind came so strong that it lifted him high into the dark air turning him, twisting him, hurling him; faintly over the wind's howl he heard: *don't Bigger don't don't* At a moment he could not remember, he had fallen; and now he lay, spent, his lips parted. (LA 933)

The original rape scene shows the contradiction of Bigger's despair in the broken-up syntax. It inscribes in the text the contradiction between Bigger's drive and his mind, Bessie's resistance and her final yielding. The abstract fullness and wholeness of his former musings come into a brutal enactment in the illusory possession of the other's body:

> Yes. Bessie. His desire was naked and hot in his hand and his fingers were touching her. Yes. Bessie. Now. He had to now. *don't Bigger*

don't He was sorry, but he had to. He. He could not help it. Help it.
Sorry. Help it. Sorry. Help it. Sorry. Help it. Now. She should. Look!
She should should should look. Look at how he was. He. He was. He
was feeling bad about how she would feel but he could not help it now.
Feeling. *Bessie.* Now. All. He heard her breathing heavily and heard
his own breath going and coming heavily. *Bigger.* Now. All. All. Now.
All. *Bigger…* (LA 664)

The ambiguity as to who utters the words makes for a totally different
reading from the revised passage. The italics are both his ("*Bessie*") and
her voice ("*Bigger*"). Bigger pleads for a "look" from her that would
sustain his existence. He is not "sorry for Bessie," but apologizes. He
is sorry. He cannot help himself. He also seems to be admonishing
himself and the utterance "Help it" could be ascribed either to him
or to Bessie since it echoes her many *don't*. The repetitions and the
rhythm mimic the crescendo of orgasm and end on the impossible
desire for total instantaneous possession, an untenable present: "all,"
"now." From the modernity of this text to the corrected version, the
effacement of the poetics of the text has made room for the hack-
neyed metaphor of the horse. Recalling the stereotype of the stallion,
the stud of racist discourse, it stands in total contrast with the sea
metaphors of their previous sexual encounter. Yet the economy of
the text makes the reader reflexively and mechanically go back to the
scene of Mary's murder. In opposition to that scene where the two
white women's blindness creates a void only filled by the racial and
sexual ideology of rape, this plea for a look on the part of the black
woman is a desperate call for the founding of the black male subject:
"she should should should look." Bigger's "He was" must indeed be
measured up against the "But what I killed for, I *am*" (LA 849) of
the final pages.

CONCLUSION

The restoration of the excised passages allows for a reappraisal of
Richard Wright's initial plans to include an explicit sexual component
in the complexity of Bigger Thomas's psychic makeup as well as in
the depiction of interracial relations: it illuminates the text's possible
adventures, its genesis as process. In a novel where female blindness—
Mary Dalton's mother's—is a metonym for racial-sexual violence and
hatred, the forced blindness of the readers who did not see, could not
see, what had been erased reverberated the guilt of innocence that
the text ironically denounces. Projections, phantasms of the sexuality

of the other, obscure the relationship between black men and black women within the general omnipotent economy of the white gaze. Thus, censorship must be reassessed as a complex gesture that did not rest content with deleting sexually explicit material but played on the notions central to Wright's writing: overdetermination, intraracial and interracial sexuality, the black male subject's psychic makeup, and the traces of the sexed body in the text. It robbed readers of a poetics of emotions that told the truth of the racial subject.

Notes

1. The text used is Arnold Rampersad's 1991 edition in The Library of America, abbreviated as LA followed by the page number. The 1940 Harper edition is referred to as either the 1940 edition or the Harper edition. On the difference between genetic criticism and textual genetics, see Grésillon, 7–31.

2. The excision of the political should be assessed. A second step should question the autobiographical text of *Black Boy* (1945). The intervention of the Book of the Month Club to have Wright change the structure of his autobiography *American Hunger* (finished in 1943) also alters that text. See Thaddeus. A further question bearing on genre is that of the impact of these changes in relation to the status of the text as autobiography or fiction. Since a complete critical genetic study falls outside the scope of this paper, I will rely on a few examples. For a thorough analysis of editing and reception, see Cossu-Beaumont.

3. The essay itself underwent several changes as it was delivered four times in two weeks as a lecture, then published in condensed versions or separately as a pamphlet (Kinnamon, *New Essays* 2; LA 913–14).

4. Keneth Kinnamon (1990) has assessed the borrowings from the press (5) and commented at length on the changes in the introductory scene, the deletion of the closing section, and the impact of Fisher's introduction presented to Wright as a fait accompli. Other critics, since then, take these changes into account in their reading of the novel. See, for instance, Hakutani.

5. Wright sent the outline of *Native Son* to Harper and Brothers in February 1938 (LA 911). The first draft of 576 pages was completed by October 24 (Kinnamon, *New Essays* 5).

6. For an analysis of censorship in Hurston's *Dust Tracks on the Road*, see Raynaud.

7. Toni Morrison makes a similar provision for Beloved in her eponymous novel.

8. Kinnamon explains that the following sentence in Max's speech was excised for it referred too explicitly to ejaculation (*New Essays* 15–16). The thematics and problematics of voice cannot be fully explored and require further attention.

9. There are actually three visits to Bessie.

10. Dawahare asserts that the reader should take at face value Max's assertion that Bigger's relationship to the world is masturbatory: "Was not Bigger Thomas's relationship to his girl a masturbatory one? Was not his entire relationship to the whole world on the same plane?" (LA 468) (458). I argue that the text makes the reader read Bigger's contradictions.

11. This scene was retained in the galleys and changed only in page proof (Kinnamon, *New Essays* 14).

12. Critics that have assessed Wright's depiction of female characters are Harris; Baker; Johnson; and Dawahare.

13. The Harper edition had three long sections that bore on the fear that the body could be discovered in the ashes. They were crossed out in the final version. See LA, 930 (532.29–30), LA, 931 (55.13–14), LA, 932 (604.11–12). A closer analysis of these enlargements and the reasons for their deletion should be conducted. Their disappearance reduces the incidence of Bigger's guilt and weakens the thematics of the body as "bones" and "ashes" in relation to the elemental presence of fire, a powerful symbol alongside sea imagery and the whiteness of the snow.

14. The section between brackets has been excised from the Harper edition.

BIBLIOGRAPHY

Baker, Houston. "On Knowing Our Place." *Workings of the Spirit: The Poetics of Afro-American Women's Writing*. Chicago: Chicago UP, 1991. 102–30. Print.

Bloom, Harold, ed. *Richard Wright: Modern Critical Views*. New York: Chelsea, 1987. Print.

———. *The Critical Response to Richard Wright*. Westport, CT: Greenwood, 1995. Print.

Butler, Robert. "The Function of Violence in Richard Wright's *Native Son*." *Black American Literary Forum* 20.1/2 (1986): 9–25. Print.

Cossu-Beaumont, Laurence. *Richard Wright (1908–1960) à la Recherche du Temps Présent; Projet, Oeuvre et Réception*. Diss. Université de Paris 7, 2004. Print.

Dawahare, Anthony. "From No Man's Land to Mother-land: Emasculation and Nationalism in Richard Wright's Depression Era Urban Novels." *African American Review* 33.3 (1999): 451–66. Print.

Doane, Mary Ann. "Ideology and the Practice of Sound Editing and Mixing." *The Cinematic Apparatus*. Eds. Teresa de Lauretis and Stephen Heath. London and New York: Macmillan and St. Martin's, 1980. 47–56. Print.

Elmer, Jonathan. "Spectacle and Event in *Native Son*." *American Literature* 70.4 (1998): 767–98. Print.

Fabre, Michel. *La Quête Inachevée de Richard Wright: Biographie.* Paris: Lieu commun, 1986. Print.

———. "Beyond Naturalism?" *Richard Wright: Modern Critical Views.* Ed. Harold Bloom. New York: Chelsea, 1987. 37–57. Print.

Gates, Henry Louis, Jr., and Anthony Appiah, eds. *Richard Wright: Critical Perspectives Past and Present.* New York: Amistad, 2000. Print.

Grésillon, Almuth. *Eléments de Critique Génétique: Lire les Manuscrits Modernes.* Paris: PUF, 1994. Print.

Hakutani, Yoshinobu. *Richard Wright and Racial Discourse.* Columbia: U of Missouri P, 1996. Print.

Harris, Trudier. "Native Sons and Foreign Daughters." *New Essays on Native Son.* Ed. Keneth Kinnamon. Cambridge, MA: Harvard UP, 1990. 63–84. Print.

JanMohamed, Abdul R. "Negating the Negation as a Form of Affirmation in Minority Discourse: Richard Wright as Subject." *Cultural Critique* 7 (1987): 245–66. Print.

Johnson, Barbara. "The Re(a)d and the Black: Richard Wright's Blueprint." *The Feminist Difference: Literature, Psychoanalysis, Race and Gender.* Cambridge, MA: Harvard UP, 1998. 61–73. Print.

Kinnamon, Keneth. "*Native Son*: The Personal, Social, and the Political Background." *Phylon* 30.1 (1960): 66–72. Print.

———. *New Essays on* Native Son. Cambridge, MA: Harvard UP, 1990. Print.

Lacan, Jacques. *Les Quatre Concepts Fondamentaux de la Psychanalyse. Le Séminaire.* Livre XI. Paris: Seuil, 1974. *Four Fundamental Concepts of Psychoanalysis.* Trans. Alan Sheridan. Book XI. New York: Norton, 1978. Print.

McNallie, Robin. "Richard Wright's 'Allegory of the Cave': *The Man Who Lived Underground South.*" *Atlantic Bulletin* 42.2 (1977): 76–84. Print.

Merleau-Ponty, Maurice. *Le Visible et l'invisible.* Ed. Claude Lefort. Paris: Gallimard, 1964. Print.

Miller, Eugene E. "Authority, Gender and Fiction." *African American Review* 27.4 (1993): 687–91. Print.

Mulvey, Laura. "Visual Pleasure and Cinematic Narrative." *Screen* 16.3 (1975): 6–18. Print.

Patterson, Orlando. *Slavery as Social Death: A Comparative Study.* Cambridge, MA: Harvard UP, 1982. Print.

Raynaud, Claudine. "'Rubbing a Paragraph with a Soft Cloth'? Muted Voices and Editorial Constraints in *Dust Tracks on a Road.*" *De/Colonizing Subject: Politics and Gender in Women's Autobiography.* Ed. Julia Watson and Sidonie Smith. Minneapolis: U of Minnesota P, 1992. 34–64. Print.

Ross, Marlon B. "In Search of Black Men's Masculinities." *Feminist Studies* 24.3 (1998): 599–626. Print.

Shepherdson, Charles. "A Pound of Flesh: Lacan's Reading of *The Visible and the Invisible*." *Diacritics* 27.4 (1997): 70–86. Print.

Silverman, Kaja. *The Acoustic Mirror: The Female Voice in Psychoanalysis and Cinema*. Bloomington: Indiana UP, 1988. Print.

Sjorgen, Britta. H. *Into the Vortex: Female Voice and Paradox in Film*. Champaign: U of Illinois P, 2005. Print.

Thaddeus, Janice. "The Metamorphosis of *Black Boy*." *American Literature* 57.2 (1985): 199–214. Print.

Toles, George E. "Alfred Hitchcock's *Rear Window* as Critical Allegory." *boundary 2* 16.2–3 (1989): 225–45. Print.

Wright, Ellen, and Julia Wright. Letter to the *Times Literary Supplement*. *Times Literary Supplement* (31 Jan. 1992) in Butler, 1995. Print.

Wright, Richard. *How "Bigger" Was Born. Richard Wright: Early Works*. Ed. Arnold Rampersad. New York: Library of America, 1991. Print.

11

"The Astonishing Humanity": Domestic Discourses in the Friendship and Fiction of Richard Wright and Carson McCullers

Julieann Veronica Ulin

Richard Wright and Carson McCullers's first encounter came in the *New Republic* in August of 1940, the same year *Native Son* was published. Wright reviewed McCullers's debut novel, *The Heart is a Lonely Hunter*. He wrote,

> To me the most impressive aspect of *The Heart is a Lonely Hunter* is the astonishing humanity that enables a white writer, for the first time in Southern fiction, to handle Negro characters with as much ease and justice as those of her own race. This cannot be accounted for stylistically or politically; it seems to stem from an attitude toward life which enables Miss McCullers to rise above the pressures of her environment and embrace white and black humanity in one sweep of apprehension and tenderness. (Wright, "Inner Landscape" 18)

Wright greatly admired McCullers's first novel, situating her among such literary forbearers as Gertrude Stein and Ernest Hemingway, and stating that "her quality of despair is unique and individual; and it seems to me more natural and authentic that that of Faulkner." Strong praise indeed. Wright's favorable review of *The Heart is a Lonely Hunter* initiated a two-decade friendship and his subsequent relationship with McCullers influenced her development as a writer and her choice of subject matter. In a 1941 column in *Harper's Bazaar*, titled "Books I Remember," McCullers noted that

Richard Wright "in his books about the problems of the Negro, has surely staked a new mine of literary material" (McCullers, "Books I Remember" 125). Yet McCullers's treatment of racial housing discrimination in her final novel, 1961's *Clock without Hands*, proved far less palatable to her contemporary critics than the works focused on individual loneliness for which she was lauded. While McCullers in 1940 had been hailed as a wunderkind with the publication of *The Heart is a Lonely Hunter*, critics now mourned the trajectory of her career, in which her "exuberant studies of freaks and grotesques gave way to a sober dramatization of Southern racial problems."[1] I, like Wright in his above review, reject this claim that McCullers's interest in individual loneliness is ever entirely excluded from an investigation of race in the South. Her most sustained and forceful depiction of racial housing discrimination comes in her final novel *Clock without Hands*, which owes much to her relationship with Richard Wright and her firsthand knowledge of his experiences of housing discrimination in the United States.

McCullers and Wright shared the same house for over a year at 7 Middagh Street in Brooklyn, New York. The house operated as an artist colony nicknamed February House because so many residents were born in that month.[2] McCullers's *New York Times* obituary notes the extraordinary residents of February House and its role in McCullers's development:

> From time to time the boarders there included Christopher Isherwood, Richard Wright, Thomas Mann's son, Golo, Oliver Smith, Jane and Paul Bowles, and such unclassifiable artists such as Gypsy Rose Lee. Miss Lee provided the cook, W. H. Auden kept house and all chipped in on the groceries. In and out of the house at all hours were such people as Anaïs Nin, Leonard Bernstein, Salvador Dali, Marc Blitzstein and Aaron Copeland. ("Carson McCullers Dies at 50; Wrote of Loneliness and Love" 40)

Richard Wright, his wife Ellen, and their baby Julia moved into the house in June 1942 and left in mid-August 1943. In her fascinating 2005 study of the history of February House, Sherill Tippins notes that the house had "developed a reputation as the greatest artistic salon of the decade" (Tippins xiii). Denis de Rougemont, author of *Love in the Western World*, noted that "all that was new in America...emanated from that house, the only center of thought and art that I found in any large city in the country." Though offering an otherwise comprehensive look at many of the house's inhabitants,

Tippen unfortunately devotes only these five sentences to Wright's stay in February House:

> The novelist Richard Wright, who was entranced by Carson when he finally met her, moved to 7 Middagh Street with his family in 1942. While their neighbors had appeared remarkably tolerant of the wild goings-on at the house in previous years, occupancy by a black man, his white wife, and their baby daughter was another matter. Stones were thrown at the windows, and the coal deliverer, himself African American, resigned rather than serve someone of his own race. Nevertheless, it was Wright who chose to leave the house after a year. He found it too painful, he said, to witness Carson's self-destruction through drinking and George [Davis's] dangerous adventures among the bars and brothels of Sand Street. (Tippins 250)

To the extent that McCullers appears in any of Wright's biographies, she is mentioned only in relation to Wright's decision to move from Middagh Street because of his concern over McCullers's influence on his daughter Julia.[3] This limited view seriously curtails investigations into the creative exchange between Wright and McCullers. Though Wright lived only a year in February House, it was long enough to leave a significant impression on McCullers and to provide the inspiration for her final novel.

For her part, McCullers appears to have been quite unaware of the effect her drinking had on Wright's decision to move and attributed his move to Paris to his desire to escape the relentless housing discrimination in the United States (*I N G* 43).[4] In her unfinished autobiography, *Illumination & Night Glare*, McCullers writes with great tenderness for Richard Wright and emphasizes the effect housing had on his life:

> Another writer who was particularly dear to me is Richard Wright. . . . I met him in the house in Brooklyn when he moved in with his wife and baby. As usual there were no decent places for [Negroes] to live. Later, we resumed our friendship in Paris where he lived until his sudden death. His death always gives me a sense of the great fragility of human life. . . . Dick and I often discussed the South, and his book, [Black Boy], is one of the finest books by a Southern [Negro.] He said of my work that I was the one Southern writer who was able to treat [Negroes] and white people with the same ease. (*I N G* 64)

After moving from the Brooklyn house they shared with McCullers, Wright and his family continued to suffer housing discrimination. In

Wright's 1951 essay "I Choose Exile," he details his desire to purchase a home in the United States, and the continual frustration of this desire to acquire a home in the United States. In the typescript of the unpublished essay housed at Yale's Beinecke Library, Wright writes: "I want the right to hold, without fear of punitive measures, an opinion with which my neighbor does not agree" (Wright, "I Choose Exile" 2). The conceit of the neighbor proves a particularly rich one for Wright; the neighbor has the power to punish and is a source of danger. In discussing the reasons leading to his decision to leave the United States, Wright recalls searching for a house in New England during the spring of 1946, finding one in Connecticut, and being unable to purchase the home because of his race. Wright was furious. It probably recalled to him his experience in New York in the spring of 1935 during the writer's congress: "I asked about housing accommodations and the New York John Reed Club members, all white members of the Communist party, looked embarrassed. I waited while one white Communist called another white Communist to one side and discussed what could be done to get me, a black Chicago Communist, housed" (Wright, *Richard Wright: Later Works* 330). Wright is given an address by one of the members, but when he arrives a "white man opened [the door], took one quick look at my face, then pushed the door almost shut again, as though in desperate defense of himself and his home" (Wright, *Richard Wright: Later Works* 331). Wright wanders the streets of Harlem, is told by passersby that there are no hotels available to him, and eventually ends up in the YMCA. In "I Choose Exile," he notes, in France by contrast, "During a period of months I entered hundreds of French homes and not once did I encounter any anger or surprise when my dark face stood framed in a French doorway" (Wright, "I Choose Exile" 15). In France, he writes of an altogether different experience with his neighbor, "I openly confess that, as an American Negro, I felt, amidst such a milieu, safe from my neighbor for the first time in my life" (Wright, "I Choose Exile" 11).

Wright composed "I Choose Exile" around the time when McCullers begins her decade-long work on *Clock without Hands.* This, her last novel, appears the year after Wright's death, and is fully indebted to his experience of "choosing exile" as a result of U.S. housing discrimination. The similarities between *Native Son* and *Clock without Hands* are numerous. Both novels are focused on a sustained exploration of the intersections among race, housing, and democracy. Both feature black central characters —Wright's Bigger Thomas and McCullers's Sherman Pew—who work as domestic servants in the homes of wealthy white community leaders. The black domestic servant in both *Native Son* and in McCullers's final novel embodies the paradox of being what Toni Morrison terms at once "curiously intimate and unhingingly separate" (Morrison 12). As in Wright's *Native Son*, on which *Clock without Hands* depends, the figure of the black domestic servant in the white house enacts tensions at the center of U.S. democracy. *Native Son* and *Clock without Hands* both rely on a murder courtroom case, which is as much about miscegenation as the murder.[5] Both contain scenes of violence against animals (the iconic opening scene between Bigger and the rat; Sherman Pew lynches a dog). In addition, both Bigger Thomas and Sherman Pew dream of attending aviation school, and "flight" figures prominently in both texts.[6]

Perhaps most significantly, both *Native Son* and *Clock without Hands* are fixated on the politics of the domestic space in which both Bigger Thomas and Sherman Pew work as servants. McCullers, like Wright, recognized the hypocrisy of a nation that simultaneously imagines itself as a democracy and maintains a Black Belt. She also chooses to textually situate the contradictions of the nation's democratic claims through the racial/spatial transgressions of a black domestic servant protagonist. Both Sherman Pew and Bigger Thomas violate boundaries related to property—Bigger by trespassing into Mary Dalton's bedroom, Sherman by purchasing a house in a white neighborhood. These offenses are punished by death. While an understanding of *Native Son* and Bigger Thomas's position within the text is impossible without attending to Wright's construction of housing discrimination throughout the novel, actual acquisition of property beyond the Black Belt is never a possibility for the Thomases in the text. When Bigger is asked why he has killed Mary Dalton, he replies that "they were crowding me too close; they wouldn't give me no room" (Wright, *Native Son* 496). We can certainly read this sentiment literally in terms of the domestic policing that occurs along the Black Belt. However, in McCullers's *Clock without Hands*, set thirteen years after *Native Son*'s publication, Sherman Pew employs Richard Wright's exact strategy for acquiring property in New York. Thus, McCullers's novel deals with the implications not of transgressing a spatial boundary within the house of the Daltons but of acquiring a home in a white neighborhood—implications that she was aware of through her relationship with Richard Wright.

In the two decades between Wright's *Native Son* and McCullers's *Clock without Hands*, racial tensions over racial proximity and home ownership had not abated, despite the fact that the ability to continue racially segregating housing based on "gentlemen's agreements" was overturned in 1947.[7] That same year saw the publication of *Race Bias in Housing*, sponsored by the American Civil Liberties Union, the National Association for the Advancement of Colored People, and the American Council on Race Relations. This text outlined the intersection between housing discrimination and the democratic project. As Charles Abrams argues, "It was in housing that segregation received its greatest impetus and momentum. Once rooted there the segregation pattern spread unarrested" (Abrams 7). Abrams sets the inequalities of the housing system against the broad democratic claims of the United States. "Present policy," he states, "will either lastingly fix the segregated pattern, with all its hazards for the future, or recreate, at long last, an environment worthy of a democratic nation. In that sense federal housing policy involves more than housing; it has become a proving ground on which the practical validity of a great ideal can be demonstrated" (9). Recalling Richard Wright's discourse of the danger posed by the neighbor, Abrams points out that "the Negro servant once afforded a convenience to those he served by living in a back-street nearby. *But welcome as a servant he became intolerable as a neighbor*" (Abrams 10, emphasis mine,).[8] Since a servant does not exist as an owner, s/he is not a full citizen, and is therefore insignificant. Ownership in America has always signified power, with homeownership in particular providing not only a possession of property but a sense of economic security, familial stability, and a basis for long-term investment.[9] McCullers's *Clock without Hands* traces the evolution of Sherman Pew from a domestic servant to an occupant of a house in an all-white neighborhood.[10] The novel takes place in 1953–54 in Milan, Georgia, against a backdrop of lynching, voter intimidation, and the push for school integration that causes the mixed-race Sherman Pew to live in "a stasis of dread and suspense" (McCullers, *Complete Novels* 741). In 1954, the U.S. Supreme Court would strike down the "separate but equal" doctrine of public education. The terror lying just below the surface of McCullers's text is less the notion of equality, which would appear ludicrous to many of the novel's characters, but rather the judicial dismantling of the doctrine of *separation*.

Sherman Pew's blue eyes and mixed-race status are frequently commented upon throughout the novel, and evoke Zygmunt Bauman's concept of the stranger as one who destroys a worldview constructed through strict binary divisions:

> Some strangers are not, however, the *as-yet-undecided*; they are, in principle, undecidables. They are the premonition of that "third element"

which should not be. These are the true hybrids, the monsters—not just unclassified, but unclassifiable. They do not question just this one opposition here and now: they questions oppositions as such, the very principle of the opposition, the plausibility of dichotomy it suggests and the feasibility of separation it demands. They unmask the brittle artificiality of division. They destroy the world. (Bauman 59)

Thus, the stranger operates as a hybrid category and is seen as fundamentally unknowable. With his gray blue eyes and his dark skin, Pew embodies this "brittle artificiality of division." The stranger, Bauman goes on, must be "tabooed, disarmed, suppressed, exiled physically and mentally." That Sherman Pew is of mixed race in *Clock without Hands* makes him a candidate for all of the above. In troubling the strict racial divisions, Pew is the destroyer of the community, which defines itself through these imagined binaries. Pew serves as a marker for both internal and external chaos, representing for those around him bodily and national disease and deterioration. In the course of the novel, the reader learns that Pew is the child of a black man accused of raping a white woman and then murdering her husband. The white woman testifies that the black man killed her husband in self-defense, and that no rape had occurred, but the jury sentences the defendant to death anyway. The white woman dies giving birth to Sherman Pew, her child with the black defendant. Sherman Pew is the embodiment of racial transgression, product of a union not between a "black and alien invader" and his rape victim, as the prosecutor in *Native Son* will characterize Bigger's crime, but between two lovers of different races, and serves as a reminder that boundaries between the races may be willingly transgressed.[11]

From the novel's opening, in which white pharmacist J. T. Malone is diagnosed with leukemia by his Jewish doctor, the breakdown of racial divisions is linked with the specter of disease. In the visit in which he is diagnosed, "[Malone] realized for the first time that Dr. Hayden was a Jew" (613). Disease and race become inextricably bound together, as Malone envisions the fixed pattern of his life as subject to infiltration and destruction, whether by perceived outsiders or diseased cells:

> The realization that Dr. Hayden was a Jew seemed of such importance that Malone wondered how he could have ignored it for so long....When Dr. Hayden came on his rounds, Malone watched him with dread—although for years he had been a friend and customer. It was not so much that Kenneth Hale Hayden was a Jew as the fact that he was living and would live on—he and his like—while J. T. Malone

had an incurable disease and would die in a year or fifteen months. (614)

That Malone recognizes his blood as infiltrated by disease at the moment at which he identifies his doctor as Jewish is a significant intersection, and initiates his dual doubting over Hayden's pronouncement that "maybe soon they will find a way to control diseased cells" (613). This recognition of his body as a site of invasion initiates Malone's journey in the novel because of the correlating recognition it affords him of the "invasion" around him. His fear of the invaded body textually precedes his meeting with Sherman Pew, and this twin discourse of disease and invasion precipitates and fuels the insidious efforts throughout the text by Malone to reassert the spatial racial boundaries.

Malone's increased anxiety over race at the moment of his diagnosis is immediately followed by his meeting with Sherman Pew, "an encounter that upset him strangely" because of Pew's "unnatural appearance" (McCullers, *Complete Novels* 617). Malone is shocked by Sherman's "same" blue eyes, which, although the identical shade to his own, appear "unnatural" in the boy's face. The shock of the blue eyes signals a blend that suggests a threatening invasion and recall Bauman's stranger:

> The impression on Malone was such that he did not think of him in harmless terms as a colored boy—his mind automatically used the harsh term bad nigger, although *the boy was a stranger to him* and as a rule he was lenient in such matters. When Malone turned and they collided, the nigger steadied himself but did not budge, and it was Malone who stepped back a pace. They stood in the narrow alley and stared at each other. The eyes of both were of the same gray-blue and at first it seemed a contest to outstare each other. The eyes that looked at him were cold and blazing in the dark face—then it seemed to Malone that the gaze flickered and steadied to a look of eerie understanding. He felt that those strange eyes knew that he was soon to die. (*Complete Novels* 617, italics mine)

The curious encounter between Sherman Pew and Malone is more unnerving for Malone because of the territorial cost to him. It is he who must step backward, caught off guard by the boy's unwavering stance.

The bodily and social sense of terror and invasion that overtakes Malone following his diagnosis and his meeting with Sherman Pew leads to an obsessive search for order and fixed lines of domestic demarcation between races: "Often he would walk aimlessly around the streets of the town—down through the shambling, crowded slums around the cotton mill, or through the Negro sections, or the middle class streets of houses set in careful lawns. . . . . Sometimes, and dimly, Malone felt that he blundered among a world of incongruities in which there was no order or conceivable design" (615). Malone's search for sturdy lines of demarcation rests in his ability to see and distinguish the town's "Negro sections." He visits with his friend, the Judge, who is more than happy to issue warnings in his prophetic language about threats in and to the South, which he argues is "in the vortex of a revolution almost as disastrous as the War Between the States" (619):

> The wind of revolution is rising to destroy the very foundations on which the South was built. The poll tax will soon be abolished and every ignorant Nigra can vote. Equal rights in education will be the next thing. Imagine a future in where delicate little white girls must share their desks with coal black niggers in order to learn to read and write. . . . The Federal Housing Projects are already the ruination of the real estate investors. They call it slum clearance—but who makes the slums, I ask you? The people who live in the slums make the slums themselves by their own improvidence. (619)

When Malone tells the Judge of his blood disease, he replies: " 'A blood disease?' Why, that's ridiculous—you have some of the best blood in this state" (620). Even Malone's explanation of his diagnosis hints at considerable anxiety about race:

> "The slide showed it was leukemia. And the blood count showed a terrible increase in leucocytes."
> "Leucocytes?" asked the Judge. "What are they?"
> "White blood cells."
> "Never heard of them."
> "But they're there." (621)

The rising tide of unknowable organisms, which, for all the attempts to ignore them, are there despite "some of the best blood in the state," signifies the anxiety expressed by the Judge and others in fending off what they see as invading hordes. It is worth noting here that the etymology of the word "leukemia" comes from the Greek words "leukos" and "heima," meaning "white blood;" Malone is dying of too much white blood. Given his type of cancer, caused not by a tumor but rather by the circulation of malignant cells, the disease cannot be isolated and removed but rather refutes boundaries and circulates freely. Reviewers of *Clock without Hands* staunchly objected to what they saw as two competing narrative threads—one involving the diagnosis and death of Malone and the other involving Sherman Pew.[12] These reviewers repeatedly failed to see that the specter of disease in the text afflicts only the white characters and is continually associated with collapsing boundaries and invading malignant cells. Far from a competing narrative, the discourse of malignant and uncontrolled cells and disease is the dominant framework through which many of McCullers's white characters (with the notable exception of the Judge's grandson) interpret Sherman Pew's position in the town.

In her construction of Sherman Pew, McCullers returns to Wright's *Native Son*, in which the black domestic servant works for a wealthy citizen of the community. Despite his fear and wrath over the racial "revolution" in the South, the Judge is happy to hire Sherman Pew as his servant. McCullers crafts their relationship to suggest the degree to which the pre-Civil War social organization continues to dictate interracial relationships. The Judge asks Sherman, "Do you think you would make me a good amanuensis?" (695). When Sherman appears confused about the word's meaning, the Judge clarifies, "An amanuensis is a kind of secretary." In fact, the word amanuensis is of Latin origin and means literally "a slave at hand." The Judge repeatedly uses the word in lieu of the term "servant." What emerges in the consideration of this word is that it is Sherman Pew—not just the dying Malone—who lives according to the titular clock without hands, which cannot measure the temporal advancement between the 1850s and the 1950s. The Judge talks to Sherman of his dream of reparations made to slaveholders, and Sherman listens "trembling with insult and fury" (McCullers, *Complete Novels* 739). When the Judge asks him to write letters to the congressmen and statesmen requesting reparations and the restoration of the value of the Confederate money, Sherman refuses in a series of exchanges that suggest the book's title be read in terms of its relationship to racial history in the United States, and not exclusively (or even primarily) as a reference to Malone's impeding death. The Judge's plan for revaluing Confederate money would, as Sherman tells him, "turn back the clock for a hundred years" (739), but the Judge insists that reparations for the devalued currency would turn the clock forward a century (748). Sherman counters, "I won't be a party to turning the clock back almost a century" (748). Later, the Judge tells Sherman he has grown so contrary that "you wouldn't give me the time of day if you were just in front of the town clock" (750). Sherman later refuses again to write the Judge's letters because "the idea is queer and would turn back the clock" (752). What emerges in a consideration of these multiple references to time is that the novel's title speaks less to Malone's impending death than to the lack of progress in the century for black Americans.

Aware of the fact that the Judge reads him in light of the social and racial codes of the 1850s, Sherman Pew becomes obsessed with forcing the Judge to "notice" him. Here, McCullers radically departs from Wright's Bigger Thomas, whose dominant aim within the space of the Dalton home is to remain invisible; Sherman Pew desires to rebel against racial constructs and be noticed at any cost. As *Clock without Hands* progresses, Sherman Pew becomes obsessed with the idea of being "noticed," which will only occur if he moves beyond the racial spatial constraints. When Sherman substitutes water for the Judge's insulin, he manages to affect the Judge's body, yet, "it was not even *noticed*" (793). Sherman's desire to rebel against racial constructs displays his longings, "[w]anting to go out of line and afraid, wanting to be *noticed* and afraid to be *noticed*" (783). The Judge is also oblivious to the fact that Sherman has discovered the secret of his mixed parentage in the Judge's office files: "Not being a *noticer*, the Judge did not *notice* Sherman's shaken face and trembling hands" (781).When he kills Jester's dog by hanging it from a tree, he thinks: "Why don't nobody care about me? I do things, don't nobody *notice*. Good or mean, nobody *notices*. People pet that goddamn dog more than they *notice* me. And it's just a dog" (784, all above emphasis mine). His final decision to rent a house in the white section of town is ultimately a strategy to achieve recognition at any cost:

> A Negro family moved into a white neighborhood and they were bombed....And slowly [Sherman Pew] started to go out of line. First he drank water at the white fountain in the courthouse square. No one seemed to *notice*. He went to the white men's room at the bus station. But he went so hurriedly and so furtively that again no one *noticed*. He sat in a back pew at the Baptist Church. Again, no one *noticed* except at the end of the service, and an usher directed him to a colored church. He sat down in Whelan's drugstore. A clerk said, "Get away, nigger, and never come back." All these separate acts of going out of line terrified him. His hands were sweaty, his heart lurching. But terrified as he was, he was more disturbed by the fact that nobody seemed to *notice* him except the clerk at Whelan's. Harassed and suffering, I've got to *do something, do something, do something* beat like a drum in his head. (782, emphasis on "notice" mine)

Home, for Sherman, becomes the site of his "doing something," the final move that cannot be ignored and demands notice precisely because it is staged around the acquisition of a home "out of line" rather than servile occupation of a domestic space or housing within fixed racial boundaries.

McCullers's Sherman Pew acquires his home in a manner similar to Wright's eventual acquisition of a home in New York City. On Friday, February 13, 1945, Wright and Ellen succeeded in purchasing a home on Charles Street in the Village. As Addison Gayle writes, black Americans were unable to rent or buy in the Village, so

> the Wrights were forced to engage in subterfuge: on the advice of their lawyer, the couple was established as "The Richelieu Realty Co." "President and sole owner of the corporation is Ellen Wright, wife of the author, Richard Wright, who has acted as agent for the real estate firm." When the neighbors discovered who the real owners of the house were, they attempted to prevent the family from moving in: one such attempt involved an offer to buy the house at almost double its cost. (Gayle 176)

Margaret Walker adds that "Wright's success in raising money in one day, six thousand dollars in cash, made [his wife] Ellen's negotiations possible, and before anyone could realize the property was being sold to a black man they had accomplished the fact. Wright crowed with glee over their success" (Walker 194–95). McCullers's protagonist engages in his own subterfuge; intent on securing some reparations of his own, Pew "was writing a letter with the 'calligraphy of an angel.' He was writing an Atlanta agency in order to rent a house in Milan in the white man's section" (McCullers *Complete Novels* 784). It is this final move into a home beyond the fixed racial boundaries that results in an explosion of violence against Sherman as a way of reasserting those lines: "He moved in the middle of May and at last he was noticed."[13]

In reaction to Sherman Pew's move, a meeting is held in Malone's pharmacy. The atmosphere is carnivalesque, and the Judge opens with an address to the men as "leading citizens of the community, as property owners and defenders of our race," and goes on to raise fears of black strangers moving in next door, sitting next to whites on the bus, and of their own wives carrying on with "black bucks" (788). The language again is that of invasion; the fear is of a group "moving in right next door" in defiance of zoning laws (789). The collective "fraternity of hate" gathered in Malone's pharmacy offers an alternate construction of the nation, one united against the acquisition of property by others and one very familiar to readers of Wright's *Native Son* (McCullers, *Complete Novels* 789). The picture of the nation mobilized against the attempt of a stranger to make the nation his or her home recalls the rhetoric of disease infiltrating the body. Fittingly, the pharmacy provides the meeting place to discern how to eradicate the threat, again uniting racial discourse and disease in the novel. Sherman Pew's new neighbor volunteers to bomb Sherman's new home.[14]

When Jester, the Judge's grandson, goes to warn Sherman of the coming attack, he finds him in "an ecstasy of ownership," with Sherman insisting on showing Jester his new suits, bedroom furniture, and baby grand piano: "The house was suddenly all of Sherman's world....He had to busy himself with furniture, with things, and there was always this ever present sense of danger and the ever present sense that he would never back down. His heart was saying, *I have done something, done something, done something*" (McCullers *Complete Novels* 792–93). The conversion of house to home is at the center of Sherman Pew's brief final and damned project. On the night of the bombing, Sherman lights a fire because "the fire had looked cozy and homelike to him" (792); the fire that signifies home for Sherman Pew contrasts the fire of Sammy Lank's homemade bomb that will destroy it.

In Pew's final moments alive, McCullers references a passage from Richard Wright's *Black Boy*, the book of his she most admired. In *Black Boy*, Wright writes: "The penalty of death awaited me if I made a false move and I wondered if it was worth-while to make any move at all. The things that influenced my conduct as a Negro did not have to happen to me directly; I needed but to hear of them to feel their full effects in the deepest layers of my consciousness" (Wright, *Richard Wright: Later Works* 165). Here, we see Wright's clear understanding of the strict limits in which he is permitted to act and his internalization of the narratives of those who rebel against those constraints. Like Wright, Pew is aware of "the penalty of death," which accompanies a move beyond the line:

> Sherman knew every lynching, every violence that had happened in his own time and before his time, and he felt every abuse in his own body, and therefore lived in his stasis of tension and fear. Otherwise he would have thought of the plans of the old Judge as the product of a senile mind. But as a Negro living in the South...he had been exposed to such real horror and degradation that the wildest fantasies of the old

Judge seemed not only possible, but in Sherman's lawless land, almost inevitable. (741–42)

Pew's answer to the "horror and degradation" shows McCullers's deepest tribute in the text to Richard Wright. In a conversation between Pew and Jester, Pew speaks of the conversion of the stories of black oppression into an aesthetic record: "I register every single vibration that happens to those of my race. I call it my *black book*" (676, italics mine). Here, McCullers flags Richard Wright's black book *Black Boy* explicitly and Wright's storage of memories in the "deepest layers of his consciousness." Pew, like Wright, suffers and expresses the violence directed at members of the black community who move beyond the line. Pew converts this suffering into the vibrations of music on the piano. When the Judge's grandson, Jester, warns Pew that the coming mob is serious, Pew relies, "Serious, man?" Sherman began to pound middle C on the piano. "Me who kept a *black book* all my life, and you talk about serious? Did I tell you about vibrations? I vibrate, vibrate, vibrate!" (794, italics mine). Pew's piano stands for this same continuity through vibration, and he is playing the baby grand when Sammy Lank hurls the first of two homemade bombs at his singing throat.[15] After Sherman's body is removed from the charred house, "the crowd moved in. They hauled the baby grand out in the yard. Why they did not know" (McCullers, *Complete Novels* 795). The murder of Sherman Pew is somehow incomplete without the gutting of the home and the destruction of the piano, the aesthetic conduit of his own black book of suffering, horror, and degradation.

Sherman Pew refuses to reconstruct the slave system by existing in an invisible periphery; he instead constructs his own home in a manner that demands visibility and notice. In doing so, he knowingly invites death, but forces this death to be a murder committed in his own home. Whereas Wright's Bigger Thomas murders Mary Dalton in an effort to sustain invisibility, Sherman Pew is murdered because of his effort to assert his visibility. Whereas Bigger can find his purpose and identity only in his murder—the only means through which he is afforded recognition—Sherman demands this recognition through home ownership. If Bigger declares at the conclusion of Wright's novel, "But what I killed for, I *am*," Sherman Pew may be said to declare, "What I died for, I am." A decade after Wright's "I Choose Exile," Sherman Pew instead takes a room.

If Pew's individual attempt to subvert housing discrimination practices fails, McCullers closes her novel with the judicial end to another form of segregation and an acknowledgement of the crumbling barriers impossible to forecast in *Native Son*. *Clock without Hands* ends with the Judge's radio address in response to the unanimous Supreme Court decision (in *Brown v. Board of Education* of Topeka, Kansas) on May 17, 1954 in favor of school integration In ending her novel with this decision, McCullers shows the multiplicity of collapsing barriers (at least legislatively). The decision, furthermore, is one that cannot but be noticed. *TIME* covered the momentous decision in its May 24, 1954 issue, stating that of all of the Supreme Court decisions, "none of them so directly and intimately affected so many American families. The lives and values of some 12 million school-children in 21 states will be altered, and with them eventually the whole social pattern of the South" ("The Nation: 'To All on Equal Terms'" 21). Chief Justice Earl Warren read from his opinion that "today education is perhaps the most important function of state and local governments...It is the very foundation of good citizenship" ("The Nation: 'To All on Equal Terms'" 22). In response to the decision, the author of the *TIME* article notes,

> The loudest roars came from Georgia.... Out of Georgia's statehouse came a tirade from Governor Herman Talmadge: "The United States Supreme Court...has blatantly ignored all law and precedent...and lowered itself to the level of common politics...The people of Georgia believe in, adhere to, and will fight for their right under the U.S. and Georgia constitutions to manage their own affairs...[We will] map a program to insure continued and permanent segregation of the races." ("The Nation: 'To All on Equal Terms'" 22) [16]

It may be no accident, then, that McCullers sets her novel in her native Georgia, although certainly the reaction against segregation in schools was far from geographically contained. In *The Sin or Evils of Integration* (1962), the Reverend Louis E. Dailey writes that the day of the Supreme Court decision "was the blackest day in the history of the South, if all the potential evils which it holds are carried to their fruition" (Dailey 85). In ranting not unlike the Judge's, Dailey goes on to state that school integration will destroy the integrity of the white home through moral and cultural degradation: "No greater discrimination can be made upon a race than...to compel such a race to associate its children in school with others of a different color. They know that race will lower the moral level of their children, corrupt their language, and final debauch the moral level of their home life" (88). The horror of integration is for Dailey almost unspeakable, the profound violation of the founding principles of the nation: "It is hard to find descriptive language with which to paint the black, infamous discrimination that is now being pressed upon a people whose ancestors did so much to bring America into existence" (94). The connection between housing and educational segregation are linked both in McCullers's novel and in the Court's decision. Later that same month, the Supreme Court would extend the rationale behind the decision in favor of school integration and against "separate but equal" facilities to include public housing. *TIME* reported on May 31st that the Court "upheld a California Supreme Court decision ordering the San Francisco housing authority to admit eligible applicants to public low-rent housing projects without regard to race or color" ("The Supreme Court: Six Steps Forward" 18).

In the fever of his hate, and with the knowledge that he must make a historic speech against school integration, the Judge can only sputter out fragments of the Gettysburg Address, which Abraham Lincoln delivered on November 19, 1863. While the Judge only recites the first two paragraphs, the speech in its entirety is worth considering for its textual implications, following as it does the murder of Sherman Pew and the bombing of his home. It is what is left off the page and beyond his understanding that seems the most significant not only in relation to the textual death of Sherman Pew but in light of McCullers's tribute to the life and exile of Richard Wright:

> But in a larger sense, we cannot dedicate—we cannot consecrate—we cannot hallow—this ground. The brave men, living and dead, who struggled here, have consecrated it, far above our poor power to add or detract. The world will little note, nor long remember what we say here, but it can never forget what they did here. It is for us the living, rather, to be dedicated here to the unfinished work which they who fought here have thus far so nobly advanced. It is rather for us to be here dedicated to the great task remaining before us—that from these honored dead we take increased devotion to that cause for which they gave the last full measure of devotion—that we here highly resolve that these dead shall not have died in vain—that this nation, under God, shall have a new birth of freedom—and that government of the people, by the people, for the people, shall not perish from the earth. (Grafton 103–04)

This passage, when seen in the context of the closing pages of *Clock without Hands* and following the murder of Sherman Pew in response to his presence in the white neighborhood, rhetorically aligns Sherman Pew with those "dead...that this nation...shall have a new birth of freedom." The text suggests that the "unfinished work" and the cause for which he "gave the last full measure of devotion" was ultimately one of homemaking.

Clock without Hands, published the year after Richard Wright's sudden death gave Carson McCullers "a sense of the fragility of life," offers a tribute to Wright and to his struggle to find a home in the United States. The novel also affords McCullers a chance to return to and rewrite the conclusion of *Native Son* twenty years after the novel's publication. In the courtroom's closing arguments in *Native Son*, Max appeals to the jury to see blacks as a collective—he asks that the jury's "eyes leave the individual" and instead "encompass the mass" (364). This plea is vehemently rejected by McCullers's omniscient narrator. At the conclusion of *Clock without Hands*, the Judge's grandson, Jester Clane, soars above the earth in the airplane both Bigger Thomas and Sherman Pew dream of piloting. Only from the vantage point of Jester's airplane does "the earth assume order" and "the surrounding terrain seem designed by a law more just and mathematical than the laws of property and bigotry" (797). But this larger perspective "from a great distance" is far from the answer McCullers offers. Instead, her narrator states, "From the air men are shrunken and they have an automatic look, like wound up dolls. They seem to move mechanically among haphazard miseries. You do not see their eyes. And finally this is intolerable. The whole earth from a great distance means less than one long look into a pair of human eyes. Even the eyes of the enemy" (798). McCullers's call in 1961, in her final novel, is for a human connection and recognition between individuals, the denial of which led to Wright's decision to live in exile.

In his defense of Bigger, Max states that "these twelve million Negroes...are struggling within unbelievably narrow limits to achieve that feeling of at-home-ness for which we once strove so ardently" (463–64). Two decades after the publication of Wright's *Native Son*, McCullers's *Clock without Hands* portrays a country in which "at-homeness" for black Americans remains elusive. As Toni Morrison argues in *Playing in the Dark*, the ability to ignore is critical to a comfortable belief in the complete success of America's democratic principles: "There is still much national solace in continuing dreams of democratic egalitarianism available by hiding class conflict, rage, and impotence in figurations of race" (64). Precisely this blindness occurred in the early reviews of *Clock without Hands*, in which critics simply refused to see Sherman Pew and the racial dynamics in the text as anything beyond a distraction. Situating McCullers's final novel in relation to Wright's *Native Son* and *Black Boy* and in light of their personal relationship brings to the fore a reading of McCullers's work focused not on individual loneliness but on the social and racial dynamics of the postwar United States that drove Richard Wright into exile. If, to return to Charles Abrams, federal housing policy operates as "a proving ground on which the practical validity of a great ideal can be demonstrated" (9), seeing Sherman Pew as the textual center of the novel and noticing his relationship to the domestic space destabilizes the belief in the success of the democratic tenets of a nation that tantalizingly holds out and withholds the promise of home.

Today, the house that Wright and McCullers once shared at 7 Middagh Street in Brooklyn is gone—replaced by a Brooklyn-Queens Expressway overpass. But to recall this shared domestic space allows for an extension of Wright's literary legacy to include Carson McCullers, for whom Wright's favorable early review shaped a trajectory that her contemporary critics mourned, but which we may now reconsider and celebrate.

NOTES

1. Cf. *The Times* obituary for McCullers, September 30, 1967, pg. 4. This obituary is characteristic in its restatement of many reviews of *Clock without Hands*, which was dismissed by critics for failing to focus exclusively on the theme of individual loneliness. Critics either completely ignored Sherman Pew (many not even mentioning him by name) or read his presence as purely symbolic. In a representative piece in the *Manchester Guardian Weekly*, W. J. Weatherby suggested that in McCullers's work, "negroes [are] merely a local symbol of how we are all segregated in one way or another." Weatherby, "Uh-Huh, Uh-Huh," 14. In seeing McCullers in relation to Wright's mentorship, I hope to correct this misreading of McCullers's depiction of black characters in her novels.

2. Cf. Rowley, *Richard Wright: The Life and Times*, 282.

3. Addison Gayle mentions McCullers only to identify her "frailness, constant illness, and emotional problems" as the reason Wright moved his family from 7 Middagh Street (Gayle, *Richard Wright* 143) and to make a brief note of her visit to Wright in Paris (199). Fabre covers McCullers in just a few sentences (Fabre, *The Unfinished Quest* 244–45, 314). In her biography of Wright, Margaret Walker notes McCullers only briefly in a list of Southern writers, and again in another list of four southern women writers employing the conventions of the Gothic Novel.

4. The Sylvia Beach Papers at Princeton University contain an article from a New York magazine, titled "Wright to Live and Write Permanently in Paris Home" dating from the year *Native Son* was filmed. In the article, Wright states, "I want to live here [in Paris] until I die. There is no city on earth like it. It is the most human of cities in a world bent upon destroying

humanity." "Wright to Live and Write Permanently in Paris Home", 86. As if to emphasize that from which Wright seeks to escape, an advertisement caddy corner on the right upper side from the article features a black man and a light-skinned black woman for new Nadinola DeLuxe, greaseless bleach cream, which promises results after one jar. "Lightens skin fast…counteracts shine!" the ad boasts. A cloud bubble under the picture of the couple reads, "Men can't resist LIGHT, LOVELY skin!" The text underneath encourages consumers to: "Now treat your skin to the amazing bleaching and clearing action of this delightful new kind of cream!… *Watch day-by-day improvement*!"

5. Cf. also Wright's treatment of miscegenation in "Big Boy Leaves Home" and "How Bigger Was Born."

6. An excerpt from *Native Son* focusing on Bigger's desire to fly appeared in New York's *PM*, edited by Ralph Ingersoll, alongside an article on the exclusion of black workers from jobs in the defense industry. The *PM* reporter writes, "We print one moving passage from *Native Son* here, because it has special meaning to a country arming against Fascism. We are making Bigger Thomases every day. We make them by barring Negroes from the Army, from the Navy and from the Air Corps. We make them by depriving Negroes of jobs in defense industries. And Bigger Thomases don't make soldiers for democracy." "If Bigger Wasn't Black," 12. The excerpt was from pages 14–19 in the first edition, from Bigger's "Look!" to his "That's when I feel something awful's going to happen to me…" McCullers too casts her black protagonist as being jealous of his white friend, who is taking flying lessons and believes every adult has "a moral obligation to fly." McCullers, *Complete Novels*, 670. The racial prohibitions surrounding flight not only prevent entry into defense positions, but extend the boundary of the Black Belt into the heavens. No small wonder then, that Bigger's "Flight" in the novel's second part is a failed one.

7. Shelley v. Kraemer (1948) ruled that the decisions of the Supreme Court of Missouri and the Supreme Court of Michigan must be reversed. The decision states: "We hold that in granting judicial enforcement of the restrictive agreements in these cases, the States have denied petitioners the equal protection of the laws and that, therefore, the action of the state courts cannot stand. We have noted that freedom from discrimination by the States in the enjoyment of property rights was among the basic objectives sought to be effectuated by the framers of the Fourteenth Amendment."

8. The postwar era saw much violent action against attempts at integration even when that integration was judicially mandated. An illustrative example occurred in 1947 in the northwest area of Birmingham, when city officials refused to grant a permit to an African American couple who had built a house on land that had been zoned for white residences. The U.S. District Court ruled this action unconstitutional, but less than three weeks after the ruling, the house was bombed. Despite the

Court's decision, permits for African American houses continued to get withheld, and seven houses purchased or built by African Americans were bombed. No arrests were made. A city ordinance eventually created a "buffer strip" 150 feet wide to separate white and black zoning areas. Glazer and McEntire, *Studies in Housing & Minority Groups*, 64.

9. In his 1972 sociological case study of metropolitan Jacksonville, William A. Stacey concluded that preventative ownership has a direct effect on a sense of membership within the community: "Finally, theoretical consideration should be given the black male. This group is obviously the most alienated in society. In this study, the opportunity to become a homeowner had a significant effect on the black male's sense of powerlessness." Stacey, *Black Home Ownership*, 83. See also Lipsitz, *The Possessive Investment in Whiteness*.

10. For a contemporaneous examination of the tensions surrounding housing and educational desegregation, see Senior, *Strangers—Then Neighbors*. Senior includes an appendix "How the Schools Can Help" with respect to desegregation. He formulates an argument of "Cultural Democracy" in 1961 that anticipates many contemporary discussions of cosmopolitanism. See especially the chapters "The Contemporary Stranger" and "Ourselves as Neighbors" and pgs. 47–51 ("Integration in Schools"), 39–41 ("Cultural Democracy"), and 15–16 ("Negro Migration").

11. It is worth noting here that *Native Son* also focuses on a murder trial that is as much about miscegenation. Cf. 476, 481.

12. Critics objected to Sherman Pew's storyline as *interfering* with that of the other protagonists. One reviewer takes issue with Pew himself, wondering at his rage: "Another [character] who contributes *more than his share* is a Negro whose blue eyes show white blood in his parentage. He is the Judge's pampered servant, but in his heart he has hatred for those he serves, even though the service is light and his treatment considerate." "Two Old Men of the South." A review entitled "Well-Told Story of Two Men" by Harry T. Moore, which appeared in the *Boston Herald*, does not even mention Sherman Pew by name, but focuses on the two white male protagonists and refers to Pew only briefly as "the blue-eyed Negro boy who becomes a martyr to his own extravagant dreams." Moore, "Well-Told Story of Two Men," 9.

13. In a November 1967 pamphlet written in the aftermath of widespread protests over urban slum conditions, "The Negro, the Small Group, and Our Slum Problem," by former president of the New York Urban League and author Arthur C. Holden, he writes: "The Negro's new self-consciousness is now reaching out for self-realization. Primarily, Negroes have been demanding that the pressure of discrimination, that have held down his development be removed" (2). New York Urban League Correspondence.

14. For a contemporary account of a house burning in retaliation for an African American moving into an all-white housing development, see

Peck, "On Being Prejudiced in a Lily-White Community." During the construction period on his Long Island home, businessman Clarence Wilson twice had his house set on fire and had his insurance policy cancelled, before eventually deciding to move to spare his wife and children the violent atmosphere.

15. A possible other intertext for McCullers here is Wright's "Long Black Song," in which a black man chooses to remain in his home with the knowledge that an angry mob is coming to set it aflame.

16. The June-July 1954 issue of *The Crisis* reprinted the text of the Supreme Court decision, a history of the five cases that led to the decision, and a map of the United States indicating (1) states that require segregation, (2) states that permit segregation in various degrees, (3) states prohibiting segregation, and (4) states that have no specific laws on segregation. Georgia was among the states requiring segregation in public schools. In the Georgia in which McCullers sets *Clock without Hands*, African American children constituted 32.2 percent of public school enrollment, and as of 1950 made up 30.9 percent of Georgia's overall population; see "Some Basic Facts," 344–45.

Bibliography

Abrams, Charles. *Race Bias in Housing*. New York: University Microfilms, 1947. Print.

Bauman, Zygmunt. *Modernity and Ambivalence*. Ithaca, NY: Cornell UP, 1991. Print.

"Carson McCullers Dies at 50; Wrote of Loneliness and Love." Obituary. *New York Times* 1967. Print.

Dailey, Louis E. *The Sin or Evils of Integration*. New York: Carlton, 1962. Print.

Fabre, Michel. *The Unfinished Quest of Richard Wright*. New York: Morrow, 1973. Print.

Gayle, Addison. *Richard Wright: Ordeal of a Native Son*. 1st ed. Garden City, NY: Anchor Press/Doubleday, 1980. Print.

Glazer, Nathan, and Davis McEntire. *Studies in Housing & Minority Groups*. Publications of the Commission on Race and Housing. Berkeley: U of California P, 1960. Print.

Grafton, John, ed. *Abraham Lincoln: Great Speeches*. New York: Dover, 1991. Print.

"If Bigger Wasn't Black and If He Had Money and If They'd Let Him Go to Aviation School, He Could Fly." *PM* 7 May 1941: 12. Print.

Lipsitz, George. *The Possessive Investment in Whiteness: How White People Profit from Identity Politics*. Philadelphia: Temple UP, 1998. Print.

McCullers, Carson. "Books I Remember." *Harper's Bazaar* 75.5, 1941. Print.

———. *Complete Novels*. 1961. New York: The Library of America, 2001. Print.

————. *Illumination and Night Glare: The Unfinished Autobiography of Carson McCullers*. Madison: U of Wisconsin P, 1999. Print.

Moore, Harry T. "Well-Told Story of Two Men." *Boston Herald* 17 Sept. 1961, sec. 3: 9. Print.

Morrison, Toni. *Playing in the Dark: Whiteness and the Literary Imagination*. New York: Vintage, 1993. Print.

"The Nation: 'To All on Equal Terms.'" *TIME* 24 May 1954: 21–22. Print.

Peck, James. "On Being Prejudiced in a Lily-White Community." *The Crisis* 61.4 (1954): 215–18, 50. Print.

Rowley, Hazel. *Richard Wright: The Life and Times*. 1st ed. New York: Holt, 2001. Print.

Senior, Clarence. *Strangers—Then Neighbors: From Pilgrims to Puerto Ricans*. New York: Freedom, 1961. Print.

Shelley V. Kraemer, 334 U.S. 1. U.S. Supreme Court 1948. Print.

"Some Basic Facts for an Understanding of the Problem of Integration." *The Crisis* 61.6 (1954): 344–46. Print.

Stacey, William A. *Black Home Ownership: A Sociological Case Study of Metropolitan Jacksonville*. New York: Praeger, 1972. Print.

"The Supreme Court: Six Steps Forward." *TIME* 31 May 1954: 18. Print.

Tippins, Sherill. *February House*. Boston: Houghton Mifflin, 2005. Print.

"Two Old Men of the South." Book Review. *Detroit News* 17 Sept. 1961. Print.

Walker, Margaret. *Richard Wright, Daemonic Genius: A Portrait of the Man, a Critical Look at His Work*. New York: Warner, 1988. Print.

Weatherby, W. J. "'Uh-Huh, Uh-Huh': W. J. Weatherby Talks to Carson McCullers." *Manchester Guardian Weekly* 29 Sept. 1960: 14. Print.

Wright, Richard. *I Choose Exile*. JWJ MSS 3. Box 6. Folder 110. Richard Wright Papers. Series 1. Writings. Articles, Essays and Reports, New Haven, CT. Print.

————. "Inner Landscape." *Critical Essays on Carson McCullers*. Eds. Beverley Lyon Clark and Melvin J. Friedman. New York: MacMillan, 1996. 17–18. Print.

————. *Native Son*. 1940. New York: Harper Perennial, 1993. Print.

————. *Richard Wright: Later Works*. New York: The Library of America, 1991. Print.

"Wright to Live and Write Permanently in Paris Home." Box 236 Folder 5. Sylvia Beach Papers. 1887–1966. Rare Books: Manuscripts Collection, Princeton University, Princeton, NJ. Print.

12

When Wright Bid McKay Break Bread: Tracing Black Transnational Genealogy

Gary Holcomb

The consensus among Richard Wright scholars now deems that the existing literary critical approach to the author's work is overdue for reevaluation, and, above all, it's time for an analytic outlook that is adept at charting the author's trajectory through his expatriate years. I would add that reassessing Wright's final decade and a half as self-imposed exile would benefit from a fresh reconsideration of his disposition with respect to other black émigré authors, and not necessarily obvious associations.[1] Wright's relationship vis-à-vis Harlem Renaissance author Claude McKay is a case in point. Some black Atlantic scholarship has recorded the cosmopolitan parallels between Wright and McKay, notably Michel Fabre's and Tyler Stovall's seminal studies of the 1990s, but the correspondences between the two black authors could do with additional reflection, a pursuit that tacks across the swells of established practices. My interest is in articulating the genealogical relationship between McKay as recuperated transnational father and Wright as self-exiled, prodigal, *transnative* son. To be sure, matching up McKay and Wright qualifies as a counterintuitive undertaking, as the two interwar phase notables are characteristically coupled in *radical* counterpoint. Wright and McKay are critically paired off in opposition not merely as historical figures but also as historic figurations, as emblematic and therefore antithetic representatives of their respective moments. Over and above gaining a new understanding of these two authors by reexamining their contrasts and contretemps, in other words, an important reason for reconsidering the two authors together is because black literary criticism has digested the

essence of their differences, ultimately transforming it into a diagnostic certitude. In order to contemplate this literary odd couple as
a kind of transnational father and son, it is essential to speak to the
question of their vivid discord. It is necessary to do so because—
again, persisting with a counterintuitive logic—distinguishing their
divergences brings into focus their *confluences.* What requires deeper
reflection is the subject of McKay and Wright's cosmopolitan con-
vergences, transnational pas de deux that merit more attention than
cross-listings in academic indices, or even the critically fertile historical clustering. In view of the fact that the current *transnational* critical focus would yield a reassessment in ways established modes aren't
equipped to pursue, the time is presently right for thinking through
the unread correspondences between the two black authors.[2]

Speaking of *unread* correspondence, I begin with a little known, if
enlightening, piece of mail. On September 12, 1944, Claude McKay
shared with Ivie Jackman a seven-year-old still-galling reminiscence
of Richard Wright.[3] Writing of an encounter that had taken place in
1937, in the vicinity of the west 135th street Harlem YMCA, McKay
witheringly relates that Wright invited him " 'to have a bowl of soup,'
as he put it." A gesture of esteem and comradeship, proposing to
partake of a bowl of soup was a customary invitation extended by
one brother leftist to another during the ascetic, proletarian-inflected
1930s. McKay, the once-renowned Harlem Renaissance writer,
recounts that he turned down the invitation to convene over the min-
imal meal, in effect giving the fiery young writer the cold shoulder.
By 1944, McKay knew well whom he had given the brush-off back in
1937. Just a few months after the encounter of these two black lumi-
naries, in February 1938, Wright would publish *Uncle Tom's Children*,
a book that anticipated his becoming the most successful black writer
in the United States and, eventually, the most famous black author in
the world. Indeed, by 1944, at the time of this correspondence—with
Native Son (1940) in print and *Black Boy* (1945) imminent—Wright's
sun was at its zenith while McKay's star had plummeted. The reason he begged off Wright's offer of the austere repast, McKay says,
was because the younger author had been "very rude" when the two
served together on the Federal Writers Project during the mid-1930s.
However brusque Wright in fact may have been, the portrayal of him
as a young man with bad manners was the older author's way of char-
acterizing their ideological differences. Where in 1937 Wright was a
committed Marxist, McKay, the once-dedicated black Bolshevik, had
become ardently anticommunist. McKay sees the younger author as
having been in the pocket of the Communist Party USA; this much

is suggested by prickly irony. Recognizing the figurative implications in the circumstances, McKay makes the most metaphorically of the anecdote by adding disapprovingly about Wright: "He knew from which side his bread was buttered."

Another way McKay conveys the conditions that motivated his snubbing of Wright is by relating another anecdote. The story is of Wright's involvement with the magazine *New Challenge*, in that same year, 1937. As McKay communicates this story, one may discern in *sotto voce* an implicit parallel narrative of his own earlier experience with a radical periodical. While McKay's prior effort is somewhat familiar, the story of Wright's taking over *New Challenge* is well known, largely owing to the testimony of critics such as McKay. Dorothy West and some friends started *Challenge* in 1934, but by 1937 she wanted a more up-to-date publication. Wright and McKay, along with journalist Henry Lee Moon, vied for control over the magazine. When all parties sat down to discuss the periodical's future, McKay tells Ivie, he "could scarcely get in a word" because Wright, "according to the Communist formula," dominated the conversation. In the end, she asked enfant-terrible Wright to edit the revitalized version, relaunched as *New Challenge* (Fabre, *Unfinished* 142–46). Wright intended to meet the "new challenge" before him by truly radicalizing the serial publication. From McKay's standpoint, however, Wright's tactic to transform West's magazine was precisely the kind of tactless Communist commandeering the elder author found objectionable among the 1930s generation of young rebels. McKay characterizes West as being "in a dither" over Wright asserting control of her magazine, and then conveys to his correspondent that, "after one number," Wright "killed it." Wright helped the Party acquire the magazine, McKay says, but "they couldn't make a Communist out of Dorothy," and the upshot was the periodical's failure.

The anecdote "scarcely" veils a parallel narrative about the letter's author, moreover, as McKay himself had pursued an analogous undertaking during the early 1920s, at a time when *he* was the enfant terrible and foremost black literary Communist. Ivie, sister of Harlem Renaissance insider Harold Jackman, would have been just as familiar with this story. Named by publisher Max Eastman coeditor of the *Liberator*, McKay wanted to remake the liberal periodical into a more militant—to his mind, more legitimately Marxist-oriented— publication by intensifying its concentration on proletarian mixed-race concerns. McKay claimed that when he and coeditor Michael Gold fell out over the future of the magazine, the result was that he felt compelled to abandon his position as editor (Maxwell 95–124). If it was fair on McKay's part to portray Wright's attempt to adjust *New Challenge* as a kind of *killing*, it is likewise correct to depict McKay's effort to renovate *The Liberator* as a stab at *killing off* a dying gene pool to engender a stout new strain, the same sort of action Wright had attempted.

As Wright was, like McKay, an ardent collector of leftist inner circle gossip, it is a virtual certainty that he was also aware of the story of McKay's unsuccessful attempt to overhaul *The Liberator*. McKay's remarking on Wright's controversial editorial effort points to this likelihood. Though the older author undoubtedly would have refuted that a parallel could be made, that is to say, McKay's focus on Wright's maneuver iterates his own past attempt. The importance of McKay's experience as coeditor of *The Liberator*, as it impinged on his personal, professional, and political existence, can't be underestimated. McKay's past editorial decision had brought about the most momentous turning point in his life, generating the impetus for his restless ramblings through Germany, Russia, France, Spain, and Morocco, indeed his nearly twelve-year-long existence as a black expatriate author. In spite of McKay's unsympathetic portrait of a colleague, moreover, Wright's request that the senior author sup with him in 1937 must be recognized as more than mere casual courtesy. Wright doubtless was abrupt with McKay during the 1930s. A trait the two had in common was the displaying of stormy temperaments and uncompromising, electric intellects, dispositions that led to colliding violently with others, even close friends and advocates. Most interesting is McKay's still tuned-in penchant for a spot of streetwise psychoanalysis—that is, the pivotal if implied perception at the crux of his *New Challenge* anecdote that terrible-infant Wright's Freudian-inflected wish was to *kill* the fathers of the previous generation. Yet Wright's bidding McKay to break bread, what side it was buttered on notwithstanding, nonetheless signals the younger writer's wish to commune with the older author. The gesture signals the author of *American Hunger*'s craving for the comradeship of a crucial black revolutionary forebear. Wright's invitation effectively signifies an appreciation for the pioneering intellectual work of a black literary father, a suggestion that McKay's letter obliquely acknowledges. It is worth asking to what extent McKay's effort to convert a liberal magazine into a radical periodical Wright thought of as a model when, acting with like determination, he set about engaging in a comparable action, and to what degree McKay, the avid analyzer, was cognizant of this.

This is not to say McKay's indignation wasn't understandable, as Wright was more than "very rude" to the older author in 1937.

Where McKay ardently disapproved of the Marxist movement in which Wright enlisted, in like measure Wright wrote off the Harlem Renaissance, the cultural movement with which McKay was identified. Indeed the source for Wright's dismissing of 1920s black literary culture is among the most familiar denunciations of the Harlem Renaissance. In October 1937, Wright published his black Marxist manifesto "Blueprint for Negro Writing" in that same ill-fated if momentous issue of *New Challenge*, the magazine he "killed." The essay's categorical trashing of the "so-called Harlem school of expression" (203), as a movement dedicated to "pleading with white America for justice" (195), situates the black Social Realist author radically in opposition to the previous generation's example: "Negro writing in the past has been confined to humble novels, poems, and plays, prim and decorous ambassadors who went a-begging to white America" (194). Wright contends that New Negro writers subordinated their art to white capital interests, in the form of patronage and related varieties of submission to the ascendant hegemony. He argues, in effect, that the New Negro movement failed because its often-stated aims—to meliorate the situation of the hard-pressed black masses—could not be achieved through such cordial expression as folk-informed art and what he characterizes as timid belles lettres. Wright is certainly thinking of Zora Neale Hurston's output, as in that same busy October he also attacks her over the role of black writing in *New Masses*. Hurston profited from the backing of patrons such as Charlotte "Godmother" Mason and Fannie Hurst. But even more contentious, he accuses the author of *Their Eyes Were Watching God* (1937) of practicing a kind of literary minstrelsy.[4] Along with the entire cohort of New Negro notables, his Tommy Gun, wide-ranging denunciation of the Harlem Renaissance necessarily also targets the likes of McKay, who benefited from several white supporters, including the Leninist Max Eastman. Wright's condemnation therefore inescapably includes McKay's radical Marxist sonnets as well as the revolutionary black proletarian novel, *Home to Harlem* (1928), and core radical Négritude text, *Banjo* (1929).

McKay's soreness, moreover, certainly was intensified by another piece included in Wright's edition of *New Challenge*. That same packed-out if fatal issue included Harlem Renaissance critic Alain Locke's harsh review of McKay's memoirs, *A Long Way from Home* (1937). Locke accuses McKay of "Spiritual Truancy," to cite the article's title. As much as any other New Negro figure, Locke encouraged seeking and indeed pursued white patrons, such as Charlotte Mason (Rampersad 147). In a remarkable about-face, Locke, the past molder of New Negro aesthetics and identity, declares that black authors of the 1920s "should have addressed themselves more to the people themselves and less to the gallery of faddish Negrophiles" (85). As a matter of fact, Wright solicited the review from Locke, hoping for an endorsement of his own view of "the Harlem school" from one of its former leading lights. In a July 1937 letter, Wright writes to Locke, exhibiting a tendency to mix metaphors: "I do hope you will feel free to enter the ring with both hands loaded when you review MacKay [sic]....Since you know that Harlem school so thoroughly, we felt that you were the only possible person to handle such a book." The review undoubtedly inflamed McKay, a personality given to fits of fury—an ire, sometimes, as I said above, even aimed at close friends.

Although such severe criticism coming from one of the principals of the New Negro Renaissance clearly helped finally bury it, Locke's role could be little more than lieutenant in Wright's offensive. Wright's radically remodeling "blueprint" should be recognized as a—if not *the*—chief source of the idea that the Harlem Renaissance failed to achieve its aims, a critical departure I call the *failure thesis*. The failure thesis intensified after Wright's dismissive characterization of the Harlem Renaissance, reaching decades beyond the 1930s. And it is important that, as one may see from Locke's assessment, not only postrenaissance writers like Wright rejected the New Negro movement. One of the movement's foremost New Negroes, Langston Hughes, also felt that the Harlem Renaissance fell flat. In the "Black Renaissance" section of his first autobiography, *The Big Sea* (1940), published three years after Wright's Marxist prolegomenon, Hughes wryly observes of the renaissance that he played a crucial role in fashioning: "The ordinary Negroes hadn't heard of the Negro Renaissance. And if they had, it hadn't raised their wages any" (228). Hughes's withering rebuke is, in harmony with Wright's, a Marxist critique of the Harlem Renaissance, though for Hughes it is the renaissance as professed in Locke's most influential contribution to *The New Negro* (1925). The essay authoritatively titled "The New Negro" hastens to allay anxieties by reassuring that the African American civilian is by nature conservative and only a "forced radical" on "race matters" (11). By this Locke means to convey that the New Negro is not fixed on violent rebellion, as transpired during the previous decade in Ireland and Russia, upheavals still chilling in the minds of a white readership whose benevolence has limits and a black bourgeois leadership fretful about disconcerting those charitable if nervous whites. In this repudiation of the renaissance he helped style, that is to say, Hughes is speaking from across the barricades of the 1930s, from the other side of a radical shift toward Marxist polemical art. During the 1930s, Hughes abandoned the New Negro aesthetic, the order Locke established, in favor of a committed proletarian poster-board poetry, agitprop drama, and a Marxist-inflected fiction, a straight-shooting leftist literature, ideological ammunition discharged on behalf of the masses of African American folk on the breadlines.

During the same period Hughes and Locke rejected the artistic awakening they had participated in forging, another leading New Negro author grew to be just as reproachful of the Harlem Renaissance and, in contrast to Hughes's committed leftism and Locke's passing liberalism, as remorseful as he had become of Communism. In other words, McKay also played a part in portraying the Harlem Renaissance as a flop. In *A Long Way from Home*, an autobiography published in the same year Wright drafted his "Blueprint for Negro Writing," McKay articulates his decision to desert Harlem in 1922 as being brought on by his antipathy for the African American cultural awakening centered there, culminating three years later with the publication of Locke's *The New Negro*, a text that represented, similar to Hughes's view, the distorted leveling of diverse black voices. McKay's ambivalence about his role in the renaissance inheres in his inability anymore to "distill" poetry from his experience:

> …now that I was legging limpingly along with the intellectual gang, Harlem for me did not hold quite the same thrill and glamor as before. Where formerly in saloons and cabarets and along the streets I received impressions like arrows piercing my nerves and distilled poetry from them, now I was often pointed out as an author. I lost the rare feeling of a vagabond feeding upon secret music singing in me. (114)

For McKay, being "pointed out" as one of the Talented Tenth—"the intellectual gang" charged with enforcing conformity to rigid renaissance values—portends the taming of roguish Harlem into becoming a fetish commodification of blackness. According to McKay, after so many years of struggle and relative obscurity, at the moment when he was poised to benefit from recognition as a foremost writer of a major movement, he abandoned Harlem for Europe, ultimately relocating to Left Bank Paris. The reason for his flight, he insists, was due to being interpellated as a Harlem Renaissance author. Once an external designation is given to his insurgence, the revolution dies and the motivation for the poetry grows stale. An apposite Prohibition image, he is no longer able to *distill* poetry from his Harlem experience.

In view of such eminent New Negro writers broadcasting the idea that the Harlem Renaissance was an unmitigated debacle, it shouldn't be surprising that the failure thesis emerged fully formed and robust at the birth of black literary criticism. A resilient brainchild, the failure thesis appealed widely: to writer, philosopher, and historian alike. In "The World and the Jug" (1963), and in his own act of positioning himself—ironically while disclaiming Wright as an inspiration—Ralph Ellison begins with the presumption that the Harlem Renaissance fell short of the mark. A still controversial essay, Ellison emphasizes the importance of white literary moderns such as Ernest Hemingway in his pursuit of the writing technique he needed to create *Invisible Man* (1952). The essay was published in *The New Leader*, and was written in response to leftist critic Irving Howe's similarly controversial criticism of Ellison, "Black Boys and Native Sons" (1963). As Ellison disavows Wright's literary influence, his critique of Howe nevertheless expresses an implicit agreement with Wright's renunciation of the New Negro generation's stimulus, an understood articulation of the failure thesis. Although not exclusively concerned with New Negro phase writings, Harold Cruse's Black Arts period *The Crisis of the Negro Intellectual: A Historical Analysis of the Failure of Black Leadership* (1967) may be identified as a failure thesis critical source text by virtue of the fact that following Cruse's philosophical study, successive iterations of the renaissance identity "crisis" and "failure" emerged. Consistent with Wright's view, Cruse's crisis was a 1920s black nationalism that relied on white collaboration; therefore, black intellectuals were incapable of effecting social change through the cultural arts during the New Negro Renaissance. Speaking from the late 1960s, Cruse, in characteristic overstatement, judges that the "failures" of the Harlem Renaissance "left a dismal heritage for the current generation and a monumental problem to solve in the future" (83). While Cruse's conservative and historically unreliable black-nationalist text established the rough strokes for African American literary criticism, David Levering Lewis's well-researched *When Harlem Was in Vogue* (1981) is the source text for Harlem Renaissance studies in its present manifestation. Referring to the Harlem Renaissance as "the Golden Age" (103), the primary metaphor for Lewis's early eighties historical study is the idea that New Negro cultural producers formulated an art for art sake aesthetics. Though he does not directly broach the subject, the ghost in the discourse of Lewis's inquiry, the unspoken idea, is nevertheless the failure thesis. Orienting itself in an art for art's sake philosophy, Lewis's Harlem Renaissance turned away from political questions, and in this way resonates with Ellison's implied and Cruse's overt estimation that the 1920s sacrificed politics for art.

By the late 1980s, however, the failure thesis was becoming controversial. Houston Baker would endeavor to salvage the renaissance by disputing the idea that it failed to make the grade. *Modernism and the Harlem Renaissance* (1989) argues that black modernist modes must be assessed as the product of the African American vernacular tradition rather than ascendant Western textual forms. Whether it materially improved the bleak situation of black people during the 1920s is not, for Baker, a very rewarding question. A forward-looking feature of Baker's poststructuralist-informed study is a troubling of the notion that the 1920s black cultural awakening should be reduced to a binary doctrine of success/failure. Over the last decade, scholars of radical leftist history, confronting the perception that black intellectuals of the 1920s solely practiced a politically disengaged art, have presented the most compelling critique of the failure thesis. In *New Negro, Old Left: African-American Writing and Communism between the Wars* (1999), William J. Maxwell retrieves the radical leftist history of the renaissance and thereby challenges the notion of a monovocal, purely aesthetically driven New Negro movement, and presents instead a Harlem Renaissance dedicated to insurgent revolt.

Despite compelling charges of arrant reductiveness, the failure thesis is a supposition possessed of a hearty shelf life. Indeed, the assumption of failure still persists as a starting point for how the Harlem Renaissance is defined in black literary studies.[5] A long-standing supposition in African American literary critical studies has it that with the advent of the 1930s, an abrupt and total break of artistic and political principles took place. The prevailing critical mechanism not only takes as a certainty that black writing of the Great Depression decade departed in virtually every way from that of the Harlem Renaissance, but that indeed the impetus for the progressive literary transformations of the 1930s was expressly articulated in opposition to the previous decade's aims and achievements. Most telling is that both sides of the argument rely on the same diagnostic trope. Praise for the Harlem Renaissance sees the cultural awakening of the 1920s as a kind of aesthetic movement that was able to remain pure of ideology, while the Great Depression is perceived as being contaminated by the crudely polemical, as black art that was serviced to macropolitical objectives. The bifurcated, banal metaphor of the virgin and whore exposes the problematic in this logic, as this decade-antithesis schematic promotes a received mutually identifying contrary. Such is verified by the fact that, conversely, for those who privilege the 1930s over the 1920s, the opposite argument exists simultaneously. It is just as reductive to flip the binary, that is to say, trimming down 1920s black literary art as naive and depicting 1930s writing as, in contradistinction to the Harlem Renaissance, heroically engaged. In other words, when it comes to reading between-the-wars black writing, the idea that one decade was on the right track and the other misguided above all spells out the limitations of the established critical mechanism. Although the impression of a chaste Harlem Renaissance and an impure Great Depression persists, the more prevalent critical postulation is that black art of the 1930s surmounted the naïveté of the 1920s. The apparently unremarkable factor in the compound notion of absolute rupture and antithesis is the impression that black writing of the 1930s owed nothing to its immediate antecedent, that not even the ragged scrap of 1920s literary inheritance is observable blowing in the hot raging winds of the 1930s. At the core of the rupture theory is the critical convention that the Harlem Renaissance failed to achieve its ends. Though stated four decades ago, Cruse's verdict that the Harlem Renaissance "left a dismal heritage" continues to resonate in the composite notion that an apolitical, naive art led the 1920s by the nose and a committed politics piloted 1930s black writing. The storied rift between Wright and McKay is among the narratives deemed to exemplify both the schism scheme and failure claim, and this view is fortified by the fact that the two authors themselves act as primary sources for the idea.

As a critical logic, the failure thesis is fairly effortlessly unpacked by cataloguing politically engaged New Negro literary art. Alain Locke's was not the only or even necessarily primary vision of the New Negro movement. In the same year as Locke's *The New Negro*, 1926, W. E. B. Du Bois insisted in the pages of the most influential black journal in America, *The Crisis*, that New Negro art manifestly must be political in content. I add the italics to emphasize what I see as Du Bois's unmistakable intention to turn conventional opinion on its head: "I do not care a damn for any art that is *not* used for propaganda" (296). By "propaganda," Du Bois plainly doesn't have in mind the term's typical English designation: misinformation, half-truths, cant. *Propaganda*, for German scholar Du Bois, means to agitate for something progressive.[6] Angelina Weld Grimké's black feminist, antilynching drama *Rachel*, written in 1915 and performed in 1920, serves as an emergent example of renaissance radical writing, as the "prim" play, as Wright would have it, anticipates Du Bois's notion that all black art should openly stir up opinion and advocate radical change. Jean Toomer's *Cane* (1923) must be recognized as a revolutionary work by any definition, whether in terms of content or form, aesthetics or ideology. As Charles Scruggs and Lee VanDemarr say in *Jean Toomer and the Terrors of American History* (1998), Waldo Frank's American transnationalism appealed to Toomer, as his friend's revolutionary poetics complemented the black author's radical articles for the Socialist paper *The Call* as well as his attendance at the "worker's university," New York's Rand School, in 1918 (48). Mark Whalen adds that Frank's radical poetics "also offered [Toomer] a political application for what he had experienced in Georgia," that is, while researching for the writing of *Cane* (75). Indeed, what makes writing *radical* is necessarily a contested site. Although for this discussion the concept is of necessity limited to the subject of explicitly political art, it is also useful to consider the notion of what qualifies as radical writing according to broader conditions. Even work by black aesthetes, art-for-art-sake advocates, and sometime avant-garde authors—granted their targets were the postulations about the role of black art generated by first-generation New Negroes such as Du Bois and Grimké—also confronts reactionary hegemony. A case in point is Wallace Thurman's relentless interrogation of skin politics, *The Blacker the Berry* (1929), a novel that appeared at the end of the renaissance phase. To cite Amritjit Singh, "Thurman's Harlem Renaissance is one of the most radical and uncompromising responses from a black writer in the 1920s to the denials of African American personhood and individuality through racialization" (9). Disseminated by such authors as Grimké, Marita Bonner, and Alice Dunbar-Nelson, furthermore, among the most radical developments of the New Negro decade was black feminism and a related women's sex reformism, including the black lesbianism of Mae Cowdery's writing.[7] Even the author at whom Wright expressly aimed his assault on the Harlem Renaissance, and who next to writers like Hughes would be most accurately described as politically conservative, Zora Neale Hurston is presently recognized, due to writings like "Sweat" (1926), as a forerunner of black feminist writing. The sort of status Hurston acquired following Alice Walker's publicizing of her as literary mother in *Ms. Magazine* during the mid-1970s is founded on the author and folklorist's import as black feminist forebear. McKay's radical poetry and fiction most palpably challenge the idea that the New Negro movement was unconcerned with politics, however. But what needs to be added is McKay's merging of what I call elsewhere a form of "queer black Marxism," a black transnational art that assails right-wing hegemony from three united, mutually invested revolutionary fronts. Like that of black feminist authors, writing by queer black New Negro writers such as McKay, Thurman, and Cowdery confronted not only white supremacy but also exposed the ideological duplicity of black conservatism. New Negro writing was essentially, necessarily political.

All of the above, however, does not decisively put to rest the notion that the Harlem Renaissance failed. Exposing the binary opposition inherent in the failure thesis trope doesn't essentially invalidate the idea that the renaissance fell short, only that the language used relies on received discourses. Likewise, New Negro writers may have been politically engaged, but it doesn't necessarily follow that their dedication resulted in constructive social transformation. The legacy of the failure thesis is persuasively met by highlighting the transnational arcs where Wright and McKay, two authors responsible for it, traversed. In pursuing this logic, I believe I can not only finally dispel the failure claim, but, more important, can show that New Negro literature helped shape the radical rhetorics of the 1930s, that in crucial ways vital characteristics of 1930s black writing may be seen as an consequence of the 1920s. This critical act may provide an example for additional inquiry. Notwithstanding the Harlem Renaissance writer's own ambivalence about the New Negro movement, McKay's *instance* serves as the most persuasive challenge to Wright's writing off of the renaissance and consequently, at the very least, unsettles the notion of its alleged failure. I argue for this viewpoint because the New Negro Renaissance, as the Négritude writers recognized, set the stage for black transnationalism, a view of the black world Wright played a strategic role in mapping. The present transnational compass reading supplies the most effective means for illuminating the flaws in the 1920s–1930s schism premise and associated 1920s failure supposition. Seeing the Harlem Renaissance and progressive Depression era as contraries in fact shrinks the 1920s and 1930s to reductive literary-historical chronotopes, telescoping a view that impoverishes the cosmopolitan complexity of the interwar period. Where my essay into the question of Wright and McKay means to advance a new mode of thinking about the relationship between the two authors, pairing them necessarily means to do more than even initiating a reassessment of the way black literary studies communities see these two writers in relation to one another. My view is that reconsidering the affiliation between McKay and Wright through a lens adjusted by the transnational focus may also assist in thinking again the interaction between the writing of the Harlem Renaissance and Great Depression phases. While my intention is to fine-tune the critical focus to review the black literary interwar phase through the transnational lens, however,

I mean to do so by means of a black intercontinental analytical instrument set to the historical realities of interwar phase political force fields. In spelling out the limitations of original philosopher of transnationalism, Randolph Bourne's disregarding of both "the tricky question of African American citizenship" and "the worlds of color outside the United States' borders," indeed Bourne's centralization of a "*European* diaspora" (53), Michelle A. Stephens's *Black Empire: The Masculine Global Imaginary of Caribbean Intellectuals in the United States 1914–1962* (2005) effects a working definition of black transnational studies. Yet even with Stephens's call for a more concentrated focus on the ideological in "black empire," transnational studies has not spoken substantially to the *authentic* radical, political, and aesthetic concerns of the 1920s.[8] In truth, black transnational studies has been following the received wisdom of both the decade schism and failure theory, failing to perceive the opportunity to interrogate one of the primary targets of transnational criticism: the environmental limitations inherent in period and related studies. An inquiry into McKay and Wright's hemispheric intersections indeed may uncover vital truths about black authorship during the interwar period.

It is essential first to catalog the expatriate, transnational parallels between McKay and Wright, both material and materialist. During the early 1920s, McKay traveled to Europe and attended the Fourth Congress of the Third Communist International in Moscow, and about a year later settled in the French capital—actions that prefigure Wright's radicalism and residence in Paris. In France, McKay wrote *Home to Harlem*, the first bestseller by a black author in the United States, a novel that in its way made almost as big a splash as *Native Son*. Though typically characterized as merely an enjoyable, somewhat sensational Jazz Age chronicle of Harlem rent party and speakeasy subcultures, *Home to Harlem* in fact not only poses a radical confrontation with white supremacist ideology but also challenges what McKay deemed already retrograde notions of black literary art and social value. Unconcerned with advancing the situation of the African American bourgeoisie, in other words, *Home to Harlem* is the first extended fiction to portray the experience of the Black Diaspora proletariat, who are, kin to the black migrants in *Native Son*, compelled to be classified lumpen only as a consequence of racial politics: Jim Crow and his blood relation, American imperialism. The novel also chronicles the experience of Caribbean immigrant groups and queer black subculture, indeed indicating that these three countercultures—African American working class, Caribbean migrants, and black queer—coexist and even help shape one another's concepts of self-determination. Like Wright, McKay's geographical journeys molded his literary expeditions. Using Paris as his headquarters, McKay took a number of trips to such destinations as Antibes, Nice, Toulon, and, most important, Marseilles, a black Atlantic port-of-call where he set two novels. Though less successful in popular terms than *Home to Harlem*, Marseilles-set *Banjo* nevertheless became a crucial Négritude source text for black transnational art. And his still unpublished, unread, and in ways most overtly political novel, *Romance in Marseille* (c. 1929–1932), portrays black Leninist vanguard attempts to organize Vieux Port transnational itinerant black migrant laborers—African, African American, and Caribbean—into becoming part of a clued-in international proletariat.[9] It is noteworthy that the plot of *Romance in Marseille*, like *Native Son*, was based on an actual incident, when McKay successfully acted on behalf of an African dockworker friend who filed a legal suit after losing his legs due to the negligence of a transatlantic shipping company. The most estimable character in the manuscript's pages is a black Leninist cultural worker based on a fusion of Senegalese Communist labor organizer Lamine Senghor and McKay himself. McKay lived in France for the greater part of the 1920s, like Wright, interacting with yet ultimately seeing himself as detached from the white expatriate community. He also spent a considerable amount of his expatriate period in Spain, anticipating Wright's valuing of the Iberian country for its "pagan" qualities. During his last three years abroad, the Jamaican colonial dwelled mainly in Morocco, where he interacted with leaders of the Trans-Saharan Arab Renaissance and learned firsthand the lessons of anticolonialism in Africa (Holcomb 63). Before heading back to Morocco, McKay returned to Paris in 1929 to reunite with the New Negro illuminati and mix with the Négritude intellectuals. All told, McKay remained in Europe and North Africa for nearly the same duration of time that Wright resided in Paris, indeed spending the majority of this, for the most part, self-imposed exile in the City of Light. Like Wright, McKay's restlessness permitted him to perceive the revolutionary potential in the transnational.

Wright's obligation to McKay may be perceived in the moment the African American author set foot on French soil. On his first trip to Paris in 1946, Wright met Aimé Césaire and Leopold S. Senghor for the first time, and was so taken with their movement that when he returned a year later he would sponsor the Négritude journal *Présence Africaine* (Fabre, *Unfinished* 316–20). By the mid 1950s, Négritude, partly owing to Wright's influence, would become more politically active, and Wright helped to organize the International Congress of

Negro Artists and Writers, a group responsible for establishing the politics of African decolonization (Rowley 477). Eventually, Wright would, like McKay, travel to Africa, a trip that resulted in *Black Power* (1954). It may be true that technically McKay never reached *black* Africa, as the Jamaican author lived in Morocco for most of 1930 to 1933. Yet it should be noted that McKay, testing the language of a nascent radical transnational poetry, rejected the idea that Morocco wasn't authentic Africa, asserting that the racial designation given North African peoples was a device of racialist scientific taxonomies, not a reflection of cultural and genetic reality in Tangier, Fez, and Casablanca. The most visible transnational intersection between Wright and McKay, however, may be traced by returning to Wright's relations with the Négritude poets and philosophers, as the central text of the politically engaged postwar period was Ousmane Sembene's *Le Docker Noir* (1956). As Tyler Stovall comments in *Paris Noir: African Americans in the City of Light* (1996), the Négritude intellectuals saw *The Black Docker* as a novel that owed equally to *Native Son* and *Banjo* (197). McKay's *présence* preceded Wright's, paving the way for the latter to participate in inventing the rhetorics of black transnationalism.

Despite Wright's clear assertion that the New Negro movement fell short politically, McKay's revolutionary politics also may be appreciated as radically anticipating Wright's. In Jamaica, McKay became stirred by the philosophy of Fabian Socialism, but his genuine engagement with militant politics occurred as a result of experiencing U.S. racism. He was a member of the underground union the Industrial Workers of the World (IWW) in 1919, when he wrote such poems as "If We Must Die" and, by the time he reached the Soviet Union a few years later, was identified by the Bureau of Investigation as a Communist. McKay's 119-page FBI file is in some ways a more reliable source for its subject's radicalism than his own 1937 memoirs, *A Long Way from Home*, as the book takes pains to obscure his past and reinvent its uneasy author. Around the time he was a member of the IWW, McKay also helped found the equally secretive African Blood Brotherhood, indeed modeling the clandestine black transnational organization on the Wobblies. He generated radical journalism for Sylvia Pankhurst's *The Workers' Dreadnought* while residing in Britain during the early 1920s and interacted with a range of radicals in the London-based International Socialist Club. Acting as a confidential emissary for the Brotherhood and hoping to meet with Lenin, McKay traveled to the Soviet Union in 1922. By the time he arrived, the Bolshevik leader was gravely ill, but McKay did interview

Trotsky, whom Lenin had appointed Commander of the Red Army and People's Commissar of War. McKay and Trotsky discussed how black intellectual workers, after the fashion of a Leninist philosophy of vanguardism, could go about radicalizing the working, peasant, and colonized black masses of the Americas and Africa, a strategy McKay planned to share with the Brotherhood (Holcomb 39).

Both Wright and McKay have served as exemplars for black intellectuals who finally saw through leftism as an oppressive force dedicated to work against the interests of black peoples. But this interpretation is as reductive as the Harlem Renaissance failure thesis. Indeed it is an assumption fastened epistemologically to Black Arts period black nationalism, a philosophy that has been habitually articulated against an anti-imperialist internationalism. Related to the notion that Marxism infected New Negro arts, African American chauvinism is the ideological source of the failure thesis, as the most egregious aspect of the New Negro movement, from a particular corner of 1960s black nationalism, was the Harlem Renaissance's dealings with and therefore corruption caused by white intellectuals. Such a gesture lumps the likes of conservative "Negrotarian" Carl Van Vechten, author of the controversial *Nigger Heaven* (1926), with the radical Max Eastman. Until the mid to late 1930s, McKay was simultaneously a black nationalist and Marxist internationalist, among the school of black intellectuals of the interwar years who, like C. L. R. James, did not see these two revolutionary philosophies as reciprocally excluding (Callinicos 62). Like Wright's break with the Communist Party USA during the 1940s, McKay's quarrel with Communism during the 1930s was specifically a break with the institutionalization of Party ideology, in McKay's case the Stalinist, that is, post-Leninist, consolidation of a form of Soviet nationalist power. As was his friend and fellow traveler Eastman, author of the mournful *Since Lenin Died* (1925)—a text that is simultaneously despondent about Lenin's demise as well as the future of international Socialism—McKay was a follower of Trotsky. McKay's commitment to the Jewish Ukrainian philosopher's permanent revolution thesis as it could be applied to the situation of the black masses lasted nearly ten years longer than his own anxious autobiography indicates.

To my mind, Wright's disavowal of New Negro writing as a stimulus in fact serves as the most persuasive argument for its inspiration. Just as the 1920s–1930s theory of total rupture and 1920s failure thesis unravel when subjected to inquiry, it wouldn't take an extended analysis to expose the flaws in Wright's black modernism, his perception of himself as rootless, as unattached to the previous generation of black cultural producers. It is illuminating that Wright's disciple, Ellison, does precisely that to his own patrimony, Wright's stimulus—Ellison's was a lesson well learned. But most important is to trace the hemispheric lines of flight McKay and Wright followed in their pursuit of a revolutionary black transnational writing, and to chart the routes where their travels, geographical but, more important, philosophical, traverse. Doing so should occasion the question of whether the Bandung World Richard Wright of the expatriate years would have existed without the previous instance of Claude McKay. Recognition of McKay's insistence may be traced to a gesture as seemingly slight as an invitation to a senior writer to partake of a bowl of soup. And evidence for Wright's gratitude paradoxically may be perceived in McKay's refusal of the offer to share a simple meal. The senior author could not, on that Harlem day in 1937, contend with Wright's Communism. Nevertheless, Wright saw in McKay a literary progenitor, and evidently believed, though sentient he had attempted to assassinate this father, that it was worth the risk of being rebuffed to extend the invitation. It is instructive that, a few years after McKay recalled his exchange over breaking bread, Wright would produce a manuscript that was originally planned to be the second volume of *Black Boy*. It would be posthumously, and appositely, titled *American Hunger* (1977). The "hunger" of the title is the desire to feel related to others, to refuse being made to feel like a black Camusian stranger, an exile, a foreigner in one's own land, an interloper and outcast. Indeed, from the Chicago-located *Native Son* to Paris-produced *The Outsider* (1953), the theme of Wright's work is the black human subject's search for relations, to feel at "home" in the world—the same theme of McKay's prose period, from *Home to Harlem* to *A Long Way from Home*. Indeed, the two met on the transnational terrain, a vista from which it is possible to survey black human subjectivity in global terms. In McKay's prior international expedition across the black Atlantic, one may detect a portion of the wellsprings for Wright's later radical transnational vision. An understanding of this suggests a new departure point for inquiries into Richard Wright.

Notes

1. A prevalent theme of panels and presentations at the June 2008 American University of Paris International Richard Wright Centennial Conference was the necessity for a revaluation of Wright's expatriate period writing.

2. Related to reassessing the writing of Wright's émigré phase at American University of Paris's Wright Centennial was the subject of his role as transnational author, two sessions being devoted to this topic: "The Black Atlantic: Transnationalism and Transatlanticism" and "Wright: The Global and the Transnational."

3. Cooper quotes the germane portion of this letter in his biography of McKay (362).

4. See Wright's "Between Laughter and Tears," and for Hurston's response see her review of *Uncle Tom's Children*.

5. The opening paragraph of the preface to Wintz and Finkelman's two-volume *Encyclopedia of the Harlem Renaissance* (2004) acknowledges that the idea of failure overshadows even contemporary views of the movement.

6. The phrase *für etwas Propaganda machen* means "to agitate for something." The inflection of this idiom may be negative, neutral, or positive, depending on its usage.

7. Patton and Honey's *Double-Take: A Revisionist Harlem Renaissance Anthology* (2001) provides a sampling of key black feminist and women's sex revolution texts by Bonner, Cowdery, Dunbar-Nelson, Grimké, and Hurston.

8. Though an unquestionably valuable contribution to black transnational and Harlem Renaissance studies, Edwards's *The Practice of Diaspora: Literature, Translation, and the Rise of Black Nationalism* (2003) argues that a globally oriented black nationalism during the interwar period posed a radical alternative to black Marxist internationalism, in effect superseding black Marxism with a kind of cosmopolitan black nationalism. Certainly a form of worldwide black nationalism challenged the predominance of black Marxist ideology, most spectacularly the populist Pan- Africanism of Garvey's Universal Negro Improvement Association. But to argue that it supplanted black leftist internationalism is a misleading contention. During the interwar period, black nationalism and black Marxism were competing forms, yet often those pledged to one simultaneously subscribed to the other.

9. I devote a chapter of *Claude McKay, Code Name Sasha: Queer Black Marxism and the Harlem Renaissance* to McKay's unpublished novel.

BIBLIOGRAPHY

Baker, Houston. *Modernism and the Harlem Renaissance*. Chicago: U of Chicago P, 1987. Print.

Callinicos, Alex. *Trotskyism*. Minneapolis: U of Minnesota P, 1990. Print.

Cooper, Wayne F. *Claude McKay: Rebel Sojourner in the Harlem Renaissance*. New York: Schocken, 1987. Print.

Cruse, Harold. *The Crisis of the Negro Intellectual: A Historical Analysis of the Failure of Black Leadership*. 1967. Ed. Stanley Crouch. New York: New York Review of Books, 2005. Print.

Eastman, Max. *Since Lenin Died*. New York: Bon, 1925. Print.

Edwards, Brent Hayes. *The Practice of Diaspora: Literature, Translation, and the Rise of Black Nationalism*. Cambridge, MA: Harvard UP, 2003. Print.

Ellison, Ralph. "The World and the Jug." *New Leader* 46 (1963): 22–26. Print.

Fabre, Michel. *From Harlem to Paris: Black American Writers in France, 1840–1980*. Urbana: U of Illinois P, 1991. Print.

———. *The Unfinished Quest of Richard Wright*. 1973. Urbana: U of Illinois P, 1993. Print.

Federal Bureau of Investigation. Claude McKay file, no. 61-3497. Assorted documents dated 16 Dec. 1921 to 31 May 1940, obtained under provisions of the Freedom of Information Act. 119 pages. Print.

Grimké, Angelina Weld. *Rachel: A Play in Three Acts. Selected Works of Angelina Weld Grimké*. Ed. Carolivia Herron. Schomburg Library of Nineteenth-Century Black Women Writers. Oxford: Oxford UP, 1991. 123–209. Print.

Holcomb, Gary Edward. *Claude McKay, Code Name Sasha: Queer Black Marxism and the Harlem Renaissance*. Gainesville: UP of Florida, 2007. Print.

Howe, Irving. "Black Boys and Native Sons." *A World More Attractive*. New York: Horizon, 1963. 98–110. Print.

Hughes, Langston. Introduction. *The Big Sea*. 1940. By Arnold Rampersad. New York: Hill and Wang, 1993. Print.

Hurston, Zora Neale. Rev. of *Uncle Tom's Children* by Richard Wright. 1938. *Richard Wright: Critical Perspectives Past and Present*. Ed. Henry Louis Gates, Jr. and K. A. Appiah. New York: Amistad, 1993. 3–4. Print.

———. "Sweat." *Fire!! A Quarterly Devoted to the Younger Negro Artists* 1.1 (1926): 40–45. Print.

———. *Their Eyes Were Watching God*. Philadelphia: Lippincott, 1937. Print.

Lewis, David Levering. *When Harlem Was in Vogue*. New York: Knopf, 1981. Print.

Locke, Alain. "The New Negro." *The New Negro*. New York: Boni, 1925. 3–16. Print.

———. "Spiritual Truancy." Rev. of *A Long Way from Home*, by Claude McKay. *New Challenge* 2 (1937): 81–85. Print.

Maxwell, William J. *New Negro, Old Left: African-American Writing and Communism between the Wars*. New York: Columbia UP, 1999. Print.

McKay, Claude. *Banjo: A Story without a Plot*. 1929. Print.

———. *Home to Harlem*. 1928. Print.

———. Letter to Ivie Jackman. 12 Sept. 1944. Ivie Jackman–Harold Jackman Papers. Trevor-Arnett Library, Atlanta University.

———. *A Long Way from Home*. New York: Furman, 1937. Print.

———. *Romance in Marseille*. 1929–1932. Unpublished MS. Miscellaneous Claude McKay Papers. Schomburg Center for Research in Black Culture, New York Public Library.

Patton, Venetria K., and Maureen Honey, eds. *Double-Take: A Revisionist Harlem Renaissance Anthology.* New Brunswick, NJ: Rutgers UP, 2001. Print.

Rampersad, Arnold. *The Life of Langston Hughes: Volume 1: 1902–1941, I, Too, Sing America.* New York: Oxford UP, 1986. Print.

Rowley, Hazel. *Richard Wright: The Life and Times.* New York: Holt, 2001. Print.

Scruggs, Charles, and Lee VanDemarr. *Jean Toomer and the Terrors of American History.* Philadelphia: U of Pennsylvania P, 1998. Print.

Singh, Amritjit. "Introduction: Wallace Thurman and the Harlem Renaissance." *The Collected Writings of Wallace Thurman.* By Wallace Thurman. New Brunswick, NJ: Rutgers UP, 2003. 1–28. Print.

Stephens, Michelle A. *Black Empire: The Masculine Global Imaginary of Caribbean Intellectuals in the United States, 1914–1962.* Durham, NC: Duke UP, 2005. Print.

Stovall, Tyler. *Paris Noir: African Americans in the City of Light.* Boston: Houghton Mifflin, 1996. Print.

Walker, Alice. "In Search of Zora Neale Hurston." *Ms. Magazine* March 1975: 74+. Print.

Whalan, Mark. "Jean Toomer and the Avant-Garde." *The Cambridge Companion to the Harlem Renaissance.* Ed. George Hutchinson. Cambridge: Cambridge UP, 2007. 71–81. Print.

Wintz, Cary D., and Paul Finkelman, eds. *Encyclopedia of the Harlem Renaissance.* 2 vols. New York: Routledge, 2004. Print.

Wright, Richard. "Between Laughter and Tears." Rev. of *Their Eyes Were Watching God* by Zora Neale Hurston. *New Masses* (5 Oct. 1937): 23–25. Print.

———. *Black Boy: A Record of Childhood and Youth.* New York: Harper, 1945. Print.

———. *Black Power: A Record of Reactions in a Land of Pathos.* New York: Harper, 1954. Print.

———. Letter to Alain Locke. 8 Jul. 1937. Alain Locke Papers. Moorland-Spingarn Research Center, Howard University. Print.

———. *Native Son.* New York: Harper, 1940. Print.

———. Uncle Tom's Children: Five Long Stories. New York: Harper, 1938. Print.

13

The Political Art of Wright's "Fire and Cloud"

Robert Shulman

In the political art of "Fire and Cloud," ideas and general implications emerge plausibly from and in response to powerful, highly charged actions and choices. The Depression is in the foreground of this prize-winning story, set in the rural South, written in 1936–1937, and published in 1938.[1] From the start of "Fire and Cloud," in the central character's initial remarks and in the folk song he's singing to himself, the Rev. Taylor shows he knows his people are hungry and the white relief officials are refusing to help. Although the Rev. Taylor is moderate and deeply religious, the situation is alive with political, Marxist implications. Wright succeeds in creating a suggestive situation and a character who is politically receptive but not committed, who is aligned with his people and his religious tradition but in a way that allows Wright to explore ideas more radical than the troubled, moderate Rev. Taylor is willing to accept. Wright assumes that we know about the radical Southern Tenant Farmers' Association and the role of Communist Party organizers in the South.[2]

"Fire and Cloud" turns on the issues connected with the protest march the communist organizers have proposed and that Rev. Taylor is considering. "Mabbe," he thinks, "ef five er six thousan of us marched downtown we could *scare* em inter doin something! Lawd knows, mabbe them Reds *is* right!" (355). Because it allows Left writers to bring radical ideas to a dramatic focus, the protest march is one of the basic motifs in the iconography of the 1930s Left—Meridel Le Sueur's "I Was Marching" is only one of dozens of marvelous examples (Shulman 67–73). For Wright as a black writer working within the Communist Party, the political issues are complicated by the tension between race and class. For all his troubled moderation, the Rev. Taylor has an incipiently revolutionary consciousness in that he feels strongly that "the white folks jus erbout owns this whole worl" (355)—and he wants to do something about it. But for him, the contest is not between owners and workers, as in the communist, Popular Front tradition, but between *white* owners and oppressed black people. The underlying ideological question the story poses and eventually resolves is whether or not the marchers will enact the Popular Front ideal of black and white together or are the five or six thousand "us"—that is, black people—opposed to the whites who own everything.[3]

Before he opens up this central concern and the equally controversial issue of democratic versus Leninist leadership of a mass movement, Wright gives an independent version of the Popular Front's involvement in traditional Americanism. Recall that in the years 1935 through 1939, the Popular Front's slogan was "Communism is 20th-Century Americanism." Wright makes the Rev. Taylor acceptable to a broad range of readers partly by showing that his protest is religiously grounded in the venerable American tradition of the Jeremiad.[4] We've fallen off from God's ways, the classic Jeremiad preacher tells us, as Jonathan Edwards does in his powerful "Sinners in the Hands of an Angry God," and unless we change, the Jeremiad preacher goes on, God will punish us.

At the end of the story, Wright brings alive Edwards's hell-fire vision but at the start he is more moderate. In Wright's initial Marxist, Popular Front version, "the Good Lawds gonna clean up this ol worl some day!" the Rev. Taylor says, without saying, as he does later, "theys gonna burn in Gawd Awmightys fire!" (356, 393). At first, Taylor's God is peaceful, not wrathful, but He is also radical. "Hes gonna make a new Heaven n a new Earth! N Hes gonna do it in a eye-twinkle change! Hes gotta do it! Things cant go on like this ferever! God knows they cant!" (356). In the accents not only of the Jeremiad but also anticipating liberation theology, for the Rev. Taylor, God sanctions radical change. The Good Lord may be the source, moreover, but the people are the instruments, so that the Rev. Taylor aligns the respectability of traditional Christianity with the Marxist commitment to revolutionary "eye-twinkle change" to establish "a new Heaven n a new Earth."

Working within the Popular Front tradition, Wright also dignifies the Rev. Taylor by endowing him with a mythic American past. He is the Moses of his people, a hard-working patriarch who plowed the rich earth and prospered. In this fertile, postslavery America, "the

Promised Land," he and his brothers own their land and experience an unalienated oneness with the earth because "the earth was his" (357). This mythic version contrasts with the view that "the white folks jus erbout owns this whole worl" and even more with the Depression hunger and uncooperative white officials who have betrayed "the Promised Land." Like Marx on precapitalist economic formations, Wright has the Rev. Taylor posit unalienated ownership and an unalienated relation between the individual and the land.

The Rev. Taylor, moreover, is deeply rooted in the values and imagery of classic American republicanism, of the sanctity of personal ownership, hard work, and the tilling of the virgin land, an individualism modulated by the Rev. Taylor's concern for the well-being of the black community and for black people as God's flock, his variation on the republican theme of a balance between the individual and community.[5] Wright legitimizes the Rev. Taylor's demands by giving them the sanction of the most traditional secular and religious values in American culture. On this view, what is at stake in the protest march is a reinstating of an earlier, mythic harmony the hunger and the white people have disrupted. The hunger and the hostile white officials are believable symbols of the larger breakdown of capitalism as it exists in the Depression South. For the Rev. Taylor, abolishing private ownership is not the issue but rather reestablishing an earlier cohesion the Depression and the whites have destroyed. Wright has effectively tapped into the concerns of the Popular Front by aligning them with the Jeremiad and republican traditions of mainstream Americanism to make the radical vision of "Fire and Cloud" emerge as understandable and acceptable to a wide range of white, middle-class Americans. He has simultaneously affirmed the dignity of African American religion as a sustaining force both for the Rev. Taylor and his community.

For the Rev. Taylor and his congregation, the immediate problem, however, is what to do about their hunger, which comes to mean, what to do about the demonstration. The communist organizers, Green and Hadley, one black, the other white, want Taylor to sign his name to a leaflet calling for the march. The white mayor and police chief have come to make sure Taylor plays their game. Another opposing force is Deacon Smith, a Judas figure who undermines Taylor within the congregation to advance his own position.

For his part, Taylor has a nuanced, democratic view of his position as a leader. When Green challenges him to explain what he is going to say to the mayor, Taylor says, "Ahma tell em ef they march Ahma march wid em. Ahma tell em they wan bread" (370). The mayor, however, wants Taylor to prevent the march. He invokes their traditional patriarchal relation. Southern blacks needed a white protector, and the mayor and Taylor have played this game before, with Taylor receiving benefits for his people in return for accepting white control. In a beautifully rendered ballet of deference and resistance on Taylor's part, implied threats on the mayor's, and overt threats from the police chief, Wright brings alive the complexities of Taylor's relation to the white establishment. He functions under the hegemonic gaze of the "cold grey eyes" (375) that repeatedly embody the power of white officialdom, a power reinforced by the police chief's view that "a niggers a nigger! I was against coming here talking to this nigger like he was a white man in the first place. He needs his teeth kicked down his throat!" (378). Wright skillfully deploys an interplay of perspectives to place Taylor in a sympathetic light. Taylor's radicalism comes modulated by the simple need for food and contrasts with what from a white Northern perspective is the arbitrary, unreasonable response of the white mayor and police chief.

Translated into intense action, this response emerges as the underlying politics of terror. Wright frames a crucial scene of archetypal white Southern violence with a contrasting episode in which the members of the black community eloquently empower themselves as responsible, democratic citizens.

"Ain nobody leadin us *nowhere!*" said Deacon Bonds.
"We gwine *ourselves!*" said Deacon Williams. (383)

This view harmonizes with Taylor's sense of his own role as a democratic leader. From the point of view of the black community, "the toiling masses" of communist discourse are "the people," and "the people" do not need a Leninist vanguard. Equally important, the black people in "Fire and Cloud" are a democratic counter to the police state tactics of the South, tactics that in 1938 strongly suggest the American equivalent of Nazi terror.

As he does again and again, Wright gives a vivid sense of white Southern terror. He focuses powerfully on the repeated physical violence—"a blow came to his right eye.... The heel of a shoe came hard into his solar plexus. He doubled up, like a jackknife. His breath left, and he was rigid, half-paralyzed" (385). But Wright also does justice to the violation of Taylor's personality and his status as a democratic citizen.

"Say, yuh cant do this!"

"Get your Goddam mouth shut, you bastard!...You think you can run this whole Goddam town, don't you? You think a nigger can run over white folks and get away with it?" (385)

"The nigger lesson" the whites conduct features a prime symbol of white domination, the whip. The blows intensify until "he felt he could not stand it any longer; he held his breath, his lungs swelling. Then he sagged, his back a leaping agony of fire" (389). The "fire" of the title is partly this fire on Taylor's body.[6]

As he returns home, "like a pillar of fire he went through the white neighborhood." Because he has been goaded into hatred and thoughts of destructive revenge, now the fire image of the Jeremiad fuses Biblical connotations with a subversive sense of Sherman's fiery march through Georgia, subversive because it is a black preacher, not a white general, who is "like a pillar of fire." As Wright continues, he has Taylor even more fully turn the fire outward from his own body into an aggressive image of rebellious, God-sanctioned retribution. "Some day theys gonna burn," Taylor thinks. "Some day theys gonna burn in Gawd Awmightys fire!...Fire fanned his hate" (393). Taylor's hatred and desire for a cleansing, divinely driven revolutionary fire are at once understandable and hard for white readers to deflect, even as the prospect of a merited racial conflagration is not one a white audience can look forward to with much anticipation. Wright has this powerful, threatening version of the Jeremiad and of liberation theology play off against the compelling and finally more hopeful struggle at the end of "Fire and Cloud."

Taylor is "like a pillar of fire" partly because the fire on his back, the deep imprint of white oppression, drives his vengeful, rebellious desire to see them "burn in Gawd Awmightys fire." His "fire" is personal in that he himself has experienced the worst of white oppression and the fire is also a public symbol with Biblical, historical, and Marxist connotations. In a thirties version of liberation theology, this fusion of the Biblical, of the Jeremiad, and of the Marxist animates Taylor's impassioned cry, "Gawd, ef yuh gimme the strength Ahll tear this ol building down! Tear it down like ol Samson tore the temple down!" The structure deserves to come down because, in another fusion of the Biblical, the Jeremiad, and the Marxist, the whites "fatten on us like leeches! There ain no groun yuh kin walk on that they don own! N Gawd knows tha ain right. He made the earth for us all!" (393).

This communal affirmation has a Marxist ring but the critique of exploitative ownership again polarizes white owners and black people, not owners and workers as two opposed classes. Because Wright does not insist on the racial issue, however, the passage can easily be read in a more orthodox Marxist way, with the emphasis on the communal, without reference to race—"He made the earth for us all." Period.

As Wright develops this tension between race and class at the climax of "Fire and Cloud," in opposition to Taylor's son, who wants to get his friends and fight back with guns, Wright has Taylor struggle toward a nonviolent but nonetheless rebellious response. The situation is a familiar one for radicals. The abuses are urgent; the gun—a cadre's immediate, violent rebellion—is appealing. Taylor, however, argues that "yuh cant do nothing *erlone*, Jimmy!" (396). But Jimmy feels passionately that "thingsll awways be like this less we *fight*!" (397). In this model situation for testing revolutionary aims and tactics, Wright has Taylor repeatedly stress that "the people" are crucial. When we act alone, he tells Jimmy, "the white folks....kill us like flies. It's the *people*, son! Wes too much erlone this way! Wes los when wes erlone! Wes gonna be wid our folks" (397)—"our folks" as opposed to "the white folks." As a democratic leader, Taylor is not so much opposing premature violence as he is the separation from the cohesive power of "the people."

Wright has Taylor become increasingly eloquent in his celebration of "the people." Even before it became a staple of Popular Front discourse, for Wright "the people" as a focus for Left discourse was made an issue by Kenneth Burke in his controversial address at the 1935 American Writers' Congress, which Wright attended. Burke argued that since most Americans disliked hard labor, the Communist Party's rhetorical stress on "workers" or "the toiling masses" was counterproductive. Burke instead advocated a symbolic emphasis on "the people," a phrase he believed promoted unity and avoided the divisiveness and negative connotations of "proletariat" or "worker." Wright has Taylor give "the people" all of the rhetorical resonance Burke hoped for but with a significant racial undertow that compromises the unity the phrase celebrates (Burke 87–94).

"It's the *people*!" Taylor reiterates, "theys the ones whut mus be real t us! Gawds wid the people! N the peoples gotta be real as Gawd t us! We cant hep ourselves er the people when wes erlone....All the will, all the strength, all the power, all the numbahs is in the people! Yuh cant live by yoself!" (398). So far, so good: as opposed to the individualism of personal success achieved through hard work and property ownership, a set of work ethic and republican values he had previously advocated, Taylor now offers the communal value of "the people," sanctioned explicitly by God and implicitly by Marx, Kenneth Burke, and the Popular Front.

But again, who are "the people"? From the Christian and Marxist perspective of liberation theology, "the people" are all of us, particularly the oppressed who know no color. The problem is that for Taylor, "mah people" like the earlier "our folks" are black people, as they are when Taylor tells Jimmy, "let nothin come tween yuh n <u>yo</u> people. Even the Reds cant do nothing ef yuh lose yo people" (398). The rhetorical force of Taylor's unifying paean to "the people" dominates but does not do away with this important racial qualification.

Wright has a delicate rhetorical situation, a black speaker simultaneously addressing two audiences, a black audience in the story and a predominantly white and presumably liberal or radical reading audience. For the black speaker, there is no difference between "mah people" and "the people," as Taylor reminds us when he concludes, "he wanted to talk to Jimmy again, to tell him about the black people" (399). For the white reading audience, however, Wright has to blur the racial distinctions and stress the universality of communal Christian-Marxist affirmation and protest. Wright himself is pulled in these opposing directions.[7]

In "Fire and Cloud," he has no reservations about the affirmative, democratic, and revolutionary role of the oppressed black community. He creates a situation in which ordinary black people can plausibly say in response to the question, "is we gonna march?"

> "Them white folks cant do no mo than theys already done."
>
> "They cant kill us but once!"
>
> "Ahm tired anyhow! Ah don care!" (402)

This model for revolution both confirms and qualifies the Communist Party's commitment to the revolutionary potential of black Americans—confirms because they are oppressed and ready to revolt, qualifies because they do so not as workers but as blacks.

Wright goes on to take a stand on another controversial issue by reinforcing the black community's commitment to democracy. He stresses that they have decided on their own, that they are not being led or manipulated. Deacon Smith accuses Taylor of leading "po black folks downtown t be killed" (402). In contrast both to the pervasive white denigration of black capacity and more particularly to the Stalinist-Leninist privileging of the leader and the vanguard, Wright emphasizes that

> "Ain nobody leadin us nowhere!"
>
> "We goin ourselves!" (402)

Near the climax of his narrative , Wright then has the Rev. Taylor
return once again to give a new meaning to the central symbol of
the fire and to the key passage when "like a pillar of fire" he "wuz
limpin thu white folks streets. Sistahs and Brothers," he declares, "Ah
knows now! Ah done seen the *sign*! Wes gotta git together. Ah know
whut yo life is! Ah done felt it! Its *fire*! Its like the fire that burned
me las night! Its sufferin! Its hell! Ah cant bear this fire erlone! Ah
know now whut t do! Wes gotta git close t one ernother! Gawds done
spoke! Gawds done sent His sign. Now its fer us t ack" (404).

For Taylor, the fire of his own beating and oppression comes to
embody all of black life. Now, however, the fire leads not to the earlier Jeremiad, the retributive burning in "Gawd Awmightys fire,"
the hate-fanned destruction of the entire white structure, but is
transformed into the militant, cohesive action of the protest march.
Taylor's immediate audience is his black congregation, so that the
plea for communal action is first to his black community. But because
Wright merges Taylor's speech with the joining of whites and blacks
in the march, he ends with an affirmative, Popular Front image of
"black and white marching" (405). The earlier problem about black
people as "*the* people" has been resolved. Similarly, the earlier "pillar
of fire" is rearticulated and transformed in the hymn the black and
white marchers sing, the "sign" Taylor has seen of militant, cooperative action:

> So the sign of the fire by night
> N the sign of the cloud by day
> A-hoverin oer
> Jus befo
> As we journey on our way…(404–05)

The "sign" of the fire and cloud and the marching of blacks and
whites together are a hopeful, inspiring forecast of a new world
emerging from the rendered oppression and rebellion in the old
world. Wright concludes this radical vision with a final reaffirma-
tion of democratic leadership. Defeated, the mayor "wants to see the
leader up front." But Taylor has the satisfaction of making the mayor
come to him, in the ranks (406).[8]

In view of Wright's personal rejection of what in "Blueprint for
Negro Writing" he calls "the archaic morphology of Christian salvation," it is worth emphasizing that in his political art he does full
justice to the Rev. Taylor as a dedicated black preacher whose imagery
and speech rhythms emerge from a long tradition of black religious

oratory (39).[9] Wright gives imaginative life to his understanding that one of the two sources of African American culture is "(1) the Negro church" (39). The Rev. Taylor's religion, however, is suffused with revolutionary implications deriving from Wright's Marxist tradition. This complex fusion of the Christian and Marxist makes for a compelling anticipation of liberation theology, not the least of Wright's achievements as a pioneering political artist.[10]

In concluding the 1938 edition of *Uncle Tom's Children* with "Fire and Cloud," Wright ends with a hopeful, affirmative vision that suggests a radical resolution for the suffering, violence, and negation of the earlier stories.[11] He is not doctrinaire and he gives full play to what in "Blueprint for Negro Writing" he calls "the problem of nationalism in Negro writing," especially in his rendering of "the fluid state of daily speech" (40, 41). The politics of "Fire and Cloud" are radical, Christian-Marxist, and democratic, not authoritarian. Despite his implied criticism of Leninist views of leadership, more than in any of his works, in "Fire and Cloud' Wright nonetheless uses, in his words, "a Marxist analysis of society" to "create the myths and symbols that inspire a faith in life" and "to buttress him with a tense and obdurate will to change the world" (43, 44). He has the Rev. Taylor "exultingly" end "Fire and Cloud" with Lenin's affirmation, "*Freedom belongs t the strong!*" (406).[12]

NOTES

1. In 1937, "Fire and Cloud" won the *Story* magazine first prize for stories by Federal Writers Project workers. In 1939 it won an O. Henry Memorial Award. On dates and awards, see Fabre 134, 156, 188. "Fire and Cloud" has nonetheless received very little detailed criticism. As James Giles points out in "Richard Wright's Successful Failure: A New Look at *Uncle Tom's Children*," Wright himself is partly responsible, because of his disparaging remarks about *Uncle Tom's Children* in "How Bigger Was Born" (256). Ralph Ellison, for his part, argued in "The World and the Jug" that Wright "found the facile answers of Marxism before he learned to use literature as a means of discovering the forms of American Negro humanity" (qtd. in Caron 1). James Baldwin further undermined interest in "Fire and Cloud" and Wright's work in general through his influential attack on the tradition of protest fiction in "Everybody's Protest Novel." See also Baldwin's "Alas, Poor Richard" in *Nobody Knows My Name* and "Many Thousands Gone" in *Notes of a Native Son*. Pervasive cold war anticommunism also discouraged critical attention.
2. For details, see Robin D. G. Kelley.

3. For Abdul R. JanMohamed, on the other hand, "the story is . . . designed to explore the role of death in Taylor's political metamorphosis from an acquiescent, fearful man to one who is proud, rebellious, and politically more sophisticated" (64). Keneth Kinnamon provides a balanced understanding of Taylor's dilemma in *The Emergence of Richard Wright: A Study in Literature and Society* (101, 104). For other treatments of the politics of "Fire and Cloud," see, for example, McCall 27–34; Brignano 19–20, 132–33; Zirin 1–6; Maxwell 170–73; and Caron 1–16.

4. On the Jeremiad tradition, see Bercovitch.

5. On American republicanism, see, for example, Wood; Pocock; Bailyn; Appleby; Banning; Isaac; Robert Kelley; and Kramnick. In Maxwell's view, Taylor presents "a yeoman's paradise in the tradition of both Jeffersonian pastoralism and black folk ideology" (172).

6. The beating, humiliation, and "nigger whipping" Wright dramatizes in the American South of the 1930s are part of a pattern that includes the torture at Abu Gharib and Guantanamo, the relation between police and minorities in cities such as Los Angeles and New York, the lynching documented in Allen et al., and the behavior of American soldiers in the Philippines during the Spanish-American War. The disciplinary practices under slavery and Jim Crow after Reconstruction are crucial.

7. Almost every study of "Fire and Cloud" quotes passages on "the people" without, however, examining the sources and conflicting meanings encoded in this key word. See, for example, Hakutani 56–57 and Kinnamon 103, 105.

8. Critics repeatedly say that Taylor "leads" the protest march but Wright is clear that Taylor acts as part of a democratic group, in the ranks and not "leading." See, for contrast, Hakutani 55; JanMohamed 63, 67; and Caron 8, 10.

9. See in the present collection Gary E. Holcomb, "When Wright Bid McKay Break Bread: Tracing Black Transnational Genealogy" for insight into Wright's relation to Claude Mckay and *New Challenge*, the journal Wright edited and which first published "Blueprint for Negro Writing."

10. Because of its Marxist resonance, the version of liberation theology Wright brings alive in "Fire and Cloud" is closer to the version developed within the South American Catholic Church in the 1960s than it is to the black liberation J. H. Cone celebrates in "Black Theology as Liberation Theology" or that Caron draws on in "The Reds Are in the Bible Room."

11. On the aesthetic success of the sequence of stories in *Uncle Tom's Children*, see Giles. For positive readings of the ending of "Fire and Cloud," see Kinnamon 103 and Walker 12–13. For negative evaluations of the ending, see McCall 33; Young 230; and JanMohamed 68.

12. See Maxwell 172.

Bibliography

Allen, James, et al. *Without Sanctuary: Lynching Photography in America.* Santa Fe: Twin Palms, 2000. Print.

Appleby, Joyce. "Republicanism and Ideology." *American Quarterly* 37 (1985): 461–73. Print.

Bailyn, Bernard. *The Ideological Origins of the American Revolution.* Cambridge, MA: Harvard UP, 1967. Print.

Baker, Houston. *Modernism and the Harlem Renaissance.* Chicago: U of Chicago P, 1987. Print.

Banning, Lance. "Jeffersonian Ideology Revisited: Liberal and Classical Ideas in the New American Republic." *William and Mary Quarterly* 43 (1986): 3–19. Print.

Bercovitch, Sacvan. *The American Jeremiad.* Madison: U of Wisconsin P, 1978. Print.

Brignano, Russell Carl. *Richard Wright: An Introduction to the Man and His Works.* Pittsburgh: U of Pittsburgh P, 1970. Print.

Burke, Kenneth. "Revolutionary Symbolism in America." *American Writers Congress.* Eds. Henry Hart et al. New York: International Publishers, 1935, 87–94. Print.

Callinicos, Alex. *Trotskyism.* Minneapolis: U of Minnesota P, 1990. Print.

Caron, Timothy P. "The Reds Are in the Bible Room: Political Activism and the Bible in Richard Wright's *Uncle Tom's Children.*" *Studies in American Fiction* 24 (1996): 1. Online.

Cone, J. H. "Black Theology as Liberation Theology." *African American Religious Studies: An Interdisciplinary Anthology.* Ed. Gayraud Wilmore. Durham, NC: Duke UP, 1989, 177–207. Print.

Cooper, Wayne F. *Claude McKay: Rebel Sojourner in the Harlem Renaissance.* New York: Schocken, 1987. Print.

Cruse, Harold. *The Crisis of the Negro Intellectual: A Historical Analysis of the Failure of Black Leadership.* 1967. Ed. Stanley Crouch. New York: New York Review of Books, 2005. Print.

Eastman, Max. *Since Lenin Died.* New York: Bon, 1925. Print.

Edwards, Brent Hayes. *The Practice of Diaspora: Literature, Translation, and the Rise of Black Nationalism.* Cambridge, MA: Harvard UP, 2003. Print.

Ellison, Ralph. "The World and the Jug." *New Leader* 46 (1963): 22–26. Print.

Fabre, Michel. *From Harlem to Paris: Black American Writers in France, 1840–1980.* Urbana: U of Illinois P, 1991. Print.

———. *The Unfinished Quest of Richard Wright.* 1973. Urbana: U of Illinois P, 1993. Print.

Federal Bureau of Investigation. Claude McKay file, no. 61-3497. Assorted documents dated 16 Dec. 1921 to 31 May 1940 obtained under provisions of the Freedom of Information Act. 119 pages. Print.

Giles, James. "Richard Wright's Successful Failure: A New Look at *Uncle Tom's Children.*" *Phylon* 34 (1973): 256–66. Print.

Grimké, Angelina Weld. *Rachel: A Play in Three Acts. Selected Works of Angelina Weld Grimké.* Ed. Carolivia Herron. Schomburg Library of Nineteenth-Century Black Women Writers. Oxford: Oxford UP, 1991. 123–209. Print.

Hakutani, Yoshinobu. *Richard Wright and Racial Discourse.* Columbia: U of Missouri P, 1996. Print.

Holcomb, Gary Edward. *Claude McKay, Code Name Sasha: Queer Black Marxism and the Harlem Renaissance.* Gainesville: UP of Florida, 2007. Print.

Howe, Irving. "Black Boys and Native Sons." *A World More Attractive.* New York: Horizon, 1963. 98–110. Print.

Hughes, Langston. *The Big Sea.* 1940. Introduction. By Arnold Rampersad. New York: Hill and Wang, 1993. Print.

Hurston, Zora Neale. Rev. of *Uncle Tom's Children.* By Richard Wright. 1938. *Richard Wright: Critical Perspectives Past and Present.* Eds. Henry Louis Gates, Jr. and K. A. Appiah. New York: Amistad, 1993. 3–4. Print.

———. "Sweat." *Fire!! A Quarterly Devoted to the Younger Negro Artists* 1.1 (1926): 40–45. Print.

———. *Their Eyes Were Watching God.* Philadelphia: Lippincott, 1937. Print.

Isaac, Jeffrey C. "Republicanism vs. Liberalism? A Reconsideration." *History of Political Thought* 9 (1988): 349–77. Print.

JanMohamed, Abdul R. *The Death-Bound Subject: Richard Wright's Archaeology of Death.* Durham, NC: U of North Carolina P, 1990. Print.

Kelley, Robert. "Ideology and Political Culture from Jefferson to Nixon." *American Historical Review* 32 (1977): 531–62. Print.

Kelley Robin D. G. *Hammer and Hoe: Alabama Communists during the Great Depression.* Chapel Hill: U of North Carolina P, 1990.

Kinnamon, Keneth. *The Emergence of Richard Wright: A Study in Literature and Society.* Urbana, IL: U of Illinois P. Print.

Kramnick, Isaac. "Republican Revisionism Revisited." *American Historical Review* 87 (1982): 629–64. Print.

Lewis, David Levering. *When Harlem Was in Vogue.* New York: Knopf, 1981. Print.

Locke, Alain. "The New Negro." *The New Negro.* New York: Boni, 1925. 3–16. Print.

———. "Spiritual Truancy." Rev. of *A Long Way from Home,* by Claude McKay. *New Challenge* 2 (1937): 81–85. Print.

McCall, Dan. *The Example of Richard Wright.* New York: Harcourt, Brace, 1967. Print.

Maxwell, William J. *New Negro, Old Left: African-American Writing and Communism between the Wars.* New York: Columbia UP, 1999. Print.

McKay, Claude. *Banjo: A Story without a Plot.* 1929. Print.

———— *Home to Harlem.* 1928. Print.

————. Letter to Ivie Jackman. 12 Sept. 1944. Ivie Jackman–Harold Jackman Papers. Trevor-Arnett Library, Atlanta University.

————. *A Long Way from Home.* New York: Furman, 1937. Print.

————. *Romance in Marseille.* 1929–1932. Unpublished MS. Miscellaneous Claude McKay Papers. Schomburg Center for Research in Black Culture, New York Public Library.

Patton, Venetria K., and Maureen Honey, eds. *Double-Take: A Revisionist Harlem Renaissance Anthology.* New Brunswick, NJ: Rutgers UP, 2001. Print.

Pocock, J. G. A. *The Machiavellian Moment: Florentine Political Thought and the Atlantic Republican Tradition.* Princeton, NJ: Princeton UP, 1975. Print.

Rampersad, Arnold. *The Life of Langston Hughes: Volume 1: 1902–1941, I, Too, Sing America.* New York: Oxford UP, 1986. Print.

Rowley, Hazel. *Richard Wright: The Life and Times.* New York: Holt, 2001. Print.

Scruggs, Charles, and Lee VanDemarr. *Jean Toomer and the Terrors of American History.* Philadelphia: U of Pennsylvania P, 1998. Print.

Shulman, Robert. *The Power of Political Art: The 1930s Literary Left Reconsidered.* Chapel Hill: U of North Carolina P, 2000. 67–73. Print.

Singh, Amritjit. "Introduction: Wallace Thurman and the Harlem Renaissance." *The Collected Writings of Wallace Thurman.* By Wallace Thurman. New Brunswick, NJ: Rutgers UP, 2003. 1–28. Print.

Stephens, Michelle A. *Black Empire: The Masculine Global Imaginary of Caribbean Intellectuals in the United States, 1914–1962.* Durham: Duke UP, 2005. Print.

Stovall, Tyler. *Paris Noir: African Americans in the City of Light.* Boston: Houghton Mifflin, 1996. Print.

Walker, Alice. "In Search of Zora Neale Hurston." *Ms. Magazine* March 1975: 74+. Print.

Whalan, Mark. "Jean Toomer and the Avant-Garde." *The Cambridge Companion to the Harlem Renaissance.* Ed. George Hutchinson. Cambridge, MA: Cambridge UP, 2007. 71–81. Print.

Wintz, Cary D., and Paul Finkelman, eds. *Encyclopedia of the Harlem Renaissance.* 2 vols. New York: Routledge, 2004. Print.

Wood, Gordon S. *The Creation of the American Republic.* New York: Norton, 1969. Print.

Wright, Richard. "Between Laughter and Tears." Rev. of *Their Eyes Were Watching God* by Zora Neale Hurston. *New Masses* (5 Oct. 1937): 23–25. Print.

Wright, Richard. *Black Boy: A Record of Childhood and Youth.* New York: Harper, 1945. Print.

——. *Black Power: A Record of Reactions in a Land of Pathos.* New York: Harper, 1954. Print.

——. "Blueprint for Negro Writing." 1937. *Richard Wright Reader.* Eds. Ellen Wright and Michel Fabre. New York: Harper & Row, 1978. 36–49. Print.

——. "Fire and Cloud." *Richard Wright: Early Works.* New York: Library of America, 1991. Print.

——. Letter to Alain Locke. 8 Jul. 1937. Alain Locke Papers. Moorland-Spingarn Research Center, Howard University. Print.

——. *Native Son.* New York: Harper, 1940. Print.

——. *Uncle Tom's Children: Five Long Stories.* New York: Harper, 1938. Print.

Young, James O. *Black Writers of the Thirties.* Baton Rouge: Louisiana State Press, 1973. Print.

Zirin, Annie. "Richard Wright: Using Words as a Weapon." *International Socialist Review* 14 (2000): 1–6. Online.

14

RICHARD WRIGHT AND THE CIRCUMCARIBBEAN

John Lowe

All art is propaganda.

— W. E. B. Du Bois

Richard Wright, whose *Native Son* exploded across the American literary firmament like a grenade in 1940, has always been noted as a master of propaganda, and his lifelong commitment to writing as a force for social change has rightly been studied in depth. This critical approach, however, has often hampered a full appreciation of Wright's full arsenal of talents, for he is also fully versed in all the techniques of rhetoric, poetry, and narrative viewing. Wright this way can assist us as we reconfigure him into hemispheric and transatlantic ways, for he always appealed to writers outside the United States through both his propaganda and his craft. Further, Wright had an especially strong influence on Caribbean writers, who were, in many cases, making an argument through their art against European colonial oppression. I need not detail here how often a parallel has been made between the racial system of pre-civil rights U.S. South and the colonial histories of the Caribbean, which were equally, but differently, structured around racial division. To show this influence, I will subsequently demonstrate a similar trajectory for the Barbadian novelist George Lamming, whose autobiographical novel *In the Castle of My Skin* seems a veritable homage to Wright, who indeed wrote the introduction for *Castle* when it appeared in 1953. Setting these two texts together reveals the many similarities between Southern and West Indian rural life, diasporan commonalities, and multiple instances of literary invention that stem from racial oppression.[1] Wright, Lamming, and other writers of the CircumCaribbean use an experimental aesthetic to refigure history. Valérie Loichot has recently referred to this process as using textual reconstructive processes that work to recapture and rewrite history and genealogy (Loichot 2).

Wright often spoke of the United States, the Caribbean, and Africa as a kind of triangular Black Atlantic. In an interview with George Charbonnier in 1960, he claimed, "It is American Negroes, from the South of the United States and the Caribbean, who brought the idea of black nationalism to Africa....We feel we are not really at home in our country. This is the origin, logically enough, of black national-ism. It begins with Marcus Garvey [a Jamaican] in the United States. After Garvey and W. E. B. DuBois, George Padmore [from Trinidad] was at the root of this idea" (Kinnamon 228). Thus the idea of black "homelessness" for Wright is a hemispheric, rather than a U.S., phe-nomenon, and Lamming, who immigrated to England, would seem to him to be a fellow traveler in this respect.

A corollary to this approach is that Wright and Lamming found their genius in their native settings, and that much of their great-est writing achieves its stature through shrewd, occasionally majes-tic, employment of Southern and Caribbean culture, flora and fauna, folklife, weather, history, and language. Further, these testimonies came from memory, conjured up in exile, as Wright wrote after immi-gration to Northern cities, and later, to Paris; Lamming penned his works from London, after an initial exile to Trinidad.

Ample proof and examples for these assertions may first be found in one of Wright's greatest achievements, *Black Boy* (1945), the first part of the overall autobiography that concludes with *American Hunger*. The narrative's intricate aesthetic modes of narration, symbolism, sequence, image, and structure all contribute forcefully to the book's overall propaganda, but also to a powerfully moving and satisfying artistic product. My reading will take advantage of several recent stud-ies of Wright and the aesthetics of propaganda as well as new theories of the "local" as a component of the transnational and global. Finally, in light of Wright's increasing uneasiness in the United States, his already formidable record of international travel, and his eventual exile in Paris (which finds a parallel in Lamming's relocation to London), where he wrote three novels and several nonfiction books, *Black Boy* deserves to be read as a text that transcends its ostensible boundaries, for even though Wright situates it in the Mississippi that he knew all too well, its relentless exploration of the shaping of black identity in a Western society spoke and continues to speak to people of color throughout the black diaspora. One of those who heard this "call" was Lamming. Wright must have seen these lines of connection when he was asked to write an introduction for *Castle*, an exercise that summoned up his memories of, and meditations on, the "South of the South."

Wright never set a novel in the Caribbean, but his introduction to *Castle* recognizes that the account of Lamming's Barbados undergoing transformation from rural to industrial society—and its effect on the protagonist—was much like Wright's own life story in *Black Boy*. Wright declared: "I, too, have been long crying these stern tidings, and when I catch the echo of yet another voice declaiming in alien accents a description of this same reality, I react with pride and excitement, and I want to urge others to react to that voice. One feels not so alone, when, from a distant witness, supporting evidence comes to buttress one's own testimony" ("Introduction" ix). Wright's use of the term "echo" could be translated as "response," one made after the "call" of *Black Boy*. We might also note the temporal frames of the two texts. Wright's text by no means concerns his entire life; rather it concentrates on the years 1912–1927 (his first four years are understandably briefly summarized). Similarly, Lamming's novel, circling around the crucial year of 1937–1938, would seem to concern a similarly formative period in his youth, from about 1936 to 1946, encompassing his ninth birthday and his departure for Trinidad.

Wright came to Lamming's novel after some useful explorations of the Barbadian's inland sea. In 1950, Wright had traveled to Curacao, and then to Haiti. He met many prominent writers, and started plans for a film on the liberator Toussaint L'Ouverture, whose life had been immortalized in C. L. R. James's *The Black Jacobins* (1938). This program would have united Wright's growing interest in diasporan history and his desire to demonstrate the richness and variety of black cultures in his adopted homeland France, which of course had a special interest in the Francophone Caribbean. His plan to play the leading role in the film speaks of his identification with Toussaint. The project never developed, but Michel Fabre has shown that Wright took copious notes for it while in Haiti and intended to write about the history of the country, causes of its poverty, and the despair of its young people (Fabre, *The Unfinished Quest* 352). We should remember that there was much interest in Haiti in the 1930s, for a variety of reasons. Orson Welles mounted a famous version of *Macbeth* set there, with the three witches transformed into voodoo priestesses. The production was a sensation, and Richard Wright made a special trip to New York to see it. His review in the *Daily Worker* noted that the play gave black actors work, and white audiences could hardly object to the subject matter, since it was the work of the Bard (Rowley 553n7).

Wright's visceral experience with poverty made him align quite naturally with many writers in the Caribbean. As Lamming once stated, "The Novel has had a particular function in the Caribbean. The writer's preoccupation has been mainly with the poor; and fiction has served as a way of restoring these lives—this world of men and women from down below—to a proper order of attention...there was also the writer's recognition that this world, in spite of its long history of deprivation, represented the womb from which he himself had sprung, and the richest collective reservoir of experience on which the creative imagination could draw" ("Introduction" *Castle* xxxvii). Lamming had seen an impressive testimony to this utterance in *Black Boy*; other African American writers, however, had made the same point. For Hurston, the truest repository of black culture lay in the "Negro farthest down." In the U.S. South and the Caribbean, this figure was situated in what Jamaican Claude McKay called a "peasant culture," one that originated in slavery and the factory of the plantation. As Lamming stated, "We inherited a region which was not designed for social living. It was intended exclusively for production...a source of fortune for hostile strangers" (Drayton 78), a commentary that is equally relevant to the rural South of Wright's childhood.

Sensing these connections, in a 1940 interview, Wright declared, "It is necessary that the black community of Latin America unite with that of North America. In this way, they will both come out ahead...An association of American writers is needed...the creative writers of the Latin American world should stand shoulder to shoulder with the creative writers of the English speaking peoples in the fight for Liberty and Justice" (Kinnamon 33).

Wright expanded his hemispheric travels in 1940, just as *Native Son* was astonishing and/or infuriating readers across the United States. He and his first wife Dhimah, her two-year-old son from a previous marriage, and her mother Eda joined their friends Lawrence and Sylvia Martin in Cuernavaca, Mexico. The Martins found the Wrights a rental property that only cost twenty-seven dollars a month. The trip South was accomplished by sea, on the *SS Monterey*, so Wright encountered the full majesty of the Caribbean physically, as a link between the South and Latin America, and he saw the similarities between the oppressive hacienda system and the plantation system back home. Wright found the weather and the foliage remarkably like that of Mississippi. As he wrote his boyhood friend Joe Brown, "Mexico reminds me a lot of the South. The climate is wonderful" (*Letters* 9). Rejecting the house the Martins had located as too small, he installed his family in a villa with a swimming pool, and started learning Spanish (Rowley

195–96). Wright was no doubt impressed by the magnificent murals at the Palace of Cortés by his fellow modernist and socialist, Diego Rivera, which depicted the Conquest of Mexico.

Wright eventually got beyond his palatial digs when he joined John Steinbeck and Herbert Kline on a scouting trip for locations; the latter two would film *Forgotten Village*, about Mexico's rural poor, which the three saw in abundance in Michoacán state. Race was not an issue in Mexico, where Wright lived in comparative freedom and luxury. When he left the country for good, he took a train to San Antonio; once in the States, he had to ride in the Jim Crow car, and was baited by train personnel (Rowley 208–09), a striking contrast that helped shape his concept of Latin culture as opposed to that of the South.

Like many of his fellow African American writers, Wright was always alert, in his travels over the globe, to parallels that existed between diasporan peoples. More recently, many members of the black diaspora have discovered a common North American/ Caribbean heritage, especially as they have come together in great cities of the Hemispheric North, but also, increasingly, in those of the U.S. South. The common folklore, in particular, has been a source of connection and community, and this phenomenon demonstrates the soundness of Edouard Glissant's observation that folklore, rather than myth, enables people to repossess historical space and to create a worldview that is both fortifying and useful for social change. Further, Antonio Benitez Rojo has helpfully situated the concept of performative style as a distinction of Caribbean culture, and has asserted that much of the power of Atlanta's Martin Luther King came from his understanding and practice of a performing art much like that of the Caribbean (24). As Paul Gilroy has forcefully argued, Wright eventually came to see that colonial oppression—particularly of people of color—was inextricably intertwined with the patterns of Jim Crow America. Further, "this enthusiasm for an emergent, global, anti-imperialist and anti-racist politics need not be seen as a simple substitute for Wright's commitment to the struggles of blacks in America. He strives to link it with the black American vernacular in a number of ways" (Gilroy 148).

Nor should we ignore Wright's equally profound conception of physical space, which always occupies a central place in his representations. As geographer John Berger has declared, "Prophecy" (which he considers a central activity of engaged political fiction) "now involves a geographical rather than historical projection; it is space not time that hides consequences from us. To prophesy today it is only necessary to know men and women as they are throughout the whole world in all their inequality. Any contemporary narrative which ignores the urgency of this dimension is incomplete and acquires the oversimpli-fied character of a fable" (Berger 40).

When critics approach *Black Boy*, they rarely mention the inscrip-tion, which is from Job: "They meet with darkness in the daytime/ And they grope at noonday as in the night..." Those who do consider the passage naturally link it with the didactic aspect of the Book of Job. However, we might do well to reconsider these lines as profound, eloquent, and representative of Wright's intent to craft his story with equally powerful and aesthetic rhetoric. Although he had contempt for organized religion, he had been steeped in the Bible, and his con-stant use of biblical allusion throughout his career speaks to his rever-ence for the magnificent literary resource of scripture. Certainly the majestic and anguished complaint of Job before a seemingly indiffer-ent (or even malevolent) God spoke to him in a powerfully personal way, especially in terms of his mother's intense suffering.

Black Boy makes it clear that Wright owed much of his biblical lore to his Granny, a strict Seventh-Day Adventist. In an intriguing pas-sage, Wright manages to render the majesty of the biblical imagery and rhetoric he absorbed, while simultaneously boasting about its failure to win his soul: "Her church expounded a gospel clogged with images of vast lakes of eternal fire, of seas vanishing, of valleys of dry bones...of God riding whirlwinds...a salvation that teemed with fantastic beasts." Yet at the end of this long, bravura passage, which in facts catalogs images and metaphors that Wright would repeatedly use in his own work, he asserts, "I was pulled toward emotional belief, but as soon as I went out of the church and saw the bright sunshine and felt the throbbing life of the people in the streets I knew that none of it was true and that nothing would happen" (89). Ah, but he came to see, however, that this apocalyptic language could indeed be harnessed to describe the many terrible events that *did* happen during his lifetime. And indeed, later in the narrative, he tells us he passed much time in his room poring over the Bible in an attempt to come up with some new verses for hymns, a process designed to win Granny's favor, but also one that trained him for typologically driven literary symbolism. This in fact leads him to write his first story, an incoherent tale about the suicide of a young Indian maiden. When his female neighbor fails to understand it, he is pleased, smiling the satisfied and superior smile of the artiste.

This prefigures Wright's later attempt at extended narrative, a florid tale entitled "The Voodoo of Hell's Half-Acre." The title alone signaled a use of alliteration, attention getting pyrotechnics, and an effort to mine CircumCaribbean exotica. He came to see, however, that the quotidian called out for presentation even more urgently: "There is a great novel yet to be written about the Negro in the South; just a simple, straight, easy, great novel, telling how they live and how they die, what they see and how they feel each day; what they do in the winter, spring, summer, and fall. Just a novel telling of the quiet ritual of their lives. Such a book is really needed" (*Letters* 13). Implicit in this statement is his own sense of having failed to compose such a work, since his novels had been more focused on the terrible quotidian ravages caused by racism. And yet we can find myriad passages in his work that do indeed render a sense of black Southern life, a traditional mode of living in concert with the land and the seasons. This is not to say, however, that those passages are where we should look for evidence of Wright's artistry; he was equally adept at rendering apocalyptic scenes of racial conflagration. His artistry, like that of the biblical sages, spanned the sublime and horrific, and the coloration of these differing effects was drawn from the same artistic palette, which was inspired by the realities of his native South.

As Wright sketches in aesthetic shorthand the "lessons" he learns as a teen in Mississippi, he summarizes, "I learned to lie, to steal, to dissemble. I learned to play that dual role which every Negro must play if he wants to eat and live" (*UTC* 13). Throughout the sketch, Wright plays variations on the black man's predicament of always being caught between Scylla and Charybdis—a situation that presents the victim with the possibilities of both psychic and physical trauma. Further, the lack of a father, coupled with an unmanning matriarchy at home, limits any kind of male paradigm Richard can follow. Lamming's G. has a similar experience, but lives only with his single mother. In both books, the lack of a father stands for the lack of a strong identification with a homeland, for in the U.S. South and Barbados, white culture, which defines all standards and importantly, publically shared history, denies people of color a place in either the past or the present apart from servitude and submission. As we know, Lamming actually had a stepfather; he subtracts him from G.'s story, perhaps in emulation of Wright, but also possibly because he wished to emphasize the quest for manhood by foreclosing the presence of an immediate source in the family.

The negative readings of black folk that one might extract from such representations multiply in another passage. Certainly one of the reasons many people give for not going forward to read other works by Richard Wright is their strongly negative reaction to one notorious section in *Black Boy*. It goes like this: "After I had outlived the

shocks of childhood...I used to mull over the strange absence of real
kindness in Negroes, how unstable was our tenderness, how lacking
in genuine passion we were, how void of great hope, how timid our
joy, how bare our traditions, how hollow our memories...Negroes
had never been allowed to catch the full spirit of Western civilization..." (32) The passage, however, is situated in the past and follows a description of his departure from the orphanage, when his
mother is shocked by his indifference to the children he is leaving
behind. But as the narrator explains, "I kept my eyes averted, not
wanting to look into faces that hurt me because they had become so
thoroughly associated in my feelings with hunger and fear" (32). One
should remember too, that *Black Boy* is an aesthetically shaped product that draws much of its power from its creation of a proud, lonely
hero, one much akin to those created by Wright's future Parisian colleagues, Jean- Paul Sartre and Albert Camus. Although it indeed tells
the story of one Richard Wright, it is also a selective rendition of
that person's life, and therefore artistic, and perhaps, in some cases,
actually fictional. We would also do well to remember that all these
charges against the black community are contradicted at many other
junctures in Wright's fiction and nonfiction, both before and after he
wrote this text. It is a testimony to the power of his aesthetics that we
take this passage so seriously, as it builds on a particular moment in
the young boy's life to extend outward to poetic social commentary.[2]
Moreover, it is contradicted time and again within this very book;
when Richard's mother suffers a debilitating stroke, the neighbors
nurse her, feed the children, and wash their clothes as they wait for
family to arrive. And indeed, seven of the eight children come, from
Detroit, Chicago, and various southern cities, another rebuke to the
indictment that is so often used to condemn Wright.

We should also recall Wright's comments about black stereotypes,
which this book was designed to combat; as he charged, "There is
something serious to be said about this legend that all Negroes are
kind and love animals and children...that legend serves to protect
certain guilt feelings about the Negro. If you can feel that he is so
different...naturally happy...and...smiles automatically you kind
of exclude him...from the human race...you don't have to feel bad
about mistreating him" (Kinnamon 65).

We might locate a rationale for this particular mode of presentation
at this point in the book by looking at Wright's previously expressed
theory of fiction, in his famous 1937 "Blueprint for Negro Writing."
There, he notes that merely holding a mirror up to an historical
period is not always effective: "The relationship between reality and

the artistic image is not always direct and simple. The imaginative conception of a historical period will not be a carbon copy of reality. Image and emotion possess a logic of their own" (48). This highly aesthetic posture says much about Wright's concept of propaganda that is also art. Similarly, George Lamming feels that the political violence that erupted in 1937 in Barbados, Trinidad, and Jamaica fueled a Caribbean literary renaissance, "a creative literary explosion...its source may be found in the collective grievances that were beginning to bear fruit through political action" (Drayton 117).[3] *Black Boy* ends in precisely the same way as *Castle*, with the protagonist preparing to leave his Southern home (Barbados/Mississippi) for the north (Chicago/London), although in Lamming the initial destination is the neighboring island of Trinidad. There is a key difference, however; Wright's narrator speaks to us out of isolation and alienation, totally alone; "G.," the narrator of *Castle*, ends his text in dialogue with old man Pa, who similarly is leaving on a journey, but one quite different, as he is heading to what he calls his "final resting place," the alms-house. After the old man bestows a paternal kiss on "G's" head and departs, the narrator tells us: "The earth where I walked was a marvel of blackness and I knew in a sense more deep than simple departure I had said farewell, farewell to the land" (303). Both narrators, however, would seem to agree with Wright about their own part of the larger "South": "The environment the South creates is too small to nourish human beings, especially Negro human beings" ("The Handiest Truth" 3).

The narrator's language, however, suggests that he is aware that the kiss of the father has symbolized the "marvelous blackness" that produced and sustains him—that is, his racial and folk heritage. Significantly, it is rooted in the "black" earth, in a particular place, Barbados, the Caribbean, "south of the south," as Wright might have said. And indeed, in his introduction to Lamming's novel, Wright begins his commentary by praising the author's "charged and poetic prose" (ix).

Wright, by contrast, at the end of *Black Boy* addresses the reader with a lengthy and powerful confession that is similar in spirit to Lamming's: "I was not leaving the South to forget the South, but so that someday I might understand it, might come to know what is rigors had done to me, to its children...deep down, I knew that I could never really leave the South, for my feelings had already been formed by the South, for there had been slowly instilled into my personality and consciousness, black though I was, the culture of the South. So in leaving, I was taking a part of the South to transplant in alien soil, to see if it could grow differently, if it could drink of new and cool rains...perhaps to bloom...And if that miracle ever happened, then I would know that there was yet hope in that southern swamp of despair and violence..." (228).

Remember too, that this term "the South" could easily apply to the CircumCaribbean world in general, a vast region drastically affected by the history and curse of slavery and plantation culture, a fact that Wright obviously understood. His effort to "escape" later came to encapsulate not only the restrictions of the Northern United States but also the hemispheric culture of racism. His flight to Paris and ultimately his engagement with the struggles of people of color in both Europe and Asia exponentially expanded his sense that any struggle for liberation would have to go beyond the bounds of the narrowly national concept of culture. Lamming similarly fled not only first Barbados, then Trinidad, but also the Caribbean and the Western Hemisphere, all arenas of black diasporic oppression, whether at the hands of Jim Crow in the United States, or under the ostensibly "civilizing" strictures of white British colonizers.

As Curdella Forbes and others have indicated, studies of Lamming—like those of Wright—for too long concentrated on his political role, particularly in terms of nascent Caribbean nationalism; this blinkered tradition has prevented a wider view of the global implications of his work. Forbes zeroes in on the great period of nationalism in the Caribbean—the 1950s through the 1970s—and demonstrates how one can, as she does in her own project, read Lamming in a transnational context through gender.[4] One can easily employ this same stance, with comparable results, with Wright, who similarly constructed an aesthetic framework built on metaphors of gender, particularly masculinity, as was the case with Lamming. It is worth noting, however, that Forbes's study concentrates on Lamming's later novels, rather than on *Castle*, which she sees as overtly invested in masculine gender formation, whereas the later novels, beginning with the female protagonist of *Season of Adventure* (1960), interrogate the masculinist traditions of the West Indian novels that Lamming ironically had seemed to typify with 1953's *Castle*. Similarly, Wright, at the end of his life, was demanding that more attention be paid to the black woman's story, and his last published novel, *The Long Dream,* and its unpublished sequel, *Island of Hallucinations*, provide strong female characters who speak with urgency and power about women's plight and rights.

In their metaphors of the "black earth" that has nourished them as children, both writers provide a foundation for this later concern with women, and for the strong role the central figures' mothers play in each text. We also notice that while both writers centrally employ a poetic sense of earth, and its link to life, Lamming situates it as foundation, while Wright expands the metaphor, proleptically envisioning a "blossoming" from this black garden, once a transplantation has taken place. Certainly one way to read this passage is to see Wright figuring not just his own individual being, but the "blossoms" of his book-length works of fiction, novels, which I would argue, are always deeply rooted in his southern past, especially *Uncle Tom's Children*, *Twelve Men*, and *The Long Dream*. The Chicago novels are also profoundly Southern, despite their setting, and the nonfiction Wright composed after exiling himself to Paris—especially *Pagan Spain*—are based on a Southerner's reaction to landscapes, cultures, and climates that he constantly compares to those of the South, and no wonder, as sensory and intellectual triggers summon forth powerful and inescapable memories, part of what Wright "was taking…to transplant" in the passage cited.

It is worth noting, however, that despite the nostalgia both writers occasionally evince for the folk/peasants of their Southern homes, each man takes pride in an ability to shake free of any tie to a particular locality. Wright asserted in *Black Power*, "I like and even cherish the state of abandonment, of aloneness; it does not bother me; indeed, to me it seems the natural, inevitable condition of man, and I welcome it. I can make myself at home anywhere on this earth" (xxix). Similarly, Lamming claimed, "This may be the dilemma of the West Indian writer abroad; that he hungers for nourishment from a soil which he (as an ordinary citizen) could not at present endure. The pleasure and paradox of my own exile is that I belong wherever I am" (*Pleasure* 50). The two in this sense presage Homi Bhabha's more recent pronouncement of a "third space" between the colonizer and the colonized (Bhabha 36–39).

Certainly the absence of fathers in these two texts speaks eloquently of the "historyless" aspect of colonized cultures, whose economic deprivations often result in fathers abandoning their families. The rootlessness of Wright's matriarchal family throughout his early life finds complementary expression in Lamming's narrative, even though "G." and his mother are comparatively stable, for in neither case do families own land. Instead, they are embroiled in a form of sharecropping, in a culture where white families hand down the large parcels of land from generation to generation, renting to peasants who may stay, if permitted, or who may—especially in the U.S. South—move frequently from place to place. In Barbados, Lamming shows us, more extended residence is possible, but only at the pleasure of the landlord, who inhabits the "castle" that lords it over the peasants from the hill.

One wonders if Wright was thinking of these overt resemblances in his introduction to the first edition of Lamming's text, when he stated that the story was "a symbolic repetition of the story of millions of simple folk who, sprawled over half of the world's surface and involving more than half of the human race, are today being catapulted out of their peaceful, indigenously earthy lives and into the turbulence and anxiety of the twentieth century...when I catch the echo of yet another voice declaiming in alien accents a description of this same reality, I react with pride and excitement...One feels not so much alone when, from a distant witness, supporting evidence comes to buttress one's own testimony" ("Introduction" x).[5] Wright's use of the words "pride" and "echo" strongly suggests that he was happy and proud to see the effect of his own work in that of a fine artist hailing from "South of the South."[6] Yet he must have been fascinated, too, to see how Lamming adapted the strategies he had used in *Black Boy* to shape a similar story that was nonetheless different because of the colonial situation, and because Lamming's narrator grew up in a predominately black culture, albeit one, like Wright's, controlled by whites.

We should be wary, however, of claims of "representation," or in Lamming's case, for a "collective consciousness." In his famous 1983 introduction to *Castle*, which needs to be considered alongside Wright's earlier one, Lamming insisted that his mode of narration was chosen so as to present the "collective human substance of the village" rather than an individual consciousness (x). Simon Gikandi has forcefully argued that the community pictured in the novel, as in Wright's tale, is fractured in various ways, and that the narrator's self-portrait is designed, in fact, to show how difficult the struggle always is to differentiate the self from the master scripts of any traditional community, scripts that are inevitably mixed and in conflict (Gikandi 75), In Lamming's case, his culture was breaking down under the pressures of modernization, while Wright's world was disappearing because of the increased pressures of Jim Crow culture and the resulting Great Migration to the North, which the narrator joins at the end of the book. Gikandi's overall observation that "attempts to investigate family and communal history through narrative are bound to meet the issues of alienation, emigration, and exile" (77) have equal relevance to *Black Boy,* and for that matter, to Wright's last masterwork, *The Long Dream,* suggesting that conditions in both the South and South of the South, based in the residual history of slave cultures, bear much in common, and produce similar social outcomes and destinies.

But there is a key difference between Southern and Caribbean black disdain for their fellow "folk"; the standard employed is not necessarily that of white neighbors, but of the Empire. The Barbadians who were trained in England return home "stamped like an envelope with what they call the culture of the Mother Country" (27). As this passage follows the scenes depicting cruel actual mothers, we perhaps are meant to see a link between the colonizing mother culture and the overly harsh actual mothering.

We should also attend to the complicated relation between Lamming and Wright. As we have seen, Wright had a keen interest in the Caribbean arena of the black diaspora, and his enthusiastic introduction to *Castle* in 1953 was appreciated by Lamming, who of course admired Wright as one of the preeminent modern writers. According to Wright's most recent biographer, however, Wright was disturbed when he came home one day and found the handsome Lamming in deep conversation with Ellen Wright. Always jealous of his wife, despite his own well-known philandering, Wright again got upset when he returned home a week later and Ellen wasn't there, which led him to have Vivian Mercer call Lamming's hotel to find out where he was (Rowley 478–79). It seems likely, however, that Lamming never knew of this aspect of their relationship, for he dedicated his 1972 novel, *Natives of My Person*, to Margaret Gardiner and in memory of Richard Wright.

Despite the debts I have traced on Lamming's part to Wright's *Black Boy*, two important Lamming critics have not drawn this connection, although both Supriya Nair and Sandra Pouchet Paquet speak briefly of Lamming's reliance on the "collective characters" Lamming employs, who in this regard resemble Wright's Bigger Thomas of *Native Son* (Wright said this character was based on "many Biggers") (Paquet, *The Novels of George Lamming* 5; Nair 6). Importantly, however, Nair points to the ways in which Lamming's angry narrative attempts to create a history for the "historyless," that is, the colonized peoples whose place in western chronicles has been erased by the colonizer. Nair reminds us of Fanon's pronouncement that it is the settler who "makes history" in the colonized land, but a history the settler always identifies as part of the mother country's. Thus, Fanon charges, the "settler" "skims off. . . . violates and starves" (51). Nair adds that this skimming of history parallels the skimming of material resources (Nair 79–80), and both Wright and Lamming illustrate this point repeatedly in their "alternate" histories.

Exiles

A penultimate matter: both of these books were written by men who had fled into exile from their native homelands—Wright from Mississippi, Lamming from Barbados. Lamming's initial relocation to Trinidad was soon followed by permanent relocation to London. Wright, after years of political and literary work in Chicago and New York, finally went into exile in Paris, where he took on a new identity as a kind of elder statesman of the black literary diaspora. Exile was a stance, a topic, and a frame of mind for each man. Lamming, in his book-length *The Pleasures of Exile*, declared, "The exile is a universal figure...We are made to feel a sense of exile by our inadequacy and our irrelevance of function in a society whose past we can't alter, and whose future is always beyond us...To be an exile is to be alive" (*Pleasures* 24).

Edward Said has famously remarked, "Exile is strangely compelling to think about but terrible to experience. It is the unhealable rift forced between a human being and a native place, between the self and its true home: its essential sadness can never be surmounted...The achievements of exile are permanently undermined by the loss of something left behind forever." Following Bourdieu's concept of *habitus*, "the coherent amalgam of practices linking habit with inhabitance," Said suggests—here following Theodor Adorno—that the only home available, after exile, is in writing (Said 173–84).

Some years ago, Robert Stepto identified key strands of the slave narrative, which many find to be the fundamental structure for much of black literature of the diaspora. These elements are "the violence and gnawing hunger, the skeptical view of Christianity, the portrait of a black family valiantly attempting to maintain a degree of unity, the impregnable isolation, the longing and scheming to follow the North Star resolved by boarding the 'freedom train,'" and "the narrator's quest for literacy" (Stepto 533). If we change the "North Star" and freedom train to Lamming's boat bound for London, we have a symmetry of effects in our two life stories that indeed bears resemblance to the classic slave narrative, which ends in flight—but to freedom, not to exile. We should note, however, that hunger of all sorts plays a far more salient role in Wright than in Lamming. Still the predominant note in both the nineteenth and twentieth century forms is writing. Lamming's equation of exile with life bears within it an implicit endorsement of writing as life. But as he usefully notes, the situation of an American black exile— and he uses Baldwin, not Wright, as an example—is different from a black West Indian in London, for the latter has to fight the imposition of the fiction that British culture is *his* culture, and that he will be judged by his mastery of it (he should know English literature, for instance, not Caribbean), and also that in Barbados there is no sense of being an oppressed minority, for blacks are the majority. While one may be condemned by blackness to poverty, one is not singled out for specific punishments for the fact of blackness, as in Wright or Baldwin's United States (*Pleasures* 33).

The escape into exile for both writers thus permits former Calibans to become Prospero. These two Shakespearean figures long fascinated Lamming, whose island background steered him to the play. As he has stated, "There is no landscape more suitable for considering the Question of the sea, no geography more appropriate to the study of exile" (*Pleasures* 96). Mastering Prospero's books can lead to sorcery, but it is compromised if it involves cutting off one's racial and cultural heritage. Perhaps for these reasons, Richard Wright came to feel ever more isolated in his adopted home of France, and at the end of his life he was considering relocating elsewhere. His last completed but unpublished novel, about *The Long Dream*'s Fishbelly sinking into a life of squalor in France, is appropriately entitled "Island of Hallucinations," and it is indeed a study of exile. Both Wright and Lamming, after their removal from their native homes, found in exile an opportunity and a curse, and this situation inflected everything they wrote.[7]

Finally, I believe Lamming would approve linking *Black Boy* and *Castle*. In an interview, he professed to be disturbed and "astonished" at the exclusion of Afro-Caribbean literature from Black Studies courses in the United States: "It should be an immediate cultural concern for the United States, because the Caribbean is part of the Americas…it would really be incomplete to think in terms of what has happened to the development of Black expression both politically and culturally without considering the role of the Caribbean, of the West Indian intelligentsia in exile in the United States, in that development. If you take a period like the Harlem Renaissance, you would not think of that without thinking of the importance of West Indian migration to Harlem, particularly the influence of Claude McKay and Marcus Garvey" (Drayton 75).

When Lamming refers to "what has happened," he returns again to the concept of literature as an alternate history, and his emphasis on the links between the United States and the Caribbean bespeaks a need for consideration of the entire cultural region, but also its "fragmented" history, which is symbolically registered in the passage examined earlier where "Pa" rehearses the hemisphere-spanning Middle Passage.

This concept of the fragmented histories of people of African descent has been powerfully addressed by Edouard Glissant: "In the face of a now shattered notion of History, the whole of which no one can claim to master nor even conceive, it was normal that the Western mind should advance a diversified Literature, which is scattered in all directions but whose meaning no one could claim to have mastered...Literature is not only fragmented, it is henceforth shared. In it lie histories and the voice of peoples. We must reflect on a new relationship between history and literature. We need to live it differently" (77). In the moving, disturbing life narratives of Wright and Lamming, we find a model for this reconnection of "fragments," and for living this *vita nuova*; their palettes of fire irradiate what begins as propaganda into pyrotechnic aesthetics of identity.

Notes

1. In a longer essay, I have given a more extended comparison of these two books, which I must abbreviate here (Lowe 553–80).
2. Similarly, Yoshinobu Hakutani has suggested that in *Black Boy*, Wright is intent on displaying his experiences "with naturalistic objectivity, rather than from a personal point of view" (115). I concur.
3. Lamming's point might be reversed as well, since his presentation of the riots, which did indeed lead to modernization and correction of the more egregious problems of the time (Nair 101) played a part in subsequent movements for social change. It is likely too that Lamming's novel and his much fiercer nonfictional speeches and essays that followed had effects on both the political and literary climates. There is no question that we can say that for *Black Boy* and many of Wright's other works.

    Still, we should remember that both *Black Boy* and *Castle* conclude with figures leaving the land. "Richard" flees to Chicago, while Pa, Trumper, and G. all vacate the village for disparate new locations. The peasant spokesman, the shoemaker, also disappears. In the long light of history, however, readers today see these earlier struggles and flights as prelude to the independence of Caribbean nations and the monumental achievements of the Civil Rights movement in the United States, and the advent of a New New South that has fomented a reverse migration of African Americans back to the Southern locales of their ancestors.
4. In this effort, she is following the vanguard of postnationalist studies by Sandra Pouchet Paquet (2002), Belinda Edmondson (1999), and A. J. Simoes Da Silva (2000).
5. We should not be surprised that Wright was eager to read Lamming's book. Always interested in the lives of other people of color in foreign lands, during the early days of World War II, Wright wrote Claude Barnett, who headed the Associated Negro Press, that he wanted to cover the war in Russia, China, or India: "I would like to get stories of how the brown, red and yellow people are faring, what they are hoping for, and how their attitudes are likely to influence the outcome of the war in Europe" (Rowley 235).
6. Because of Wright's hostility to Zora Neale Hurston for her supposedly romantic, poetic vision of folk culture, one wonders at the apparent

hypocrisy of his stance here, where he praises Lamming for precisely the things he criticizes Hurston. For instance, he lauds Lamming's "poetry" of "outlandish names of his boyhood playmates: Trumper, Boy Blue, Big Bam, Cutsie, Botsie, Knucker Hand, Po King, Puss-in-Boots, and Suck Me Toe," whereas we remember the book Wright damned, Hurston's *Their Eyes Were Watching God*, includes characters named Motor-Boat, Sop-de-Bottom, Tea Cake, Bootyny, and Stew Beef.

7. On the other hand, two late letters from Wright to his editor outlined the third novel in his Fishbelly series, in which Fish chooses Yvette over Marie-Rose, and settles for a time in Africa, where their son is born, shortly after Fish's mother arrives. The entire family then returns to the United States, hoping for a final and true integration into American life. The novel was to conclude with the choices faced by Fish's son—life in Europe, New York, or in Mississippi with his grandmother? (summary from Fabre, *Quest* 486). The projected trilogy would have pulled in the three points of the black Atlantic, and by circling back to a presumably transformed United States, seemingly ended the trilogy, which began, typically for Wright, in fear, ending in some kind of hope, a trajectory perhaps prompted by a kind of wistfulness on Wright's part at the end of his life. We might see somewhat of a parallel in Lamming's eventual return to the Americas.

BIBLIOGRAPHY

Baugh, Edward. "The West Indian Writer and His Quarrel with History." *Tapia* 8, 9 (1977): 6. Print.

Benitez Rojo, Antonio. *The Repeating Island: The Caribbean and Postmodern Performance*. Trans. James E. Maraniss. Durham, NC: Duke UP, 1992. Print.

Berger, John. *The Look of Things*. New York: Viking, 1974. Print.

Bhabha, Homi K. *The Location of Culture*. New York: Routledge, 1994. Print.

Edmondson, Belinda. *Making Men: Gender, Authority and Women's Writing in Caribbean Narrative*. Durham, NC: Duke UP, 1999. Print.

Fabre, Michel. *The Unfinished Quest of Richard Wright*. 2nd ed. Urbana: U of Illinois P, 1993. Print.

———. *The World of Richard Wright*. Jackson: UP of Mississippi, 1985. Print.

Fanon, Frantz. *The Wretched of the Earth*. Trans. Constance Farrington. New York: Grove Weidenfeld, 1963. Print.

Forbes, Curdella. *From Nation to Diaspora: Samuel Selvon, George Lamming and the Cultural Performance of Gender*. Kingston: U of the West Indies P, 2005. Print.

Gikandi, Simon. *Writing in Limbo: Modernism and Caribbean Literature*. Ithaca, NY: Cornell UP, 1992. Print.

Gilroy, Paul. *The Black Atlantic: Modernity and Double Consciousness*. Cambridge, MA: Harvard UP, 1993. Print.

Glissant, Edouard. *Caribbean Discourse: Selected Essays.* Trans. J. Michael Dash. Charlottesville: UP of Virginia, 1989. Print.

Hakutani, Yoshinobu. *Richard Wright and Racial Discourse.* Columbia: U of Missouri P, 1996. Print.

Kinnamon, Keneth, and Michel Fabre. *Conversations with Richard Wright.* Jackson: UP of Mississippi, 1993. Print.

Lamming, George. *Conversations: Essays, Addresses and Interviews, 1953–1990.* Ed. Richard Drayton and Andaiye. London: Karia, 1992. Print.

———. *In the Castle of My Skin.* 1953. Ann Arbor: U of Michigan P, 1991. Print.

———. *Natives of My Person.* 1972. Ann Arbor: U of Michigan P, 1995, Print.

———. *The Pleasures of Exile.* 1960. Ann Arbor: U of Michigan P, 1995. Print.

Loichot, Valérie. *Orphan Narratives: The Postplantation Literature of Faulkner, Glissant Morrison, and Saint-John Perse.* Charlottesville: UP of Virginia, 2007. Print.

Lowe, John. "Palette of Fire: The Aesthetics of Propaganda in *Black Boy* and *In the Castle of My Skin.*" *Mississippi Quarterly* 61.4 (2008): 553–80. Print.

Nair, Supriya. *Caliban's Curse: George Lamming and the Revisioning of History.* Ann Arbor: U of Michigan P, 1996. Print.

Paquet, Sandra Pouchet. *Caribbean Autobiography: Cultural Identity and Representation.* Madison: U of Wisconsin P, 2002. Print.

———. *The Novels of George Lamming.* London: Heinemann, 1982. Print.

Rowley, Hazel. *Richard Wright: The Life and Times.* New York: Holt, 2001. Print.

Said, Edward. *Reflections on Exile and Other Essays.* Cambridge, MA: Harvard UP, 2000. Print.

Simoes Da Silva, A. J. *The Luxury of Nationalist Despair: George Lamming's Fiction as Decolonizing Project.* Amsterdam: Rodolfi, 2000. Print.

Stepto, Robert. "I Thought I Knew These People: Richard Wright and the Afro-American Literary Tradition." *Massachusetts Review* 18 (1977): 525–41. Print.

Wright, Richard. *Black Boy.* New York: Harper, 1945. Print.

———. *Black Power: A Record of Reactions in a Land of Pathos.* 1954. New York: Harper Collins, 1995. Print.

———. "Blueprint for Negro Writing." 1937. *Richard Wright Reader.* Eds. Ellen Wright and Michel Fabre. New York: Harper and Row, 1978. Print.

———. "The Handiest Truth to Me to Plow Up Was in My Own Hand." *PM Magazine* 4 Apr. 1945: 3. Print.

———. Introduction. *In the Castle of My Skin.* By George Lamming. New York: McGraw Hill, 1953. Print.

———. *Letters to Joe C. Brown.* Ed. Thomas Knipp. Kent, OH: Kent State University Libraries, 1968. Print.

AFTERWORD

I.

Upon his death in 1960, Richard Wright had already begun to describe a future where knowledge would be expanded far beyond the limitations of the autonomous national subject. Despite his initial misjudgment of complex relations between tradition and modernity, he envisioned a future as one where race would be central to the aspirations of a transatlantic modernism, and where cosmopolitanism might come to be reconceived as something solid, and as meaning more than simply being detached from one's country. His vision anticipated the current revisionist scholarship on modernisms being dispensed by such critics as Joseph B. Entin (*Sensational Modernism*, 2007), Sara Blair (*Harlem Crossroads*, 2007), Michael Thurston (*Making Something Happen: American Political Poetry between the Wars*, 2001), Edward M. Pavlic (*Crossroads Modernism: Descent and Emergence in African-American Literary Culture*, 2002), and George Hutchinson (*The Harlem Renaissance in Black and White*, 1995). Wright's position is echoed in Michelle Stephens's view on what is embedded in "African-American Modernisms": "[an] awareness of the text and the artwork as inextricably intertwined within, and in dialogue with, a modern racialized social reality" (307). African American modernists built from social realism a "black modernity which could be perceived and performed in multiple modes, genres, and registers" (318).

Yet this position can only be understood in relation to how Wright anticipated "a modernism that knows we have never been modern" (Brown 187). For Wright, we have never been modern most crucially in a social and racial sense that would equate being modern with having mastered a new humanitarianism. Wright realized that the only acceptable modernism to which to aspire was one fully cognizant of social equity and justice. As several essays here attest (Miller, Maxwell, Rabinowitz, and Ulin), Wright's modernism uncovers the "crime[s] of modernity" (Brown 184): the inexorable pursuit of pecuniary power as well as the failure to find and identify any kind of social essence. Wright's modernism reveals a world image—a modernity overflowing with racism, violence, a kind of repository of "that which fundamentally determines subjectivity," as Rabinowitz puts it. Adding to this, Wright's cultural definitions of a modern identity highlight the importance of poverty—an additional uncovering—not only as a "critical category" (Jones 148) but also as a literary frame for organizing and analyzing race and culture. Wright's fictional and autobiographical engagements with poverty, running from Mississippi to Chicago, from (present-day) Ghana to Jakarta, especially when combined with race, unsettle literary-historical categories. Wright encompasses a modernism in which the majority of his characters exist outside the structures of ownership and where families cannot be depended on as a source of stability. He embraced a modernism that positions itself against the very forces it reveals.

In its racial resignification, Wright's sense of modernity, as argued variously by Butler, Lowe, and Shulman, envisions shared problems of human existence at the same time that it seeks to recover an ethical and social function within literary and cultural debates. In Wright's efforts to investigate consciousness, his modernism is part of a continuum "where the subject is repeatedly overwhelmed in its encounter with the turbulence of urban transformation" (Brown 182). Soto and Davis demonstrate the shifting presentations of Wright's urban spaces and places, whose values are contingent upon the changing demographics of race, class, and ethnic migration in the 1920s and 1930s. In this vein, Wright's terrible cities can be usefully interpreted as versions of the high modernists' dislocation and destabilization of the self. These same spaces can also serve as sites that provide new modes of envisioning a self that departs from conventional understandings of American national identity.

II.

In contrast to Ralph Ellison, the overall impressions that Wright has of America were ultimately informed as much by his absence from his country of origin as from his presence on American soil. With respect to his promotion of interethnic exchanges and his attempt to deal honestly with the ravages of racism and colonialism, his disorientation and distress—as related in *Black Power, The Color Curtain*, and *White Man Listen!*—provide alternative legacies to those of *Black Boy* and *Native Son*. As Cornell West argues, these literary-journalistic works emphasize Wright's "secularity," "rootlessness," and "exilic consciousness" (viii–ix). They speak both to his "third way" and to the "unpopular truths" produced from his commitment to the ideals of enlightenment cosmopolitanism. As Cassuto, Charles, Joyce and Maxwell have stressed, Wright's exilic fiction, running from *The Outsider* and *Island of Hallucination* to *The Long Dream* and *A Father's Law* offers an African American participation in modernism, focusing on many of the material conditions that shaped racial politics in mid-twentieth-century America. His most aggressive postwar nonfictional and fictional strategies for imparting his impressions center on the unmade, the repressed, and the eliminated.

Wright uncannily anticipates some of the present-day theorists on concepts of cosmopolitanism and postcoloniality. Paul Gilroy's anti-generalizing revisionist impulses are as evident in Wright's works as is Homi Bhaba's consciousness of space and spatiality, concepts that have been explored further by authors in *Richard Wright: New Readings in the 21st Century*. Most interestingly, Appiah, an early critic of *Black Power,* describes the work as "a projection of Wright's own failings" (*Collection* 194), a response of "the fury of the lover spurned" (*Collection* 201).[1] Appiah's recent writings on Afrocentrism, race, and pluralism, nonetheless explicitly rely upon some of Wright's central views in *Black Power* and *The Color Curtain*. For example, Wright argues that race is a construct, a superimposed category, not a biological reality: " 'racial' qualities were but myths of prejudiced minds" (*Black Power* 79).

In his essay, "Race, Pluralism, and Afrocentricity" (1998), Appiah similarly argues:

> . . . I think it is clear enough that a biologically rooted conception of race is both dangerous in practice and misleading in theory. African unity, African identity need securer foundations than race. (116)

By the same token, Wright insists that Africa must surmount both its "gummy tribalism" and the "psychological legacy of imperialism" (*Black Power* 412) before it can enter "modernity" and face its future. Appiah delivers a parallel directive in his critique of the Afrocentrists:

> [The Afrocentrists] require us to see the past as the moments of wholeness and unity; tie us to the values and beliefs of the past; and thus divert us from the problems of the present and the hopes of the future. ("Race" 116)

Wright strongly urges that evidence and reasoning must triumph over "racial" and "tribal" differences. As he puts it, "There is nothing that can be said when one faces men in whom there is a total mobilization of all the irrational forces of the human personality" (*Color Curtain* 491). Appiah's description of flawed identity politics is again in accordance with Wright's formulations:

> One temptation, then, for those who see the centrality of these fictions in our lives, is to leave reason behind: to celebrate and endorse those identities that seem at the moment to offer the best hope of advancing our other goals... ("Race" 116)

Wright never ceased to be impassioned and vocal in his advocacy of African liberation movements and in his condemnation of the brutal legacy of slavery and colonialism that he observed in the Gold Coast colony, an insistence that risks going unnoticed in Appiah's assessment of Wright's travel writings. To counterpoint interpretations of Wright's internationalism and cosmopolitanism, which have perhaps not done due diligence to his prescience, this volume has emphasized Wright's enduring insistence upon his "transnational" subjectivity (Lowe), his "*transnative*" status (Holcomb), and "the essential humaneness" (*White Man Listen!* 704) of his activist and literary efforts. Put more succinctly, Wright's work has long spoken for many who believe, like Gilroy, "that race has never had a stable existence, and that experience and identity in the world have always been transcultural and international" (Ernest 244).

Finally, this collection has intended to reignite the debate on Wright as a transnational modernist, to pick up where one of the central critical collections on Wright (*Richard Wright: Critical Perspectives Past and Present*, 1993) left off. In the preface to that collection, Henry Louis Gates Jr. argues for the powerful shaping force of naturalism as Wright's dominant literary epistemology and mode. While he concedes that Wright "may also have been responsible for the shaping of a literary modernism" (xiii), he does not pursue the idea, returning quickly to his focus on Wright as a "compelling" naturalist. *Richard Wright: New Readings in the 21ˢᵗ Century* takes up Gates's suggestion concerning Wright's modernist tendencies and reframes the debate on Wright's literary origins and legacies. In so doing, the volume portrays Wright's instrumental role in locating notions of race within larger hemispheric and colonial genealogies and repositions his legacy within critical discourse on literary modernity.

NOTE

1. See Paul Gilroy, *After Empire: Melancholia or Convivial Culture?* (Abingdon: Routledge, 2004); Homi Bhabha, "The Vernacular

Cosmopolitan," *Voices of the Crossing: The Impact of Britain on Writers from Asia, the Caribbean, and Africa*, ed. Ferdinand Dennis and Naseem Khan (London: Serpent's Tail, 2000) 133–42, and "In the Cave of Making: Thoughts on Third Space," *Communicating in the Third Space*, ed. Karin Ikas and Gerhard Wagner (New York and London: Routledge, 2009) ix–xiv; Anthony Kwame Appiah, "Rooted Cosmopolitanism," *The Ethics of Identity* (Princeton and Oxford: Princeton University Press, 2005), 62–79. See Richard Wright, "Tradition and Industrialization: The Plight of the Tragic Elite in Africa," *Présence Africaine.* 2nd series 8–9–10. Special issue (June–November): 347–60, for a condensed version of Wright's views on these issues.

Bibliography

Appiah, K. Anthony. "Race, Pluralism, and Afrocentricity." *Journal of Blacks in Higher Education*, 19 (Spring 1998): 116–18.

———. "A Long Way Home: Wright in the Gold Coast." *Richard Wright: A Collection of Critical Essays*. Ed. Arnold Rampersad. Upper Saddle River, NJ: Prentice Hall, 1995.

Brown, Bill. *A Sense of Things: The Object Matter of American Literature.* Chicago: U of Chicago P, 2003.

Ernest, John. *Chaotic Justice: Rethinking African American Literary History.* Chapel Hill: U of North Carolina P, 2009.

Gates, Henry Louis. Preface. *Richard Wright: Critical Perspectives Past and Present*. Eds. Henry Louis Gates, Jr. and K. A. Appiah. New York: Amistad, 1993. xi–xvi.

Jones, Gavin. *American Hungers: The Problem of Poverty in U.S. Literature, 1840–1945.* Princeton and Oxford: Princeton UP, 2008.

Stephens, Michelle. "African American Modernisms." *A Companion to the Modern American Novel.* Ed. John T. Matthews. London: Wiley Blackwell, 2009. 306–23.

West, Cornell. Introduction. *Three Books from Exile:* Black Power, The Color Curtain, *and* White Man Listen! By Richard Wright. New York: Harper Perennial, 2008.

Volume Bibliography (2000–2010)

Richard Wright: New Readings in the 21ST Century

The following consists of highly recommended secondary sources on Richard Wright from 2000–2010. This bibliography is intended to be suggestive rather than comprehensive.

Biographies

Rowley, Hazel. *Richard Wright: The Life and Times.* New York: Holt, 2001.

Bibliographies

Kinnamon, Keneth. *Richard Wright: An Annotated Bibliography of Criticism and Commentary, 1983–2003.* Jefferson, NC: McFarland & Company, 2006.

Book-Length Critical Studies
(devoted to Wright or containing chapters or sections on Wright)

Baker, Houston A. Jr. *Turning South Again.* Durham, NC: Duke University Press, 2001.

Blair, Sarah. *Harlem Crossroad: Black Writers and the Photograph in the Twentieth Century.* Princeton and Oxford: Princeton UP, 2007.

Brewton, Butler E. *Richard Wright's Women: The Thematic Treatment of Women in "Uncle Tom's Children," "Black Boy" and "Native Son."* New York: Academica, 2010.

Campbell, James T. *Middle Passages.* New York: Penguin, 2006.

Coleman, James. *Faithful Vision: Treatments of the Sacred, Spiritual, and Supernatural in Twentieth-Century African American Fiction.* Baton Rouge: Louisiana State UP, 2006.

Dawahare, Anthony. *Nationalism, Marxism, and African American Literature between the Wars: A New Pandora's Box.* Jackson, MS: Jackson UP, 2003.

Edwards, Brent Hayes. *The Practice of Diaspora: Literature, Translation, and the Rise of Black Nationalism.* Cambridge, MA: Harvard UP, 2003.

Entin, Joseph B. *Sensational Modernism: Experimental Fiction and Photography in Thirties America.* Chapel Hill: U of North Carolina P, 2007.

Folks, Jeffrey J. *From Richard Wright to Toni Morison: Ethics in Modern and Postmodern American Narrative.* New York: Peter Lang, 2001.

Hakutani, Yoshinobu. *Cross-Cultural Visions in African American Modernism.* Columbus: Ohio State UP, 2006.

Hricko, Mary. *The Genesis of the Chicago Renaissance: Theodore Dreiser, Langston Hughes, Richard Wright, and James T. Farrell.* London and New York: Routledge, 2009.

Hakutani, Yoshinobu. *Cross-Cultural Visions in African American Modernism.* Columbus: Ohio State UP, 2006.

Janmohamed, Abdul R. *The Death Bound Subject: Richard Wright's Archaeology of Death.* Durham, NC: Duke UP, 2005.

Jones, Gavin. *American Hungers: The Problem of Poverty in U.S. Literature, 1840–1945.* Princeton and Oxford: Princeton UP, 2008.

Rabinowitz, Paula. *Black and White and Noir: America's Pulp Modernism.* New York: Columbia UP, 2002.

Richardson, Riche. *Black Masculinity and the U.S. South: From Uncle Tom to Gangsta.* Athens: U of Georgia P, 2007.

Robinson, Cedric J. *Black Modernism: A Critical Study of Twentieth Century Negro American Authors.* Chapel Hill: U of North Carolina P, 2000.

Tolentino, Cynthia. *America's Experts: Race and the Fictions of Sociology.* Minneapolis: U of Minnesota P, 2009.

Warnes, Andrew. *Richard Wright's Native Son.* London: Routledge, 2007.

Weiss, Lynn. *Gertrude Stein and Richard Wright: The Politics of Modernism.* Jackson: UP of Mississippi, 2001.

Articles

Atteberry, Jeffrey. "Entering the Politics of the Outside: Richard Wright's Critique of Marxism and Existentialism." *MFS Modern Fiction Studies* 51.4 (Winter 2005): 873–95.

Bingall, Elizabeth. "Burbanking Bigger and Betty the Bitch." *African American Review* 40 (Fall 2006): 475–93.

Butler, Robert James. "The Loeb and Leopold Case: A Neglected Source for Richard Wright's *Native Son*." *African American Review* 39 (Winter 2005): 555–67.

Cappetti, C. "Black Orpheus: Richard Wright's 'The Man Who Lived Underground.'" *MELUS* 26.4 (Winter 2001): 41–68.

Carson, Warren. "They Don't Look So Good, Mistah': Realities of the South in Richard Wright's *Black Boy* and Selected Fiction." *CLA Journal* 47 (March 2004): 299–309.

Dubek, L. "'Til Death Do Us Part: White Male Rage in Richard Wright's *Savage Holiday*." [Part of a special issue: Richard Wright]. *The Mississippi Quarterly* 61.4 (Fall 2008): 593–613.

Elder, Matthew. "Social Demarcation and the Forms of Psychological Fracture in Book One of Richard Wright's Native Son." *Texas Studies in Literature and Language* 52.1 (Spring 2010): 31–47.

Gaines, K. "The Mixed Perception of 'Black Power.'" [Part of a special issue: Richard Wright, Citizen of the World: A Centenary Celebration; Review essay]. *Southern Quarterly* 46.2 (Winter 2009): 145–51.

Gibson, Richard. "Richard Wright's *Island of Hallucination* and the 'Gibson Affair.'" *MFS Modern Fiction Studies* 51.4 (Winter 2005): 896–920.

Griffiths, Frederick. "Ralph Ellison, Richard Wright and the Case of Angelo Herndon." *African American Review* 35 (Winter 2001): 615–36.

Gussow, Adam. "'Fingering the Jagged Grain': Ellison's Wright and the Southern Blues Violences." *boundary 2* 30.2 (Summer 2003): 137–55.

Hakutani, Yoshinobu. "Richard Wright, Toni Morrison and the African Primal Outlook on Life." *Southern Quarterly* 40 (Fall 2001): 39–53.

Henninger, K., Zora Neale Hurston, Richard Wright, and the Postcolonial Gaze. *The Mississippi Quarterly* 56.4 (Fall 2003): 581–95.

Hicks, Scott. "W. E. B. Du Bois, Booker T. Washington, and Richard Wright: Toward an Ecocriticism of Color." *Callaloo* 29.1 (Winter 2006): 202–22.

Higashida, Cheryl. "Aunt Sue's Children: Re-viewing the Gender(ed) Politics of Richard Wright's Radicalism." *American Literature* 75.2 (June 2003): 395–425.

Hogue, W. Lawrence. "Can the Subaltern Speak? A Postcolonial, Existential Reading of Richard Wright's *Native Son*." *Southern Quarterly: A Journal of the Arts in the South* 46.2 (Winter 2009): 9–39.

Iadonisi, R. "'I am Nobody': The Haiku of Richard Wright. *MELUS* 30.3 (Fall 2005): 179–200.

Jackson, C. L. "Tougaloo College, Richard Wright, and Me: Teaching Wright to the Millennial Student." [Part of special issue on Richard Wright]. *Papers on Language & Literature* 44.4 (Fall 2008): 374–81.

Joyce, Joyce Ann. "'What We Do and Why We Do What We Do': A Diasporic Commingling of Richard Wright and George Lamming." *Callaloo* 32.2 (Spring 2009): 593–603.

Karem, Jeff. "I Could Never Really Leave the South": Regionalism and the Transformation of Richard Wright's *American Hunger*."*American Literary History* 13.4 (Winter 2001): 694–715.

Lowe, J. W. "The Transnational Vision of Richard Wright's *Pagan Spain*." [Part of a special issue: The South in a Global Context]. *Southern Quarterly* 46.3 (Spring 2009): 69–99.

Perez, Vincent. "Movies, Marxism, and Jim Crow: Richard Wright's Cultural Criticism." *Texas Studies in Literature and Language* 1.3 (Summer 2001): 142–68.

Peterson, Christopher. "The Aping Apes of Poe and Wright: Race, Animality, and Mimicry in 'The Murders in the Rue Morgue' and *Native Son*." *New Literary History* 41.1 (Winter 2010): 151–71.

Rambsy, H. "Richard Wright and the Digital Movements" [Part of a special issue on Richard Wright]. *Papers on Language & Literature* 44.4 (Fall 2008): 365–73.

Relyea, S. "The Vanguard of Modernity: Richard Wright's *The Outsider*." *Texas Studies in Literature and Language* 48.3 (Fall 2006): 187–219.

Roberts, Brian. "The CPUSA's Line and Atmosphere: Did Ellison and Wright Walk It as They Breathed It as They Wrote?" *Journal of Narrative Theory* 34.2 (Summer 2004): 258–68.

Robin, Lucy. "'Flying Home': Ralph Ellison, Richard Wright, and the Black Folk during World War II." *Journal of American Folklore* 120.477 (Summer 2007): 257–83.

Robinson, Whitted. "'Using My Grandmother's Life as a Model': Richard Wright and the Gendered Politics of Religious Representation." *The Southern Literary Journal* 36.2 (Spring 2004): 13–30.

Rowley, H. "Richard Wright's Africa." *The Antioch Review* 58.4 (Fall 2000): 406–21.

Smethurst, James. "Invented by Horror: The Gothic and African American Literary Ideology in *Native Son*." *African American Review* 35 (Spring 2001): 29–40.

Stringer, D. "Psychology and Black Liberation in Richard Wright's *Black Power* (1954)." *Journal of Modern Literature* 32.4 (Summer 2009): 105–24.

Tolentino, C. "The Road Out of the Black Belt: Sociology's Fictions and Black Subjectivity in *Native Son*." *Novel* 33.3 (Summer 2000): 377–405.

Tuhkanen, Mikko. "Richard Wright's Oneiropolitics." *American Literature: A Journal of Literary History, Criticism, and Bibliography* 82.1 (2010): 151–79.

———. "The Wager of Death: Richard Wright with Hegel and Lacan." *Postmodern Culture* 18.2 (January 2008).

Ward, J. W. "'Native Son': The Novel and the Plays." [Part of a special issue: Richard Wright, Citizen of the World: A Centenary Celebration]. *Southern Quarterly* 46.2 (Winter 2009): 40–45.

Yukins, Elizabeth. "The Business of Patriarchy: Black Paternity and Illegitimate Economies in Richard Wright's The Long Dream." *MFS Modern Fiction Studies* 49.4 (Winter 2003): 746–79.

CRITICAL VOLUMES

Andrews, William L., and Douglas Taylor, eds. *Richard Wright's "Black Boy (American Hunger)": A Casebook*. New York: Oxford University Press, 2003.

Bloom, Harold, ed. *Richard Wright, New Edition*. New York: Chelsea House, 2008.

Butler, Robert, and Jerry Ward, eds. *The Richard Wright Encyclopedia*. Westport, CT: Greenwood, 2008.

Graham, Maryemma, ed. *The Cambridge Companion to the African American Novel*. Cambridge: Cambridge UP, 2004.

Graham, Maryemma, and Jerry Ward, eds. *Cambridge History of African American Literature*. Cambridge: Cambridge UP, 2011.

Mitchell, Hayley R., ed. *Readings on Native Son*. San Diego, CA: Greenhaven, 2000.

Smith, Virginia Whatley, ed. *Richard Wright's Travel Writings: New Reflections*. Jackson: UP of Mississippi, 2001.

OTHER CRITICISM

Detloff, Madelyn. *The Persistence of Modernism*. Cambridge: Cambridge UP, 2009.

Davis, James C. *Commerce in Color: Race, Consumer Culture, and American Literature, 1893–1933*. Ann Arbor: U of Michigan P, 2007.

Djel, Kadir, and Dorothea Löbberman, eds. *Other Modernisms in an Age of Globalization*. Heidelberg: Universitätsverlag, 2002.

Ernest, John. *Chaotic Justice: Rethinking African American Literary History*. Chapel Hill: U of North Carolina P, 2009.

Green, Tara T. "Richard Wright." Edited and introduced by David Seed. *A Companion to Twentieth-Century United States Fiction*, 342–51. Oxford, England: Wiley-Blackwell, 2010.

Moglen, Seth. *Mourning Identity: Literary Modernism and the Injuries of American Capitalism*. Stanford, CA: Stanford UP, 2007.

Morgan, Stacy I. *Rethinking Social Realism: African American Art and Literature, 1930–1953*. Athens: U of Georgia P, 2004.

Mullen, Bill V., and James Smethurst, eds. *Left of the Color Line: Race, Radicalism, and Twentieth-Century Literature of the United States*. Chapel Hill and London: U of North Carolina P, 2003.

Trodd, Zoe, ed. *American Protest Literature*. Cambridge, MA: Harvard UP, 2006.

CONTRIBUTORS

Robert J. Butler is Professor of English at Canisius College in Buffalo, New York, where he teaches American, African American, and modern literature. He is the author of *Native Son: The Emergence of a New Black Hero* (1991), *The Critical Response to Richard Wright* (1995), *Contemporary African American Literature: The Open Journey* (1998), and *The Critical Response to Ralph Ellison* (2001). He has coauthored two books with Yoshinobu Hakutani, *The City in African American Literature* (1995) and *The Critical Response in Japan to African American Writers* (2003). He has also coauthored *The Richard Wright Encyclopedia* with Jerry W. Ward, Jr.

Leonard Cassuto is Professor of English at Fordham University and author of *Hard-Boiled Sentimentality: The Secret History of American Crime Stories*, which was nominated for the Edgar and Macavity Awards and named one of the Ten Best Books of 2008 in the crime and mystery category by the *Los Angeles Times*. His most recent book is *The Cambridge History of the American Novel* (2011), of which he is General Editor. A columnist on graduate education for *The Chronicle of Higher Education*, Cassuto is also an award-winning journalist, writing about subjects ranging from science to sports.

John C. Charles is Assistant Professor of English and Africana Studies at North Carolina State University. He has published essays on Alain Locke, Ann Petry, and Zora Neale Hurston; is the guest editor for a special issue on Richard Wright in *Obsidian III: Literature in the African Diaspora;* and is completing a book-length manuscript entitled *Talking Like White Folks: Sympathy and Privacy in the Post WWII African American White Life Novel.*

Alice Mikal Craven is Associate Professor of Comparative Literature and Film Studies at the American University of Paris. She has published articles on the works of Chester Himes, race and spatial dimensions in the film *In the Heat of the Night* for the *Tamkang Review,* and on issues of race and otherness in *Titus Andronicus* for the journal *Shakespeare*. Her articles "Richard Wright's 'Island' of Silence in *The Long Dream*" as well as work on Richard Wright's influence on Parisian *banlieues* aesthetics are forthcoming in 2011.

Thadious M. Davis is Geraldine R. Segal Professor of American Social Thought and Professor of English at the University of Pennsylvania. She is the author of *Games of Property: Law, Race, Gender, and Faulkner's "Go Down, Moses"* (Durham, North Carolina: Duke University Press, 2003), *Nella Larsen, Novelist of the Harlem Renaissance* (Baton Rouge: Louisiana State University Press, 1994; paperback 1996), and *Faulkner's "Negro": Art and the Southern Context* (Baton Rouge: Louisiana State University Press, 1982), and the editor of numerous reference texts, including the coedited *Satire or Evasion: Black Perspectives on Huckleberry Finn* (Durham, North Carolina: Duke University Press, 1992). She edited and wrote the introductions and explanatory notes to the Penguin Classic editions of Nella Larsen's *Passing* (1997) and *Quicksand* (2002).

William E. Dow is Professor of American Literature at the Université Paris-Est (Marne-la-Vallée) and is teaching at The American University of Paris. He is the Managing Editor of *Literary Journalism Studies* (Northwestern University Press) and has published articles in such journals as *Publications of the Modern Language Association, The Emily Dickinson Journal, Twentieth-Century Literature, ESQ: A Journal of the American Renaissance, Critique, The Hemingway Review, MELUS, Revue Française D'Etudes Américaines, Actes Sud,* and *Etudes Anglaises.* He is the author of the book *Narrating Class in American Fiction* (Palgrave Macmillan, 2009), and is currently completing a book-length study on American Modernism and radicalism entitled *Literary Journalism and the American Radical Tradition, 1929–1941.*

Gary Holcomb is Associate Professor of African American Literature in the Americas, in the Department of African American Studies, Ohio University. In addition to articles in such journals as *African American Review, Callaloo, Journal of Modern Literature,* and *Modern Fiction Studies,* he is the author of *Claude McKay, Code Name Sasha: Queer Black Marxism and the Harlem Renaissance* (Gainesville: University Press of Florida, 2007), which won honorable mention for the Gustavus Myers Center for the Study of Bigotry and Human Rights Book Award. He is currently coediting two critical collections: *Hemingway and the Black Renaissance* for Ohio State University Press and *Sex and the Left* for Temple University Press.

Joyce Ann Joyce, a 1995 recipient of an American Book Award for Literary Criticism for her collection of essays, *Warriors, Conjurers, and Priests: Defining African-centered Literary Criticism* (Chicago: Third World Press, 1994), is also the author of *Richard Wright's Art of Tragedy* (Iowa City: University of Iowa Press, 1991), *Ijala: Sonia Sanchez and the African Poetic Tradition* (Chicago: Third World Press, 1997), *Black Studies as Human Studies: Critical Essays and Interviews* (Albany: SUNY Press, 2005) as well as the editor of *Conversations with Sonia Sanchez* (Jackson: University Press of Mississippi, 2007). She has published articles on Richard Wright, Toni Morrison, James Baldwin, Gwendolyn Brooks, Nella Larsen, Zora Neale Hurston, Toni Morrison, Margaret Walker, Arthur P. Davis, Toni Cade Bambara, E. Ethelbert Miller, Askia Touré, Gil Scott-Heron, and Sonia Sanchez. Her fields of expertise include African American literary criticism, African American poetry and fiction, feminist theory, and black lesbian writers.

John Lowe is Professor of English and Comparative Literature, and Director of the Program in Louisiana and Caribbean Studies at Louisiana State University (LSU), where he teaches African American, Southern, and ethnic literature and theory. He is the author of *Jump at the Sun: Zora Neale Hurston's Cosmic Comedy* (Baltimore: University of Illinois Press, 1994); editor of *Approaches to Teaching Hurston's "Their Eyes Were Watching God" and Other Works* (MLA, forthcoming), *Louisiana Culture: From the Colonial Era to Katrina* (Baton Rouge: LSU Press, forthcoming), *Conversations with Ernest Gaines* (Jackson: University Press of Mississippi, 1995), and *Bridging Southern Cultures: An Interdisciplinary Approach* (Baton Rouge: LSU Press, 2005); and coeditor of *The Future of Southern Letters* (Oxford: Oxford University Press, 1996). His most recent book is *Faulkner's Fraternal Fury* (Baton Rouge: LSU Press, forthcoming), a study of birth order and sibling rivalry. He is currently completing *Calypso Magnolia: The Caribbean Side of the South,* for which he has been awarded fellowships from the Virginia Foundation for the Humanities, the Louisiana State Board of Regents, and the National Endowment for the Humanities. He is also President Elect of the Society for the Study of Southern Literature (SSSL).

William J. Maxwell, Associate Professor of English and African American Studies at Washington University in St. Louis, teaches courses in twentieth-century American and African American literatures. He has published over thirty articles and reviews, and two books: the award-winning *New Negro, Old Left: African-American*

Writing and Communism between the Wars (New York: Columbia University Press, 1999) and an annotated edition of Claude McKay's *Complete Poems* (Champaign: University of Illinois Press, 2004). He is now at work on a book for the Princeton University Press entitled *FB Eyes: How J. Edgar Hoover's Ghostreaders Framed African American Literature.* Maxwell serves on the MLA committee on twentieth-century American literature, on the editorial boards of *American Literature* and *American Literary History,* and as the book review editor of *African American Review.*

R. Baxter Miller is Professor of English and African American Studies at the University of Georgia. His many books include the internationally acclaimed *Black American Literature and Humanism* (Lexington: University Press of Kentucky, 1981), for which he wrote the historical introduction and final essay, and *The Art and Imagination of Langston Hughes* (Lexington: University Press of Kentucky, 1989; paperback 2006), which won the American Book Award for 1991. His *Black American Poets between Worlds, 1940–1960* (Knoxville: University of Tennessee Press, 1986) is an academic bestseller. In 2002, he edited "The Short Stories" in *The Collected Works of Langston Hughes,* Vol. 15 (Columbia: University of Missouri Press). Author of *The Southern Trace in Black Critical Theory,* a commissioned monograph for the *Xavier Review* (1991), he has most recently had published *A Literary Criticism of Five Generations of African American Writing* (New York: Edwin Mellen Press, 2008). He is writing the final chapter of a manuscript entitled "New Chicago Renaissance from Wright to Fair."

Paula Rabinowitz teaches twentieth-century American literature, film history and theory, and feminist and materialist cultural theory at the University of Minnesota. She is the author of a number of books including *Black & White & Noir: America's Pulp Modernism* (New York: Columbia University Press, 2002) and *They Must Be Represented: The Politics of Documentary* (New York: Verso, 1994). She is currently coediting with Cristina Giorcelli a four-volume collection of essays on clothing, fashion, and dress entitled *Habits of Being* (Minnesota) and is completing a book called *American Pulp* for Princeton University Press. In 2011, she held the Fulbright Distinguished Lectureship of American Literature and Culture at East China Normal University in Shanghai.

Claudine Raynaud is Professor of English and American Studies at the University François-Rabelais, Tours, France. She has taught in

England (Birmingham, Liverpool) and the United States (Michigan, Northwestern, and Oberlin). A Fellow at the Du Bois Institute (Harvard, Fall 2005), she headed the nationwide African American Studies Research Group created in 2004 and works at the Centre National de la Recherche Scientifique (CNRS). She is the author of *Toni Morrison: L'Esthétique de la Survie* (Paris: Belin, 1995) and numerous articles on black autobiography. Her most current publications are "Coming of Age in the African American Novel," *The Cambridge Companion to the African American Novel* (Cambridge: Cambridge University Press, 2004); an anthology of articles on Gaines's *The Autobiography of Miss Jane Pittman* (CRAFT, 2005); "Beloved or the Shifting Shapes of Memory," *The Cambridge Companion to Toni Morrison* (Cambridge: Cambridge University Press, 2007); and an article on the place of autobiographical material in James Baldwin's writing (*New Formation*, 2009).

Robert Shulman is Emeritus Professor of English at the University of Washington. He is the author of *Social Criticism and Nineteenth-Century American Fictions* (Columbia: University of Missouri Press, 1987) and *The Power of Political Art: The 1930s Literary Left Reconsidered* (Chapel Hill: University of North Carolina Press, 2000); he has also edited *Charlotte Perkins Gilman, The Yellow Wall-Paper and Other Stories* (Oxford World Classics) and *Owen Wister, The Virginian* (Oxford World Classics).

Isabel Soto is Associate Professor in the Modern Languages Department of Spain's Universidad Nacional de Educación a Distancia. She has been Visiting Scholar at Vassar College and Honorary Fellow of the Schomburg Center for Black Research and Culture. In 2000, she cofounded the independent scholarly press The Gateway Press, devoted to publishing work on liminality and text. She was an Associate Fellow of the Rothermere American Institute, University of Oxford, during 2008–2009. Her research interests are in liminality theory, African American Studies, and Transatlantic Studies. Her most recent book is a coedition, *The Dialectics of Diasporas: Memory, Location, Gender* (Biblioteca Javier Coy d'Estudis Nord-Americans, 2009). She is currently working on a forthcoming title, *Western Fictions, Black Realities: Meanings of Blackness and Modernities* (LitVerlag). In addition, she is preparing a monograph on non-Anglophone constructions of the Black Atlantic, focusing on the work of Langston Hughes.

Julieann Veronica Ulin is Assistant Professor of British and American Modernism at Florida Atlantic University. She holds a PhD in English from the University of Notre Dame, an MA in English from Fordham University, and a BA in English from Washington and Lee University. Her research focuses on the intersections between housing ordinances, property law, discourses of race and citizenship, and representations of domestic and domestic estrangement in twentieth-century literature. Her publications appear or are forthcoming in *Joyce Studies Annual, James Joyce Quarterly,* and *Hungry Words: Images of Famine in the Irish Canon.*

Index